Praise for Joseph Connolly

'Connolly has established himself as a very English comic author, in the tradition of P. G. Wodehouse' *The Times*

'Connolly unfolds a rich and compelling drama of life that is anything but everyday, with Dickensian attention to detail, trademark black humour and a genuine love for his creations' *Daily Mail*

'Connolly specialises in sardonic period melodramas whose characters he either harshly cherishes or affectionately despises — it's hard to resolve the nuance, which is part of the sour fun of reading him ... He knows exactly what he's doing, in an immensely contrived, sophisticated and satisfying game' *Observer*

'Connolly remorselessly points up social pretensions with the eye of Dostoevsky ... this satire on human behaviour is timeless' *Independent*

'A writer of considerable power and subtlety' *Guardian*

'Connolly has a keen sense of the hushed emotional tenderness of English life and our silent shattering pain' *Sunday Telegraph*

'It is Connolly's skill to get the reader to laugh at what should make you cry or at least wince' *Times Literary Supplement*

'A virtuoso performance' *Sunday Times*

'Connolly creates a sense of intimacy and collusion with his reader that is rare in contemporary fiction' *Financial Times*

'With brilliant execution Connolly plunges the reader into each of his characters' heads ... keeps the reader hooked through it all' *Mail on Sunday*

'Connolly has an extraordinary prose style. It's jaw-dropping. Shocking. Mesmerising. It's desperately and excruciatingly funny' *Ham&High*

'He remains essentially a comic noveli~~~~ ~~~~ even sinister side ... There is no other ~~~~ Connolly' *Scotsman*

Also by Joseph Connolly

Fiction

POOR SOULS

THIS IS IT

STUFF

SUMMER THINGS

WINTER BREAKS

S.O.S.

THE WORKS

LOVE IS STRANGE

JACK THE LAD AND BLOODY MARY

ENGLAND'S LANE

BOYS AND GIRLS

Non-fiction

COLLECTING MODERN FIRST EDITIONS

P. G. WODEHOUSE

JEROME K. JEROME: A CRITICAL BIOGRAPHY

MODERN FIRST EDITIONS: THEIR VALUE TO COLLECTORS

THE PENGUIN BOOK QUIZ BOOK

CHILDREN'S MODERN FIRST EDITIONS

BESIDE THE SEASIDE

ALL SHOOK UP: A FLASH OF THE FIFTIES

CHRISTMAS

WODEHOUSE

FABER AND FABER: EIGHTY YEARS OF BOOK COVER DESIGN

THE A-Z OF EATING OUT

IT CAN'T GO ON

JOSEPH CONNOLLY

Quercus

First published in Great Britain in 2000
by Faber and Faber Limited

This paperback edition published in 2014 by

Quercus Editions Ltd
55 Baker Street
7th Floor, South Block
London
W1U 8EW

A CIP catalogue record for this book is available
from the British Library

PB ISBN 978 1 78206 703 0
EBOOK ISBN 978 1 78206 713 9

10 9 8 7 6 5 4 3 2 1

Printed and bound in Great Britain by Clays Ltd, St Ives plc

Typeset by Ellipsis Books Limited, Glasgow

To Cool Cat Charles
(and all that jazz)

CHAPTER ONE

It was her legs. They were the first thing he had noticed (odd in itself, oh yes granted, no arguments there – if you knew him at all, you'd surely know that) – but looking back, as now he could and had to, it maybe wasn't her legs so much, no, as just the way they carried her over to him. That very insinuation of the hips (could it in fact have been the *hips*, then, actually? Were *they* the very first thing or things he noticed, given all the bits of her?): cleaving their way through all those motley people that were always there, and certainly had made up that very last and pointless party. And springing away from them (and we're still with the hips) – tautly suspended and practically catwalk loping – those easy, good-time, don't you think to go rushing me, cool and could-be silky legs of hers.

'It was me you were looking at, wasn't it?'

He had reminded her later, oh, a long while later – but not so late that he could not again even begin to summon up that thing he supposed was fondness – that they were the very first words he had ever heard her utter. She denied it, of course: said she had said to him something quite other – but he knew, just knew, she was wrong about that. For all sorts, oh God – so many reasons – these were words and a meeting he would never forget.

'It's not impossible . . . I felt you were over there, anyway, even if I wasn't maybe directly, er, *looking*, looking. I'm Jeremy.'

The teasing drizzle of a drinks party – soon to be maddening – was all around them, but it was just as if they were

3

alone and together, maybe deep inside a tunnel (her words were cloaked in booming).

'Just last week,' she said, 'they buried my brother. A simple ceremony, by all accounts.'

Jeremy was thinking, Did I hear that right, all that – could I have and did I? What he said was, Oh. And nor even now (or ever, face it) could he not see the way she had lowered her eyes, raised them up – was casting around, newly alert, as if for the first time registering that here were people, and that they were about her. But when she looked full at and into him, that's when he suffered somewhere strange within him the first of the convulsions this woman was destined to cause him. She nodded, before she added quite softly:

'And three days later . . . he died. My poor brother.'

Jeremy knew that his whole face had flickered and creased in true consternation. Some person had shunted his shoulder, and his head had gone along with that, but all he saw when he brought his gaze back to her was the same, quite simple passivity there.

'I'm . . . sorry,' he said – still feeling No Jesus, I must have misheard her, surely to God. So saying I'm sorry should just about cover the lot – empathy with her bereavement, yes, mm – or maybe regretting having been possibly caught out by little more than an acoustic blip (but also, if I'm not more drunk than I truly am feeling – and you, girl, are not either kidding or mad), well then in that case I rue the day that persons unknown interred or entombed your poor brother no fewer than a full three days before he succumbed to the thing that customarily occasions so utter a ceremony, whether it be simple or not. (Maybe I am, I must be – rather more drunk than I truly am feeling . . .)

'Phoebe.'

She had no more to add to any or all of it, this time round. So maybe just nudge my way a bit deeper into the demeanour of a stupid guy at a stupid party – think so?

4

And just go for it. Like his head had just gone with his shoulder: along with it.

'Can I get you a . . . you're not drinking – can I get you a . . .?'

And oh wow – just look at her eyes, what they're up to now: blazing right into him. Jeremy was warmed and then seared by that – he even heard the sizzling (yes I bloody am, yes I bloody did. Christ – it's hot, quite hot in here).

'Drink is maybe not at all a good thing. Call me Maria.'

'Well *I* bloody well like it, that's for – here, let me get you a . . . I thought you said your name was . . . didn't you just say – ?'

'What? What did you think? Do you *know* everyone here, all these people, or what? Why did you come? Why do we *do* these things, actually, Jeremy? Do you know?'

'Phoebe. Your name. You said it was – '

'Didn't. No I didn't. Why would I? It isn't.'

'But I'm *sure* you said – '

Yes I am – damn bloody sure. I'm certainly not *that* much drunker than I truly am feeling – although I'm feeling more so now, I have to admit it: more and more with every single second of this (whatever this is – I still can't say).

'No no. Freebie. I said freebie.'

'You said – ?!'

'Freebie, yup. That's what I am for you. A freebie.'

Jeremy had hardly dared look at her at all – no, not this time. He knew he was hooked (felt its tickle, feared the prick) – and when her eyes reeled him in, he would be torn away jaggedly from just everything he had. So he looked at her now, and yes, oh Christ – he was really done for.

'Maria,' is what he felt he whispered. And she agreed with that by just looking up and saying Yup.

*

And later that night – in the warm dark of early, before

morning proper came to whiten and spike it, Jeremy had lain across her lumpish, vast and preposterous bed (it must truly have been raised four or more feet from the ground – they had helped each other up and in) and pretended as well as he could to be slumped in a mature and deep wallow of contentment, but the only good sensation now dwelt just on his skin where it touched her: the rest of him felt picked out stark by a spurious alertness that presaged only the swaddled thickness of an impending hangover, to be followed solely by the huge and engulfing bloody thing itself, no bones about that, oh no – when it came, he'd know it.

But worse was the feeling of deep unease: it wasn't that he didn't quite feel *sure* of her – he was bloody *sure* he didn't feel sure of her: God Almighty, all those things she had said and done at the party (I think she's asleep, now – could be asleep, think so, by the look of her, just at this moment, she is), so I'll soon start easing the memory back into the spliced and jerky rut of the party, when I've just got one or two other things, if not quite out of the way, then at least stacked up neatly. I think it's Anne I ache for. Not that, no. What I mean is, I feel hollow and then briefly nauseous when I think of the ache she soon will be suffering because of me. Do you know what happened when I told Maria I was married? Know what she said? Nothing. She didn't say a thing. She put her tongue right on deep into my ear and said it reminded her of gnocchi.

'Her name is Anne. My wife. Her name is.'

'And it tastes salty. Nice.'

Maybe not the time to mention the children. Adrian and Donna. Their names are.

'Maria – '

'Marsha.'

'Marsha! What in hell do you mean *Marsha*! You're not telling me – '

'No – I did tell you. I said to you Maria. My name really is Marsha, though – I just like Maria so much better.'

'Look –'

'Hold me tight.'

'Maria – it's Maria, right? Why did you do that to that man? What on earth did you do it for? Hm?'

And yes, behind all that lay the wail of a huger and therefore silent eruption: what in hell is it that you'll do to *me*?

'What man?'

'What – ?! What man do you *think*? How many men at the party did you actually assault, then, Maria? I mean – I only caught sight of the one, just before we, oh God – *left*, but of course he could just have been the latest in a very long line of –'

'Are you always like this?'

'Hm? What? Like what?'

'Like this.'

'What do you mean like this? Like *what*? *What*? What am I like? I'm *asking* you, Christ's sake.'

She raised herself over him, and the flood of warmth from her breast as it teased apart the hairs on his chest made him not just gasp but of course forget. And then she said:

'Hold me tight.'

And he did.

*

And after she'd refucked him (and that is surely how it had felt to white-eyed Jeremy – bruised, he was now, somewhere around that place where mute and seemingly dead extremities connected somehow with a churned-up and inner paining that tugged him) – Maria said to him brightly that she just had to (hear her?) go and fry bacon, now. Oh Christ *don't*, had been Jeremy's moaned-out comeback – I

7

just couldn't think of food, not after all that booze and stuff, and those funny kind of, what were they – those gooey sort of canapés in little pastry cases with bits of could have been grass on top. Oh you don't have to *eat* it, she giggled (first time he'd heard it, the giggle – or seen her as she walked away from him naked – and this and that both stopped his heart). But *surely*, Maria, he had urged (and we will, then – yes? We'll settle for Maria for now, will we? Well on balance yes, was Jeremy's verdict on that – until, anyway, she emerges with something freshly minted and even barmier): *surely*, Maria, you couldn't think of, oh God – *bacon*, not now, oh God you couldn't really, could you? *No*! That's what she called back gaily from somewhere else entirely (kitchen, yes – must be kitchen, I suppose; quite a big flat, this – quite roomy, maybe) – of *course* I couldn't: anyway, I'm a vegetarian – didn't you know that? No, no – I suppose you didn't.

Explore it? Should he have? Maybe, yes, he should. Maybe right there and then he ought to have tracked her down and sought her out: what *are* all these things that you say and do? What on earth are they supposed to *mean*? Hm? And at the party – what you did, what you said – was there *meaning* here, or what? And if not – well *what*, then?

Among whatever other things he felt he might be feeling, it was confusion that clustered round Jeremy now. He well remembered peering through the first thin mists of it – when? Not that long ago – hardly more than just a couple of life-warping hours back at this party he very nearly didn't go to, when what she had done was . . . well look, no doubt Maria'd recall it quite differently (probably deny she'd even been there at all) but this is surely how it seemed to me, the way things had gone:

'So you're sure, then, yes?' I had kicked back in with. 'The wine's actually pretty all right, for once – red is, anyway – and I think I saw someone with a glass of – '

'No.' She was emphatic, Maria. But looking too so determinedly through the press of bodies and elsewhere, far beyond, that God knows, frankly, quite what she was denying. 'I need to be clear,' she had gone on, in a tone so flat and detached as to be practically spooky (had she not seemed still so physical, and therefore magnetic). 'Drink just clouds you.'

And I suppose I had been not much more than vaguely busy summoning up some or other deeply unmirthful rejoinder to that, when I was jerked by a pull at my elbow.

'Jeremy!' Hugo exclaimed – it turned out to be Hugo – 'As I live and breathe.' His face was deep pinkish, going on deeper – usual thing: drink and heat and flushed and even taken in by the simulated ecstasy that one brought to parties, and wore like a pirate's parrot.

'Hello, Hugo,' I said. 'Thought I might see you here.'

Knew I'd see him here, didn't I? Course I bloody did. That was the trouble, that was the trouble – all these parties, all these do's: same old faces, same old stuff. And I was at once reminded of Maria's maybe not at all rhetorical enquiry: why do we *do* these things?

'And this,' he blustered (Hugo's like that: Hugo docs that), 'if I am not very much mistaken, will be the lovely, um – what are you calling yourself, these days, lovely girl?'

And while I knuckled down to chuntering some over-loud guff about Oh – I didn't realize you two, um . . . *knew* one another, I was just knowing that Maria wouldn't like that, wouldn't at all care for what Hugo had said. That, of course, from the off and ever since, was always one of the things about Maria – I never did, even at the end, really know the first thing about her, and yet I often seemed to be able to divine her instincts. Not enough of them, of course, to later save me. But that, as I say, came later.

'I *don't* know him,' snapped Maria. 'And he doesn't know me. What he *means* is that I am perceived to be the adjunct of one Mister Max Bannister – and no, Hugo, he isn't here, so you can stop, now – craning your neck and drooling for favours.'

I was out of my depth, of course, but didn't really care. Although it rang a sort of bell, I was not at all sure I'd ever heard of this Max Bannister, for starters (although I did wonder, yes, what it was she meant by an 'adjunct').

'I don't know what you *mean*!' is the sort of way Hugo was going – a fake yet knowing outrage, cut by an undertone of what he could well have imagined was you-and-me flirty: another big mistake, it had seemed to me – and no, I wasn't wrong.

'Hugo,' Maria said coldly. 'Would you like to fuck me?' And in the face of his bloated 'O' of a mouth (and she sure had my attention – and yes, that of others too) she carried on implacably – though maybe no colder than coolly, now: 'You would, wouldn't you? Yes you would. But you're not going to. Know why? Because you are hideous, Hugo. Low and reptilian as well, of course, and – I am totally reliably informed – soon to be redundant. Which, strictly, you are anyway. Yes *really*, Hugo – that big thing. So it's Max, isn't it, you should really be fucking. But it's too late – far too late – even for that. The reason he isn't at the party, Hugo, is that he is yet again very busy working late. And, incidentally, finishing you off, Hugo. For the very last time.'

Hugo stared. A flicker over to me to maybe gauge just how seriously I could be taking any little part of this (not at all, surely, his eyes were pleading) – or could have been just a vain hope for some sort of shelter. But mainly he stared. And when Maria crooked her finger at him, mock-enticingly, and moved away from the two of us, he followed on wide-eyed, as I did myself. By the time we found ourselves hard by the drinks table, Hugo was already attempting some sort of complicity (can you believe it?) and oozing out bait with a softly pressured urgency.

'Look, um – Maria. What you were saying – all that stuff you were, you know – saying, about my – *job*, and everything . . . you didn't really mean – ? I mean – he *needs* me – Max wouldn't just – ?'

'Is it this Alsace you've been drinking tonight?' cut in Maria, nearly smiling.

'I – uh – *yes*, yes it is, but – '

'Well have some more then.'

And then Maria went to upend the bottle all down Hugo's front – but as his hands fluttered frantically and he veered to deflect that, I saw and knew with inexplicable alarm that she wasn't seriously inclining that bottle – no, it was not her intention to pour it out or over him. And then she swung it upwards and it cracked against his jaw and Hugo – shocked now, pitching back numbly (hurt like hell later) – took the full force and fell from view as Piers came bustling up and cried What the *hell* and *Christ*, Jeremy – is this bitch with you? Get her the hell *out*, Chrissake – Jesus, Jesus – Hugo, are you OK? Are you? Now, Jeremy, *now* – I mean it – just get her *out* of here, kay?

And I did.

*

'So who is he?' Jeremy grunted later.

Maria was pouring tea, really quite sweetly: proper tea, proper pot.

'Who's who?'

'This . . . Max – what was it? *Bannister* character.'

'Oh – you don't really want to know.'

'I wouldn't have asked.'

'He's just . . . someone.'

'Just someone. Uh huh. And me? I'm just someone too, am I?'

Maria smiled. 'You're *Jeremy*.'

And Jeremy smiled too – partly because when she did, you just had to, but also by way of gentlemanly concession of yet another small defeat in another little battle that, oddly, no one had waged. It was just that . . . oh God – this was far from being the first of these circuitous and utterly pointless exchanges: Maria could have chattered on like this for the rest of the night, and still by dawn you'd end up with nothing. Maybe give it just one more go. I don't know, though. It was that brief and fleeting mention of dawn, just there (and look at the curtains: I can make out their colour). What will Anne say? Worse: what is it that I'll end up telling her? OK, then – one more go. What's to lose? (I'm lost already.)

'So then – this Max person. He's your, what – bloke, is he?'

'What a ghastly word: *bloke.*'

'But he is, is he? And he's Hugo's boss – did I get that right?'

'Not any more he isn't. Sacked him. Told you.'

'Why did you *do* that to Hugo? You could have broken his – '

'I didn't break *anything*. People like Hugo *expect* it. Are you staying?'

Well? Am I? Well I am, yes, in that I've been putting off getting home for as long as I possibly can – and yet, oh God, the longer I leave it . . .

'Depends. What are we *doing*, Maria? What do you want of me? What are we going to *do* about this thing?'

'You *know* what I want of you, Jeremy. You know exactly what.'

'And Max?'

'Oh God do stop going *on* about him, can't you? Max is just *Max*, OK? And you're you. That's *enough*, isn't it?'

'Well *no*, not really – not at all, in fact. Look, Maria – we've got to get something straight: I'm *married*, and – '

'Marsha.'

'*What*?!'

'Some days I like my real name better – today is one of those.'

12

'Yeh? Well you're going to be *Maria*, OK? Change name once more and I'll go crazy. Oh Christ – I've completely forgotten what I was *saying* now . . .'

'Don't say anything. Just hold me tight.'

'Maria . . .!'

'Just hold me. You know you want to.'

'I *do* want to, I do – but . . . God, you know, Maria – I know it sounds a bit of a . . . well, cliché, I suppose – you see it in films, all this, don't you? These scenes. But I feel as if I've known you for . . . as if I *will* know you for . . .'

'Ever. I know. Hold me.'

'I have to go. I have to think. There's *Anne* to think of . . . don't you want to know anything about me? About her? And there are children – I have two. I can't *hurt* them – can't ever bear to *hurt* them.'

'I'm not asking you to hurt them. I'm asking you to hold me. Hold me.'

'Maria – please – !'

'Shall we go back to bed? Do you want to?'

'I have to go. Of *course* I want to!'

'Well come on, then. Come on. Come to bed and hold me tight.'

'Oh God.'

'Come *on* . . .'.

'OK, OK – all right. And then, and then – I really have to go. OK? Yes, Maria? Say yes. I leave at nine – OK? Yes? At nine sharp, I am definitely leaving.'

But I didn't.

Did, eventually. Eventually Jeremy did manage to peel himself away from that girl and her things. It had taken, the whole process, just about for ever because listen: *first*, as soon as one of Maria's cool and soothing hands had reluctantly left him, the fingers of the other would maybe snake over a shoulder, or slide into one of his – could cup his jaw or tease those stiffly electrified hairs at the back of his neck; and *second* . . . well, *second*: he just didn't want to go. But

13

then as soon as he had actually done it (I am *out*, yes out of there – down those stairs, away from the warm and back in the street) and conducted a rapid roll-call of not just his parts but also the state of them – then so did he feel more chilled and alone than ever he could recall; and not as he first thought by the dread of going on home – facing what had to be faced there, no – but by the very emptiness that gapingly filled him. He blinked in the consciousness of knowing that being without Maria just simply had no point: it felt all wrong and it had no *point*. And yet before the party that he nearly didn't go to, he had not even known she had ever been born. But everything, all of it, seemed different now.

Better get home to Anne and the kids: hear firsthand what it is I'm going to say. (How can it be that this girl has got me? It's not as if she's even very nice.)

*

'Christ, you know,' laughed Max, 'I really do think Hugo must have lost his bleeding mind. You listening, Feebs? Says you said I'd chucked him from the company – some-thing – and then you upped and clocked him with a bottle! Didn't think you was even going to that bash – why did you?'

'Because I was bored. Wasn't going to. And then I did. Because big shot Max Bannister was *working* again – remember? Anyway – just can't stand that creep. What did you say to him?'

'Didn't get much of a chance to say *anything* to him, did I? Bloke marches in, first thing this morning – looking bleeding rough, I gotta say – '

'Oh *shit* . . .'

'What?'

'Spilt drink. Doesn't matter. Go on.'

'Always spilling *something*, aren't you, Feebs?'

14

'Oh Christ sake don't keep *calling* me that. I keep on telling you *Marsha*. Anyway – spilling you, soon.'

'What? What say? Spilling what? And you can fuck off with your bleeding *Marsha* caper, baby – I call you Feebs cos it's your sodding *name*, isn't it? Phoebe? Isn't it?'

'Max. I just don't want to talk to you any more. Kay? Just don't want to. Don't want you to be here.'

'Charmed. Anyway – off soon. Meeting. So – you give Hugo a smacking or didn't you?'

'What did he say to you? And you don't seem to *get* me, Max – I mean I don't want you *around*.'

'Yeh – you said. Bleeding polite. No – what he said to me was – barged right in, like I say, and he says OK Max You Bastard – nice, ay? OK, Max you *bastard*, he says – I've got the fucking truth, you bloody *bastard* – so now I'm really warming to the guy, aren't I? So I start in with Hey Hey Hey – don't know what the fuck you're *talking* about, do I? And he goes Oh Yeah Like Hell – she told me the lot. Anyway, he says – and he's really worked up now, telling you: veins standing out on him – anyway, he goes – what you can do is you can stuff your crap bloody job where the stars don't twinkle, mate – you're not sacking *me*, you bastard, cos I'm *out* of here. Amazing or what? And I'm like going, *excuse* me? Didn't know what the prat was on about, did I? So he's really kicking into me now, you know – so I just bloody let him have it: *Hugo*, I said, I don't know who's been telling you what, and I don't much care about whether you think you're junked or tendering your thing – *resignation*, right? But you're dead on the money on one score, my friend – you're fucking out the door, that's for bleeding sure. Should've seen his face!'

'So he's gone?'

'Not many. Too right. Then he starts going for me physical! Soon put paid to that little caper. Ow ow ow, he goes – once I'd dotted his bloody i's for him, cheeky sod. And he's, like – first your bird fucking brains me with a bottle, now you've gone and broken my bloody nose! Ha ha. Gotta laugh. Prat.'

'Yeah he is. He tried it on with me one time, you know.'

'Yeah? Bastard. Should've told. Would've done for him, period.'

'Yeh well. He's out now. And so are you, Max, by the way. So are you. Not so much big time as all the way, yeah?'

'What you on about *now*, darling? I own the bloody *company*, don't I? Ay? So what you talking about now, then, Feebs?'

'I mean, Max, you're out of my life. From last night. When you wouldn't even come to a party. Again.'

'What's . . . this? You joking or what, Phoebe?'

'*Marsha*, you bastard! No, Max. No joke. I don't – do I?'

'Phoebe – *Marsha*, honey: talk to me. What's got into you, hey? Not like you to do all this on me. Not your number.'

'I do all this when it's *over*. Haven't you got a meeting to go to, Max?'

'Hm? Oh fuck it – meeting can wait. Listen, Feebs – '

'They never waited for you before, though, did they, Max? Your bloody day and night endless important *meetings*. Hm? And if you call me that just one more time I walk right *now* and that's the end of me, I'm telling you.'

'You're . . . not kidding me, are you, love?'

'Got it. Not.'

'But listen – hey: *lisssen* – you and me, we're all right! We're OK, us. Look, let's go and have a spot of – let's go over to Sophie's . . . you like it there, yeh? Give ourselves a really boozy lunch, ay? Ay? How about it? Then we come home and I'll change your mind. Press all the right buttons. Sound good?'

'Sounds . . . laughable. *Laughable*, Max. Understand: I'm not telling you I want more attention – I used to, all the time I used to, but now I just don't. Want any. Want *out*. Too late. I'm not saying Hey – let's talk it *over* – no, Max, I'm not. I'm simply informing you that it has *ceased*. As from last night.'

'As from last night . . . Just like that. *Ceased*.'

'Correct. So why don't you go to your meeting, hm? And then when it's over – well then you'll know that we are too.'

'Look . . . Marsha, love . . .'

'Bye, Max. Some of it was nice.'

'Don't . . . leave me, baby. Don't just walk.'

'Bye. I won't say See You.'

'Here – you got another bloke or what, you *bitch*?'

'Yeah.'

'Yeah! Yeah! What you fucking mean – *yeah*?! Since bloody when, you slag?'

'As from last night. Told you.'

'As from . . . Christ, it's not fucking *Hugo*, is it?'

'Oh God, Max – you just don't see *anything*.'

'Yeah? Oh yeah? Well let me just tell you, you *cunt* – I see *this* – I see *this* – I see bloody *you* for exactly what you bloody are, you . . . you –'

'I go now.'

'So who is he? Hey? Who is he, this Mister Bleeding Wonderful? What's so fucking great about him, hey? He got money? Who is he? What does he *do*?!'

'What he does, Max, is he calls me Maria – which is one step further on. This is what I need and all I want, just now. It's not important if you don't understand.'

Maria turned and easily walked away. Max bloody knew he – Christ yes – had one helluva lot more than *this* to hit the cow with, but found himself caught up and dumbed by the sidle of her hips, and the long legs idling away from them. His mouth was still wide open and silent as the door kissed shut quite softly behind her.

*

And then I just did, then, did I? Go home? Jeremy had often wondered at this from the distant vantage point of what could never, even then, be thought of as anything ever close to a haven, no – simply later on, is all. Time helps. Helped me along, anyway – until it comes full circle and turns and confronts you and trips you up just one more time, it can generally be relied on to do that thing people always assure you it will: heal – or anyway make it blunter and hurt less. But when you are actually in the midst of a spotlit scene that's ticking away, ticking away – even if it's horrible (and that episode with Anne, the one I'm thinking of that time when I went home the next day, God it was – it was horrible, that) – everything seems so utterly *natural*, no matter how strange: completely unalterable, like the lie of the down as it glistens on your forearm. What is good, though, is that after seemingly ages (but maybe only just long enough) every prickled and all-too-see-through hair begins to bunch up and thicken, before blurring into fur and softening the worst of it: a protection of sorts, and one needs and hugs it. But as you play your part, second by second in the here and now – ah well then, then there can be no defence at all, not then: you're out there, stark and alone – knowing it's real, though barely believing it can be.

And it just had to be a Saturday, didn't it? Adrian and Donna – not at school: doesn't exactly help, does it? Well – didn't matter awfully much in Donna's case, if I'm being quite frank here. She was five then, just on – and I don't know if it's just with little girls (always more difficult with Adrian) but I always found that if you just smile in their direction and keep on fishing out treat after treat from your secret store of goodies, they just about swallow down anything, some kids – though that glint of doubt shows me clearly that they don't wholly trust themselves for doing so, let alone you, for needing their collaboration.

Adrian, though – different, quite different. Thirteen he was then, pretty close (*very* close, in point of fact, because his birthday was due, I will always remember, on the Thursday of the following week – wasn't there for it: gone by then). And he's always seemed older than his years, has

Adrian – always regarded him with an air of awe, maybe respect (and sometimes, inexplicably, even fear: my very own son – odd or what?). And yes, I well know that the gap between the two kids was seen to be a long one – nearly eight years, yes that's long – used even to joke about it in the old (old) days: Waaaal, I'd drawl – you get so *tired*, don't you, ay? Started off as a joke, anyway (don't things, often?), but soon it had become uncomfortably close to the heart of the matter: just ask Anne. No – don't bother: she'll tell you herself – she is, I'm told, unstoppable now. She'll say to you something like (I can well imagine) – Oh *Jeremy*, poor *Jeremy* – had a permanent *migraine*, poor darling; well – not *permanent* permanent: lasted from when I joined him in bed at night-time until he bounded up and out in the morning, eager to be simply anywhere else at all! Something, I should think, on those lines. And she had a point, be fair. It's not that I found her unattractive, as such – it was just that she was, well – *Anne*, if you see what I'm saying. And mother to Adrian and Donna. And God, they both of them – facially, you know – are so much like her it's weird, I'm telling you. Particularly Adrian. The looks he sometimes gives you – like that one that kissed me full in the face and shamingly dead centre when I did eventually get home that first morning after that first night with Maria (no hint of migraine then, I recall: came like a train – came again like another one). And look at Anne, now – just look at her, will you? Same expression as the boy – same exactly. Same face, you see: same accusatory and heavy-veiled eyes – and yes, almost certainly, same dark thoughts lurking behind them (leaving suspicion way behind, and closing in fast on outright condemnation).

I lit a last cigarette – exhaling, I thought reasonably coolly. I never did smoke heavily, but without knowing it, I was poised on giving them up completely – that very hour and quite without trying (along with so much else – all, indeed, I ever had). Anne was fiercely grinding down a lemon half on the Juicy Salif – that jaunty and gunmetal squeezer – something, I know it sounds silly, I had asked her never to do. I'm odd, I think, among my fellow designers in that I always feel that these beautiful objects are best left alone – whatever their function: chairs or shelves, vases and bowls – even lamps and bottles, sometimes. Don't make them work, is what I'm thinking: why don't you just let them be? Not Anne. Not only would she sprawl all over the Charles Eames lounger, or recklessly nudge Corbusier's masterpiece, the chrome and leather Grand Confort, hopelessly out of square – she'd even deck them with newspapers and, oh God – *cushions*. This hurt me – and I don't really care how that comes over. And yes of *course* I now see that this is maybe – not maybe – just why she did it. Any other time and my opening line could well have been, Anne – Anne? Listen to me, Anne: I've told you, what – how many times is it now? We've got *other* squeezers, haven't we? Hm? We even bought that electric juicer. So why the Starck? Hey? Tell me please. Of all the gadgets, why the one that's just perfect in repose? Yes – I did, with Anne, find myself sounding quite as arch as that, and sometimes a good deal more so. Only with Anne, I think (and ever-increasingly, I now see, towards what I didn't really know would be the end). But with four hard eyes, now, burning right into me (and Donna would not be long in catching up) that is not what I thought I should say. What would have come, I couldn't tell you (I remember an almost hysterical giddiness, something approaching a mad excitement – so eager was I still to be first to hear just exactly what it was I might go for) – because it was Anne, tossing the lemon rind almost into my gleaming Brabantia wastebin (the chromework now streaky, I just had to observe) – who looked up and nearly at me and spoke:

'Hugo rang. Said he saw you. Good night?'

'Daddy,' said Adrian – truly gravely – 'have you *really* just come in from last night this morning?'

'Hugo?' I heard, the second I said it.

'Something about someone hit him and he's lost his *job*? In a terrible state, sounded like.'

What was this voice of hers *saying* to me? That's what I was busy working out.

'Hugo?' I said again – which was thoroughly absurd, this time round.

'*Daddy*?' insisted bloody Adrian. 'Have you? Really just come home now for the very first time since last night?'

'Wasn't a *bad* party. As these things go. Usual crowd. Should've come! Met someone called – can't recall his . . . new face. Insisted we go on to some bloody club or other, couldn't tell you where. Hellhole. Potential client, though, so I thought I ought. God *knows* where the time went.'

Ah. So *that's* what it was I was going to say.

'Daddeeeee!' piped up little Donna, God love her and save her. 'Did you *bring* me anything? Daddeeeee? Did you?'

'And me!' shot in Adrian (no slouch when it comes to handouts: wouldn't believe he'd been judge and jury just two seconds earlier).

'Of *course*, my angels – would I forget you? Never really ever known quite what it is that Hugo actually *does*, you know – never really thought to ask him. You seem to know him better than I do. Can be a hell of a bore – and worse when he's pissed.'

'Piss,' pouted Donna, 'is *naughty*.'

While I was laughing like a madman at that – it got me off, didn't it, for the moment, saying any more? – Anne started looking at me deeply: made the whole of my head twitch, when she did all that – could almost feel the insistent probing, like a dentist's cruel and gleaming tool (scraping away, scraping away) as all my nerve-ends clenched and cowered.

'*Piss* isn't naughty!' poo-pooed Adrian, at his most elevated and worldly. 'Piss is just crap.'

Anne had the goodness to say *Adrian* – short and

reproving – and I did, I think, snigger at the flicker of utter confusion across dear little Donna's big and trusting eyes. And then, as they do, she forgot it all completely.

'Well where *is* it, Daddeeeee?' she now was singing. 'My present – where is it?'

'Shouldn't expect *presents*,' Anne was more or less grunting. 'Just because your father's been out all night . . .' (and now, by God, those two bloody piercing eyes of hers had bored their way right between mine – were nearly out the other side) '. . . why should we expect him to give us *anything*?'

'But he *said* . . .' protested Donna, close to tears, now.

'And I *meant* it,' was the magnanimous retort from her great grand father. Who legged it up the stairs to his study as fast as he decently dared (thank Christ Round One's in the bag) – for there was his life-saving cache of Smarties and trolls, Pez dispensers, key-rings, felt pens, dollies, toy cars, sticker sets and comics (never much of anything too beautifully packaged, though – just couldn't bear it when they tore them apart).

While he sat at his desk – one hand cradling his newly aching temple, the other rootling around for just the right level of diversionary tactic and conscience-appeaser (not so derisory as to be scornfully everyday, nor so lavish as to nakedly betoken a crime on his part) – Jeremy suddenly caved in with a rush of tiredness and just the temporary easing of a tension that would soon be back in place, to keep him alert and protect him. And it shocked him when all of that was slid away and in came lust – the sudden vision of Maria's long and cool and warm-hot thighs (and silky, yes – they had been silky) just before they had locked themselves to each side of his face, the appalling softness of her skin making his pre-dawn stubble ache first, and then sting. It was her legs – that and the way they had carried her over: those legs of Maria's were walking all over him.

Which would seem odd, as I say, to anyone who knows me at all. Always more of a . . . well, if you press me – breast man, I suppose. And bottoms, oh yes: bottoms are good. *Protrusions*, I suppose, were always it. Legs? Well – legs, very pleasant, of course, but like ours they just *hang* there, right? Not really wholly central to the issue, to my way of thinking. Take Anne, in the old days: it was weeks before it dawned on me she even *had* any legs (mind you, she wore trousers a lot – in those damn near impossibly distant days, she did). No – it was those tits of hers that knocked me in the eye. Women always know, don't they, which bits it is of themselves they ought to promote? Three-quarter length, oh – just *anything*, really, always denotes that the woman in question is none too pleased with the general situation in the hip and thigh department. Trousers? Boots? Problems with the ankles, or at the very least the calves. (And I'm at one in sympathy for them on this score, believe me: a thick ankle, and no matter how dainty the foot, it is rendered as a hoof – this isn't heartless: there are simply no two ways about it.) Does she never wear a sundress, even in a heatwave? Hammy upper arms – and very possibly dappled, by way of a bonus – rather in the manner of those fattier rounds of Italian sausage (you know the type – pinkish and whitish whorls – with rather worrying flecks of green). But, on the brighter side, if you're talking pierced navel, miniskirt, high-heeled strappy things, painted toenails, spray-on jeans or clingy little tubey tops – then all you see (play your cards right) is very much all you will be getting – and jolly nice too.

Take Anne, as I say: very first time I saw her . . . well: *I* say it's the first time, anyway – she's always firmly maintained in that way of hers that *No*, Jeremy, *no*, actually – we met, oh God, *weeks* before that, *weeks* – at the Regatta, don't you remember? You *must* remember, surely? How can you not? Well no I *don't*, as a matter of fact – I don't at all. I remember you at that restaurant, what was it, some bloody restaurant I took you to – The Bear, fairly sure. It was our first meeting – don't interrupt – and you had this, never forget it, plunging bright blue top on. Your breasts, Christ, they looked fantastic: I just couldn't wait to – *No*, Jeremy, *no*, she always came back with: that was simply *ages* later – and anyway, if it was our first date at a restaurant – Compleat Angler, actually – it *can't* have been the first time we met – well *can* it? Talk sense. And the top wasn't *blue* – I never wore blue, not in those days, I didn't – and certainly not *bright* blue, that's for sure. It was emerald green, that top – I remember it so well. Peter Jones, I got it: forty-two pounds – thought it was a fortune, at the time. Really wish I'd kept it, now – but you remember when I had that massive chuck-out? All those piles and piles of clothes I gave to Oxfam or one of those that time? God I *so* wish I hadn't, now – but you do that, don't you? Just suddenly feel you've got to be shot of it all. And *God*, Jeremy – I don't know where you got *plunging* from – what sort of a girl did you think I was? Didn't *do* plunging – it just . . . fitted, that's all. You were just a randy young devil, and that's the way you saw it. (That's what you were. What you were. You were.)

And no, for the record, I don't remember any sort of a 'chuck-out', massive or otherwise. Should I? Really? Well I *don't*. I just remember the very first time I saw you in The Bear in this plunging bright blue top and your breasts, oh Christ – your breasts just looked to me simply *fantastic*.

So here was just one snapshot of Anne and me, sort of together, and looking back on the good times from the decent and not yet chilling distance of the More-Or-Less-Still-OK-Times – albeit the Nothing-Much-To-Write-Home-About-Times (those Hey: The-Whole-Of-Life-Can't-Always-Be-A-Honeymoon-Times) – but not too long after that came the pitch and toss of the ups and downs (left you feeling green and sick of it) and then soon the downs became truly mystifying: how could it be we kept on having them, without the recurrence and grace of ups to fall from? It all got even worse when she said I was a liar. Not just a liar, she was at pains to make it clear – but a *Liar*, a *Liar*, a *Liar*, bloody Jeremy – you two-faced lying *bastard*.

'Look . . .' I had sighed and groaned the first time (although Anne, of course, would say this was, oh Christ – no *way* the first time, not by a bloody mile – yeh yeh, but whether it was or not it really might as well have been: they were all the same, these acid and endless confrontations. Stale, sour – oozing rawly and going nowhere). But here was almost mellow: this was before some unseen hand had dumped the vinegar in favour of napalm – when instead of the shock of the barb of a spite-tipped dart, one came to be burst by the evisceration of a dumdum bullet marauding all over one's insides – this ultimately savage game of bagatelle laying waste with each ricochet any outstanding internal organs. Yeah.

So anyway, back to then: *Look*, I said – listen to me, Anne. I think we should maybe have a little talk. Hm? Get things straight. Where do you *get* all this 'lying' business from, hm? I don't lie. Why should I lie to you, hey? What do I stand to *gain* from it? You really have to ask yourself all these things, Anne. I mean, here I stand accused – but why, Anne? *Why*?

'Oh *fuck* off, Jeremy, you pompous lying *prat*. You *know* what I mean – you *know* it. I'm looking at your face right now and I just *know* that you know what I mean and that I *mean* it. All these women – all these *women* of yours, Jeremy – who *are* they? Why do you *do* it? Who *are* they? What about the children? Don't you *care* about them? Adrian isn't a *baby* any more – he sees things, knows things. Don't you *care* about any of that? Why do you *do* it?'

'Of course I – *God*, Anne – I really can't believe you're

saying all of this! There *aren't* any other "women" – of course there aren't.'

And before – some years before – I might've tacked on: 'It's *you* I love: *you*, Anne. Why can't you see that?' But there are limits. And anyway, I knew by now she'd be well revved up to drive back in:

'Yeah? Oh *yeah*?' (Had just taken down far too large a glug of Rioja – sort of thing she did, times like this.) 'So tell me about Dubai then, Jeremy. Dubai – yes? Last summer. You remember?'

'I remember perfectly well – '

'Oh fuck *off*, Jeremy, you lying bastard. Are you telling me – ?!'

'I'm telling you – '

'Oh fuck off fuck off fuck *off* – bastard bastard *bastard*.'

Well what can I tell you that you don't already see? Symptoms of a deeper malaise? Is that what all this was? It would be facile and convenient to say so now, I suppose. All it did then was drive me nuts. I mean look – Dubai, yes OK – let's take Dubai. I was out there that summer – redesigning a rather splendid hotel for, need I say, extremely important clients who are very, very exacting (and for that sort of money, so they bloody well should be). But as far as *Anne* was concerned I was off having an affair in the sun! I mean, hey, look – of course there were one or two *girls* involved (well there always are, aren't there? Part and parcel) but it was nothing like she *thinks*. Plus, of course, it's rude to refuse when they're offered. Shocking breach of etiquette, I shouldn't at all wonder. Christ – give me a *break*, here: all I do is my *job*, you know? As well as I bloody well can, to raise my own family I hope in a decent manner and what do I get? Hey? Grief. Grief is all I get – that and *accusations*.

'Even when we went to Tony and Sheila's that time – '

'Oh *please*, Anne, spare me – not Tony and bloody *Sheila's* again . . .'

'I'll never *forget* the shame. Where's *Jeremy*, everyone was saying. Where's good old *Jeremy* got to? And where *had* sodding good old fucking Jeremy got to – hey?'

'Anne . . .'

'Well we soon all found out, didn't we? In the spare – oh God – *bedroom* with that bloody *Ulrika* – drunk and giggling and practically fucking her on the *floor.*'

'Oh don't be so *stupid*, Anne, God's sake – I've told and told you – I was just helping her find her *coat*, is all, and – '

'Yeah? *Yeah*? Well it wasn't very likely you'd find it stuffed down her *knickers*, was it, you bloody lying bastard! And Jesus – You were so bloody pissed you actually said out loud to her – everyone heard it in the doorway – her legs were around your bloody neck and you actually said to her "Pretend you don't *know* me"! I mean – *Jesus*, Jeremy!'

'I never said any such thing. Look – !'

'Oh fuck off. I'm going to bed. Do the lights, for once. *Bastard.*'

And yes, as I say – here was before it turned nasty. All nonsense what she was saying, of course. Her name was Gilda, for a start. Nice girl. Saw her, yeh, once or twice afterwards (well you have to – they don't like it if you don't) but then that was very surely that. I don't know why or how Anne keeps thinking that something *meaningful* is going on. What is it that gets into these women, at all?

*

I suppose, if I'm honest, I thought it would be like that for always. I didn't ever expect a thing like Maria to amble her way into my life. Does anyone anticipate so utter an occurrence? Maybe some people do – wait and pace and yearn for such a thing, their longing palpable, and therefore repugnant. Hopelessly destined for disappointment, of course – but it would maybe help them a lot if they could know in advance that any realization of this one sweet dream was only a brief and dazzling postponement of the very same end.

So that day – it might as well, now, be a lifetime ago (certainly mine, anyway, seems to have passed) – when I did eventually get back from that first night with Maria, Anne did not take at all long to see that here was different. Quite quickly, Adrian and Donna were deflected from the scene (Go and watch *The Lion King*: oh *God*, Mum – not *The* Lion *King* again – why can't we ever get any *new* videos like Nathan Fieldlander? Because we're not bloody billionaires like Nathan Fieldlander's people, that's why – now go and watch the bloody *Lion King* while me and your father *talk*). And then it was time for the horrible:

She was twitchy, agitated – practically bouncing amid the sleek and gleaming curves of the Mies van der Rohe sidechair (to which, quite frankly, she contributed nothing – though here is not quite so direct nor personal a slur as it may at first seem: in common with all these lovely things, as I'm forever saying, the chair looked so much better unadorned). That said, she didn't *actually* have to jerk up and down in it, like that: just because it is cantilevered doesn't make it a rocking chair, as I had long ago given up on admonishing her.

'So,' she opened. 'This "potential client" you met. What's her name?'

'Maria. I think.'

I said it as simply as I could (the postscript was involuntary). I didn't exult in its music – hoped that there was no inference that here was anything approaching the most beautiful sound I have ever heard (nothing like that) – though nor did I wish it to seem that the name had been forcibly wrung from me. It was the sheer immediacy of my response, though, I could see, rather than any nuance of delivery – this is what made the spark of shock and maybe fright light white in her eyes (possibly I should have been a liar?) – her intake of breath momentarily delaying whatever it was she just knew she had to get out of her next, or die.

'I want you gone.'

Anne's eyes were holding his gaze; Jeremy felt he could bear their glare for absolutely not one second longer, and yet he held it, transfixed. He hoped to God she'd have some more to say on the matter, but to break his awful fascination he coughed and muttered, Yes: I'm going. Her eyes were still hard, but glassier now – though her chin, it surely seemed to Jeremy through the blur of his mesmery, was quivering – or maybe just readying to talk at him again.

'So . . . she must be really pretty special, this . . . Maria: you *think* . . .'

Jeremy looked about him for something to look at.

'She's – '

'Special enough to take the place of your children. Oh of *course* I realize that just *any* of your pick-ups would be *more* than adequate to take the place of your *wife* – I mean, what *am* I, after all – ?'

'Anne – '

'But for some little – *tart* to just walk in and rob two children of their admittedly woeful *father* – well, she must really be something. Quite a . . . *cracker* – yes, Jeremy? Nan will be *so* disappointed.'

Jeremy looked up sharply, and in genuine surprise. However this awful thing was to have gone, here was surely a non-name he hadn't expected.

'Nan? *Nan*? What – you mean *Nan*, Nan? What the hell has she got to do with it?'

'Well I *imagine*, Jeremy, that she thought your sordid little affair was actually, oh God – *going* somewhere – well they do, these young girls, don't they? But when she discovers you're – '

'Wait! Now you just wait a bloody minute. Let's just get

this straight – we are talking about *Nan*, yes? As in Adrian and Donna's nanny – *that* Nan? You must be *mad*.'

'Unless there's some *other* Nan you've been screwing,' threw away Anne, at her most freshly rancid. But then her lip curled up and she turned on him viciously: 'Oh come *on*, Jeremy – you're not going to *deny* it, are you? Why bother? Why bother denying *anything* any more? You're leaving me, aren't you?'

'Nan! Nan is about nineteen years *old*, Christ's sake! I've never even so much as – !'

'Oh *balls*, Jeremy – you're besotted with each other: it's absolutely as plain as – *Christ*, I only kept her on because it's so impossible to *get* nannies, these days – but I suppose, yes, she'll go anyway, now. Now that *you're* not here any more.'

'Anne. Believe me. You're dreaming. What the hell anyway are we talking about *Nan* for, for Christ's sake? We should be talking about – '

'Who? About who, Jeremy? Me? No – not rubbish little me, surely: what's to say? Your children? Well – you've never talked about them before, so why should you start now?'

'Anne – that's – !'

'Or is it the *girlfriend* we should be talking about? Shall we do that? I don't think so, Jeremy, no. I think I should find that just slightly distasteful. Can you be gone by tomorrow?'

Jeremy gaped at her. Tomorrow. Well can I? Can life really happen so that I am more or less here today, and utterly gone tomorrow?

'Well do *try*,' Anne went on – although the forcedly playful malice was quitting her now, and her lips were hardening into a snap-shut box. They opened again grudgingly, but nothing came. She got up to go off (where?) and although Jeremy was mightily relieved that she'd done so, he still rose – maybe to stop her. Neither of them for an instant moved – Jeremy aware of his stricken posture only when whatever had him was broken by young Adrian's voice from the door.

'What on earth are you two standing in the middle of the floor for?'

'Daddeeeee,' cooed Donna, running up to him and wrapping her arms around his legs and nuzzling his stomach, like she did. 'I want to be a big lion when I'm older. Grrr! Grrr!'

Jeremy glanced over to Anne, and his eyes of a sudden felt huge with despair. She shook her head once, and looked down; then she turned and walked to the door as Adrian rushed up to her with urgency in his eyes: Mum? Mum? What's up? What's wrong? At least, thought Jeremy – maybe not just then, maybe later as he once again went over and over it – *someone* is aware of, if not quite what she's feeling, then at least the fact that she feels at all. Anne gave in to a strangulated sob, just before she reached the door – and as Adrian ran to her, filled with hurt and enquiry, Jeremy caught sight of just her retreating calf, which seemed to him so white and strange – as if it were part of an altogether alien body. He tousled Donna's hair, like he did, as his mind said Christ: what now?

Jeremy and Anne spoke just once more that night. She had not yet quite finished piling up all of his clothes on to the bed in the small room, by the time he had eventually come there – knowing full well it was where he had to be.

'When,' said Anne, 'did you meet her? Is this the Dubai one? Or a newer one?'

'I didn't take *anyone* to . . . I told you . . .'

And then he did look full at her – feeling so strong a charge, this time, as their eyes just fused – and it is difficult to say which one of them first was spun into amazement as Jeremy mumbled to her . . . Last Night. Is When. I Met Her. You see, he thought (as Anne seemed so eager to leave as to be roughly pitching herself out of the room and into the hall), it's just that I've been bowled over – which is why I do find myself just standing here, stunned, and utterly unable to do anything for either of us.

*

And then I remember thinking Well – well well: could maybe have been the following morning, this, when I said Well, oh yes – really quite a lot, and sometimes right out loud, to no one (sometimes keeping it barely inside, not even for me). And also – Right! *Right*, I kept on muttering, in a grim and manly this-is-it and please let me feel, oh God – *determined* sort of a way. The actual nature of the resolution never came through, though; if I hugged to me just the one coherent idea (and when I cast my mind back, all coherence lay just out of reach) it was no more than on the lines of You Know What, Don't You, Jeremy Old Lad? This is all a bit *quick*: it doesn't (can't, can it?) altogether amaze me that I'm leaving – for people such as myself (and I think I know what I mean by that) all it really ever can be is no more than only a matter of time. So no – not that, then. What gets me is this: it's just that I'm doing it *now*, when what I feel is not quite ready.

And then I gasped at my new insight and confronted myself hugely with knowing exactly *why* I leave: I'm not just *quitting* this place, am I? Not walking, turning my back, giving two fingers or ripping us up – because listen to me, will you: I *give* a monkey's! What I am is *exiled*: the bitch has got rid of me – I am ordered to go. Well isn't that the case, pure and simple? 'Can you be gone by tomorrow?' – were not those her very words? Not quite, is it, the reaction of a woman half-crazed by passion – on the verge of desolation at the threat of being cloven in twain? I don't think so. No one could level at her the charge of being *clingy*, is all I'm trying to say here: right? And as for all that nonsense about *Nan*, well – clearly the woman's deranged. I mean I

32

thought of it, yeh sure – but Jesus, she's not much more than a kid, Nan; plus, she didn't seem remotely interested – and why, in fact, should she be? It's not as if I'm *young*, or anything.

So how I shall maybe do this, then, is shuffle, yes shuffle – move with diffidence and finger just one or two things both lovingly and longingly, heavy with an adult burden of what must surely be the longest hour of all. And I would more or less happily have gone along with some of that – already, I recall, there were pinpricks of salty pain all over my eyeballs, so tenderly did I feel for me, now – but that was the point when Adrian arrived: Adrian, it was clear, wanted words with me (mine, yes, but one or two of his own were queuing up, I could see, in not that orderly a fashion).

Adrian plonked himself firmly – but had to be, didn't it, irritatingly askew in the Wassily chair (and how many times had Jeremy told and told him that if he hangs his knees over the suspended leather strap arms, like that, the tension will be lost – the tensile strength, yes? – and along with it the lean and spare but utterly cubic lineament of the whole ensemble?).

'So . . . Adrian?' Jeremy opened. He figured he had to: boy would otherwise have gone on glaring at him for ever.

'Is it *true*?' was Adrian's accusation – and yes, Jeremy would have betted on something along those lines, for here, it must be understood, could be no desperate cry for reassurance – nothing approaching the tentative first steps to a stupefied denial. Adrian had him, and he knew it. He was like that at draughts – towards the endgame, when wherever you went it didn't at all matter because, look – it was as plain as day: Adrian's crown was going to dance all over you, scooping up all of your remaining forces. (And no doubt at chess as well, Jeremy wouldn't know: never ever learned the game.) For now, he seriously played at levelling with the twin barrels of his son's big gun, staring down the frankly open soon-to-be-loathing, this well fortified by a smug and just-try-and-get-out-of-this-one goading – this all seeming to Jeremy, now, hardly less than a full-frontal offensive, which had to be met head-on.

'Well *is* it?' prompted Adrian – giving it a little bit of a twist rather too early on, was Jeremy's judgement. And *yes*, he fooled with the idea of going through all of the 'Well now, Adrian – it rather depends what you mean by *it*, doesn't it really?' sort of stuff – all the 'Is *what* true, Adrian – what exactly is it you're asking me?' kind of garbage. But why? In order to defer quite what, precisely? Because a deferment was surely all it would ever have won him: any hope of a deflection was out, quite out – he saw that.

'Yes,' said Jeremy. 'I think . . .'

Adrian was perplexed – and no, it gave Jeremy no joy at all as he physically registered that flicker of confusion momentarily contorting so very young and earnest a face that really had no business in concerning itself, not yet, with all this murk and horror. The sweetness of a boy's stupidity – or anyway the shelter of faking it – should be preserved for longer, much longer than this.

'You *think* . . .?'

'No – sorry,' Jeremy was quick to amend. 'Don't mean "I think". Don't know why I said it. I do that. Yes, Adrian – I'm sorry, but it's true.' And what mad force could possibly have made him tack on: 'Not, of course, your mother's fault'? The spark of affront in Adrian's eyes soon clouded over, though, as they settled back down into a distant distaste, just at the very edge of easy contempt.

'When are you going?'

'People seem to be in rather a hurry . . .'

'Are you going today? This morning?'

'Jesus.'

'Mummy says not to hate you and that you're not to blame.'

'And *you* think?'

'I think – if you're not to blame, then who is? Of *course* I know it's not Mummy's fault, it never can be – so who does that leave? Me and Donna is all that's left.'

'Oh Adrian – it's just not *like* that – it's not a question of ... look, you know it'll break my ... I'm not actually *enjoying* any of this, Adrian, no matter what you may think – and no, no – please don't say Well why are you *doing* it, then, because in a sense, in one very *real* sense, Adrian, I'm not doing ... anything. It's just – things just sometimes *happen*, you know? Yes? It's like next year – look at next year. When you leave prep school, hm? And go on to, we hope, Westminster. Yes? It's not that your prep school is no *good* any more, is it? Not that they're chucking you *out*. See? What I'm saying? And Westminster – well, of course we all *want* it to be, you know, as good as everyone says it is, but we don't yet actually *know*, do we? For sure. Until you're there and sort of *doing* it, well – we just won't, will we? You're moving on, Adrian, simply because ... well, because it's *time* to: see? It's just that time, is all. And maybe that's how it is with me. Can you maybe try to think of it like that? Do you think?'

'But it's not ... oh Dad, it's not the same thing at *all*, though, is it? Is it? It just *isn't*, is it?'

Jeremy sighed, and looked at the boy. 'Not really. No. No – you're right: it's different. Completely. Oh God look – I just ... it's all a bit *quick*, this, for all of us, and I don't frankly – OK, Adrian, OK: I'll be frank with you, yes? Man to man. I don't *know* if what I'm doing is ... all I can do is go with the flow – and no I *don't* mean that to sound – oh Christ, I *am* taking all this very seriously, of course I am, it's just that it's a bit sudden for me too, you know – and who knows? Maybe all I'll do is go away for a day or two, have a bit of a – you know, *think*, and then, um, come back again and all this will be no more than – '

'But you're not. That's not what you're doing, is it?'

'Um. No. No, it isn't.'

'I thought you were being straight with me?'

'I was. I was. It started *out* straight . . .'

'I have to go and help Mum, now. She's seeing to all your clothes, and stuff. Are you going to be with a woman? Donna said to ask you.'

'*Donna* – ?!'

'And she also said . . .'

'Mm? Yeh?'

'You still owe us for the past five weeks' pocket money. Will we still get that when you're gone? Expect not.'

'Oh God, Adrian . . . Here. Take this. Take it. And this is for Donna.'

'God, Dad . . .!'

'Just take it.'

Jeremy felt a pang of pure love and maybe remembrance as the expression on his young son's face went so fast from grave to almost radiant, his fingers closing fast on the twenty-pound notes. With the unchecked grin all over him, Adrian whooped just once, turned away and bounded up the stairs to seek out his mother. He found her where he knew she was: kneeling on the floor of the small bedroom, still busy seeing to all of Jeremy's clothes, and stuff. When she saw Adrian, she smiled and – quite as promised – passed to him the Stanley knife, so that he too could have a go.

*

And now I'm here. Slumped over my drawing-board in Maria's back extension, just as I seem to have been for (and I get this feeling from way outside me) far too long. I am trying to do the very simplest thing, here, and somehow I keep on failing. I don't get any more the huger commissions, not now I don't: *pitch* for them, yeah (well – not lately, not now: after the first and then the second tranche

36

of rejections, you just don't trouble any more – and anyway, word gets round: in this game, the word is all).

I don't know what it is – they seem to be going for altogether younger and more wide-open concepts, these days. Or so, I think, that last one said. Not long after moving in with Maria, I went for that hottest of hot new Docklands restaurants – not just the interior, but the front and side elevations and most of the landscaping too. But even as I was talking them through the quite searing specification, leading on up to what I felt sure, then, was a totally mind-blowing *coup de théâtre* (back-lit and sometimes wholly illusory walls and frangipani-scented air ducts were just one throbbing part of it – can't now recall even so much as the nature of the trigger for such impulses as I had) – I just knew that the clients were almost palpably yawning: they did not intrude upon my detailed explosions – nor did they enquire if I had given any thought to such as staff uniform, nickable ashtrays or monogrammed stemware (and I had, I had – but all my print-outs and spreadsheets were left unexplored).

Not long after, I heard a whisper that someone with money unlimited high up in the arts world (Getty Museum – that was the word) was taking delivery of a forty-million-dollar private jet, and now he was seriously in the market for a state-of-the-art interior that would render Hefner's old Big Bunny of the Sixties the sort of cool and cloistered enclave from whose cellars the likes of Chartreuse might come. So of *course* I went big-time for that – well wow: what designer wouldn't? Hey? You name me one. Didn't get it – as, I suppose by now, was just about inevitable.

It was maybe around then I began to lose it – and no, I'm not, of course I'm not (how could I be?) *blaming* Maria in even a small way for any of this, but still now I feel sure that I might just have persisted if only she had ever liked even one of my ideas – approved my artwork (applauded just any of my dazzling conceptions). Or – if she didn't at all go for the sort of thing I did – then at least, maybe, if she could just have brought herself to keep a bit quiet about it. But no:

'And this,' she'd say – stabbing with disdain at whatever it was I'd just come up with, some new club (and using the fine steel tip of one of my Rotring pens to do it – no matter that I was constantly beseeching her just never to touch them). 'What in hell is *this* supposed to be?'

'It's a – well, what it *will* be is an endless and serpentine banquette. Inspiration, I suppose, was that Dali sofa – you know the one: red and pouty – Mae West's lips? But the idea is, you take the fullness, right – the whole sort of erotic *engorgement* of the original, yeah – but make it sinuous and sort of *enclasping*, so that when people first come in, down the stairs, the first thing they feel is a kind of – '

'Jeremy. What in fuck is it that you're actually *talking* about? What people like to sit on is *chairs*, yeh? Why don't you lot ever get that? I go somewhere – club, bar – then what I want is a chair, OK, and some dumb table to stick my drink. So where are the *tables* in this nightmare dive of yours?'

'I've tried quite hard to update the concept. What there is: look here – see those? There will be hundreds of these twenty-mill toughened glass cantilevered ledges at all different levels – all curved, a bit Noguchi – and as the temperature alters and shifts, then all these different deep pastel colours come into play. It'll be very exciting because – '

'Wrong, Jeremy – wrong. This is where you get it all wrong. People aren't – they just *aren't* excited by any of this. *Designers* may be – but humans, believe me, just aren't. I don't know anyone, Jeremy, who goes somewhere for a drink and ends up having orgasms over bloody sofas and no Gucci *ledges*. And who in fuck's Mae West? Because I'm telling you – if she isn't an It girl or in the charts, you may as well forget it because she won't even be *coming* to your

poxy little bar, will she? And without people like that –
you're *dead*, mate.'

Jeremy could only glance up, and just then he noticed
two things about her: the scorn implicit in her stiffened
nostrils drained him and made him awash with lust – and
also that her breasts, you know, were really quite small
(when honestly compared to those of others). Her legs, of
course, remained the thing – and he owned that he wanted
her most when he watched them amble away from him,
and not when he lay crouched and rutting between each
shank, gasping as if for breath, if not just a modicum of
mercy.

Sex had been just everything, when Jeremy first had
come here – and this remained true (though only, he supposed, in the sense that now it's all there was). Arrival had
been so strange, and not strange. He had come to Maria so
naturally, and yet just one day before he had been sitting
at home, with wife and children (all of them soon busy, it
later transpired – those loved ones of his – coldly
destroying all he most cared for; Anne had even, Jeremy
can still barely bring himself to tell you, sawn into pieces
a Mackintosh Hill House chair, and then wrapped up and
posted him the bits. She could at least have sold it – if its
presence had offended her, and she felt unable to grant
him custody: Christ alone knows that these days, Jesus, the
money would be useful).

He had known zero about this Maria, absolute zero –
and now, after all this dead time together, he could only
wonder at what could never really be termed the sum total,
totting up as it did to little more than nothing. Her real
name *was* Phoebe; so she hadn't, that time they met, said
she was a freebie (which she wasn't, no no – expensive,
very, in all sorts of ways). And her brother? The buried
alive one? Couldn't tell you – wouldn't even begin to
hazard. She did refer to his funeral, just one more time –
the funeral (if it took place – if there ever was a brother,

living or dead) which she had not attended. Told me that just as the coffin was halfway lowered into the cold and dark, the brief trill of a mobile phone shrilled from within it. And then, she added with drama: it *stopped*.

'It stopped? Stopped ringing? Christ. But Jesus – why was he buried with a mobile bloody – ?'

'You're not paying *attention*, are you, Jeremy? This wasn't just *any* old funeral, was it? Hm? He was *alive*, I tell you – alive. All it means is he answered the phone. Don't you see? Someone rang him, as he went to his grave. Poor soul.'

Well as I say – your guess is quite as good as mine. One other time – yeh, bit pissed, otherwise I never would have dared – I said Oi – Maria (because I still called her that, yes, I suppose because it had become my own personal name for her) – Hey Maria, listen: some time during the three days before he croaked, this brother of yours – what did you say his name was? – why didn't he call up the fire brigade on his mobile and get them to come and dig him out? She looked at me hard and said *Gross*. She went on really staring cruelly, and soon she came out with *Sick*. Then she laughed as if at an absurdity and said Anyway – I doubt he could get a signal, down there; his name was Des – but he had a lisp, so whenever he said it it came out as Death.

You figure it out – I've tried and tried and I can't. We were eating a couple of steaks I'd done at the time – I'm no cook, believe me: steak in a pan is more or less it – and it was then that I was suddenly hit by the thought: Maria? Maria? I thought you said that time you were a vegetarian? No, she said; just no, is what she said. What, I stumbled on – No, you *didn't* say that? Or No, you *aren't* one? Oh – Just eat and be quiet, was all I got to that. And all I could think was Why on earth do I find me here with her? When what I clearly am is nearly alone.

And what of Maria herself? What, I wondered, could she be getting out of my being in her place? I'm even now not too sure about that. At the beginning, she seemed smug in a tower (all of her own erection) simply on account of my having become an *installation*. Whatever I gave her – I shouldn't ever think much, in the real sense – seemed to be enough and more so, at first: at first, it certainly did. We stayed in a lot – my work I'd left to go and hang (she had nothing to carp at, till I took it up again) – and the money I spent, I don't care to think of. Sent even more to Anne, of course – who said she couldn't work, now, because of the children: she'd sacked Nan the nanny (well of *course* she had, she insisted – how now could she share the same roof as her? A constant reminder of my serial infidelity? Jesus). I paid the mortgage – dreaded Adrian getting into Westminster (the reverse of how I used to think – but time and circumstance can do that, reverse things – and also: have you seen what they *charge*, these places?). Maria, well – I suppose this Max Bannister character must have kept her, before: certainly she seemed to have no money of her own (paid her mortgage, too). No job, or anything: her sole occupation was assassinating mine.

We'd gone out, too: pictures, eating, parties. I went off the parties fairly soon, though. Sometimes she'd catch sight of some man she decided was on a par with the devil, and it was all I could do to restrain her from physically consigning him to hell. She still loves going to them, though – the parties. These days I simply pass straight on to her whatever invitations I sometimes receive (few, so very few, just lately – because word gets round: in this game, the word is all).

Last night. She went to one. Party, I mean. I only mention it because, well – it's morning, now: coming up to eleven, and she hasn't yet shown. It's not that I'm worried, or anything – not per se; I mean Christ: grown-up woman – look after herself, yes? It's just that I feel cold in a way that is new to me. I have been lonely, I now know, for just about ever, but never quite that other thing – alone; and it is the threat of this ultimate coldness that now I am feeling. Wife. Children. Clients. And the woman who walked right up to and away with me: they seem to be gone. And you know what? Without people like that – you're *dead*, mate.

CHAPTER TWO

'Christ Oh God, Hugo – *please* take your hand away from there – get *off* me, Christ's sake, will you?'

This was Anne, exclaiming in that way she had now – a desperation born of the shock of fracture and ground down further by sheer and utter day-to-day weariness – they bonded together and exerted this permanent hold on the larynx: her cawing voice, she would swear, always now a good few shrill degrees higher than ever it had been (and lurking behind it, the threat of breaking).

'Oh but *Anne*, you gorgeous thing – how can I? How can I? How can I possibly keep my hands away from you when all I see is so much undulating loveliness?'

Anne slammed down two plates (she was drying plates) and turned on the man.

'Oh *crap*, Hugo – get the fuck *off*. They're *my* breasts – mine. Go and play with your own flabby breasts, bloody Hugo. Jesus – there's so much *pork* on you, these days – they're *acres* bigger than mine. And no oh *no* – *please* don't go through all the *further* crap of looking at me *hurt*, like that. I've got the kids' *teas* to do, Hugo, and Adrian is fixated on peanut butter but it's got to be *crunchy*, right, oh Jesus – and *Donna*, Donna won't even *look* at crunchy, not now she won't – will she? Will she?'

'Anne – '

'*Oh* no – not Donna. Got to be *smooth*, hasn't it? And she's gone right off Penguins – it's all KitKats now and I have to – it's me who has to keep all this in my *head*, Hugo – there's only me to *do* all this and it *changes*, it keeps on changing from day to day, and not just the food, no no – if it was only the food, then maybe I could . . . but their *clothes*, my God – they're so damn fussy about their *clothes*, and particularly Adrian. It used to be the girls, didn't it? It was girls who were always meant to be so terribly particular – but Jesus, you should just sit down and listen to Adrian, some time. *This* must have creases, but this must be just *folded* – and all his stuff, all these shirts and things have *writing* all over them and it drives you mad, simply *mad* when you're ironing it all because you just can't help yourself reading and reading the same few stupid words over and over again – "Converse", that's one of them – and "N Y City" and "Total Sport" and Jesus oh Jesus – it's all the reading I ever *do* any more – just don't do *anything* any more – and *then*, even then – they don't *thank* you, do they? You never even get so much as a syllable of *gratitude* out of them, do you? Kids? All you get is "Oh yuk there's *brown* in the toilet" and it's no good my saying Well that's because neither of you ever shits straight *down* – and anyway, I haven't *got* to the lavatory yet, it's Tuesday I do the loos – and it's *lavatory*, Adrian: lavatory or loo – what do they teach you at that bloody stupid school of yours? No no – no good at all, because they think that home should be like all those hotels their bloody *father* used to take them to before he just walked out and left us all to *live* like this. I *try* – I *try* to explain: *look*, Adrian, I tell him – '

'Anne – '

'Oh fuck *off*, Hugo, and listen: *Adrian*, I say – you know the circumstances, don't you, hm? Mummy can't *afford* a cleaner any more, can she? Or a nanny. Because Daddy won't let us have them any more because he's *left* us, he's *left* us and he's spending all his money on some *showgirl* and probably buying up more stupid *chairs* and things – although I do keep telling them they mustn't *blame* him, I do say that, because I don't actually think it's right: children taking sides. And Adrian just doodles in the dust – he

44

keeps on drawing on the furniture with his finger: everything says "Clean Me"! Everywhere I look I see "Clean Me", "Clean Me" – and I can't keep up with it, I just can't, I can't, I *can't*!'

Hugo, in a bid to quieten her, if not quite shut her up, held wide his arms – his face hung heavy with a curtain of fond understanding – and this time, with an anguished sob and the rolling of wet and injured eyes to heaven, she actually went for it.

'Oh Hugo! Oh Hugo! I *hate* living like this. Hate it hate it hate it! How could that bastard have *done* this to me?'

'*Anne,*' soothed Hugo – holding her now, and cloaking his thoughts with an even darker velvet. 'Anne . . . Anne . . . Anne . . .'

'Hugo . . . Hugo? Stop *touching* me, you bastard. Take your hand *away* from there. How many times have I got to keep on *saying* it?'

And then she was gone from him, as Hugo had known she would just have to be. Her voice now was cranked up close to cracking, and that meant that soon . . . ah no – it was *now*: already she had launched into the declamatory:

'What *is* it about you men? Why are you so all *over* us one minute and somewhere else entirely the next? Why can't a woman ever just know where she *is*?!'

'*I* would never leave you, Anne – you know that.'

'You *can't*, can you, Hugo? How can you leave me? You're not even *here*. Which I wish you'd get into your head. Oh Jesus – that's the door. Adrian's back from school and I haven't even . . . Oh God and he'll go *mad* if he has to wear the same shirt again tomorrow and I forgot to do the white wash, and anyway there's no more Comfort – oh get out of the *way*, you stupid man, Hugo –'

And then Hugo was really alert – even fright was teasing him – because suddenly Anne was silent, and her look was cold and hard and coping with incredulity. They both were hearing 'Mum?' – 'Mum' was being called out from maybe the hall. And then she hissed at him (and venom was there – simply phials of it):

'You've . . . eaten it. You've *eaten* it!'

'Hm? Oh . . . that. Well it was only a bit of bread and – '

'Only a bit of . . .?! It wasn't only a bit of *bread*, Hugo, you fat greedy *bastard* – it was the *last* of the bread and it had Adrian's crunchy peanut butter on it and he's *here* now and what am I going to *do*? What shall I *say* to him? Please tell me! Ah – here he is now – *you* explain, Hugo: you explain to Adrian just exactly what it is you've *done*!'

And as Anne sat down and wept and then howled and held on tight to her racked-up ribs, Hugo and Adrian just looked at one another, and there wasn't even so much as a question between them.

*

It can't go on, Anne just sat there thinking: not like this, it can't. She thought these hard words often, without ever being sure – not, you know, really clear in her own *mind* – quite what it was she was meaning. And here it was again, that feeling now, as she gazed at herself candidly in this rather lovely and oval mahogany mirror she had once and long ago spotted, haggled a bit for and got: sneaked it into the house, and with drama and lip-set adamance had hung it as prominently and she hoped as jarringly as possible in what she could only wince to remember she had quite unselfconsciously termed the 'family room'. (*This*, she had said pointedly to Jeremy, is *furniture*. It is made of polished wood and has a pretty banded inlay; why does everything you keep on telling me is a magnificent example, oh God – cutting-edge *design* have to be made out of steel and slate and what looks like bits of *saddles*?)

Anne had finally got Donna off, and Adrian too was asleep; in his *room*, anyway – what he did there was entirely up to him. Well look – face it: she couldn't *for ever*, could she, be telling him it was *school* in the morning and for God's sake put out the *light* and why oh God *why* do you have to have that perfectly ghastly music blaring into the *night*? (And if he didn't want to brush his teeth, well then sod him, quite frankly. He wants to grow up to be a handsome young man with yellow and rotting teeth and bleeding gums well then that's just got to be *his* affair, I'm thinking now – I can't be nannying him *all* my life, can I? There must for me be more than that.) And it's just the same with his reading: Mister Masters had made it perfectly plain in that last English report of his that if there was to be any hope at all with Westminster, then he really had to use these holidays to get down to some serious reading – and, more important than that, actually *understanding* what it is that's being *said*. And you go on, don't you, till you're blue in the . . . and why is it, actually, that children just don't seem to comprehend that it's *their* future, *their* lives – God knows it's no skin off my . . . and *honestly*, Adrian, I say to him, you are, don't you think, just a wee bit on the *old* side now for all these *comics*, hm? And what does he say? What does he do? He just *looks* at me – looks at me that way he does as if all *my* years on earth (and please, oh God, don't get me on to the *age* thing) amount to absolutely and precisely nothing – and then he curls up his lip in that perfectly revolting way (sure he got it from some damn film or other) and says to me (and you haven't *heard* condescending, not till you've heard Adrian like this, I'm telling you) Graphic *novels*, Mum – they're called graphic novels: don't you know *anything*? Don't *I* know anything?! Oh that's good, that is – coming from a bone-idle thirteen-year-old, that just really has to be *the* most . . .! And anyway, it's his *father* who should be dealing with all of this, this boy thing, not me. Isn't it enough I've got a little girl to tend to? And not just tend, but defend as well – shield her from the odour of threat and abandonment that is just everywhere, now. He's *gone*, and he sends no *money* – and all of us are just *left* here and it can't, it can't, it can't go on – no way, no way: not like this, it can't.

*

I'm calmer, now – these days, I am. I was only like that then, when all of it was new to me. It takes time, you know, to realize that a man has really *gone* – left you (finished). And it's hard too to quite put a finger on what exactly happened when he was actually around; it's just the fact that he is no longer that seems to make everything so utterly different. Worse, oh yes worse – no doubt, now, about that, although it pains me to even think it. At first, I tried – I really did try to be, oh . . . not positive, no (I'm not that big a fool), but at least to attempt to point up some of the *advantages*, here: no more kowtowing to a profitless buffoon – no longer having to worry if I knocked some stupid and angular chrome thing a centimetre out of parallel (not that I gave a toss either way about what he once actually termed – God, Jeremy, you're such a bogus shit – his aesthetic *hurting* – can you believe it?) It's just that whenever anything was, in his eyes, *wrong* – he'd go on and on and on about it until, oh God, you'd just want to take an axe to the whole bloody lot: which subsequently, I more or less did – that farce of a Mackintosh chair, anyway (stupid bloody thing – couldn't even sit on it; wish I'd sold it, now – these days, the money would be useful).

And money: he sent no money. Said he had none. Well, I expect he didn't – not after lavishing on this *woman* all the designer clothes, and the holidays and the dinners and the surprises and the treats and all the other, oh God – *things* these demolishers of lives seem to expect as their unassailable due ('Look at all the people I have just ripped up and trodden on – pay me, please, and handsomely'). And what about Adrian and Westminster? That's what's worrying me now – an anxiety that will keep on winkling

48

in, under what puny defences are not really left. I mean –
what? Adrian's going to work really hard and pass the
entrance exam, is he (well actually, on current progress, and
given his attitude, emphatically no – but let that lie while I
get to the point); and then his big-shot no-hope two-faced
fork-tongued pig-shit absentee father is going to turn round
and say Oh well *done*, Adrian, prime effort, brilliant – but
things being the way they are, old chap, no can do, hope
you understand: why not throw a petrol bomb into Mother-
care, next time you're passing, and possibly we can wangle
you a place in Borstal. Great, isn't it? He sees a pretty face
and just goes for it: all that's ugly is left behind him.

And everyone's draining me white: the children, yes –
but it's hardly their fault, is it? They have enquiring *minds* –
famous for it. So when Adrian says . . . well, like he did yet
again, just the other day:

'Why, Mum, has Dad actually gone? We don't even *see*
him any more. I thought he'd come back. Is he never
coming back, then?'

'He hates us,' said Donna, with that nearly usual, now,
big-eyed defiance – her own words forcing those eyes to
crumple before they widened again, wet now and made
glassy by whatever awful thing she had conjured up behind
them.

'Doesn't – of course he doesn't,' tried Anne. 'It's just that
he feels that for now – and no, Adrian, I don't know how
long "now" will be – he just has to be . . . somewhere else, is
all. Doesn't *hate* us, course not. Loves us. In his way.'

'I heard you saying to Hugo he was a *bastard*.'

'Well, Adrian,' allowed Anne – quite at her most reasoned, 'he *is*, of course – but that doesn't necessarily detract
from the facts of the matter.'

'What does that mean?'

Don't know, thought Anne: just made it up. Couldn't
understand, even as I was saying it. And I don't even care if
he changes his mind, now, and *does* come back, because I'm

simply not having him, not now I'm not: at the beginning, I might have (for the sake of the children? No – for the sake of the money), but not now I won't, no way. Wouldn't have him back in the house. If we still *have* the house. I pass him letters from the mortgage company: they arrive quite frequently, now.

'And why did Nan have to go too?' went on Adrian – relentless, settling again to trundling down the ruts of a much-travelled road – and in spite of all Anne's pleading, he always got into it when Donna was around (think of your little *sister*, Anne had once implored, and Adrian had come back deadpan: I am).

'I miss Nan,' Donna practically sobbed. 'I miss Nan even more than Daddy. When is Nan coming back to us, Mummy? Does she hate us too? Are she and Daddy together, somewhere?'

Anne just shook her head. No: Nan was the *resident* tart, you see, little Donna, who Daddy chose to screw while he was here – but now that Daddy's *away*, well – he's jolly busy screwing quite another tart altogether! Like he always has done – God knows how many times, or where – Dubai, oh yes – but that was just one of them. (Men for you, isn't it? In a bloody nutshell.)

*

'You're too young to understand.'

'Not,' protested Donna.

'Oh you are, you are,' Adrian insisted – quite his most urbane and assured, now: he always was, when it was just the two of them. 'You see, what you don't see is what Mum is actually *saying* without, you know, actually *saying* it. You're too young to get it.'

'Get *what*, Adrian? Say sorry to Barbie for not kissing her.'

'Look – I don't think Dad's *ever* coming back. It's just us, now. It's what men do, when they get older. Loads of my friends don't have dads any more – well, they *have* them – see them at weekends, mostly, but they don't actually live at home any more. You grow out of it.'

'Say it. Say sorry.'

'Oh, *Donna* . . .!'

'Say it.'

'Sorry. Sorry, Barbie, for not kissing you – kay? I expect I'll do the same, when I get older. Just go. It's actually pretty cool, sort of. If you're a man.'

'You're going to Westminster. Are you not coming back too?'

'Oh – I'll be back. Westminster's just a school – I mean when I'm *older*, older.'

'What's a bastard?'

'It's in Shakespeare. Means shitty.'

'Rude. Rude word. What's shake-sce?'

'Spear. Old writer. Right pain, actually. You're lucky, Donna – you don't have to *do* all this stuff, yet.'

'Mummy's always sad.'

'Yeh. And in a temper. Dad's fault.'

'He should have said sorry for never kissing her. *Is* he a bastard, then – Daddy? Is he? Is he shitty?'

'Dunno. Expect so.'

'And what about Hugo? He always brings sweets.'

'Oh *Hugo*! He's just *sad*. Not like Mum's sad, I don't mean – just *sad*, sad – you know? Tragic.'

'What's that mean?'

'That's sort of Shakespeare too. He's a tragedy. It means completely hopeless, really. Totally crap.'

'Rude word! Shitty crap! Shitty crap!'

'Ssh – Mum'll hear and start up again. I know! I'm going to get all my Action Man stuff.'

'Don't! He drove his car into Barbie last time, and it messed up all her plaited hair with *beads* in.'

'That's what Action Man *does*, isn't it? Honestly, Donna – you're just still too young to *get* it.'

*

'*Look*,' Hugo had said – the very day after Jeremy had gone, Hugo was there, pleading his case. 'Look: *he* may be a bastard, Jeremy – yes he is, he is – but *I'm* not, Anne. I'm not like him. I'm different. I'm nicer.'

'You're a *man*, aren't you?' And yes, Anne thought – I might as well sneer: Hugo will take it.

'Not all men are the same, Anne – you know that. Why are you saying all this? You *know* I'm not like that.'

'I don't know *anything* any more, and I don't much care. Don't put your glass there, Hugo – it's going to leave a mark.'

'You sound like – '

'*Don't*, Hugo: just don't say it. Right?'

'Right. Won't. But you do. But never mind all that – all right, all right: you *don't*. But *answer* me, Anne. Will you? Will you do this for me? *Please*, Anne – I just can't approach him now. Christ – I actually told him where he could stick his bloody job, don't know why I did, I just did – and Max, believe me – he just isn't the sort of person who will easily forget it. But if *you* talk to him, Anne – '

'But why on earth *me*, Hugo? I only met the man once, and that was just ages ago.'

'Yeh but he'll *see* you, he'll listen to you – me, he won't even take my calls. Been trying him all bloody morning.'

And so it was that Anne – not even knowing why – had rung up Max Bannister and arranged to meet him for a chat over lunch (Yeh, he had said – *course* I remember you, darling: *choice*). Look: her husband, Jeremy, had the day before met a woman and walked out on her and his family, and now, apparently, Anne was (was she really?) – at the wheedling insistence of the ineffectual and frankly con-

52

temptible Hugo – seeing his ex-boss, whom she didn't even know, in a bid to get back the man's job. Why did she agree to do such a thing? Maybe, could it have been (and now she could ask herself candidly) that she realized that at some point a beholden and solvent Hugo might not, despite everything, be such a bad thing to have in her grip? Don't know. Maybe. Don't know.

And even as she was setting out to meet this Mister Bannister (I wonder if I ought to have my hair chopped short again?) Anne very nearly phoned to call the whole thing off. Her mind was flashing a neon embarrassment (I can't *possibly* just coldly do this – and why should I anyway? What the hell is Hugo to me?) then idling back into a somnolent resignation: Why the hell not? What on earth does it matter what I do or who I speak to? My husband Jeremy has just this week met a woman and walked out on me and my children – so what else can hurt?

But still, but still – she very nearly phoned to call the whole thing off: the cordless was here and tight in her hand, one finger raised up for stabbing. And then she laid it down and thought Oh sweet Jesus – let's just *do* it.

*

So why do I say Yeah when this bird from nowhere just phones me up right out of the bloody blue? I'll tell you for why, son – cos right at that bloody moment in my life if I hadn't had a jaw with bleeding someone, I dunno – can't, you know, sort of put it into kinda thing, words . . . it was all this bloody Phoebe business – doing my bloody head in, couldn't barely believe it. I mean *look* at it, is how I was thinking: this time yesterday, I'm shacked up all neat and tight with her – and no, don't get me wrong, I'm not saying she's an angel or nothing, but which of them are? Ay? You ever ran into Little Miss Bleeding Perfect? You been around a bit you come to know that not never you going to get a full house. Know what I'm saying? So Phoebe, right – spends money like there's no wossname, admitted – could be a right bloody haughty cow too, when she felt like it . . . but Christ, what a plus side, son: she looked really good with you, Phoebe did: classy. Take her bloody anywhere, is what I'm saying to you – hear? And the long climb up those bloody legs of hers, Christ: that, and she fucked like a rabbit.

And then she's gone. Met a bloke – and she's off. Now look: get this. I've had a few birds in my time, you better believe it – could be more than my fair share, oh yes, I'm not denying – but me, I always treat them good, like ladies. Bung 'em some flowers, take 'em up West – always say something nice about the dress, even if it looks a bloody joke. And no one – not one of them – has ever walked out on me. You got to understand: people just don't *do* that, not to me: Mister Max Bannister just ain't for walking out on. And here – it's funny now: couple of hours before Phoebe hits me with this one, bleeding ungrateful sow, bloody Hugo walks out on me and all! No look: something you gotta know about Hugo – he's a twat, right? Total wanker. Point is, he's good at what he's paid for. He ain't no creative, nah – couldn't build up a decent campaign to save his bleeding life – but Jesus, can he sell it to the men with the money! It was Hugo what got signatures down there on the dotted line – know what I mean? I reckon it's because he's one of nature's born brown-nosers and arse-lickers, and believe me, in the ad game, you need one or two like that. So it pissed me off, right, losing the bastard – but he put me in this *position*, right? I dunno – still don't bloody get it: said I'd sacked him – Phoebe said I'd sacked him, or something – and then he starts mouthing off at me. Which no one – not anyone – ever does. Get? Not to me. So what could I do? Caught – right? Told him to fuck off. Couple of hours later, Feebs ups and tells me she's bloody off too! Met a bloke: believe it? She goes to a party in some bloody pussy-pelmet what I bloody paid for – meets a bloke and that's it: kaput. Blows me out the bloody water. So I told her to fuck off. Wish I had. Didn't want her to go, is what I was feeling. Yeah. So. Fucks off anyway.

Next day: call comes through. Some bird called 'Anne', friend of Hugo (that's a new one – Hugo having *friends*). We met once, she says – don't suppose you remember. Too bloody right: don't suppose I do. How many people I meet in this game? So I says Yeah, oh yeah – *course* I remember, darling: *choice*. Truth is, she sounded OK – and what else did I have doing? Ay? On that day in my life. Plus – she says she's a friend of Hugo's, maybe I can get her to, I dunno – *talk* to him, yeh? Get him back and forget all the shit. (Silly tosser – he'd been phoning all day – but you don't, do you? Well you can't. You say Fuck off, you gotta be firm.)

So I'm on my way outta there, right, and then Monica starts in on me, don't she (OK, I'm not saying . . . she runs my life, granted, like a good PA should – Christ alone knows what would come down if ever *Monica* walked, yeh sure – but she can be a right pain in the butt, I'm telling you here and now: Do this, do that – be here, go there; sometimes I'm thinking she forgets who signs the cheques round here).

'Max,' she goes. 'You can't go out now – Simon Bowman's due – it's in your diary.'

'Yeh? Well tell him to shove it. Bowman's a pain in the butt.'

'He's *important*, Max. This meeting was set up *ages* ago, and you know what he's like when he's – '

'Yeh: yeh. I know what he's like – he's like a *prat*, is what he's like. Just tell him to stuff hisself. Or say I'll ring him. Do whatever it takes, Monica darling – on this day in my life, I just gotta be outta here – OK?'

Sometimes, when I end – you know, sign off like that with an 'OK', it looks like Monica's – I don't know what it

55

is with her – kind of *considering* it, or something, almost as if she's really checking that what I've said is all *right*.

'He won't like it,' is all she had left: tight-lipped and tight-arsed, that's our Monica – what a diamond.

'So he does the other thing – what the fuck I care?'

So again I ask you: why? Ay? Why? This broad from nowhere called Anne phones me right out of the bloody blue and I'm cutting appointments and sending old Monica into a right old tizz. I reckoned at the time it was fate what brought us together. That Kiss-thing. Whatever. Anyway, look – for starters, this is how it went:

I said we'd go to Sophie's, and I was very pleased with myself for doing so: good decision, very. She was knocked sideways, Anne – you can always tell. See – my world, you got to check out all the happening places soon as they hit – and Sophie's, I'm telling you, was one time nearly as hot as The Ivy: they ripped off just about everything they could from them, course, right down to the bleeding stained-glass windows (and what place still in business hasn't had a go?), but then, you know, time and all the bloody luvvies moved on a bit, and Sophie's settled down into being more, what is it – *discreet*, is what I'm meaning. Stayed right up there, oh yeah, but you felt more sort of *easy*; still costing you major damage, though – which, when you're out to nail someone (basically what lunch is about), is still, you bet it is, the name of the game, whatever other crap people try and stuff you. Also – they know me there: know what I'm saying? None of this balls about Oh dear no, *terribly* sorry, we don't have a table: I call – they got a table (always one or two kept back for VIPs: they all do this – got to). And Armand – the mater dee, yeah? Been there since when. He treats me nice. Which is why I'm always just a little bit late: I don't have to tell you the score. Bird or client (much the same: we're talking *deal*, right?) – they don't know the place, they say your name to whoever's greeting and bingo! Instant and big recognition: already we're talking kudos. Then the *real* welcome comes from Armand, when yours truly ambles through the door: total waste if you get there first.

So that's the moment I clap eyes on Anne – snug in the corner, she was. My usual table – yeh, course: not too many prying eyes, and from where she was sitting (nice little dress she'd got on – nothing great, but enough to show she had all you need) bugger all to see but me: and that's the way I like it. How was I looking? OK, not bad, pretty bloody good – and considering the trauma I been through, fucking ace. It's not just women, you know, what get bad hair days – but today (complete fluke – didn't get time for one of Trevor's historic wash 'n' blow-drys) it was looking cool – bit long, bit sexy, but classy with it – know what I mean? And the suit? Well – all my suits, they knock 'em dead, face it: coming in at twelve hundred a pop, I should bleeding well hope so.

Anne looked up when finally he arrived at the table; she was aware of both his reception and his studied approach, of course she was, but here and now came the moment she selected to raise her eyes.

'*Anne*,' announced Max – not so much sitting down as enthroning himself opposite her. He flapped out his large and stiff linen napkin, ramming it – Anne was relieved to observe – roughly over most of his knees (Jeremy had a way of, Jesus – *aligning* napkins, oh God I can't tell you: even the memory of it among so many ghastly others has set on edge the fillings in my teeth).

'You must think I'm awful,' said Anne, 'just ringing you up out of the blue, like that. Can't believe I did it.'

Max had a hand raised – maybe to stem any further disclaimers, possibly in the hope of flagging down a lost and cruising taxi.

'Ah Johnny,' he beamed at the bright-eyed, dark-haired, eager and fairly frightened young man who had drawn up beside him from nowhere. 'I think we'll have the DP, yeah? OK by you, Anne?'

Anne nodded silently – and Max thought Yeah: you know what *that* is, don't you? Got you already, haven't I, darling? Masterful: the shared and posh fizz – yet subtle, always subtly done: choice, if I may say so.

'Nah,' he went on, after Johnny had scuttled away – maybe joyous at having escaped a custodial sentence. 'Like you said – we met. Not strangers. Remember it well. You're a very memorable lady, Anne, if I may say so.'

Anne looked down. Christ this is great – she's gone for it: really lapping it up, this one (we are looking at pure doddle, my son). But you know, I like that looking down thing some birds do – I like demure. You see it in them BBC things (only good bit) when everyone's poncing about in britches and tailcoats and crap like that and talking in that stupid way they did then. Then the talent arrives, don't she – all low-cut titty dresses and waving a fan and looking down, like that: raunchy little bitches. As I say – I like demure (and this bit of totty – she's got it in spades).

'Tell you what, Anne love – why don't you get that pretty little nose of yours well stuck into the menu, ay? Check it out, see what you fancy – smoked salmon's a fucking wonder, I have to tell you, if you're into that, at all – and then we can have a good old jaw. How's that? All right?'

Nice little smile, she's got – and now she's reading through the card like a good girl, just as I says to do: like that in a woman. And the tits on her, yeh, are definitely sound. Which you need.

'Mmm,' Anne was now enthusing (is she trying, I'm wondering, to come over just a bit girly? Could be, could be). 'Scallops – divine. *Is* it "scallops", actually? Or scollops? You hear both. Ooh and look – moules!'

'Couldn't tell you, love: don't never look at neither. You don't want all that shellfish rubbish – you wanna go for some whitebait, maybe – or smoked salmon, never go wrong with that. How about a nice bit of smoked salmon to kick off with, ay? And then a, what? Dover sole? Off the bone – easy to eat, can't be bad.'

So she went for those, like he bleeding knew she would. See – you got to suss out your woman bang at square one, else you've lost it. This one – she wants to be guided. Nah – scrub that: she wants to be *told*. And I'm here to tell her – got it? It's easy if you know what you're about (and you got the moolah to back it up, course. Birds, most birds, without cash you're dead: they smell it off of you. Just look at the way she's eyeing up the Dom bloody Perignon: aye aye, she's thinking: aye aye. And she's clocked the Rolex – course she has. You can see it all over her, plain as you like).

'*Armand*, my dear old mate,' set up Max, now, at the man's quite effortlessly sidelong approach. 'Like you to meet a very special lady friend of mine – Anne, this is Armand: very much the man to know around here. Ain't that right, Armand?'

'Any friend of Mister Bannister's is most welcome,' smiled Armand – and Max was frankly marvelling at the way he just came out with it: so cool, you know? Totally *discreet*, is it, but mega-*sprauncy* with it – know what I'm saying? 'The champagne to your liking, madame?'

'It's ace, Armand,' came back Max. 'Now listen, Armand – I think we're ready to order. Smoked salmon, twice – no *bits* with mine, you know how I like it. Maybe the lady'd like all the stuff comes with it . . . nah, don't think so. We'll have it as it is. The sole, then, I think – make them big ones, ay? You know how I like it. And a few sauté – couple of beans, few other bits, yeh? Choice selection, is what we're after.'

'Off coss, sore. And would you care to see the wine?'

'Stick with this. Shout when I wanna nother bottle.'

'Off coss. *Thank* you, Mister Bannister. Madame.'

See? Come to somewhere like Sophie's, and wall-to-wall respect is what you get. Tell you something else – and correct me if I'm thing, but I don't think the two is unrelated. This is it: since I walk through the door, I'm not any more thinking about Phoebe: up till now it'd been like a hook in my head, churning me up. Point is, this Anne is *responding* – making me remember who I am again. And maybe Feebs was right on one score – I *was* staying in and working too much, cutting the parties – yeh, all of that. Well – let's get it straight: I wasn't never cutting nothing *key* (I ain't that bloody green), but still – yeh, s'pose – I wasn't putting my face about as much as I could've done. Here's a big for instance: I go to the party the night before, then Phoebe don't get to fuck and fuck off with her bleeding Mister Wonderful (wouldn't have let her out of my sight for a minute – never ever did, till lately). But then look at this – if I'd listened to sodding Monica, I'd right now be up to my eyes in some crap of a pitch with Simon bloody Bowman – and instead of all that I'm being *revered* again, like I know I ought to be: Armand, he's looking after me really nice, and Anne – well, Anne, she's seeing me for what I really *am*. And after Phoebe, that's a good feeling, deep down.

'Happy with the salmon? Best in London – telling you.'

'Mm – it's really – '

'Yeh yeh – it's triffic, you don't have to tell me. So how come you know Hugo, then, Anne? What a punishment for a sweet young lady like yourself – knowing bleeding Hugo! You gotta be, what – thirty-eight? Late thirties, ballpark figure – am I right?'

'I, uh – sort of right . . . thirty-five, actually. Next birthday.'

'Yeh yeh – I'm never wrong. You look younger. Sweet sixteen and ain't never been kissed, ay? You married, or what? Split up? Like me – I'm split up. Christ – you're not with bleeding *Hugo*, are you? I couldn't bloody stand it!'

'*No* – no no, Jesus no – not with Hugo. I'm married – well, until *yesterday* I was *sort* of married, anyway . . . now I don't know. I suppose not.'

'My bird's fucked off too. Can't understand it, frankly.

60

You know what James Bond said once? You don't, do you? Tell you – he said in restaurants, right, there's no problem buying as much blooger caviare as you can bloody well eat, but you just try getting enough fucking toast! It's the same with this salmon – never enough brown bread, I'm thinking. I'm a big one for brown bread and butter, me.'

'Max, um – look, I might as well come straight to the, er . . . Hugo was hoping you might give him his job back – and no, don't ask me why *I'm* asking you, because I honestly couldn't tell you. Even why I'm here. Terrible, really . . .'

'But you like being here, don't you? With me? Don't you?'

'I . . . it is a lovely restaurant.'

'It is, it is: they treat you good, here. Ever you want a table, you just mention my name to Armand. So Hugo was "hoping", was he? He's a great little white hoper, Hugo is. An optimist. Now don't get me wrong – there's nothing wrong with looking on the bright side: Christ, you don't do that, you'd get up in the morning, slash your bloody wrists. But what I'm saying is, yeah – you gotta be *realistic*. Capeesh? No good going round just *hoping* for things – you gotta get out there and grab them by the nuts. You with me?'

'I think I see what you mean.'

'I *know* you do: know you do. I look at you, I see an intelligent lady. Great *looks*, oh yeh granted – but also, you got a good little brain up there, Annie – see it a mile off.'

'Anne. It's Anne, if you don't, ah . . . Sorry to sound . . . it's just that I really can't *stand* "Annie" – never could.'

'Anne – Annie: whatever pulls your trigger, darling. Now Hugo – I'll give you a for instance, this optimistic side of him. Every morning, right, we all have a meeting – maybe eight, ten, dozen of us. Everyone pitches in with what he's got, and then after – cuppla cappuccinos – we kick it around, chat, have a doodle – I'm a bit of a doodler. You

61

doodle? No? Me – do it all the time: space rockets, I do – don't ask me – and dollar signs and Snoopy – you know? The dog cartoon? Peanuts? I do him when he's on his back on the kennel: breaks me up. But Hugo, yeh – he gets out *The Times*, OK, folds it up neat so's the crossword's on his lap, and then – and this is it: *he gets out his pen!*'

'Uh huh. And . . .?'

'No, Annie, no – you're not getting it. Never, but never, has Hugo ever understood even one of those bloody stupid clues – but every single day, out comes that fucking pen of his. See what I'm saying? No point in optimism, if there just ain't no fucking *hope*.'

'Yes. I see. So what you're saying is . . . there's no hope of Hugo ever getting back his job, right?'

'*Nah*! Nah – not saying that at all. Oh! Oh! Look at that bloody Dover sole – blimey, I know I said big . . . I say, Oi! Johnny! I know I said *big*, but I didn't order no bloody *whales*. Heh heh! *Whales* – yeh?'

'They look gorgeous.'

'Best in London: telling you. Nah – Hugo comes back any time he likes, silly sod. Dunno why he left. Tell you who's *definitely* walked, though, and that's my bird. Don't wanna burden you, or nothing, but it chokes me up. All I done for her. Christ, she was a right mess, Phoebe, when I first took her in. Felt *sorry* for her – know what I mean? Give you a few beans, there, Annie? Spuds? No? Well look, we'll just leave them all in the middle and who wants takes, yeh? Yeh – telling you, she was one of them – an, er – *wreck-chick*, way back then. You know – them skinny birds what don't eat nothing. Filled out nice since – give her her due. But then she starts playing around, don't she? Well – she had to go. I'm like that – can't stand no hanky-panky. I says to her fair and square: Oh-Ewe-Tee spells out, darling – sling it. Hurt at the time, yeh – blimey, seems longer ago than . . . but what I feel now is, I dunno, a kind of *relief* it's all over. You know what I'm saying?'

'I do. Yes I do, actually – know exactly what you mean. I was dreadfully cut up too. My . . . husband . . . he'd clearly met someone else, he was just so *preening* – and so once I, you know, *confronted* him with it – God, I can't believe I'm telling you all this – it was all Oh *Christ* she's wonderful, she's marvellous, she's this, she's that . . . *well*, I said, if she's so bloody *fantastic*, Jeremy, go to her, why don't you? Just *go!*'

'Good for you. You done right. Well shot of him. Jeremy must be an all-time loser – playing the field when there's something so lovely as you at home, Annie. You're a vision, you are.'

'Oh . . . God's *sake*, Max . . .'

'No – straight up: mean it. Look, OK – cards on the table. I'm a very successful businessman, rich, good-looking, so they tell me – all that – and I don't tolerate no messing, and people respect me for being *hard*, a hard man, you know? But deep down – underneath – I'm a soft touch, a pussycat – bit of a romantic. I am. Truly. And you, Annie – no no, come on, let me say it – you're a right bloody stunner. What's more – you got balls. I look at you, I see a lady what goes into life with her legs wide open – yeah? What's wrong? Annie? You gone all quiet.'

*

Seems ages ago now, that lunch – and although it had been quite possibly one of the most offensive, not to say deep-down queasy experiences of Anne's entire life on earth (and maybe, thinking about it, just for these reasons) she remembered pretty well every single heave-inducing detail right to this day. The day she was finally going to ring him up, Mister Bannister, and then say Yeah, OK – OK, then: *yeah*.

But Christ – that man! Can you *believe* such people actually *exist*? I mean: conceited or *what*? The word 'flash' might have been invented solely for his personal enjoyment. I mean to say, do you suppose he *ever* just slips out for a quiet bite to eat somewhere – well, if not *normal* (too much to hope for, I suppose) then at least just a little bit *discreet*? God Almighty – I couldn't believe it when he said to meet at Sophie's . . . I mean, apart from being dizzyingly trendy and wildly expensive it's also famous for never, just never having a table available, so already big points were being scored – messages sent out, yes? And why? He didn't *know* me, did he? Whatever he said I just *knew* he didn't remember me, of course he didn't – why on earth should he? One chance meeting at a party? So what was going on? And Christ, I felt even more uneasy when I got there and that creepy head waiter (what did he say his name was? Peanuts? No – *Almond*, pretty sure) oiling all over me: Jesus, it was as if any woman who was lunching with Max 'Call-Me-God' *Bannister* just had to be the luckiest bit of skirt on the planet! That bloody little 'mistress's' table he shoved me into – practically *displaying* me, as if to say Greetings, Sacrifice – have you met Slab, at all? I'm sure you'll get on (house on fire – yes?).

And then when the man finally arrived, well God – I nearly *died*; I mean – I don't know quite what I was expecting, but Jesus, he was so *small* – I mean really, really short, you know? Funny little legs – and pretty dumpy with it. And why do men with so little hair always have it long and wispy and *urghh* at the back? (I bet he sometimes ties a bow in it – he'd be the one who still does.) And a tonic suit? In mauvy blue? I don't think so. Mind you, it went so utterly perfectly with that great big knuckleduster of a watch he was wearing halfway down his hand as to be almost a *parody* of whatever ghastly sub-species we've actually got here: on anyone else it could only have been one of those, you know – garish knock-offs you see for sale out of suitcases in places like Florence and Bangkok (you can pick them up for nothing). But here was the guy you've always wondered about: the prat who laid out thousands for the *authentic* horror.

And his voice! Now look, living in London you get to hear just about every accent you care to mention – I know that, I know that – and on television, these days, it seems that unless you're a regional with horribly strangulated vowel sounds and practically no consonants at all (or else Irish or Scots or something else sort of *northern*) then you quite simply don't get a job at all. But *this* – my God, I could barely make out what the man was *saying* – apart from when he called me bloody *Annie* all the time and all his ghastly swearing and horribly lewd allusions (some of them I still go crimson even to *think* about: legs wide *open*?! Ex-*cuse* me? *Are* there such people left who come out with such things? Well there's sure as hell one: Max bloody Bannister).

Couldn't even *order* for myself! Well of *course* I couldn't, naturally not – how could such a Pretty Little Thing even begin to make an informed decision about what she actually wants to *eat*?! Everything about me was 'little' or 'pretty' – not pretty enough, however, for him to rate me as anything much less than forty years old (couldn't take his eyes off my tits, though) even though I'm only bloody thirty-eight (I think I told him younger – can't even remember, now). Not quite sure what we ate – I remember I didn't get scallops, though (scollops?), simply because he, *he* didn't go for shellfish! Oh yeh – sole is what we had. I remember now because he made such a big bloody deal of wanting them the size of a bloody whale – and they were absolutely delicious, I have to say, but most of his he just left, in the end.

Some of the things he came out with, oh yuk. One point he tells me – actually *tells* me, no mucking about – to stop tapping my nail on the rim of a side-plate (didn't even know I was doing it). Don't you ever, then, I came back – just about as sneeringly sarcastic as I could possibly

manage (waste of time, of course – water off a duck's arse) –
have any sort of nervous tics or habits? Or are you just
absolutely flawless, Max? I used to bite my nails, he says
('Niles', is what it came out as), but now – get this, big
laugh – now I've got all these people who'll do it for me! He
practically died of merriment over that one – ended up
having a coughing fit; no time at all we're surrounded by
more anxious-faced staff than you'd think a small place
like that could actually employ. Are you all *right*, Mister
Bannister? *Get* you something, Mister Bannister – here is
water, Mister Bannister: Christ, it made me sick. Cos there
was no water of our own actually on the table, you see,
because all we were drinking was champagne (I had mentioned something about some Still, at some point, but
obviously the message never got through, because Max,
evidently, didn't want any of that). I only discovered that it
was champagne he'd ordered when it actually arrived. I
mean – Dee-*Pee*? What in fuck's name's *that* supposed to
mean to anyone at all?

So why in hell did I go along with it? Well initially, I
suppose, for Hugo's sake (a bit) – and when Max just
breezily came out with Oh Yeah, Hugo can come back any
time he likes, I remember making a mental note: Memo –
kill Hugo for making me *do* this. And then, I don't know – I
sort of got swept up in it: maybe you do, people like that.
The only good thing about him that I could see was that he
didn't arrange his *napkin*, like bloody you-know-who
habitually did. That, and the fact that he wanted me. Ha!
Jesus – you should have seen his face at the end, though –
after the coffees and all his bloody brandies and that disgusting great cigar he had jammed in his mouth. He really
did, you know – actually expected me to go off with him to
his flat and *screw* the bastard: he was absolutely astonished
when I just smiled and walked away. He's been phoning
and phoning me every day since. Flowers? Place sometimes
looks like a funeral parlour.

But that was then, and this is now. I am desperate, and desperately sad. Adrian has passed into Westminster (tell you?) and Jeremy says he can't possibly afford it. I simply can't remember the last time I got anything new and I just can't look Donna in the face any more – she asks me for all the latest Barbie bits and pieces because all her *friends* have got them – and it's more than that, of course it is: it's the way she looks up to and right *into* me. Her father's gone – *bastard* – and it is I and only I who is trusted and relied on. And all I do is turn her down. The house is up for sale. Mention that? Oh yes. Jeremy phoned, just this morning as a matter of fact, and this time I talked to him, don't know why. I'm so used to hearing his pitiable whine on the answering machine: 'Anne? Anne? Are you there? It's Jeremy . . . please pick up, Anne . . . Anne, if you're there, please pick up – got to talk to you. Anne? . . . Anne? It's me . . . Jeremy . . . please pick up . . . Anne . . .?' And today I just did. *Anne*, he gasped: thank *God*. What's *wrong*, I snapped back, not happy in your new incarnation with Little Miss Fabulous? Not sure, he said – not sure of anything any more. I have this feeling, he says, that it can't go on. Yeah? *Yeah*?! Well that's just tough on *you*, isn't it, mister? *I've* had to go on, haven't I? Haven't I? *I* didn't get a bloody *choice*. And he goes quiet. And then he tells me about the house: says me and Adrian and Donna will be happier – better off – somewhere smaller, bit out. And I go Uh-*huh*: you think so, do you? Wrong, Jeremy – wrong: we'd all be happier if you were *dead*.

So you see my position. *Hugo*, of course – oh God, don't for Christ's sake get me on to *Hugo*. Just keeps on hitting on me, day and night. Simply because once I, yes – I suppose I egged him on just a bit – that time the bastard Jeremy had obviously tired of that little bitch *Nan* and was off with some other bloody tart in, Christ – *Dubai*. Just because of then, Hugo somehow seems to think he's got a *hold* on me, or something. Tragic. Men in a nutshell. Because look – I soon made it perfectly clear to him that I wasn't going to *do* anything, or anything (because despite what Jeremy's inflicted on me, all down the years, I just *can't*: often wish I could, but I can't).

But now, maybe . . . I can? Can I? Which is, I suppose, all of the reason why it is that right this second I'm finally going to ring up Max Bannister and say to him Yeah, OK – OK, then: *yeah.*

CHAPTER THREE

'The trouble with *you*, Nan – you know what *your* trouble is, don't you?'

'Oh God I just *hate* it when people say that!' squawked out Nan, now, plonking down her coffee mug so that both hands became free to clamp to her head in puny defence against whatever could be coming – her eyes opening wide into not quite a parody of outrage, could be, and a comic-book dread of the inevitability of Susie's soon-to-be-here put-down.

'*Your* trouble, Nan,' – and Susie was dogged, the affection in her voice by no means undermining the true note of warning.

'Don't! Please don't!' squealed Nan, screwing tight her eyes and stiffly shaking her head, like children do. 'Whenever people say that you just know they're going to tell you and I honestly, really, just don't want to *know*. I *know* I'm useless – I know I am, Susie – just please, oh God – you don't have to *tell* me.'

'You're not – oh *Jesus*, Nan,' hooted Susie, lobbing over a cushion (God, this girl: she could be so *frustrating*). Nan swiped it away from the coffee mug – she managed to, yes, but only just. 'You're not a bit *useless*, and you bloody well know it. That's the whole point – you're *too* damn useful and people smell it a mile off, Nan, and they're always – forever they're taking *advantage*. Aren't they? You know it. Like Tony is now. Your trouble is, Nan – you're just too *nice*.'

'But that's a completely *horrid* thing to be, isn't it?' And

Nan was having a good old go at being frankly appalled by so uncool a verdict, though relief was tugging upwards at her eyes, the glistening there one of tenderness for Susie. 'And I don't really think that Tony *is*, you know – it's just I think that's how most guys go on. It's just in their genes – and don't, Susie, don't start up: you know what genes I mean, so no jokes, kay? I sometimes think that, oh . . . I think men probably find me quite boring – I *am* quite boring – no I *am*, I *am*: I *know* I am. And then maybe, I don't know . . . just sort of push for more. Think it could be that. Can't really blame them.'

Susie just looked at her, in genuine pain for her sweet friend Nan. How could so giving and kind a person ever come to even *think* of herself like this? Down to the people who walked all over her: always had been – always was, so far as Susie could see, from the first time she had met her. Which hadn't, actually, been at all that long ago – impossible to think it, now: seems as if I've known her for ever. Just sometimes, you know – very occasionally – it really can be like that: you kind of collide with someone (and of course it's always when you're never expecting to) and even though you don't yet know the smallest thing about them, there is a warmth – kindled by friction and touching the two of you: a feeling that here is no more than a resumption of something started ages earlier (and maybe, in dreams, even maintained). Poor Nan, actually, had been in one hell of a state, that awful rainy morning (we've laughed about it since, oh yeh sure, but at the time it was pretty close, really, to tragic – you could see quite clearly that what Nan needed was not just soon somewhere decent to live, but a friend as well – right now and badly; and yeh, as I say, already I felt I was it).

The three of us – me, Sammy and Carlo – we'd been interviewing, oh God, seemed like dozens of people for more than two days: going *crazy*. Kylie had only been gone from the flat about a week, then, probably less (moved in with that absolutely creepy Australian doctor of hers called *Keegan* – and she called him Kiwi, which is plain ridiculous if you stop and just think about it; only went and married him, didn't she? Wasn't even pregnant. *Why*, Kyle, I'd gone – why on earth *him*, of all people in the world? He's just, oh God, so *ecchhh*; I know, she said – I know what you mean – hey, I'm not *stupid*. But he's *loaded*, OK? And I'm just so sick of my boring bloody job and he's got this *boat*, see, and everything – and look, OK, if it doesn't work out I'll just ditch him: people *do*, you know. Well there – that's Kylie for you; mind you, when she put it like that, I had to see the sense).

So anyway, we really needed to get someone else for the room pretty damn pronto, because the rent for this place, I'm telling you, you just wouldn't believe: every single month, it's a nightmare. It must be great, you know, being a landlord – just bank the cheques and ignore all the complaints. They're all complete bastards – got you over a barrel, this part of London, though, because wherever you go it's going to cost just as much – and you simply never know, do you (this is the trouble), exactly who you're going to end up with. I'm telling you, I could never ever share with someone I thought was even just slightly, even remotely *ecchhh*, boy or girl – which is why we were taking so long with all these bloody interviews: trying to weed out the sickos and the nerds and the psychos and the drags – the farts and the anals, the leches, the penniless and the bloody refugees. It's maybe those who are the worst of the lot, is what I think, because whatever it is they're running away from, it always but always catches them up, and then what have you got? Tell you – you've got jealous-crazed loonies wall to bloody wall – people locking themselves in bathrooms and threatening to swallow every pill in sight (we had one of those once, Simone – Moaning Simone – which is why now there's only some Nurofen and Eno's and those little funny blue ones for Carlo's blocked-up bottom problem – which we don't talk about, and certainly not at interview times: sometimes he's in the loo for the best part of an evening and it sounds like he's trying to give birth through his bum, or else having orgasms).

Which reminds me – killed me, this – one of the girls, can't remember her name – Julie, could be – we nearly took her on (she seemed OK – and Jesus, I was so sick, I can't tell you, of answering questions about kitchen rotas and not swiping all the milk and friends staying over and double-locking and bolting at night, but only when everyone's *in* – think I frankly might have signed up a one-legged murderer). But she turned out to be that worst of all things – a refugee. Said she was getting away from her boyfriend, mainly because he was incapable of keeping his flies zipped up. So I pressed her a bit on this (well you do, don't you? Not often you get to hear about a real live sex maniac, except on Sky) and she said No no – I'll never forget her face: no no no, she was going – chronically weak bladder, that's his problem. You rent a video, right, and he runs out of the room looking really strange about eight or nine times and you can't keep on *pausing* the thing because it completely buggers the *plot*, right, so I thought OK, Mate, she said – I'm outta here. But the thought of this serial pisser coming round to get her back, and finding during the course of a heated debate that the loo was permanently colonized by constipated Carlo was frankly too much for me, so she had to become yet another no-no. Then there was a guy – he seemed OK too, pretty good – but his name was Jonathan *Eat*, right – and God, don't ask me why but I just found this so perfectly and hideously hysterically funny that I just laughed in his face every time he glanced over and it was all absolutely *terrible*, actually, because Sammy was more or less stuffing cushions into my mouth and he, the guy, was going *scarlet*, Christ, but I just couldn't help it – and when Carlo said *Well*, Mister Eat, we're all on first-name terms here, of course – well I just nearly *died*. So he didn't make it – he practically ran: felt sorry for him, after. Still made me laugh, though.

So you can understand that by the time little Nan rolled up, we were getting kind of mad and desperate, you know? So at first I tried to tell me that it was that and only that I was feeling: Yeah Great She'll Do (now let's for God's sake just stop and have a *drink*). But that really wasn't it at all: I didn't just say Hi, to her – I remember her looking so surprised – I went Oh *Hi-i-i-i!*, like I'd known her for just – well, like I say – it was a kind of a reunion thing: like she'd come home. Not really sure if the other two felt the same – I mean they *liked* her, sure (how could you not? Everyone likes Nan – it's just impossible not to – she's always so terribly nice: which is, as I'm forever telling her, her one biggest problem – people being the way they are).

Anyway, we all had a confab and more or less said Yes to her on the spot – normally we go, you know: Yeh Great – So Anyway We've Got Your Number, blah blah blah. But the thought of Nan going somewhere else was just killing me, now, so we had another quick and whispered meeting – me, Sammy and Carlo – and we all came out of the kitchen, and Christ – we were grinning like maniacs (maybe even enough to put her off) and of course I was expecting her to say, Well OK, but I've got one or two other places to see, so can I get back to you, sort of thing. But *Yes*, is what we got – oh yes *please*, I'll take it, I'll take it: thank you *so* much. Which maybe made me think for a moment she might be a refugee, but it turned out pretty soon that she was the other thing: pushed out, evicted – practically turfed into the street, and just the day before, if you can begin to believe it. Ours was only the second place she'd seen (the first had had those blond and shiny maple floors – terribly smart – but Nan said they made everyone go clunk clunk clunk, all the time, which already was driving her crazy: that, and the place smelt of cheese. Gorgonzola, I asked her – big smirk.

73

No, she smiled back – she's really got the prettiest smile, sweet little teeth – a milder thing altogether: possibly Edam).

Anyway, she really loved our flat, which I have to say really really pleased me a lot because I'm the sort of interior designer, round here: Conran R Us. I mean the others are OK, they appreciate colour and all the rest of it (and they're *tidy*, thank God – that's one of the first things I always ask: didn't have to, with Nan), but it's really me who sort of pulls it all together, makes it work. She loved the muslin at the windows (you get it really cheaply in Brick Lane, and then you just dump it all in the bath with these really brilliant cold dyes and it just turns out *amazing*). Hee – I remember when I was halfway through doing the orange lot – I wanted it all to be a bit Buddhisty – Carlo came crashing in saying he had to, just had to try sitting on the bog because this time, he felt sure, might really be *it*. Well carry on, I said, but I can't leave any of this stuff now because it'll go all streaky and he just kind of stares at me and goes Christ, Susie – I Can't Go If You're Here – and I say Oh Jesus, Carlo, you won't be going *anyway*, will you? You never ever *do*. So – give him his due – he settles down to it and puts in a jolly good effort. I hauled out the orange stuff, rinsed out the bath and got ready for the green batch; did all those too and he was still just squatting there, all bunched-up muscles and blue with strain – when I left, oh God, just ages after. Any luck, I asked him later. He just shook his head grimly, and went into his room muttering his mantra: One Day – One Day, You Just Wait: One Day I Will. (Must be awful, really.)

And she thought the throws on the sofa were great, Nan – and the Philippe Starck squeezer in the kitchen. I remember she said her last employer (it was the wife who threw her out, bitch) had had one of those – and she had never even known that's what it *was*, which I thought was so sweet; and she just adored the rough brick fireplace which was just great because it was me who had chipped off all this really yucky sort of false pebbledash muck and found all this terrific old stuff behind it, probably covered for decades. Carlo brought back this amazing old railway sleeper (oak, pretty sure – Christ knows where he got it, weighed a ton) – and we somehow got that up (Sammy was no help – she never is at things like this, but she's absolutely brilliant at soups and puddings) and stuck up there it looked so huge and brown, like a massive Cadbury's Flake – and Carlo said with a dead straight face (you never really know with Carlo, whether he's joking or not) that if he ever did, you know – *do* it, then that's what the bloody thing would look like: it'd tear him in half, and then where would he be? He's such a hoot, Carlo – I don't know if he knows it.

Nan settled in really quickly. For me – can't talk for the others – it seemed like she'd been there for ever: couldn't remember what it had even been like, living with Kylie – and God, she'd been here for must be, what – well over a year. It was only a bit later that I discovered that Nan had been close to despair, that morning she'd turned up to look at the flat. God, she'd covered it well; glad she did, else Sammy and Carlo might have thought she was, oh my God, one of the weeping psychos, and it would've been uphill work to get her, then. What it came down to was, she just simply couldn't come to terms with the fact that she had been sacked from her nanny job (Christ, I had said – *nannying*: what a perfectly ghastly thing to be doing – I think you've maybe got to be born to it. What do you do, Susie? she'd asked me. Oh me? I'm sort of fashion PR. Much the same thing, then, she practically whispered. I've thought about that quite a lot). It wasn't that she couldn't get *another* job, or anything – Jesus, the temping agency had absolutely jumped at her, and she was doing lots of bits, right from day one. But what I didn't get at first (I reckon because I just couldn't begin to identify – children, they scare me, frankly: don't know why) was that she was really really close to this little boy and girl she'd been caring for, right, and it had practically broken her heart to leave them. When you actually live in, I suppose it must get like that. And when she got round to describing the scene, I was pretty choked up myself, have to tell you.

'But *why*, Nan: *why* did this bloody woman just give you the push? There has to be a *reason*, no?'

And Nan had thought Yes, there's always one of those – but not, oh no – not the one Anne had given me: that was just mad. Jesus – it had all started out as a perfectly normal day – normal, anyway, from Nan's point of view, although she was more than aware from Adrian and Donna's unstoppable gossip that there had very recently taken place some sort of, oh – *row*: a scene between Jeremy and Anne, but that was hardly a novelty. And he had gone off somewhere, apparently; well – Jeremy did travel a lot for his job, so here too was nothing new, nothing remotely special. How was Nan to know that Adrian and Donna were to be snatched away from her, just because Jeremy had upped and gone? That and some crazy idea stuck in Anne's head? Nan was fearful, as she fought her corner:

'But *why*, Anne? *Why*?'

'You know why, Nan.'

'Anne, I don't. I don't.'

'Nan – don't.'

'Anne – don't do this. I don't – *understand*, Anne.'

'Nan – you understand perfectly.'

'Anne – *listen* to me: I *don't*. You can't *mean* it.'

'I mean it, Anne. Nan, I mean. Oh Jesus.'

'Christ . . . !'

'No more talk: just pack up and go. If you want money – and I'm sure you do – women like you *always* do – then I suggest you contact your erstwhile lover.'

'Anne! Anne – please listen to me: Jeremy was never my erstwhile *lover*. I don't – I don't know what erstwhile *means*, but he wasn't, he wasn't – I don't understand why you're

76

doing this. It's Adrian – Adrian and Donna that are important to me: it's *them* I love, Anne – not . . . *Jeremy!*'

And it was true. She had, early on, quite fancied Jeremy, no point in denying it, but as far as she was aware, he'd never so much as even glanced in her direction, which hurt Nan only on a very superficial level – it didn't continue to trouble her – because look: she had a boyfriend of her own, naturally she did. Or at least she had had, anyway. He lived in Edinburgh, David – she had met him in August when she'd done the Fringe on the cheap, and God – that fortnight they'd had: unimaginable. But then she'd got a letter – she had just about sorted the fare and accommodation for a return trip round Christmas time, and then this letter arrived. Nan has no intention of boring you with any of the ins and outs of the thing, but the thrust was very much that David had met a nice young girl from Glasgow (daughter of friends of his parents – you remember what *they're* like) and Nan, he felt sure, would understand. She hadn't – she was hurt and sad. And nor was she getting it now (hurt and sad, here you are again) – but this time, on top of it, *my babies* are being taken away from me, and it is I who must go: all blame is mine, and I'm blameless in this.

Nan was aware that one of those sweet little pale green Aertex shirts that Donna wore to school on games days had slipped from her hand and fallen to the ground – she felt it folding softly about her ankles, before she even knew that her fingers had lifelessly let it go. And she'd need it in the morning, Donna; for rounders.

'When do you want me to go?' she heard herself asking numbly, the thud of each dead word hurting as it left her and again as she felt it rebounding. 'Have you told – ? How have Adrian and Donna . . . what have they said?'

'Look, Nan,' Anne concluded briskly, gathering up her bag and scooping into it cigarettes, cash, Wrigley's and a lighter – her hand like a claw hovering briefly over that spot where her car keys surely should have been, and then snatching them up from a glass bowl just over there, which she was certain was not where she'd dropped them. 'I really don't want a *debate*, here – I'm going through a deeply traumatic period in my life, and the sooner you are out of this house, the better I can, oh Christ – I don't know if I'll *ever* come to cope, but I know I never will if *you're* still around. Reminding me of your awfulness with that bastard husband of mine.' And then Anne reddened and wheeled back over to Nan, her eyes dragged wide as she practically barked at her: 'Jesus *Christ*, Nan – how could you have *done* this to me? I *trusted* you – I liked you, we all did. What in Christ's name did you think you were *doing*?'

Nan was stung and fearful, but she let the light of fright fade back in her eyes. She looked over to, but not quite at, Anne and repeated flatly:

'How have Adrian and Donna . . . what have they said?'

Anne was nearly out of the door, and away from here. Her involuntary grimace seemed cruel to Nan, though she saw it was probably just another part of Anne's own pain.

'Oh Jesus you don't think I've *told* them, do you? *I'm* not doing your dirty work for you, missy – dirty work is *your* department. You're the one who's walked away from this job – away from them. You're the one who's, shit – *consorted* with their father. Don't interrupt – I told you I want no *debate*. So *you* tell them, Nan – you explain the whole story to them in that perfectly lovely and gentle way of yours. And do it *now*, you bitch – because I want you gone by tonight. Clear?'

Anne flounced out – having thrown across a shoulder her final and meaningful glare – and slammed hard behind her the kitchen door. The front door, seconds later, came in for similar and summary treatment, and Nan was just left there in the silence that followed. She started and practically cried out, when a new voice cut the air.

'Mum gone, then . . . ?'

Nan turned to Adrian, needing and dreading the

expression that she knew he would be wearing. He looked up full at her, his eyes maybe trying for big consolation, but also craving an assurance that was now so way beyond her. Gradually, a mutual hopelessness seeped into each of them, and a sort of blank despair hit Nan heavily, while Adrian seemed determined to rally some fight back into his eyes – could he, at least, make one of them feel better, feel safer?

Nan touched his hair. 'Did you hear?'

Adrian turned his head, but not nearly away from the feel of her fingers. 'Some. I don't understand.'

'No,' said Nan, this one word so charged with a deep sorrow she just knew she should not be betraying – it cried out for obliteration, a vigorous and immediate pasting over with thick and gluey sheets of hearty bluster. What she should never be doing is plunging the boy down deeper – Nan knew that, yes, but how could she help it? She was filled with misery – still not tearful, but close to fragmentation. It was maybe only Donna wandering in from the TV room that served to haul Nan back from the rim of blackest disillusion – now she just had to be strong (oh please, God, make me it) – to defer at least till later the bruising and loss that could maybe be persuaded to patiently queue, and not just yet invade without mercy.

'Are there any – ? Can I have a Jaffa Cake, please?'

'Oh *honestly*, Donna!' And the edges of Adrian's voice were more roughened – far more than Nan had ever known. Some sort of fear, it could be, was making him aggressive? Before all this, Nan would have known. 'You're just such a *baby*. This is *serious*, Donna!'

'What's serious? What? Why can't I have one?'

'We're not *talking* about – oh God, Nan: *you* tell her.'

Nan was quietly replacing the lid to the biscuit jar. She stooped down to Donna, and with a near-unbearable frailty in her voice, she said to her *Here*, Donna – *here*: Jaffa Cake for you.

79

Adrian was shaking his head, as if to clear it of circling bees.

'She's leaving. Nan. She's going, Donna. Leaving us.'

Nan was instantly hot, and alert to the dark threat of agony.

'I'm *not* – I would never – ! Oh God – but it is true, Donna – Adrian – that apparently I must go. Just can't . . . believe it. Your mummy and daddy don't want me to stay any more. I honestly don't know why.'

'But Daddy's not here!' piped up Donna, expelling big crumbs of Jaffa Cake, in her eagerness to make everything clear. 'Daddy's left us – and now you're leaving us too. It's not fair: I don't *want* you to go. Tell her, Adrian – make her stop. She mustn't go – *mustn't*. Don't want you to go, Nan – don't go. It's not fair. Please don't go. Please don't *leave* us!'

Nan inhaled sharply, as if some overlooked detail had suddenly forced itself right back into her mind. A hand went up to near where her mouth hung, and she glanced down in anguish and imploringly to Adrian – but Oh! Look at the poor boy, oh God – just look at him! He doesn't – of course he doesn't – *understand*; so how can he make it all right with Donna? (Still not tearful – far too alive to the rambling prickles of this pain all over, and a terrible dread of dealing with more of it.)

'Look,' she said. 'Let's all go and sit next door?'

'Why? What's the point of that?'

'Well it's just – more . . . oh God – I don't *know* what the point is, Adrian – it's just that, well – we're all of us just standing around here in the middle of the kitchen floor, and – '

'Nan . . .?'

' – What is it, Donna, my angel?'

'*Please* don't leave us! Tell us you won't?'

Nan really did try, now – she tried so hard to smile down at them fondly, flooded with indulgence; she was aware of tense and silent seconds passing, and still the parts of her face she so desperately called on would not come anywhere close to an arrangement – would play no part in assembling the illusion. She looked up and around her for help from just anywhere, and it was only when her fraudulent and please be soothing tone cracked wide open close to the start of stuttering Jesus in heaven alone knew what – it was just at that moment that Adrian and Donna both flew to her side and hugged themselves and her so hard – and she could feel their jerking limbs, each one of them a separate detonation – and then their hot wet faces through her clothes.

Tearful, now, oh God yes – blood and my babies sucked right out of me: who (not me!) can be expected to cope with a life like this? A life like this (not for me, now) – it just can't go on.

*

And so I suppose it was with a sort of, how can I say it . . .? Maybe it was bewilderment – this overtook even hurt, those first few days. I was in a, oh God – there's probably a better word, but possibly kind of trance-like state, you know? I mean – I'd been living with Jeremy and Anne, Adrian and Donna for just simply ages: certainly shared two Christmases with them. Felt so good there, so right – never really thought about *afterwards*; should've, obviously, because if you're a nanny there's always an afterwards, and it's never ever as good as the *now* – because people grow up, things move on, but the nanny, I don't know, doesn't ever seem to *notice* all this: for her it's all as if everything stays the same.

But in whatever way change was to loom, I never ever contemplated (well who would? Everyone I told was just utterly amazed – and I was too, I was too) – no, it never so much as for a moment even occurred to me that I'd be *chucked* – that the very next day I'd have nowhere to live, nowhere to go – none of my children to tend to. At the agency, though, they were really nice: We can get you work starting any time, they said – there's a huge demand. But what about *Anne*, I remember quite feebly protesting – she'll never ever give me a reference: she really (why?) hates me. And the woman at the agency just smiled and said Hey, No Problemo, Believe Me. And then she said Don't you think you'd better see about fixing up somewhere to live (till you get properly settled)? There's a sort of accommodation agency, parallel thing, we often have dealings with – pretty reliable, not too grasping: shall I . . . would you like me to give them a ring?

Got scared again: I couldn't even remember how flat-hunting went. Did a lot of it when I was a student, of course – oh God (now it seems so funny, in a ghastly sort of way): in the Manchester places I used to doss down in, I just can't tell you! Everyone was doing dope, in those days – and you never quite knew who it was who actually lived there, and which other spaced-out crazies were just passing through. Well obviously I knew I wouldn't have to do any of all *that* again, but the agency had told me too that there was no way I could afford the sort of place I now, I suppose, felt I deep down needed, unless I was willing to share. And that single word – it had so cast me down. I *had* been sharing – sharing my whole life with both Adrian and Donna – and now I was expected to just choose new people, as well as laying myself wide open to being sniffed at and turned away. Again. And so when I came here – talked to Susie – I can't tell you what a, oh – fantastic relief I felt. I'd seen about six awful places in the space of a day (I told Susie, I think, just the one – I don't know why I did that; maybe I didn't want to come over as a footsore nomad, some sort of unwelcome refugee) and they were all just so . . . and the funny thing was, it wasn't always just the obvious stuff wrong with them, the things you'd expect; I mean yes – some were poky, dark or had a funny smell – one was fearfully noisy, I remember (right on the high street); but mainly I just felt *displaced*: no matter how nice or not nice all these places were, what in God's name did any of them have to do with *me*? Why was I sitting on someone's sofa in someone's room, engaged in I'm sure quite mutually embarrassing and totally pointless chit-chat with a series of someones with whom I might the next morning be living? Crazy – and scary, too.

And then there was Susie. I felt so at home – then, I did. And Sammy too – she seemed fine, if a little bit serious. Didn't see too much of Carlo (only afterwards I found out why: if there was ever anything wrong with this place, it was just this one-loo thing – and that in the bathroom). It's heartbreaking, really – Carlo doesn't so much use the room as more or less live in it: brings in piles of cartoon books and sort of lifestyle magazines (he's something to do with graphics, he was telling me one time, but I'm not at all sure quite what) and when he eventually comes out, there's nothing for any of us save that, oh God – so mournful expression of his. I tell you this – Susie and I decided one evening, and we weren't (honestly) even that drunk – that if he ever did, Carlo, manage a really good, world-class, truly historic . . . oh God: you know – *crap*, right, then the least we could do was throw a really good party. But so far, no show; maybe after I've gone – but it doesn't seem too likely.

And talking of parties – Susie and Sammy and Carlo did a really sweet thing for me, that very first weekend after I came here. I'd been looking after little Emily, that Friday (she's only eight, but just so spoiled I can't tell you), and Susie had said before she flew out that morning that they were renting some film for later on in the evening – can't even remember what, now (something just out on video with Hugh Grant, pretty sure, who I really really like), and so make sure you're back by seven-ish, she told me. And so dopey old credulous little me gets in around seven, as per instructions – looking, I have to say, like absolute *hell* (Emily and I had been painting each other's faces, and I'd just scrubbed mine off, oh – any old how) – and there in the big room was a fantastically laid-out sort of supper party thing, and all in my honour! I just simply couldn't believe it – there were takeaways and Chardonnay and Chianti and Beck's and candles and just everything: looked great.

And Susie's boyfriend Jake was there – we hadn't actually met before (but God – even by then I'd heard *so* much about him) – and Sammy had brought someone from work who had the most amazing long and braided hair and there was that older guy, can't remember what he was called – seemed lost in a Sixties time-warp: not actually sure if he was with Carlo or if he was Jake's friend. Not really too sure (no one is) quite what Carlo really goes for: doesn't *seem* to be gay, or anything, but he doesn't come over as too straight either, if you get what I'm saying. Susie once said that she doubted if there were the hours in the day for Carlo to start up even a mild sort of relationship, what with his freelance graphic work and his tenure of the lavatory. Poor Carlo – really shouldn't laugh because he's actually been awfully sweet to me, and particularly just lately (in the light of this new thing – my latest kick in the face from God, who I always used to believe in: a one-way thing, I'm thinking now. Why is it that He and no one else either will ever let me settle?).

*

Nan had just stood there in the middle of the room, shrugging from her shoulder the big old leather bag that hung there – excited, yes, but so aware too of how washed-out and dreggy she looked (loving Susie for having done it all, sure – but resenting just a bit how perfectly done up she was: eyeliner and earrings and that champagne floaty dress and God Almighty just *look* at me) – and hoping she'd remember all these new names: Chloe, was it? Simon?

Absolutely hopeless at names, always have been. I don't actually forget them so much as not even hear them in the first place: I just see the person's lips move in a well-meaning mime – all noise just shuts down, and from then on in I'm completely on my own.

'Don't hog all the bloody wine, Jake!' hollered over Susie, now that everyone was seated and (Thank God at last, thought Carlo darkly) reaching for and passing over plates and bowls of food ('I don't quite know,' he then came up with, 'what must happen to all this grub I shove inside me'; anyone who knew him sort of smiled and pulled a long Christ-I'll-be-sick face, everyone else just passing it by).

'Who wants red?' offered Jake. 'Christ, Susie, you're a real nag, you know that? Did you get any radishes in the end, or what?'

'The noodles are *cool*,' sighed out the girl with the long and braided hair – she made the noodles sound as if they were taking her high, and leaving her there.

'Thanks, Clodagh,' smiled Susie. 'I didn't slave over a hot stove and make them myself! You're the only one who *likes* radishes, Jake. You pig.'

Oh it's Clodagh, racked up Nan: thought it was Chloe.

'I *used* to like them,' said Sammy – slowly, even ponderously, just like she always was. 'Used to like a lot of things I don't seem to, now.'

'Oh yeh – by the way' – Jake had just thought of this – 'Tony'll be coming over later. I said it was OK.'

'Who the hell's Tony?' asked Susie. 'Here, Nan – have you had rice? Carlo – can you get another of these Chardonnays out of the fridge?'

'Oh – you don't know Tony. Great guy. American. You'll love him,' Jake assured her. 'Oh and Carlo – go to the bog *after* you get the wine, yeh? Otherwise we'll all die of thirst.'

'Oh fuck off,' grunted Carlo, who was already on his way to the one place or the other.

'It's not *funny* . . .' said Sammy, quite quietly.

'Makes *me* laugh,' grinned Jake – upping this into a guffaw when Susie half-heartedly attempted to bat him down, with a languorous hand. 'Here – this is funny too: guy at work, right . . .?'

'I'm really in the mood to see a good film tonight,' said Susie, suddenly. 'Carlo?! *Carlo*?! Where's the *wine*, Godsake?! Anyone up for *Casablanca*?'

'Overrated,' said the friend of maybe Carlo. He spoke from behind a straight curtain of seriously greying hair, and just everyone stopped to seemingly listen – maybe because these were the first words he had uttered – but despite this impromptu pause, there seemed to be no more to come.

'Why didn't he go with her on the plane at the end?' piped up Nan – laying her hand on Susie's, as she said it.

'Oh Jesus – never mind *Casablanca*!' hooted Jake. 'Listen – this guy at work – Tony and I were killing ourselves about this – oh Carlo, back at last. Did you bring the opener? Cork thing?' And then to Carlo's retreating form: 'Not staying?'

'Oh *leave* him,' hissed Sammy.

'Fuck off, Jake,' grunted Carlo – not quite audibly, as the bathroom door was practically shut behind him by the time he said it.

'What about a Bond movie?' suggested the friend of maybe Carlo.

'Oh *God* no,' deplored Susie, 'everyone'll start talking about Connery and that ghastly other one and Roger Thing, and everything – it's just *so* . . . actually, um – I'm awfully sorry, but I don't think I got your name, ah . . .?'

The friend of maybe Carlo nodded eagerly, as if he had easily anticipated that. 'It's Sid,' he said.

Susie nodded too. 'Sid. Right.' And then she turned away rapidly and did a gorblimey and just-for-Nan face, for she truly did feel in danger of exploding into one of her Jonathan Eat-type fits.

'*Look*!' mock-roared Jake, setting down his knife and fork.

'Does any of you want to bloody well hear about this guy at work or do you not? Hm?'

'Oh God don't go *on*, Jake,' sighed Susie. 'Just *say* it, if you have to – just don't keep going *on*.'

'I only went *on* because – oh look, anyway: this guy, right? All he ever does – the only thing that's ever on his mind is planning some party-type thing for his fiftieth birthday!'

There was a general feeling of maybe having just possibly missed something here, before Nan ventured cautiously Well ... you know ... fifty ... it's quite a landmark age ...?

Jake grinned broadly, practically in triumph. 'Yeh yeh,' he agreed, 'but get this: the guy's only twenty-seven!'

A random rumble of amusement was his reward for that.

'*Kidding* ...' said Susie.

'*Straight*,' affirmed Jake, chewing energetically on some damn bit of thing or other so that it could be out of the way for when he launched into the next bit: 'He's obsessed with buying old-man stuff. He's got a walk-in bath. Keeps forgetting to drain off the water before he bloody walks out again. Flat below's been flooded three times.'

'Oh *Jake*,' laughed Susie, 'you're making it all up!'

'I'm *telling* you!' protested Jake, eyes as wide as if he meant it. 'Other day, he came into work with a collapsible walking stick: said it nearly killed him.'

'How ...?' was Nan's take on this.

'Fucking *collapsed*, didn't it? Says he might replace it with one of those stand things, frame-type things ...'

'Zimmer,' said Sid with assurance – as if he was anyway maybe no stranger to at least the concept.

'Yeah that. The guy's *crazy*, I'm telling you. Says the thing he wants more than anything in the world is a Stannah stairlift – promised it to himself for this bloody fiftieth birthday of his, but now he says he doubts he can even wait that long!'

'So, what . . . he *is* mental, is he?' Susie now wanted to know.

Jake shrugged. 'Seems OK in every other way.'

'Single, I presume,' said Sammy.

'He's got a girl. Knockout. Well – not bad for her age, anyway. She's a hundred and six.'

'Oh *Jake*!' roared Susie, chucking over at him her napkin, Sid being very far from pleased when it landed in his chicken.

'You know . . .' started up Sammy – tentative and determined, rather as if steadying herself to announce to the assembly that she was finally and at last ready to renounce the shallows of the paddling pool in favour of the high-dive. 'What I think is, I really like Indian food more than any other sort of – well, Chinese, maybe too . . . Indian and Chinese are really my favourites of all, you know, these days. Used to be Italian . . . *French*, of course . . .'

'I eat pretty much everything, I do,' said Sid. 'Except offal. Can't abide offal in any shape or form.'

'Hate it,' whispered Nan.

'So after pudding,' Susie was already well into saying, 'hands up who wants to watch *Casablanca*?'

'*Liver*!' exclaimed Sid, the initial yelp soon yielding to a thick coating of near-lascivious revulsion, as he gave himself to wrapping his whole tongue around the word as if in the early stages of belching it beyond and away from him.

'*Calves'* liver's OK . . .' muttered Jake. 'Why are we actually talking about this anyway?'

'Right – well if no one's interested in *Casablanca*, then, why don't one of you suggest something else?' pouted Susie. 'And *no*, Sid – not Bond. Or shall we play a game?'

'And as for *kidneys*,' Sid stormed on (Bond was gone from him now): 'just *think* – just think of what they *do*.' And then he launched into an *Urrrrggggghhhh* so guttural and pronounced as to turn even the hardiest stomach, and render it decidedly queasy. Carlo ambled back then, having taken the latest round of bad and intensely personal news squarely on the chin, and said with idle wonder What's Wrong? Why's Nobody Talking? And Sammy mumbled something about Bodily, er – *Functions* and Carlo said Oh Yeah, Big Joke, Thanks A Lot, Guys.

Clodagh sipped some Chianti and said (quite brightly, for her) I really love your curtains, Susie.

'They're brilliant, aren't they?' enthused Susie. 'What you do is, you get this really cheap muslin from – '

'Oh *God*, Susie,' shot in Jake. '*Please* won't you spare us all your dyeing-the-bloody-curtains saga – they're only *curtains*, right? And we've all heard it, anyway.'

'Oh yeah? Oh *yeah*? Well I'd like to see *you* do something creative, Jake – just *you* try it once in a while, why don't you? God, Nan – you should just see *his* place: looks like a *tip*.'

'Is this fruit for *eating*?' enquired Sid with care. 'Or just looking at? Decorative, is it just?'

'Hm?' checked Susie. 'Of *course* it's for eating, Sid, sure. Help yourself. Honestly, Nan – *Jake's* place – '

'It's just as well to know,' intoned Sid, selecting quite studiedly a banana, his fingers darting back for a bunchlet of grapes.

'It's *not* actually like a tip,' Jake protected himself, stoutly. 'Not at all, actually, Nan – don't even listen to her. Sammy – pass up the red, could you? It's actually industrial *chic*, Susie, if you really want to know – '

Susie snorted. 'Industrial *shit*, more like.'

'Ho ho,' said Jake, quite drily. 'Hi-tech, it used to be called. With retro pop art overtones.'

'Oh Jesus will you *listen* to him!' hooted Susie. 'He means it, you know, Nan – he actually *means* it!'

'I don't *mind*, you know, *Casablanca*,' said Sammy, full of doubt. 'Or what about that other one – the one with that man, what's the guy, the quite funny one . . .?'

'What he's got,' blared on Susie, 'is old metal sort of *garage*-type shelving in that kind of grey and yucky watering-can dull dull dull finish and builders' trestles and a big sort of giant cotton reel thing right in the middle of the floor covered in old tin cans!'

'*Cotton* reel,' sneered Jake, with real contempt. 'It's an industrial ply cable drum, actually, my pet – and as far as the cans: Heinz and Campbell's. Yes? Warhol? You've heard of?'

Susie just goggled at Jake through the huge red cheek of it: her open-mouthed face said to everyone who cared to get this that of all the things that might have loomed before coming her way, she surely hadn't expected a slap in the face with a great fat slimy cod, newly netted and wet from the ocean.

'How can you – ?!' she eventually found it in her to gasp, 'how *dare* you ask *me* if I've heard of – ?!'

'Well let's just watch the film, then . . .' hesitated Clodagh. 'I've never actually *seen* it, *Casablanca*, if I'm honest. Keep *hearing* about it, of course . . .'

'It's OK,' said Sammy.

Sid selected a pip from between his teeth, placed it with precision to the side of his plate, shook his head and said Overrated.

'Nan!' screeched Susie, 'I just don't *believe* this guy – it was me who bought him that bloody green and orange *Marilyn* print, and the stupid bastard only drew a *moustache* on it – the stupid *bastard*.'

'Duchamp,' smiled Jake. 'Dada.' And he put up his hands and crossed them in protection across his face while ducking his wide eyes – only then did he feel safe in coming out with: 'Heard of?'

Susie was actually half up and making for him, and Nan could see that what had started out as maybe no more than lovers' bluster – a mutual flexing of sexually fixated muscles, a public baring of pink-flushed buttocks – had

90

at some unnoticed point turned first into something else entirely, and then quite ugly. Jake too maybe now had sensed this: while the doorbell was still ringing, he was away from his chair and half out of the room, yodelling back to the table and anyone there not siding with Susie Keep Her Off Me Will You? (She's crazy when she gets like this.)

'There's some mousse in the freezer,' Susie called out to whoever it was who maybe could be interested – smoothly switching her aborted assault on Jake into an amble to the kitchen – 'if anyone wants.' And then, more quietly to Nan, who had joined her: 'I just can't stand him, when he gets like this.'

Nan just nodded – for already it seemed natural to her to simply concur with any passing view or feeling Susie might express: she just found herself quite easily going along with whatever, before she worked out or tossed around even the gist of it. But Nan knew that earlier – just minutes back – she had been maybe not exactly avoiding Susie's eye, during those recent funny-turned-to-tetchy exchanges of hers with Jake, but certainly she had been damping down and cloaking any sign of her amusement. Nan was just so happy and relieved that Jake was there to lighten things up (all of just everything that Sammy and Chloe – Cloder, don't know how you spell it – had had to say had been frankly bringing her down; even Susie going on about *Casablanca* had soon become wearing in the extreme – Nan had just had to admit that): I just don't get all this junk about classic films. I mean – I've *seen* bloody *Casablanca*, OK, and at the end he doesn't get on the plane with her (why? No one ever tells me why) so what on earth could be the point of watching it again and again and again? With everyone saying Oh look – this is a really good bit, love this bit, and I totally adore that Kiss Is Still A Kiss thing: it's so *romantic* – and See! See! He doesn't ever actually *say* Play It Again, Sam – did you know that? Woody Allen *must* have known that, but he still used it for a title anyway (great film, that: hilarious). D'you like Woody Allen? I think he's great: the early ones were really funny and *Annie Hall* – totally blew me away: like the *cocaine*, yeah? The dreary ones got to me, though: all that Ingrid Bergman-type stuff. No no – you don't mean that: you mean *Ingmar*, the director – the other one's an actress. She was in *Casablanca*, which is an absolute classic, my favourite of all time. Everyone thinks it was Lauren Bacall in *Casablanca*, but it wasn't – she was in that other one where she hung around the doorway and did that sexy You Know How To Whistle thing; that was with Bogarde, in another of those oldies. Bo*gart*, it's pronounced – Bogarde is Sir Dirk, who's dead now too. I liked him in *Darling*. Julie Christie – she's still absolutely gorgeous, isn't she? Last person on earth you'd think would have a face-lift – but hey, why not? Life, you know – you only get one crack at it. I'm not at all sure *I* could ever have plastic surgery because I'm really scared of operations and hospitals and – *urrrr* – all of that, but look at Cher – fantastic for her age. She got an Oscar for something or other (wore that amazing dress); I can't *stand* all that Oscars and Baftas stuff (can you?) where they all dress up and slap each other on the back and thank the whole world and then *cry* when they get one. Hitchcock, you know, never ever got an Oscar in his lifetime – think it was Hitchcock. Could've been that *Citizen Kane* guy – *that* film I didn't quite get either, I think not, and yet everyone says it's just marvellous. Orson Thing. People always say that it's their favourite (Welles, Orson Welles) or else *Casablanca* but I've *seen* bloody *Casablanca* and honestly, you know: I know how it *ends* (well *why* doesn't he, huh? Nobody ever says: why didn't he just get on the *plane* with her? Huh?) and I really don't ever want to sit through all that again. And so *what*, actually, if they'll always have Paris? Because they won't: that's just junk. You never actually own even a single bit of anything that's gone because that's just what it is – it's *past* and *finished*; the only stuff we can ever lay claim to is all the white and frightening future – all those blank days and nights that can be stained or enriched by just about anything or anyone that happens along. And that, I feel fairly sure, just has to be the thrill and terror of every coming morning: the not at all *knowing* – which, well, has *got* to be good news, really, if you look at it, because think, just think, how truly awful the other thing would be. Not even seeing it is the only way we can all go on.

Nan shrugged all that away and settled down to being pleased when Jake came back in (he kind of lit up the place – you know what she's saying?).

'Everyone!' he announced from the door. 'This is Tony.' Jake clapped an arm around him and hugged hard his shoulder – and to top off Tony's jerked-in lopsidedness there slid across his face the inevitable dopey sort-of-pleased and pretty embarrassed half-smile. 'Tony: the famous Susie – who I think still loves me!'

'I *hate* you,' smiled Susie. 'Hi, Tony. This is Nan – she's just joined the asylum – and Sammy, she lives here too, and so does Carlo . . . where's . . .? Oh, well, Carlo must've just slipped out for a second – oh shut *up*, Jake, Godsake. And this is Clodagh – and this is Sid.'

Tony's eyes elongated in tune with his mouth, and the flat open palm of his hand neatly described a rainbow arc – his stylized thanks and greeting in just the one size that he hoped would fit all.

'Come and sit, Tony!' exclaimed Susie, now – comfortably back in hostess mode. 'Have you eaten? There's heaps. Jake – under the sink there's more Chianti.'

Jake was on his way there, hollering back to Susie: 'Yeah yeah – Tony will've eaten: he's forever stuffing himself, aren't you, Tony? And always this weirdo American muck. If it ain't from the good old US of A, then this boy's just outta here – right, Tony? Tell us what you had for supper.'

And Nan watched Jake now as he easily ambled back

into the room, two black bottles of wine hanging loosely from each of his large and faintly ginger-haired hands.

'They weren't actually under the sink,' smiled Jake, plonking them down. 'On the window sill. Still – at least you got the kitchen part right.'

Susie's glance was acidic – but now she was stirring molasses well into the mixture, for when she turned to Tony.

'So tell us, then, Tony: what was on the menu tonight?'

Tony sipped the wine that Jake had poured for him, smiled, stretched out his long legs under the table – the expansiveness in his face just flickering as he muttered apology for whatever it was they had briefly brushed with (Sammy mumbling back Sew-kay) – and together with a glint of far too many huge white teeth, the rich and homey voice was rumbling:

'Lima beans and fried cornbread, Susie – and maybe a cuppla Buds.'

'I had grits,' fluttered Clodagh, 'in America once.'

'Apart from their burgers,' averred Sid – hoisting his empty glass and winking alternately at Jake and a Chianti bottle – 'American food is totally overrated. I mean to say – what *are* those beans you said? Black, are they? Like in that terrible soup they do?'

Tony somehow managed to broaden his smile even further than very wide indeed – wider still, as some of them noticed, when it passed over faces and settled on Nan.

'*He-e-ey* . . .' he idled, disarmingly, 'you guys don't wanna talk about *beans* . . .'

'Too bloody right!' boomed Jake – and Nan laughed out loud at that. 'So what *are* we going to do? Not that bloody film, I hope.'

'Oh God no,' said Nan quickly – not looking at Susie, because Susie was looking directly at her (something she seemed to keep on doing).

'*Four Weddings* . . .' said Clodagh, seemingly almost to herself.

'Oh *shit*, no!' protested Jake – and although Nan was surprised to find her grin of collusion already hovering and pretty much in place, she had to quell it because she quite actually liked Hugh Grant (but even that one – oh no: *please* not again! We *know* he gets that ultimately very irritating and rather scrawny American girl in the end and the English one – not Duckface, though she was OK too – but the other one, the posh one – she quite obviously was *miles* superior: but better not say any of that with Tony here, maybe, because they could often be pretty sensitive, Americans, you know – Nan had noticed that – and sometimes over the very tiniest things).

'Coffee, everyone?' offered Susie. 'You'll have coffee, won't you, Tony?'

'*Caw*-fee,' put in Jake, sounding as at home on the range as ever he was going to.

Tony grinned over at him, closing his eyes in acknowledgement and acceptance. 'I *thank* you, Susie.'

'Right,' said Susie, getting up and stacking plates. Nan and Sammy – and soon after, Clodagh – stretched out their arms and let their fingers just hang there stupidly over a bowl of this and the last of that, keen to show willing until Susie assured them all in turn that it's OK – honestly – I can manage (truly). 'Jake's got some really good Leb, if anyone's up for it. Why don't we all play the Truth Game, if no one wants a film? Good idea? Bad idea? What do you think?'

'*Urrrr*,' shuddered Sammy, as she shook around her hair. 'Even the *smell* of that stuff makes me sick. I just don't know how you can swallow it – inhale it. I could never even do that with cigarettes, when I was at school – just kept gagging. Quite pleased, now – it's so *obviously* bad for you. Gold Leaf, they were, pretty sure . . .'

'What is this game, Susie?' Tony now wanted to know (he sounded both seduced and thirsty for more, but this was probably more politeness than genuine interest, Susie had quite rapidly concluded).

'I *think* I know . . .' thought Clodagh.

'It's pretty straightforward,' expanded Jake. 'Good for a laugh. You just put people in any old hypothetical situation – '

'And ask them – '

'Yeh, all right, Sammy – *questions*. May I go on? Sammy? Yes? Excellent. Honour bound to tell the truth. If someone thinks you aren't, they can challenge you.'

'It's better than it sounds,' promised Susie. 'I promise you.'

'Most of these so-called mind games,' warned Sid, 'are extremely overrated. They simply serve to embarrass. No more.'

'We don't *have* to play . . .' qualified Susie.

'*Course* we'll play,' Jake averred. 'Why not? Better than bloody *Casablanca*. Now then, people – roll, as it were, up: this, my friends, is the joint to end all joints – a veritable viscount in a sea of proles. Ladies and gentlemen, I feel safe in assuring you that this fine spliff – once dragged, never forgotten.'

'Oh *Christ*, Jake,' deplored Susie, 'just light the bloody thing and *pass* it, Godsake. Do two or three and then they won't go all soggy like last time. Miles Davis OK with everyone?'

'What about The Beatles?' Sid wanted to know. 'Cool – but not so *aggressively* cool as all of that dinner jazz stuff.' He drew deep on the joint that he had more or less wrested from Jake's compressed and none-too-yielding fingers. '*Sergeant Pepper*, I suggest, might well fit the bill.'

'Don't know if we've *got* . . .' doubted Susie.

'Yeah,' Jake assured her. 'It's around that heap somewhere – haven't played it for ages and ages.'

'I used to love it,' sighed Sammy. 'That and *Bridge Over*

Troubled Water. Not at all sure I do now. What I go for these days is altogether more – '

'Oh *Gawd*,' sang out Jake, his shoulders drooping in mock exhaustion.

'If I'm *boring* you, Jake,' snapped Sammy, 'why don't you just say so?'

'You're *boring* me. No one *cares* about your musical predilections, do they, Sammy? Hm? You have to face facts. We just don't *mind*.'

'Oh *leave* her, Jake,' hushed Susie. 'Oh *here* it is – great cover. Can't really see all the detail on a CD. We always used to try and identify all the people – did any of you do that? Never ever got the ones at the back – and I still can't remember who that black boxer is.'

'Ali,' said Sid.

'No – it's not him, it's not!' came in Clodagh, almost frantically. So urgent were the signals in her face that Jake even held up whatever it was he was going to barge in with (probably some nonsense about Frank Bruno, or something). 'It's – it's – oh God, it's not Ali, it's that *other* one – oh Christ: I *know* this . . .'

'Sonny Liston,' said Carlo, who was suddenly standing there.

'*That's* it,' affirmed Sammy. And then to Carlo: 'Any luck?'

Carlo shook his head in unfeigned sorrow.

'Sonny *Liston* . . .?' queried Clodagh, seemingly in a state of complete mystification. 'Who on earth is Sonny *Liston* . . .?'

'See if the coffee's perked, would you, Jake?'

'Your wish, O Empress Susie, is my command. See, Tony? I know my place. Just as well.'

Nan, who had been watching him, watched him still as he rose and grinned and stretched and yawned and scratched at his stomach and rifled his hair and walked stiff-legged from the table.

Clodagh was lying full-length on the dhurrie, her head just about propped up higher by what she had thought was a pillow sort of thing when she grabbed it, but turned out to be a not-too-thickly-folded maybe throw. 'Oh God,' she groaned – and it sounded as if she meant it – 'it's not my turn *again* to do this, is it?'

Susie clapped her hands in gleeful delight, and Jake boomed out It is, It is – It's your turn, Clodagh, and here comes the question *now*.

'All you have to do,' assessed Sammy, with an unswerving reason that was beginning to drive Nan just a little bit crazy, 'is simply tell the truth. It's not as if you have to *think*, or anything – you just come out with the answer within you.'

'Yeh . . .' agreed Jake – but grudgingly, because OK yes, that *was* the object, no point in denying it, but like all games, Christ, it was supposed to be at least halfway . . . what? Diverting? Entertaining? Some damn thing. Admittedly the Lebanese weed was taking up a good deal of the slack, here (and Tony had come with a gram or two of coke – told him to be a bit, well . . . don't flash it around, OK? Susie doesn't like it in the flat); but Jesus, when you asked Sammy, like I did last time, a question like What in the whole world would you go straight out and buy tomorrow morning, first thing, if money were no object at all – you didn't really want *this* (did you?):

'Flowerpots,' Sammy said promptly, without even blinking. 'Well actually *troughs*,' came her unsmiling qualification. 'Terracotta, ideally. I've always thought that bit of wall just outside the kitchen window looked awfully *bare*, and – '

'Yeh yeh,' broke in Jake – and testy was there, as well as real and heartfelt wonder. 'Thank you, Sammy – and goodnight.'

And now it was Clodagh's turn again (she had been fairly OK for the first couple of rounds – truthful enough, was the general feeling, and not too po-faced).

'*Sid*,' Jake was now insisting (better get Sid, was his way of thinking, before the guy's out of it completely: seemed to have been weaned on hash from an early age, and the need to suck on it had clearly never left him. 'You ask the question, this time. Anything you want.'

Sid was nodding – could have been sagely, though no one really thought so. After a bit more nodding, and maybe just a hiss and an exhalation or two, Susie was all for driving right through it with a question of her own – but Sid then rallied round (suddenly seemed awake-ish) and now that elliptical mouth of his was slowly forming words, and here now they plopped out, one by one – each a special offer, with completely free pauses in between:

'Right . . . OK, then . . . Susie . . .'

'Clodagh.'

'Clodagh, yes Clodagh . . . absolutely right . . . *Clodagh* . . .'

'Oh *Christ*,' whistled Susie. 'Someone *else* do it – we'll be here all night. Where's Carlo?'

Jake made a sizzling sound. 'Where do you think?'

'No no,' insisted Sid. 'I've got it now. I'm together. OK, Clodagh – here it is: Is there a man in this room that you fancy?'

Jake and Susie were cackling as one (this was more like it; it generally did get around to all this sort of thing, yeh, course – but Jesus, it had taken bloody ages, this time – what with bloody Sammy and her terracotta pots).

Clodagh had half risen – her sideways weight slumped on to an elbow, which didn't, to Susie, seem up to taking it for long. Clodagh was shaking her head in a seen-it-somewhere and – certainly to Nan – intensely irritating sort of USTV way: Hey-guys-I-can't-believe-I'm-*hearing*-this, was the mock-shock-horror impression she was giving –

but yeah I suppose, Nan had to concede, that a bit of theatre is just OK.

'*Yessssss* . . .' concluded Clodagh, still looking down, the last bits of head wagging still not ready to pack it all in.

'*Who*?' roared Jake.

And Clodagh looked up in Not-fair surprise, and a rush of might-as-well-be outrage. 'That wasn't the *question* – I *answered* the question and now it's my turn to ask someone else something – right, Susie? That's the rules, yeh?' And then to the rumbles of let-down. 'I *answered* the question . . .!'

'She's right, you know,' adjudged Sammy.

Susie knew this, but chucked her a fuck-off look anyway, and then she yielded into resignation. 'OK – OK, you win, Clodagh: ask your question.'

'*Right*, Susie,' agreed Clodagh, with relish – 'I'll ask Jake. Jake: have you had a rude thought – a sexy thought – about anyone in the room tonight?'

And over the groans and clamour, Jake shouted: 'No! Not guilty!'

'*Challenge*!' screamed Susie. 'I simply don't *believe* you!'

'I don't either,' laughed Tony – and he laughed louder when Jake went to punch his shoulder, and missed.

'Well of *course* I lied,' bellowed Jake. 'Of *course* I've had thoughts – '

'He's *always*,' affirmed Susie, 'got rude thoughts. He's quite filthy – aren't you, Jake? Totally sick. OK – my go.'

'Hey!' was Jake's aggrieved exclamation – spilled a bit of wine as he was slopping it out. 'How do you reckon that? *I* get to ask the question now – my go.'

'*Wrong*,' shot back Susie. 'You were challenged and you were *lying* – you *said* so, Jake!'

Jake was temporarily halted. 'Oh . . . *yeah*, but – !'

'That's the *rules* . . .' Susie was adamant. 'So my go, right? OK – let's get some *real* answers here. Nan – it's your turn to tell us, and remember you got to be *truthful* – kay? Right: who in this room do you really *fancy*?'

And as Jake started drumming up a throbbing tattoo on the table with two pairs of stiff fingers and howling like a dingo, Nan rolled up her eyes – and despite the elastic smile of protection, felt the warmth of her blushing. Susie turned to Clodagh as the hubbub subsided and explained to her quite patiently that *that's* the way to phrase them, the questions, you see – that way you don't get just a yes or a no: what you get then is a *result*.

All eyes (except Sid's, which were closed) were now on Nan, as her white and straight-fingered hands flew to each side of her face: she pressed them inwards, this forcing her mouth into an oval of mortified speechlessness. Her eyes, though alight with party laughter, were still tinged with dread – and by the time she closed them like shutters and her front teeth slid down briefly to suck in hastily on her lower lip, Susie just knew she was ready to answer. Still not sure, though, whether the entire charade had been designed with simple charity in mind – supplying the baying punters with not just their money's worth but also an interlude of lewd anticipation – or was enacted merely so that during the time it took, some or other method of evasion could be not too laughably slung together.

'So-o-o-o?' leered Jake.

'We're waiting,' prompted Sid – who seemed now astonishingly alert – radiantly, in a way that was neither needed nor natural.

'What a *shame* . . .' – it was Sammy's wistful voice (and not at all, as usual, thought Susie quite bitterly at this point, in tune with the spirit of the moment). 'Carlo's missing all this . . .'

'He misses *life*,' snapped Jake. 'Some people go out and grab it by the balls – others just hang theirs over a bog. Come on, Nan! Truth! Truth! Answer! Answer!'

'We-ell . . .' drawled Nan.

'That was disgusting, Jake,' said Sammy, shortly.

'She's going to say "no one", smiled Clodagh. 'And she *can*, you know, Susie, despite what you say – that *is* an answer.'

'Oh God's *sake*, Clodagh – don't *tell* her what she can say,' shushed Susie. 'Anyway – that's a crap answer, "no one". Isn't it, everybody? What sort of crap answer is that?'

'All I'm saying – !' protested Clodagh.

'Oh shut the fuck *up*, everyone!' bawled Jake. 'Christ's sake let her *speak*. Come on, Nan – time's up. Can't stall any longer.'

'Well OK, then,' agreed Nan. 'I'll tell you. It's . . . – ' and during the quite real and bated hush that filled up the pause, she turned her face full on to Susie's. '. . . *Tony*.'

There was a whoosh of release at the outcome (Sammy grinning – Clodagh pointing with glee, and with the other hand attempting to cover her teeth) but Jake was whooping now and urging Tony into on-the-spot and dog-like fornication, as Susie laughed and gave in fully to an I-*thought*-so smile that dragged down her mouth at one corner. Sid was just sitting there, as sad as hell.

'Gee . . .!' was Tony's only response for now. He looked a bit expectant, and then both sidelong and pleased, but Nan was busy hanging her head and shaking it – really quite Clodagh-like – in order to maybe convey to herself and others that she couldn't (hear her?) just couldn't *believe* she had said that!

Carlo wandered over to the table, wearing his usual air of amiable bewilderment. What's up, he wanted to know: what's all the excitement?

'Nan doesn't fancy you,' said Jake, abruptly. 'But then to be fair, you weren't one of the people in the room, were you, Carlo? Cos you never bloody are.'

'*Leave* him,' cautioned Sammy. 'God's *sake*, Jake.'

It turned out later (Jake said 'Jesus!') none of them knew

why Sid had been there: he seemed in the end to be the friend of no one.

*

And the very next day, Tony had called Nan up and asked her out – just as, when he kissed her as he left – he had promised to do. And all these months later, Nan didn't recall this inaugural and welcoming party for the sake of that, and nor for the fact that it marked the beginning of the truth that, until so recently, she had been going out with Tony ever since. No, thought Nan: no no. Here is my memory now (and for ever? Who knows? I so much doubt it: what *can* be for ever, actually? Is there anything left that *really* goes on?); in my memory now is just and solely Susie, and the very first time I lied to her face.

CHAPTER FOUR

Nan's lips and eyes were coping again with mounting an easy-to-swallow show of sincere appreciation, this now bolstered by the brief descent of eyelids and an affectionate simper. Tony's fingers were fingering hers, and she neither clutched at them nor withdrew – a delicate balance she had learned the hard way. Tony by now must be as cringingly aware as she was, surely, the way all of this went; if only it would make him stop *saying* it all, but it didn't – never did. He let the words hang there spikily between them – and when, beyond the simper, she made no reply, he could not once just let them fade back and soften, so that Nan could pretend to forget or not have heard them. No. He would – as she knew he was just about to – say it all again:

'Nan. Nan, honey – didn't you hear me? I *love* you, Nan my angel. Love you like I've never loved anyone before – never come close. I need you, babe – need you for ever. I just didn't ever believe this would happen to me.'

Nan got up and stepped the three paces that were all it took to reach the far side of Tony's dark and not nice room. Next door (well – just to the other side of the partition) stood a vast and rounded old American fridge, Nile green and decked with chrome like a purring and vertical Buick: huge and lush, unlike anything else here. There were always oranges in a bag inside – on that you could depend (and it was good, considered Nan, to be able to know that about just anything, now – it went so far to cushioning the rest).

She leant then idly against the plasterboard room divide,

and it slightly shivered as she dug deep a thumbnail into the tough hide of a Jaffa. Next to her was sticky-fixed a glossy gatefold from a magazine Tony had mailed to him, depicting not – at least – some oiled and fabulous torso, but a solid wall of unsmiling and upholstered black and white Nan supposed football people (menacing in helmets), their forearms crossed, each meaty pair far brawnier than thighs she had known.

'Why,' sighed Tony, 'do you never say it back?'

And why, thought Nan – again again again – do you think you have to ask that?

'Look, Tony,' she said (and did it sound more leaden than ever, this time around?), 'we're fine as we are, aren't we? Hm? Let's just leave stuff as it is. Kay?'

Tony glanced up (was he maybe frustrated? Could be seeking distraction) to one low corner of the room, and then to its opposite number. He wagged his head in a sort of speechless sorrow, just as Nan was lowering hers. It's really silly, all of this, she was thinking. It's actually more and deeper than silly, of course, but it's bloody silly too just *saying* simply any of this, isn't it? Because in whatever state she and Tony found themselves at this brittle point in their short and endless time in one another's lives, 'fine' was not only just not close, but so far away from even the general drift of the way it seemed to Nan things surely seemed headed.

But right back at the beginning, then it had been different – during those, what were they? In a way, sweet days – when Nan had been new to the flat and warmed by Susie, though still echoing with hurt and scared of caring for the succession of toddlers so briefly in her care (when still she could sense the bitter seepage of her still-love for Adrian and Donna – who were doing what, now, she wondered often, at this absolute moment – now that Nan was no longer a part of their present or their future? How odd that it could still go on, with Nan all gone).

'You wanna take in a movie?' That was the sort of thing Tony had come out with, then (and like all Americans, to Nan, that's just how he always sounded: like someone in a movie). And Nan had said Fine – because that's exactly the sort of easy thing she did want to take in: a movie, a pizza, ten-pin bowling (they did that once, and Nan had been better then Tony – strike after strike – but he didn't seem to mind, just laughed and hugged her; never went again, though) and then maybe howsabout we rent a cuppla vids, chill out back at my place with a cuppla beers, or sump'n? And that was cool too – and so was the touch of Tony's skin to her so very tentative fingers (she was chilled by the fear of again getting burned). Sex – even the shadow of that looming thing – had been blissfully lit and laughed at: they had slouched in the couch of Tony's surprisingly small and generally dispiriting bedsit, she sipping and then gulping Californian wine, and Tony eyeing her as he snorted coke. Which Nan didn't. And then she did. So bed is where they had found themselves, sometime later, their warm and lazy grins and stickily kissing shoulders assuring each of them that some sort of pleasure must have been received, and maybe given.

But then it got to Tony saying 'Why?' And 'Why Not?' – he said that too. Nan could see now the hurt-but-making-light-of-it expression that always accompanied every one of his enquiries. Not tonight, Tony, really, she would say: what do you mean why *not*? I just don't *feel* like a movie tonight, OK? I just want to be in my room on my own – I'd really like that. I can't tell you *why*, Tony, can I? It's just the way I'm feeling – I'm tired, I had a bad night, I've got to get up so early in the morning because the Jameses' twins are going on a picnic with their class and I've got to get every-thing ready. And he'd eventually nod, with huge reluctance, and give back with grudging grace – Jesus – what to Nan's mind was already hers! I mean – Christ! It's *my* time – *my* evening, isn't it? Why do I always have to come up with a reason just to do what I bloody well want with it? Huh? So after – a bit, not long later – she poured away her accumulated concoction of guff about headaches and stomach cramps and the need to rise at dawn: *why*?! she threw back at him – *why*?! Because I bloody *want* to, that's why, Tony: got it?

But. When she did decide it might not be too bad to take in yet another bloody movie, he came to regard it as a big special thing ('Tonight I got my baby back!'). And she took care, now, never even to mention any yen or enthusiasm that flitted in and out of her – for there it would be, whatever it was, just sitting there waiting: Yeh, Tony, I *know* I said I quite fancied Häagen-Dazs Chocolate Chip but Jesus Christ, this is the size of a bloody oil drum. (And where did the money come from? This puzzled – not troubled – her. The room was mean, and he never mentioned his work: this was good – most things about anyone she did not, if she was truly frank, really care to know.)

And Susie, as usual, got everything wrong (she was so very clever – so why couldn't she see what seemed to Nan to glow in neon?). Whenever Nan was alone in her room – reading maybe Catherine Cookson, which she *liked*, OK? – or else just slumped with Sammy on the sofa, zapping the remote, Susie seemed to think that it was all down to Tony having once more and again let her down and failed to call. He's jerking you around, she'd often tell her – and all you do is just take it: you know your trouble, don't you, Nan? And yes Nan did, she surely did – but whatever Susie might imagine it to be, she would not (would she ever?) come within a mile.

'You're too *nice*, Nan – that's your trouble.'

Nan just smiled. These days, that's all she did. 'I'm going to the loo, and then I'm off out.'

'Carlo's in there. I thought you weren't. Thought you said you were in tonight, no?'

'I did. I was. But now I'm going out.'

And if Susie was thinking But hang on – if not out with Tony, with who, then? Well if that's what she was thinking: let her.

*

Nan well remembered the first time with Jake – just as vividly and with so many hot and tender pangs, as if it had been the very first time with anyone in her life. (The attendant details of her actual deflowering – and Nan thought of it like that, because she remembered feeling as if she had been picked, not so much chosen as picked like a flower, yes, like that – and also like a lock . . . were now forgotten. Her real first time, mm, had been quite literally unmemorable – how many years ago, now, must all that have been? – in that to this day she remained not quite sure as to where – I think in that bit of scrubland, close to the games field – or when – GCSEs? A-levels? – and nor the real name of the reaper, as she still considered him to be. She had called him Star Trek because he had these funny ears like that Mister-Whatever-His-Name-Was in the programme; and that's as much as Nan could tell you.)

But with Jake there had been impact. As the hugeness of his wildly pumping and sweat-sweet chest came in close and covered her, as *Christ* whistled out of him and flew right in to her, she was throwing wide her wet and helpless arms and then she screwed down her eyes and concentrated hard on the deep black centre of all this happening and the clench of her thighs was making him gasp as she jerked out the words Oh God get it *done*, and she was filled up with his furiously living dark death-rattle as he fell right across her and then as he was nearly dying she had yelped at her flooding and called out gloriously – *Oh*! Oh Heaven: You Have Ripped Me Right Up. And slowly, in the still and warm, her scattered parts came back together, and she sighed out her glutton's contentment that now and at last this renegade wanting had been fed and put to rest.

It had been just after eight in the evening, when Nan had rung his doorbell. She had endured a day of thinking thinking thinking I can't, I can't, I can't – and then scurrying back to Well why not, actually? Hm? Why shouldn't I? *Want* to. I will, I will, I will; oh God I *can't*. Yes I will. I must. And as she stood there, waiting – and aware now of Jake's big voice becoming louder over the buzz of TV: OK – OK, he was saying, I'm coming, I'm coming – she still was ringing with the clamour of talk (but here I am – I have walked the walk!).

Maybe if, when Jake swung wide the door, he had been confronted and possibly butted by a blue and furry rhino, then just possibly, Nan had later considered, his face might have borne even deeper furrows of shock and puzzlement – the ripples of confusion could have shuddered more broadly.

'Nan . . .' he just about managed. 'Susie OK? Nothing wrong, is there?'

Nan stood up on tiptoe and pointed over Jake's shoulder into the room behind him as she widened her eyes into every sort of appeal. Jake backed inwards with unrehearsed and therefore large and clumsy grace and stuck on a nearly smile of sort of welcome and kind of dopey happiness that went not far in masking not just a flicker of irritation but the plangent undertone of What the fuck is *this*, now?

'Since that supper,' said Nan quite breezily – twirling around in the centre of Jake's vast and lofty space, as if coolly determining whether or not it should be allowed to continue – 'and I *don't*, by the way, think much of your so-called Truth Game – even *Casablanca* would have been better than that – Susie has been going on and on about how absolutely vile your flat is, so I thought I'd come and see it for myself. I think it's . . . *cool*.'

And Jake liked that a lot. 'Yeh,' he agreed – indicating

with one finger the can of beer in his hand, and raising his eyebrows as he did it. 'It is.'

'Love one. Is it cold?'

Jake grinned. 'Like ice. What do you take me for?'

Nan slipped into the hand-on-hip posture and chewed-up sub-Brooklyn drawl of a mobster's moll. 'A guy who likes his beers cold . . . and his babes *hot*.'

And Jake was laughing even before Nan had indulged herself with her own little drizzle of amusement – holding on tight to the bridge of her nose (gawky, now, and twelve years old). Then she stood before him, composing in turn each muscle in her face and making sure her things like breasts reasserted themselves (female, now, and – yeh, quite timeless).

'Coooool . . .' she spun out thoughtfully, touching just lightly a brushed-steel cabinet (could have been she really liked it).

'They're meant for hospitals,' said Jake quite eagerly. 'You should see the lav – prison issue. Same steel – no seat.'

'Chilly,' smiled Nan.

'Surprisingly not,' offered Jake, apparently meaning what he said. 'But I can't see bloody Carlo going for it in any big way.'

'*Warming* to the thing!' laughed Nan. And then she prompted: one eyebrow up, her lips not quite joining again, after she'd done it and the word was out: 'Beer?'

'I'll get,' Jake assured her, and made to do just that.

'What goes on up here?' Nan called after him – the flat of her hand sidling up and down the flank of a steep-pitched aluminium stairway, seemingly stretched and pinioned by taut and burnished plaited cables.

'That's where I crash out.' And before Jake ducked out of sight through the only doorspace: 'Dream my dreams.'

Standing at the fridge, Jake made himself concentrate solely on extracting just one tall frosty can of Foster's, gently hooking his foot around the door and kicking it home – and then with care peeling back the ring, seemingly intent upon the side-of-the-mouth pssst it gave off, then alert to that oozing pout of bubbles. Later, weeks later, he had asked himself frankly Well what did you *think*? Why do you imagine, for Christ's sake, she had *come*? To check out your décor? I don't really think so, Jake old lad, and I don't buy for a minute that you did either. Did you? Well *did* you? But at the time Jake had freely and devoutly given up his whole soul and rendered his being to the devoted care of this one can of beer – but it is true that he had to put just everything he had into feigning surprise (looking this way and that) and maybe a smidgen of outrage when on returning to his living space, a can hanging loosely from either hand, Nan's voice floated down to him from high in the gallery:

'Come on up!' she hailed him, fully at home with the tone and gaiety of an excited tripper. 'The view from here's just lovely!'

Jake could, he thought, say No – no no: you come down here; but he thought it only when he had heaved himself up to the top of the stairs, one arm outstretched to her, now, and holding out a beer. He had a large, very large futon up there – had it specially made in this weird place in Fulham, seven feet square and with a double-thickness filling. This still left plenty of floorspace – but yeah, oh sure (guess what?), Nan was all over it.

'I *love*,' she sighed, 'your muscles.'

'Shit,' said Jake, not knowing quite what he meant by that.

'They were the first things I noticed about you. That and your smile, which is really very kind. Come and sit down, Jake.'

'Nan . . . look . . .'

'OK, then – stand up. I don't really care either way. It won't change my life.'

'I can . . . look . . . I can sit *down* . . .'

'I don't much care, Jake. Stand up, sit down – do what you like. It's what you seem good at.'

'Look – I'm *sitting*, OK? I'm sitting. Do you want this beer or not?'

'I want . . .' and she eked out the pause as long as she dared, '. . . *you*. I know you must think I'm terrible and all the rest of it but I don't much care about any of that either. I didn't *want* to want you. But I do.'

And although now Jake was trying to sound like a benign and self-effacing cardinal, gently letting down the starry-eyed postulant, he truly really did love all of this big-time (he's just a guy, right? That's how he had explained it all away to a lapping-it-up crony at work, when all was sunk and Jake was done for. *Look,* he had exclaimed, in wide-eyed pique and desperation, both of them slugging it out with bafflement and regret – craving from fate a *break,* here: I'm just a *guy*. Right?).

'Susie,' he said, 'I think wouldn't like this . . . that's my – yike! – *ear* you're bloody chewing, Nan – Jesus. Don't do it.'

'She's not here,' whispered Nan. 'I am.'

'Isn't she meant to be your *friend*? What is it with you women? I thought you were meant to stick together. Isn't that the way it works?'

'I don't do – oh God, your neck, it's so strong . . . it's divine . . . I don't do, Jake, ever, what I'm meant.'

'Look, Nan . . . Susie: I *love* her, OK?'

'So?' And then, surprised: 'Why?'

'I just do. And she loves me, pretty sure. I know she doesn't always, you know – *act* like it . . . Jesus, Nan . . . don't . . . please don't *touch* me like that . . . I think maybe this isn't actually a great idea . . .'

Nan was now behind him and kneeling – inhaling his hair and gently hugging the big hard warmth of his chest. 'You got a better one? *Casablanca*, maybe?'

Jake smirked, and broke away. His eyes were dancing as he held off her wrists and looked on her with all the supreme cockiness of a man who just knows he is firmly in control.

'Nan,' he explained easily, 'listen to me. Whatever you do, and whatever you say, there's one thing you've just got to understand: there is no way I'm sleeping with you. Hear me? I don't mean to, oh God – *hurt* you, or anything, but that's just the way it has to be. Dig?'

And looking back on it all, from far too late and so much later, Jake vaguely remembered – he felt pretty sure – that all Nan had had to say after that was Sure – I dig. Oh no – she said one more thing: Dream Your Dreams. And then there was impact.

*

And yes, on reflection, Nan would have willingly agreed with you: not like her at all, all this – how could anyone think she didn't know that? It was just that, even at the supper thing – maybe at the touting of Tony's imminence, before even he had arrived – Nan had sensed the looming inevitability of his coming: that he would be at once attracted to her, that he would seem to just everyone the ideal guy (she knew, just knew, that Susie and Sammy later would have built it all up, and taken it apart). And hey, how cute – first proper day in a brand-new flat, a little welcoming get-together and bingo! Along comes Mister Right (oh Christ: maybe even why he was bloody invited – *can't* have been, can it? Don't know. Never asked Jake: we talk of other things). And Tony, yeah – he's OK, not saying he isn't; but what's OK, when all's said and done? I mean, when you come right down to it, if you go for OK, what are you doing, really and truly, except postponing the end of pretence – not really dealing with big disappointment, because it was surely on the way since before the beginning. Better, almost, to stay where you are – recede and shrink back into the sour cocoon of hurt, and sad.

But in Jake there had seemed to Nan to be not just a healthy and *God*, yes, mighty alternative, but something that almost straight away had come ready assembled as a driving purpose. And it had been hard, that evening, because Nan had found her eyes being dragged towards Jake by her own inner sirens; Tony was eyeing her, and so was Susie, and that is when she threw them both the one bloated herring – so red as to be bloody and high, to Nan's mind, but it was awesome the way each of them in turn just fell on it and gorged.

So she had gone out with Tony and along with it all – slept with him, sure (there was no impact) – while always at pains to underline to him as indelibly as it took that here was no commitment. OK? And Tony had said OK (before he started asking Why?) and then he had assailed her with things like he *loved* her, to which Nan just had to eventually respond, as kindly as she could – though her patience with Tony was thinning daily, quite in line with her fattening need to have Jake for always – that was nice, very nice, a kind and lovely thing to say to me, Tony, but I don't, I'm afraid, love *you*, OK, and I've never ever said I did – did I? And Tony had said No (before he started asking Why Not?).

Jake is a separate issue (but not for long) and yes, I suppose, another set of problems. He said he felt so bad, early on, about – as he put it – 'doing this to Susie'. But *Jake*, I reasoned (men can be awfully slow, no matter how gorgeous they happen to be – maybe particularly, then); *Jake*, honey, I'd go – but we're *not*, are we? Can you see? Doing anything *to* her. She's not *here*. Is she? Hm? What we're doing – it's just between ourselves. He'd nod. But not a nod of having got it, no. The next evening and the next, I'd have to go over and over the whole thing again – it was as if he was wilfully unlearning everything I'd carefully taught him to finally believe in. You get that with the toddlers, sometimes; I think it's that the comfort of recognition

– to be eased just once more through a familiar routine of exchanges – they think it's far better, could be safer, than ever moving on; it's why, maybe, we all have our favourite stories. Tell her, I'd go to him. Leave her utterly and be with me. I will, he said: I will. And then he looked sad and maybe sick. Do it *now*, I'd urge him. Can't, he'd say – it's not the right time. When is? When is, then, Jake? Don't know, he'd go – before turning away: I just don't know. (When is it ever right, to smash people up?)

And nor did Susie seem able to take my hints, and I was dropping so many of them all about her. Whenever I spent an evening in at the flat, it was usually only because she was going to be with Jake (which I didn't mind at all, at first; and then I did). Or else because I just couldn't, oh God, face Tony and all his plaintive mourning (and nor could you, not after Jake – the man is just busting with fun, I tell you, and crammed so full of vigour). But sometimes Jake just bolts the door on me: *No*, Nan – *No*, is how he goes: I just can't *stand* any more. What? *What?*, I'd be screaming (panicked – Yes, I suppose I can get like that) – *what* can't you stand? What have I *done*? No ... *no*, he'd sigh brokenly from just the other side of the panels – I mean it's *you*, you're wearing me out and grinding me down: I literally, Nan, can't *stand* any more – I just want to lie down ... I laughed out loud – it was so good to hear (and it was true, it was true – whenever we were together, I shagged him senseless). Sometimes, Susie would come back to the flat quietly, and really early. You're early, I'd go. Mm, she'd agree, quite sort of airily ... Jake was, um – tired. And I'd be: *tired*? Really? What – *again*? And Susie would nod quite sadly. (Hee hee: not surprised. Whenever we're together, I shag him senseless.)

That, then, has been the picture – or a part of it – right up until now. When it simply has to change. I'm tired of it. I'm just fed up with the people I simply don't have to know any more, while I can't get enough of the man I need (who loves me). And who I am, right this very minute, on my way to see: this, I just know, will be a night to remember.

*

'I can't tell you, Tony,' said Susie, with wide and sympathetic eyes. 'I just don't know where she is. I thought she was with you.'

In the honking snort that came right down and out of his nose, true and deep bitterness was there for all to hear – or, as in Susie's case, recoil from.

'With *me*? Nah. Ain't seen her near two days, now.'

Well, thought Susie, maybe she's trying to make a point here, Tony: it's what you get, isn't it, when you jerk people around. That's what I should say – so why, in fact, don't I? I'm always saying one thing and thinking something else entirely, and I can't be alone, here, can I?

'She'll probably phone,' said Susie. 'Look, Tony, I have to go out – but Sammy should be in a bit later, not too long. Why don't you have a drink and hang around?'

'Naw . . .' sighed Tony. 'I'll be getting back to my place. Which she hates, by the way. She said that? Hates it. I guess it is kinda scuzzy. It's not what I'd *choose*, you know?'

'Well.' laughed Susie, 'it can't be as bad as *Jake's* flat – have you been? Just awful.'

And suddenly, Tony sat down heavily, and hid his whole face behind two long, hard hands.

'Oh *Jesus*,' he practically sobbed. 'Why does she *do* this to me?'

This was not good news to Susie: had to go out, you see.

'Maybe it's what you get, Tony, when you jerk people around.'

And Tony was only marginally more amazed than Susie to hear such a thing.

'Jerk her – ?! *Me*? I don't . . . *she's* the one, Susie, not me – I just never know where I *am* with her. I *love* her, I *love* her –

116

I keep telling her I love her and all she does is not come over when she says she's coming over and tell me *not* to say I love her and lately she's started with this "don't touch me" jive and I'm telling you, Susie, I'm going kinda crazy.'

'Nan? *Nan* does that? Oh come *on*, Tony – we've got to be talking about someone else, here. *Nan's* trouble is that she's just too *nice* – whatever are you running her down for?'

'Running her *down*? I *love* the bitch, Chrissakes.'

'I think, Tony, you have to sit down and think out just what you mean. You're not making sense, you know, Tony. Really not. Look – I must go. There's beer, pretty sure – OK? OK, Tony? You OK?'

'No.'

'*Tony.*'

'OK – *Yes*. What do you want me to say? I'm in bits without her – I don't know what to do. Where *is* she? Huh?'

Susie was so, so relieved when the flat door opened and Carlo was there, wearing his habitual expression of certain knowledge that once again something momentous had happened in his absence, but he'd try his damnedest to piece it all together once someone had kindly apprised him of the nuts and bolts.

'Tony – talk to Carlo,' insisted Susie. 'I must – oh God, it's so late – I really have to *go*.'

And, not risking it, she went.

Carlo looked down at Tony, who was staring at the floor.

'You're welcome to come and talk to me in the bathroom, if you can bear it,' offered Carlo, resignedly. 'Otherwise we'll have to shout through the door.'

Carlo thought Tony might be about to be sick, and he was covered in guilt while torn, too, by the need to be in the bathroom – but it turned out he was only crying, so Carlo eagerly left him.

*

'Jake? Jake, darling – are you awake?'

Nan did not just hold his shoulder, as she hissed this at him, but gently, and then more boldly, shook it too. Jake groaned from within his half-sleep, and rolled over and into the warmth of her. The single white sheet seemed to be twisted about his ankles, and with one eye open he groped for the edge of it and tried quite weakly to haul it up and over him.

'What's that . . . what's that bloody noise?' he wanted to know.

Nan scooped back an armful of her hair, and set to pursuing this very thing: 'That's what I mean, Jake – it's someone at the door. They've rung twice already – it sounds as if they're getting impatient. Who do you think it is?'

Jake sighed, and moved in closer to Nan, the contours of her and the futon holding him tightly and keeping him safe. 'Don't care who it is. They'll go away. Not expecting anyone. Obviously.'

The ringing started up again, and a sort of knocking sound now accompanied it.

'I think you should answer it,' urged Nan.

'Oh sod it.'

'No, Jake – I really think you should. Could be a neighbour. Could be important.'

Jake opened his mouth to say one thing, but then the infernal irritation of the bell set up again its jangling and so he settled for a cursory Oh Christ Damn Them and slid himself away, and on to the floor. Standing now, he muttered darkly as he wrapped around him a towelling gown.

'If it's that bastard about my *car* again, I'll absolutely kill him,' raved Jake distractedly, his bare feet slapping coldly on the aluminium treads of his cool and shuddering suspended stairway. Temper and disgruntlement had tightened their firm hold on him by the time he reached the door (bell still ringing, the bastard, the bastard), which is maybe why he didn't fool around with any of the palaver of chains and spyholes but just swung the bloody thing open, tetchy and more than ready to deal with whatever the fuck.

Except that he hadn't been ready for this – no, not Susie: no time was good, but this, dear Christ, just had to, God, be the worst of all. He stared, just, as Susie quite huffily – and letting him know it – breezed on in and past him, shrugging off her coat as she did it and dropping it just anywhere.

'*Jesus*, Jake,' was her opening shot. 'I've been ringing and ringing. God – even you, surely, couldn't have just gone on sleeping through all of that lot? And why *have* you been sleeping, actually, Jake? Hm? I'm not *that* late. God, I need a drink.'

'Susie . . .' Jake said. It was the only word for now that he felt confident to utter. The broader implications of this raw and heart-clutching moment in his life (memorable already, before it was even partly formed) had begun to roar in his reddening ears: here was potential conflagration – once it was lit, it would know no end. How to not just damp down Susie's aggravation, but also smother the wisps of what might be coming and then (quite vital) put her out?

'You might have given me a bit more *notice*, Jake,' Susie now was quasi-sulking – her nose, quite perceptibly, coming back into joint. 'I just don't know where I *am* with you, these days, you know: it's not much fun. *Don't* come round – come round; I'm tired – I'm *not* tired . . . I'm not a bloody *taxi*, you know, Jake: I don't just *arrive* when you decide to whistle. Get me a glass of wine, would you, my sweet? You mentioned something about *champagne*, yes? So what's all the secrecy? What's the big event? Christ you drive me crazy.'

Jake's face was crawling: noncommittal corrugations and jags of perplexity were shooting all around it, and although he knew his mouth was now well ajar and stalely empty – words would have to be pushed out and through it, at least for form's sake, as well as to fill a void – he felt not at all sure that whatever they might turn out to be they would not serve only to cast him down and string him up before they had even touched the air and travelled the distance. He was not so much relieved, then – relief, if there ever was to be that, would be ages in coming – as winded and briefly grateful that Susie was up and striding (not at all in any way great, this side of things) and talking, talking – she was up, yes up, and talking again:

'And you don't *deserve* it,' she was mock-scolding him, now, 'but I've done what you asked, which is actually what made me late – that, and Tony. I don't quite actually know what this makes me *look* like, but anyway . . .'

And as Susie un-through-buttoned her blue linen shirt dress, Jake just gazed, blinking often (shutting his eyes for slightly longer, now, as if to deny or blank out whatever was coming, or maybe just demonstrably willing his quite dead brain to just, Jesus, pack in its terminal loafing and for Christ's sake, will you, come up with something – anything – and *save* me).

'Get the champagne, darling,' Susie now whispered, 'and then you can feast on *this* . . .'

She stood before him, feet well apart – which flexed her thighs, and didn't she know it – pinched, laced, hooked and bloody strapped in to what they both had often thrilled to knowing was Jake's most towering fantasy image: Susie pouted her fat pink lips right at him, as one hand dragged back and high behind her head whole skeins of hair, stray strands falling back and coating her face, clinging to her sticky eyelids. Jake's own were strained wide as he swept down from that (look, look – whatever the torment, I'm a *guy*, OK? A guy is – Jesus, though! – all I am) and ate up the swell of her white soft breasts, each cupped in and brought up short by the lacy clasp of a hard-wired corset, the criss-cross satin ribbons pointing and urging his senses down to the tightly held and rounded mound, framed by a seriously frivolous frill, its throat-stopping message underlined in bold by taut and severe suspenders (their unyielding jaws sated by stocking tops, and visibly straining). By the time Jake's wild-eyed longing had swooped him down the curves of her calves to those jack-heeled and dancingly glossy dagger-tip shoes – eight pink toes huddled into cleavages and just winking up at him, shyly – he had nearly lost his grip on a terrible and raging conflict: only now there seeped through the awed realization that what he was confronted with here just had to add up to the most appalling provocation and all he could hear was the blood thudding hard in his ears and maybe, just distantly, a mournful plangency that could be just the beginnings of his own knell of doom. Jake was choked by lust and fear and lust and cringing, the depth of his mood as he continued to stand there not even relieved half-heartedly by a frail and white butterfly of not-much-hope, hesitant and aflutter, that maybe – if only, if only he could just please judge this not too wrongly – no big and scalding harm would after all and finally be dashed into their faces, leaving them shrieking with not just pain but the dread of scars that were already forming?

Jake's heart ceased its pounding, then, and fell at once to the floor. He could hear the sigh on the stairway, and now over Susie's shoulder (and she stared at him strangely, as well she might: if his face was in tune with his being, it can barely have seemed to her sane or human) he could glimpse first one foot and then another, and now the bare legs of Nan, trailing behind and half around her the huge white bedsheet that flipped and then flapped over every aluminium tread and riser – and it was only when her very forcedly sleepy wheedling smacked into the air that Susie froze as if speared and still didn't look.

Jake knew he just couldn't come close to meeting that stab of fright and disbelief, alight and gleaming like needles in Susie's eyes, flickering once and only slightly – away from the heat of impending devastation.

'*Susie . . .*' was once again all he could manage, the one word well dripping with a distant desolation – it was as if he had agreed with heavy heart to be the one who should tell her of the recent and brutal annihilation of her parents and sisters, but now as he stood before her he knew that somehow the information had already reached out, and held her in its grip: the news had broken and so, quite soon, would she be too.

*

And for days, even weeks later, Jake had flinched away from flickerbook images of the scene that had then come down and engulfed them all; there was, of course, no hope of this, for whatever he was doing or trying very hard to, all of that just stormed his senses. He still was left wondering whether Susie would in the end have turned at all – her face had been a porcelain mask, not giving in yet to even a chink of pain, and nor did she shake from the buffeting of humiliation that could easily have knocked her sideways and down. Maybe, Jake still idly and stupidly imagined, Susie might have scooped up her dress, located her coat, and with steely intent and a suppression of all signs of wounding so absolute and awesome as to have made Jake gape and tremble, swept right out of there for good and ever (maybe so soon to whimper and crumple in a space of her own).

But Nan had spoken – not with huge regret at any aspect of the *position*, no, nor with any small hint at appeasement or even gushing and therefore watery apology. No: there was in the air, now – and it stung both Jake and Susie (their final intimacy had come to this: the recognition in each other's eyes of the white light of mutual shock as it hit them) – a sense of outrage and the icy challenge of accusation: voices from Nan that neither of them had known.

'What's *she* doing here?' came the first of these voices –

and Susie was already revolving as Nan quite coolly attained her peak of indignation. Susie's face was now made ugly by contortions so completely beyond recall – and Nan went on: 'All dressed up like a *whore*.'

And that had pretty much done it: Jake had closed down his eyes to the thud and then crunching of Susie's whole body just running Nan over (there had been impact) and the clang of Nan's bangle as it caught on maybe the handrail of the stairway served as the signal for him to snap them back open again, lured and taunted by the compulsive irresistibility of the awfulness that would surely now be rammed right up to and then, for ever, into him. The two women keeled over brokenly, a confusion of limbs and a series of collisions spiked by shrieks of protest and gaping hurt. Susie's eyes already lost to sight amid a wash of blackness – her bordello maquillage, at first just seeping, had let go its grip and soaked her face in soot, wet dark flecks flying wild and speckling the twists of sheet that Nan now kicked at and writhed away from. Once she was free of it all, she jerked away and sprawled naked, quite still for so brief an instant, mouth open and gasping and her hair in a frenzy. Jake felt in him, despite a kind of delirious detachment, the breath knocked out of her entirely as Susie – still caught tight though near bursting away from the twin clasps of satin and quite stiff lace – launched herself on top of her and raised high the stiff and bent fingers of one mad hand, bringing down sharp nails as red and as glossy as new-spilt blood, the knuckles of the other dashing away from her face the charcoal streaks of caking and her own wild hair, flailing and whipping at her cheeks.

Jake now just had to wade in before murder was done: he stepped forward woodenly and as boldly as a man so way beyond even fright can very often do, gripped and hauled at Susie's shoulders, the flood of warmth there affecting him as badly as the sight of Nan's wet and open lips and glorious breasts spilling to the sides and plumply compressed by the insistent pressure of Susie's own, still tautly encased and bearing down hard. He did not antici- pate – Jake had been far from working it out, blow by blow, all of this – that Susie might then rouse herself up and punch him so hard and sharply across the jaw: he felt with a jolt the severe abrasion of teeth ground askew, and was forced to sip with a hiss the tang of his blood.

'You *pig*, you *bastard*, you fucking bloody *shit*!' screamed Susie. And then to Nan, who was scrambling with claws from under her: 'You bloody little lousy *tart* – ! How *could* you – ?!'

'*Susie*!' panted Jake. 'Susie, Susie, Susie – Christ's sake, Susie – oh Jesus don't hit me again!' And he jarred his knee badly as he ducked down to not, as it turned out, deflect the latest tight-fisted lunge she had flung at him. 'My, oh God – my *eye*, my *eye*!'

Susie spat out at Nan as she was bent double and drag- ging at her legs, now hurting badly under the twin weight of Susie and a near-collapsed Jake – and Nan threw back her hair now sparkling with spittle and snarled as her hands made like furious crabs and flew for Susie's face.

'Just get *out* of here, Susie!' she screamed so rawly, slap- ping aside a criss-cross of defensive wrists. 'It's *me* Jake wants – not you: it's *me*, it's *me* – so just get *out* of here, will you?!'

And Susie breathed in sharply and lost all taste for the fight: she just stopped dead and all at once appeared to wither, diminishing to the point of implosion. Jake dared look at her, and then over to Nan, and all that was heard during this subsiding moment was the rasping pump of all their hearts. And what he thought was Oh God, Oh God, Oh God – I know this just has to be the worst of all moments in my entire life on earth, and yet what I want – all I yearn for – is to fuck just any of them right here and fast and really hard and *now* and then I want to grind down the palms of my hands into all the soft and yielding places that one of them will urge me to while I fuck and fuck the other one blind – really get it *done* – and then after that if I've got to die, then oh dear Christ just *let* me – because how could my life throw up again so sweetly intense and wholly frightening a time as this, which would leave me wrung and spent after all that boiling of my blood before it was set alight? Look – there's just one thing you've got to understand, here: I'm a *guy*, OK? Whatever else is bubbling, whatever large and looming thing is coming down, at base and at last all I am is a *guy*. OK?

*

And now I'm thinking – and no it didn't, since you're asking, of course it bloody didn't, take at all long in coming: course not. And now I'm thinking, just sitting here thinking . . . Nan's over there, doing her nails, still doing her nails and not, pretty sure, thinking about anything bloody at all . . . and I'm slumped on the sofa at the other end of what I really – God, I really used to believe would be my fab and ultimate bachelor pad right up until the day I eventually got around to saying to my Susie: *Well*, Susie? You know? Up for it? How about it? How about you and me kind of get . . . sort of *together*, yeh? And then? What would I have done then? Bigger mortgage, yeh probably – house, maybe, because Susie really did, you know, absolutely *detest* this place, she didn't just say it. And not only my stuff, no, but the entire space, even the very air it gave off: it wasn't, she said – never could be – *home*.

Well not now it couldn't be, no. On account of we don't even *know* each other any more – and that's, I suppose, what I just can't get my head around: simply can't believe it. So I sit and I think – and what I think is how, why, has all this happened? How could I have been so total a bloody fool? I was *happy* with Susie – loved her (still do) – so what the fuck was I doing messing about with Nan? (Christ, not long ago, Susie and me – we didn't even know of her *existence*.) And yeh yeh – I know: that *guy* thing, mm . . . but only up to a *point*, for the love of – you don't want to go screwing up your life just for the sake of a passing . . . oh Christ . . . *screw*. Do you? But that's what I've bloody well done, isn't it? Susie won't even *talk* to me, now – you think I haven't tried? Since that evening, that terrible evening . . . and I went round there, you know, later on I did. Nan was screaming the place down: *Leave* her, she was going – Christ's sake *leave* her, Jake – you're with *me* now: it's *me* you're with (which I didn't, then, actually believe). I just left her to get on with it and went round fast to plead with Susie. Who wouldn't even let me through the door. So I ran right back – I was wild with fright and I felt as if there was a hole right through me: got on the phone. How many times have I rung her since then? Thousands, bloody thousands. All I get is her posh-voiced po-faced message – know it by heart, hear it in my sleep. And when I did get back that evening, that terrible evening – you any idea what Nan had done? Tell you. Remember my futon – the kingsize job? Cut it to ribbons. Slashed it to bits. Next day she was covered with regret, oh sure: Oh *God*, Jake, she was going – I'm *sorry*, I'm so *sorry*, I didn't know what I was *doing*, I was out of my *mind*: I'll get you, get us, another one, yes? No, I said: no. Don't want another one. The whole idea just doesn't seem a good one, any more. Not any more; along with so much else, it's just gone from me, now.

So I'm just sitting here – thinking, and sometimes trying not to . . . and another thing I'm thinking is this: that if you'd upped and told me – if just, what, couple of months ago you'd bloody started telling me that some girl called *Nan* would be not just in my flat but, Jesus, actually *living* with me and that Susie would be history and not even *talking* to me . . .! Well – I'd've said you were a . . . and that's a point, that's another thing – and this thing, yeah, is just driving me crazy: if she's . . . if Susie's not with me, and not even talking – well with *who*, then? Is she? Huh? Who is listening to her now and looking, while I just sit here slumped on the sofa – and way over there, Nan is just doing her nails (and yeh, incredibly, *still* – still just doing her bloody fucking nails).

*

Do you know what I think? I think this is really cosy, really nice: I'm just loving all of this. It's probably the first time in my life I've actually not thought and *thought* about something, but just gone out and *done* it. Me: Nan. And it works – that sort of attitude really pays off, you know, because . . . well look: I've *got* it, haven't I? Got what I wanted. Just grabbed it, and here it is. And Jake too – he doesn't always act like it, I know, but deep down he feels, must really feel now that he's settled. Because people do – they go on in a rut for years and years, settling for not much at all, really, until something just comes along and blasts them out of it. And that something in Jake's case was me. Little me. And now we're together, which is – oh, I can't tell you how wonderful. A man of my own, at last. We don't even have to talk – prattle endlessly, like some people seem to think they ought to. God – sometimes, like this evening, I nearly just laugh out loud because – hee hee – it can seem like we're, I don't know – some sort of old married couple, or something – Nan and Jake, together for years and part of one another. I can just sit here, doing my nails – and I do them for Jake, because I know he just loves them when they're all red and shiny – and he can just sprawl on the sofa, quite contentedly, with not a single thought in his head, and gazing over at me, in that fond and loving way he has: it makes me feel so warm. (This is called contentment, and it's a rare thing, believe me.)

I do . . . yes I suppose I have to admit that I *do* feel just a teeny bit bad about Susie, yes I do, of course I do – but you

127

know what they say about love and war? Well it's very true, that – and of course there just has to be a winner and a loser, it's just the way of it: how it has to be. And I know what losing is, of course I do (what girl doesn't?). You remember David? Boy in Scotland? Well there – case in point. I have no doubt at all that he's very happy with whoever he's ended up with – this Glasgow girl, was it? – and jolly good luck to him, that's what I say. We were never really right for each other, I see that so clearly now – and Susie will too, in time, about Jake. But I'm not saying it won't hurt, of course it will – and yes, you might well ask why it was I had to make it hurt for Susie quite that much: sending her the fax, telling her to come dressed up like that. You see, it needed something seismic, this is why: Susie just had to absolutely *know* that Jake and me were a total item – hints, as I told you, just weren't cutting it. And when she came to see it with her own eyes and on someone else's ground, there could then be no danger of reconciliation: all that darling-I-forgive-you stuff would have wasted precious time – time that Jake and I could be spending together, building up our lives. So she had to, you see – poor Susie – exit from a scene to which there could never, never ever, be a coming back. Women will understand this: there are just some places you can never revisit. It's a shame it had to be Susie, though – of course it is. You think I don't feel that? Because she was really kind to me, when I was new to the flat. And I really did need her so badly, then, because I had no one at all, no one at all. And look – it's not *my* fault that Tony just left me so cold (and Tony? Oh – Tony, he'll get over it: men do). Or that Jake and I just *fused*, like that (my God – had there been impact!). I didn't *want* to want him: I just did. That's all.

And Adrian and Donna – it doesn't hurt nearly so much to have lost them, now. It's a funny thing, isn't it? The human heart. I'll maybe write. I hope their mother rots in hell. She got what she deserved in Jeremy, Anne: of *course* he's going to go off with all those other women – married to her, who wouldn't?

God. Oh God. Eeeee – that was . . .! I suddenly feel . . . no, I can't have seen that. Imagined it. Did I? I feel so cold and frightened – I simply can't believe it . . . no. I must be wrong. What it is – I've just done my nails, just this second finished, and when I looked up – glanced across to Jake (I just love to see him) – the expression in his eyes, all over his face, was just so . . . nearly *cruel*, you know? Almost as if he *hated* me, or something. It's OK *now* – he's grinning like anything *now*, so I'm sure, yes – oh of *course* it wasn't that, course it couldn't have been. I think what it is is I'm still a little bit insecure – I've never had a love anywhere near the scale of this one, and I'm just so scared of breaking it. Because of all the things I can do, hurt and sad just aren't among them.

Carlo was really so terribly sweet. Did I say? He came round the morning after D-Day – had with him all my things. Sat on Jake's prison loo for just about ever and – God, he's such a character, Carlo, truly a one-off – said it was very pleasant (he used that word: *pleasant*) but still, alas, it hadn't actually *worked*, or anything. And then he said – so odd, this – he said to me: *Casablanca*. Mm, I went, *Casablanca*, yeah – what about it? And then he said, Do you really not know why, at the end, Rick didn't get on the plane with the woman? And I went *God*, Carlo, what a perfectly weird time to bring all *that* up! But no, actually, since you ask, I don't – never have done: Why didn't he? And Carlo just looked at me, and went. Some people, I tell you: really really strange.

CHAPTER FIVE

'It's not, is it?' intoned Tony, darkly – chewing off each of these snub-nosed words and forcing them out, though it wounded him. 'Going to work. Is it?'

He was draped in resentment – and here's a new and extra layer of self-loathing coming down as he shakes his head with a big and blank-eyed sorrow, letting Susie's hank of soft and glossy hair shimmy away gently from his no-damn-use fingers – watching it fall back, just as things do, coating the surge of her breast which suddenly, she knew, had to be tucked out of sight.

'No,' she said quietly – some sort of generous attempt at a wistful smile, there: a stab at God, Don't blame yourself, it's nobody's fault (and yet all that filled their heads and glowed red behind their eyelids were those same and meaty portraits of each of the real and vibrant culprits, frozen in stills maybe once of their choosing, but now just fixed and unstoppable icons, always there to haunt and plague them).

What sort of level of hurt, Susie had to wonder, makes you lose your mind? Where precisely is the point when it transgresses that weak and fluid line containing the simply unbearable and gut-wrenching ache, this interspersed with a kind of waking swoon – the nearest one can ever come to the kiss of relief – and becomes that other moment, where all the bitter and mangled bits of barely blunted agony invade your head and your eyes begin roasting and you just know how wide and mad they look (the lids so dark pink and waxy, stretched taut and made raw by all the days and nights of tears)? Only two people so torn up as to be hardly hanging together could ditch their collective sanity to so spectacularly little effect, and now and so soon be chilled by the douche of reason – which hadn't had them spluttering for long (it's not as if they hadn't sensed it, lurking).

Susie buttoned her cardigan and looked down kindly on Tony, trying not to wince away from how wretched he seemed – for she must too, she must too. She believed him, now. After their bruises and weals had been made shamingly plain to one another, Susie had come to know with deep shock just how deeply Tony had felt – was still, oh God, so very much feeling: he had not been, oh no, jerking Nan around; and nor had that girl ever been – as Susie could not now accept she had believed so fervently – just too nice. And so, bound by the wire of mutual devastation, they had hugged each other and maybe, for a desperate instant, hoped for more – but the wire had been unyielding, and had simply cut in deeper. Now they were undone again, Tony and Susie, back and stranded where they felt they always would be – laid waste by the seemingly endless tracts of pain to come, and covered in hurt by those they daily faced and were forced to live in. Sometimes, they had agreed – with something approaching a lunatic joy – there were, couldn't there be, moments of numbness – a kind of drunk not quite delight; but they didn't ever last. All these were, maybe, carefully considered and tactical withdrawals enabling all those truly bad bits to be efficiently remustered and, quite without heart, sent back in.

'What're you gonna do, then, Susie?'

Tony was stirring coffee that Susie had been barely bothered with the business of making (you boil the water, you spoon the stuff in, you mix the two – how can I be *doing* with any of this, feeling the way I am?). And Tony anyway wouldn't be drinking it because hey look – what would be actually the *point*?

'Don't know,' was Susie's short and whispered answer – she combined it quite grudgingly with a tight twist of her neck, while expelling a lungful of mid-blue smoke from the latest cigarette, the latest cigarette. She shook her head, as two red fingernails were held like pincers just inside her lips as she tried to locate some maybe illusory speck on the tip of her tongue. 'Seem to have taken up smoking again in a pretty big way – gave up nearly three years ago: three bloody *years* . . . so maybe I'll just do that. They say it kills you, don't they?'

'Jesus, Susie . . .'

'Says it right there. Right on the front of the fucking packet.'

'Would you ever . . .?'

'What? Would I ever what? Do the job properly?'

'Christ no, Susie! Christ no. I mean . . . would you ever, take him back? Jake. Would you?'

Susie tightly closed her eyes and fluttered her mouth. She was maybe secretly reciting a personal mantra: Don't give in to this newest swell of sickening longing – don't move your head just slightly or even think of speaking and then soon, as all things do, it will pass. She made great play, then, of snapping alight another cigarette; the old one was lying there in a saucer, could be, burning down fast.

'No,' she said, quite unexpectedly for both of them. 'Never. I wouldn't. I couldn't. Anyway – he doesn't want to.'

'But Susie – you keep saying he's always ringing you. Why would he keep on phoning if he doesn't want – '

'Well maybe he *does* want – I don't know, do I? All I know is I couldn't. It wouldn't be . . . I just couldn't. That's all.'

Susie did not think Tony could have looked any sadder or more lacking in blood than he had done all morning, but suddenly now he certainly did – as if his plug was pulled, and anything left was seeping away.

'It's just that . . .' he started up, practically brokenly, '. . . if

Jake doesn't come back to you, then how' – and now his eyes were huge and old – 'will I ever get back Nan?'

Susie nearly spat at him *Jesus*, Tony – she doesn't bloody *want* you, does she? Haven't you learned that yet? Why do you think she went and – ?! But she halted that train of thought right there and then (*yes*, because it was killing her, but she saw as well that if any little part of it got out and into the air, this could well amount to murder).

'*Look*, Tony . . .' sighed Susie – as kindly as she was able, though knowing now there was not a lot more of this she could actually go through: after the clench of agony, there is always the weariness to come. 'I know it sounds stupid to say that the two things are not . . . *connected*, but really they're actually not, if you . . . we can't all just, oh Jesus – all swap *back*. Can we? Hm? It's just not going to *happen*.'

Tony's eyes were gleaming, but with a dangerous zeal: all over his face was the intent and quite rapt look of one who has been brought to the brink of starvation.

'Maybe,' he urged, 'we – I – could *make* it happen. Just *look* at us! It's gotta be worth a shot.'

'How? Anyway, Tony – it's not, is it, what everyone *wants*? *Nan* doesn't want it – it's Nan that's, sorry, Tony – screwing us all up. Isn't it? So how?'

'Where I come from – *money*. Money makes everything happen.'

Susie was genuinely aghast: maybe Tony's madness was more advanced than hers (of a deeper-seated nature)? Or could she just be seeing him distantly now from deep down in one of her too occasional and breathlessly clutched-at troughs of remission?

'*Money*, Tony? What in Christ's name has *money* got to do with this? How can *money* – ?!'

'Money buys. Yeh? This is *known*, Susie: this is a fact. Money buys you anything you'll ever need – it's what it's for, it's how it works. Things. People. Anything.'

'And so what you're saying is . . . oh *Christ*, Tony, what *are* you saying? Hm? It just doesn't make sense, this.'

'Well look, listen . . . I haven't worked out exactly what I mean yet – details – but Nan, you know, she was forever going on about my room – the drapes, crap like that. Why you always in jeans, she'd go – that kinda crap. What I'm saying is, she really likes good stuff, you know? Loadsa women do. *You* do, Susie. Fancy dining, limos, clothes . . . and I never gave her any of that because, because – well in one way, I guess, because I thought I was *safe*. And Jake – '

'So you're saying you just offer her *presents* and she'll come running right back to you? And what *about* Jake? What?'

'Well Jake – you know Jake. Sorry, Susie – sorry. But hey – he spends every cent he gets the second he gets it: am I right?'

Susie snorted, nearly half-hating the memory of Jake. She lit a cigarette: sucked it down, held it warm, whooshed it out. 'Mainly on that bloody awful flat of his. Jesus. The money he's spent on all that terrible *metal* junk . . .'

'Well all I'm saying is . . . you can always do with more.'

Susie gazed at Tony, not for a moment believing that she was one of the two people actually *having* so dumb a conversation.

'So which is it to be, Tony?' And her tone was more charged with scorn than if she'd maybe had a mind to prepare an alternative. 'You shower the saintly Nan with baubles? Or you bung a wedge to Jake? Christ – either way, she's bloody laughing, isn't she? Damn her.'

'Don't,' said Tony – slow and serious. 'But maybe – maybe both. Whatever it takes. What's this "wedge"? I don't know that.'

'Expression,' glossed Susie, briskly. 'Tony – I think you really *are* nuts, you know. But Jesus, hey – it's your money. You want to make a total fool of yourself, then you go right ahead. I'll chip in a fiver,' she smirked – twisting away from the (why hurtful?) smack of it – 'seeing as it's all in such a good cause. So what – are you loaded then, Tony?'

And once again, Tony's whole spirit seemed to visibly plummet – almost audibly slap on to the floor.

'This is . . . the flaw in the scheme. Why you think I go on living the way I do? I am that unique thing, Susie. I am the American who has no money. People don't think they exist, but – ' and even Tony allowed himself a screwed-up sort of smile ' – but they do. Or one does: I'm the guy.'

And Susie was thinking Well if *that's* the case then your bloody silly idea is even crazier than ever – isn't it, Tony, you fucking idiot?

'How come?' is what she said.

'I guess . . . I don't like too much to be pinned down. Know what I'm saying? Move around. One job – nother job. Bosses don't go big on that. Rented room – no possessions, you know? Plus I don't like to work! Which guys aren't meant to maybe say. But I don't. And I guess I never dreamed it would be any other way . . . but then, this girl came along . . . and I kinda, at the start, wanted for the first time to be . . . pinned down. And then, Susie, then – I *needed* it. You know? I need it *now.*'

Susie held his gaze. She had momentarily surfaced from the dark and scummy undertow of all those feelings that dragged her down – close to impaled on the just sheer wild talk (his love's not like mine). He would see soon, wouldn't he, Tony – if Susie widened her eyes into a sort of come-off-it and searched among his for anything similar – how completely looney he seemed to have gone (and quickly, too). But look, just look at him: all that she could see were furrows of fervour and a detached intensity that was jerking him elsewhere.

'All I gotta do . . . came this new deep and quite treacly rumble of his voice, '. . . is get it.'

'Get it? What? What do you have to get now, Tony? A *joke*?'

And he looked up suddenly, frankly appalled by her arrant stupidity: had she not been *listening*?

'Well, no . . .' he responded slowly, as if either to a moron or else to a japester who must surely be kidding. 'The *money*, yeah? The money. All I gotta do is *get* it. Is all.'

*

Nan had told him quite early that morning (she was up and showering, which well suited Jake, it suited him fine – to have her calling to him from amid that wet slap of soaping and storms of hiss – power shower, natch – somehow imparted a welcome distance, which made him feel what? A little bit safer; none of this he had ever known before, and although each individual prick of it had him alert and startled, if not understanding, he knew with gloom the absolute nature of what was going on, here).

'So that's OK with you, then, Jake – is it? Sure? You won't be lonely?' She padded over to the bed where still and almost purposely he lay quite tidily (it was a bed, now, just a bed – just like anyone else's bed, he sadly supposed) and she playfully patted the tip of his nose with the corner of the huge white bath sheet around her: she tripped over the edges of it as she gigglingly came at him. 'Won't be lonely? Won't pine for me *too* much, darling?'

Jake quite easily supplied the smile of affection he imagined was required. 'I'll be fine,' he assured her. 'Course. You do what you have to do.'

The towel – and her soft damp shoulders, rounded and peeping: they were signposts for sexy, quite sexy (weren't they?). And her hair – loosely piled up and only just not falling down into a tousle of disarray: moving, no? Well yes – yes yes (Jake had to, in the abstract, acknowledge all that). So why, then – and here it comes – wasn't he moved? Why was the thing that had made him bright, lifted him up, and within seconds had him scrambling his plans for the entire day and evening just her big news that here was the day of little Emmy-Lou's birthday (I did, oh God, *tell* you, Jake) and the whole family and me's going off to that *ghastly* Alton Towers place (you don't remember, do you, Jake? What is it that you're thinking of when you just go off, like that?).

'And they're bringing, God – practically the entire *class*. Cost an absolute fortune, should think.'

She had the towel half off her, fingering lightly the clothes she had laid out for the day, as a gleam of quite naughty afterthought flew into her eyes – and although she near immediately boosted and launched it over to Jake, he had long before impact sensed its despatch. Which is why he swung his legs over the (other) side of the bed, looked elsewhere and yawned – making maybe too much of scrabbling around his fingers amid the tangle of his hair (the yawning now as if from an earnest actor, told to make the business travel to the gods).

Would she have pursued it? On any other morning, almost certainly. Which is why Jake had lately taken to arriving absurdly early to work (once the place had amazed him – he had never before seen it covered in darkness) for the simple reason, as he patiently explained to her, there happens to be just an absolutely huge amount *on* at the moment and it's the only time of day you get a bit of peace to, you know, actually get to *grips* with it all without the bloody *phone* and the *fax* and the *e-mail* driving you totally mental. Kay?

But if there was one thing Nan took quite seriously (apart from Jake – apart from the burst of pride she felt and was feeling at the utter conquest of this man Jake, together with all his parts and doings) then it was her charges: the custody of little ones. Jake had been speaking to a journalist (female) one time, who had solemnly assured him that women who are crazy – you know, just ditzy – about kids usually have no real time or place for a man (as such);

which, Jake thought bitterly later, tells you all you really need to know about all these bloody journalists (female), doesn't it? So nothing in the world (well – maybe just Jake, if he'd pushed it) would make Nan late for this (it is true: she's a pro. But also, Jake felt – despite putting it down as *ghastly*, back there, Alton Towers is not a place she would hate to be).

Nan was ready, and now was hurtling in an excited and shoe-shuffling flurry: a half-chomped and marmaladey triangle of toast put down in haste – her shoulder bag swinging as she scooped it up and around her (It's great, it's great: I'll now never know hurt and sad again). Jake waved her away almost – and he caught himself feeling this, even as it was going on – in the fulsome manner of a proud though resigned (bit tired) father who, despite his pleasure at her pleasure, surely now needed his rest. And as the door slammed behind her, he closed his eyes and allowed his face the luxury of wrapping itself around a huge and cat-like grin of – not *satisfaction*, no (he hadn't had any of that since . . . well, you know: *since*), but certainly a hale and lung-filling relief: here was his space back – at least and at last it's *mine* again.

And Jesus, no – I'm not, I'm not – I'm not, since you ask, actually going even *near* work today (decided that when she was still sloshing around in the shower: I suppose she's left the soap-on-a-rope sticky and just anywhere on the sand-blasted surface. She likes all the *stuff*, but she doesn't *respect* it). It's not, actually, that I've got any sort of *agenda* going, or anything – I'm not now going to swing my whole being behind Plan B because, well . . . as must be probably pretty clear by now, I didn't really get as far as implementing, did I, Plan Bloody A: i.e. to nail down Susie, and have her for good.

You see, it's odd (I've been thinking about it, haven't I? Well of course I bloody have) because one other reason I didn't just, oh Christ, get hold of Susie and do the thing properly (apart from the fact I'm a lazy bastard – typical bloke, just a guy – yeh, just a guy) is that I *trusted* her, see. Totally did. I just knew that whatever she said she loved me, really, and although she's, Jesus – the most knockout thing you ever did see (and Jesus, oh Christ: who in God's name is she stunning right now?) she never had that air of looking *around* her. Don't know if you've ever been with girls like that – not nice, tell you. They're kind of, how can I put . . .? They're sort of *with* you, yeah – but not *really*. You know? What I mean to say is, you're around while you're around, but just anything could happen at any time at all because they're forever looking over their shoulder, aren't they? And sometimes – at parties – yours. And it never once crossed my bloody mind, did it, that some woman would ever bust it up and come after *me* because, well – (a) I'm not that great, right, and (b) I was happy with Susie. So don't, please (will you?), get me on again to all this endless Well *why*, then, caper because I don't frankly think I can go another round. And today, at least – at least today – I don't have to. OK – in the long term, yeh, nothing's changed, but look: I've got my *space* back. You know, it's odd about Nan. I'll tell you, shall I, what I think it is that's truly the oddest thing about her: she *knows* I think she's an invader – I've told her quite openly. And that she seems to *like*. I've told her too that I still love Susie – and you know all she has to say then? *No* – no, Jake, no, she goes: you don't still love her – all it is is that you *think* you do. Well Christ. What can you say to that? All I *feel*, then, Nan (I tried to start it up) – let's get this straight: so what you're saying is that all I can feel are my *feelings*, yeh? *Yeh*, she goes: *yeh*. And I come back with: And they're *wrong*, right? *Right*, she goes – you got it, Jake: all those feelings are wrong – everything you feel is wrong, except what you feel for *me* (right?).

Jake now sighed and bravely told himself Well look: Never mind. I've got a whole day, haven't I, alone in my space (so what shall I do?). And the knowledge of this had something maybe to do with why he straight away snatched up the phone – just almost at the very second it had started to ring: if Nan was not here, this could easily, so easily – well *couldn't* it – be Susie?

'*Hi!*' he nearly yelled.

'Jake,'said Tony.

'Oh Tony,' came back Jake – and a great deal more quietly, for he felt all dead again. Look, Tony – if you're ringing me up again to just cry down the phone, I'm not actually – I just can't *face* it. How's, um . . .?'

'*Proposition*, Jake: proposition. I ain't about to cry no more. And Susie? She's *lousy* – how d'you expect her to be?'

And Jake hadn't even registered whatever stupid word it was that Tony had initially thrown back at him: all he yearned to do was howl out But *I* feel lousy! I'm lousy *too*! How the hell can we both be so lousy? *I'm* just lousy because I'm without her – can *Susie* be lousy because she's maybe stuck with some louse who's behaving that lousily towards her? Jesus – what a louse! Telling you – when I get through with him, he'll know all about what it is to feel *lousy* (fucking louse).

And then Tony was practically growling: 'Ten thousand. Enough? Not dollars: pounds. Enough? You want more? What's it gonna take, Jake? What's it gonna take?'

'What the fuck are you on about, Tony?'

'OK – you're playing dumb. Cool. Well hear me: you leave Nan alone – get her back to me – and ten grand's all yours. Twenty. Twenty, Jake? Twenty K: just say the word.'

Well, thought Jake: that'll be the breakfast cocaine kicking in, I suppose. *All* I need: one free day from the clinging thing he imagines I'm *caging*, and I have to get it going by talking down a crazy. How do you play it? Whatever I say, he'll never remember – and whatever he hears he'll deny, even if he gets to making out the *words*.

'A *million*, Tony,' sighed Jake. 'Wouldn't even consider it for less.'

And then he hung up (couldn't even be bothered to humour the lad) thinking Jesus oh Jesus: why must everyone behave so *madly*?

And Tony, in his room – he hung up too: dropped the phone as if it could sting him. White hard knuckles clutched an equally determined fist, as the light of demons sprang up into his eyes. 'Right,' he muttered darkly, rolling the yellowy whites of them. 'Fine. OK, Jake. Fine. You wanna million? You do? Well then a million is what you'll fuck'n *get*.'

*

'Susie!' gasped Jake, just barely daring to believe it. 'Susie, oh Susie! Thank Christ you called!'

'I maybe shouldn't have. I nearly didn't – you *bastard*.'

Susie was as in control as she thought she ever could be. How many times had she picked up the phone, then put it down – picked up the phone, then put it down? And then (from out of the blue?) a mantle of almost serenity had descended upon her (she nearly felt the touch) and it damped down all the frenzy, allayed at least a part of her electric anxiety. I'll call him now, then, yeah? If I don't call him now I just won't ever call him and he'll stop – he's bound to stop – trying me soon because even those people who really are meaning it, from deep down within them, eventually they do, they've got to, they've got to – they have to just stop because not to would bleed them too far, whiten them to the point of frailty and emptiness. So she had picked up the phone and dialled that number, and at the first purr of distant ringing that he must be hearing, Susie slammed it right back down again. And some time (four cigarettes) after, she found herself redialling – forced the receiver hard against her ear – and it took both hands and screwed-up eyes and chewed-on lips to make her stick there and make her wait and then her wait was amazingly over and here now into her ran his sweet voice – all she had done was breathe Jake's name and straight away he gasped hers back at her (full of love, charged with a dissolving hiss of relief: she loved him so much, she called him a bastard).

'Susie – oh Susie – just talk to me. I don't care what you say – well I *do*, I *do*, of course I do – but what I mean is Don't Go, is what I mean – just go on talking to me, please Susie, go on being with me, Susie. Oh Jesus I've been so – !'

'Oh Jake. Oh Jake.'

' – *dying*, Susie, is what I was going to – oh Susie, I'm sorry, so sorry, I don't know what I've – why I – '

'I'm hurt, Jake. I'm so hurt.'

'I *know* you are, my darling. Know that. I too – different, different I know, yeh – but me, I'm in bits, Susie. Pieces. Can we end this? Please, Susie – don't say you just rang to see if I was *OK*, because I'm not, not – not OK, never OK without you, Susie. I maybe didn't . . . but I do *now*. I just know it, Susie – I can't . . . live without you. I never thought I'd have to, and now I *have* been – oh God, I'm getting this all round my bloody neck, but what I *mean* is, Susie – what I want to say is . . .'

'Say it, Jake. I'm not doing it for you.'

'Come *back* to me, Susie. For ever. I want you. For ever.'

'Just like that. And what about – ?'

'*Don't*. Don't even say the name. I feel *mad* about . . . all of it. Mad like I *must* have been. You know? I only feel sane, I only feel right with *you*, Susie. It's you. It's you.'

'Jake. We're going to have to meet. Talk.'

'Yes! Yes oh yes – anywhere. Where? When? You say.'

'What are you going to do about . . . *her*? I don't ever – I can't ever see her again.'

'No, you – no, of course you can't. I don't want to either. Sounds terrible, but I just *don't*. I never really *did* . . .!'

'Tony does. Poor sod. He's going mad.'

'*Sounded* mad. Rang me. Sounded crazy. Stoned.'

'I think he could do something desperate. I've been

142

phoning him all morning but he's constantly jammed. I just don't want him to do anything . . . terrible.'

'Like what? Oh *God*, Susie – I can't tell you how good it is just to be *talking* to you again.'

'I don't know what. Last time I saw him, he seemed just . . .'

'Oh Jesus – let's not waste time talking about bloody *Tony*. *Us*, Susie – *us*. Let's Godsake just *be* together. Yes? Yes? Say yes, Susie.'

'I do . . . love you . . .'

'Oh thank Christ! And I you, of course I do – always have done. Always will.'

'But you're not answering me, Jake. What are you going to do about – ?'

'Get rid of her. Chuck her out. Dump her. Don't care. She just doesn't *matter* to me, Susie. She's just someone who came along from nowhere and fucked us up – oh Christ – and now she's just gone. Over. Finito.'

'Really? Truly? It's so *easy* for you, isn't it, Jake?'

'*Absolutely* over. It never *was*. Susie – it's *you*, just *you*. It's just as if she never happened. And no, Susie, *no* – it hasn't been easy. Not a bit.'

'Oh God I *love* you, Jake, you utter bastard.'

'Susie – oh Susie. Let me see you. Let me come round. Now. I want you so much.'

'Jake . . . it's . . .'

'*Please*, Susie – oh God *please*!'

'Oh Jake . . . OK . . . OK. Come. But promise me – you've got to promise me about that bloody *girl* – !'

'Susie. Listen to me. There is only one thing she is. Only one.'

'Tell me, Jake: tell me. I have to *hear* it from you.'

Jake breathed deep before he came right back with a depth of feeling that rocked him:

'*History*, Susie. That girl is *gone*.'

CHAPTER SIX

There was a time, once – oh God in heaven, how long ago can it be, now? – when Reg McAuley had got up in the morning with a true good feeling: anticipation would not be over-strong, he could honestly say – an innocent and driving curiosity as to just what this new day might bring.

He idly stirred his tea, now (which means it must be just coming up to eight), as he trudged, quite puzzled, through all this again. So what (here we go – big sigh) actually *happened*, then? Hey? Was there a single moment when all that just flew right out of him, leaving him suddenly beached and just stuffed with foam, his rusting key having to be cranked around with reluctance by an unseen and automatic hand? Or had the seeds of unease been carefully sown, his early exuberance just imperceptibly shading down daily, not even a hue at a time, until gradually it became always darker for longer, and then even darker still; there must have slid in the moment, Reg could only suppose, when the last chink of light was shut down to him (blink, and he'd miss its passing).

These days, he got up in the morning *why*? Well to be out of the house and away from bleedin' Enid, oh God yes (if there's still a spur, then this is it) – but now when he settled into his cab and strapped himself in, that's all he could feel – strapped in for ever. Once, the clunk of the belt's buckle as it locked and held him – even that had close to thrilled him; he had felt not so much a cab-driver, kicking up a diesel purr and cruising the streets of London for the first fat fare of the day, no – much more like a fighter pilot, maybe – a hero in his lifetime – on a vital-to-others and blood-warming sortie, spiked by challenge and by actually quite euphoric uncertainty: driving around, meeting the people, deploring the traffic, chucking up one's eyes at the, Jesus, bloody cyclists – all the time knowing only that the mission would end maybe ten hours on, safely back at base, when he would bring down the crate, unzip his manly leathers and step out creakingly to generously deflect any wilder plaudits going. And there were always those: Enid, oh God dear Enid (can it really, this thing, be the same woman now? Did she at some time again unnoticed by Reg undergo a comprehensive body transplant that came with a complimentary personality change, her entire attitude subverted and warped by mind-bending substances?). That once effortless fondness and gratitude towards him had shrivelled now into lemon-sour not even toleration of Reg's continued existence: the resentment of his soft breath just barely stirring the air that took such care to keep its distance between them.

Was it when the children started growing up? Went their separate ways? Well – I *say* grow up, not Laverne, she never really did, not that one. Couldn't wait to leave that school of hers, nearly broke my heart. *Laverne*, I'd go – oh God, blue in the face – and the way she'd look at me as I sat there and did it (telling you – come close to breaking my heart). *Laverne*, my love, I'd be sat there going – *listen* to me, can't you? Don't be thinking I'm stupid just cos I'm your old man. I've lived longer than you, haven't I? *Learned* things. *Education* – there's nothing to touch it. Look at *me*: now, I'm not saying I done badly – wouldn't swap the cab for any life on earth (I felt that, then – oh dear God, I really did feel all that) – but me, Laverne – listen to me, girl, put that magazine down – no you *can't* go out, I'm *talking*, aren't I? See – I never had none of your chances – I was one of six, my mother was a – I *know* you've heard it, I know you have, Laverne, but it'll do you no bloody harm to hear it *again*.

My mother went *charring* to keep us all clean and decent and – I *know* you're not going to be a bloody cleaner, Laverne – good God, that's my whole point: want *better* for you, don't I? Hey? I *had* to leave school: I was the eldest – no choice. Had to put bread on the table. You know I only go on because I *love* you, don't you? Hey? Don't you? You're my little girl. And what do I always say to Pauly? Yes that's right – get a *trade*, I tell him – whatever you do, have something at your fingertips you can always turn to. Can't go wrong. Now for a girl, I know it's different, I know that – and yeh, one day in the future, *course* you'll settle down: married, kids, all that. But what you going to do in the meantime? Hey? Can't just sit around the house all day. Your old man won't always be around to take care of you, will he? You got to *think*, Laverne. You got to *plan*. Here – where you going? What do you mean – *out*? What sort of an answer is *out*? Out where? Who with? Good God, Laverne – you're only *fifteen*, you can't just – it's *dark*, Godsake – it's not *safe*. Enid! Enid! You talk to the girl – I just don't seem to be able to get *through*, no more.

But Enid, oh dear God – Enid was the last person, wasn't she? How long it been since I got through to *her*, never mind Laverne? I look back now on those years, and I tell you – I can't actually remember who I talked to at *all*. Pauly, yeh – good kid, I'm not saying – can't complain about Pauly. One day – felt so proud, telling you: nearly busting with it, I was. Says to me, *Dad* . . .? Yes, I says, what is it, son? What's on your mind? And he says How about if I do the Knowledge? Just like that – straight out the thing: you could've knocked me down with a wossname. He'd never mentioned cabbing, not once in his life – save that one time when he was still a little boy: thought I was great that day, he did (tenth birthday, could well've been), cos we went down the Zoo, didn't we, and all his friends could fit in the back. Some of them, don't reckon they'd ever been in a black cab before – you could see it was a kick for them.

Good day, that. We all had a laugh: tied some balloons to the mirror.

Nothing come out of it, though. Started talking about the Army, one time after that – and that put the fear of God into me, tell you quite frankly. What you wanna go thinking about the *Army* for, Pauly? What – I brung you up to be this healthy handsome young man (and he is, you know, he is – always a looker: girls all over him) so that, what, you can go off to Northern Ireland and get your bloody self killed? Anyway . . . all that went the way of the cab – then he says he wants to be a doctor. A doctor, I says – fine, lovely (although I had, what are they – *reservations* on this one: he's all right, Pauly, know what I'm saying? But he was never, you know, one of them scholar types – bookworm, sort of style: if there was a football around, his homework could go to buggery – what a lad, what a lad). So . . . it turns out someone tells him about all the work and the years involved, so that passed by pretty quick. He sells cars down Crawley way – nice little Vauxhall concession, seems to do OK: look – it's his life, I don't interfere.

Laverne? She went to work in a shop. And then another bloody shop. Changes jobs like she changes boyfriends. Turned out not long ago she was *living* with one of them – and I know, I know this is supposed to be the *way*, these days, but I never – not in a wossname – thought my daughter would go down that route. I thought of putting my foot down (what a laugh: from her seventeenth birthday, all she ever had to say to me was You just *wait*, Dad: you just *wait*. One year's time I'm eighteen, right, and then I can do what I bloody well want and there ain't you or no one else is going to stop me). Nice. So you can imagine, can't you, the sort of mouthy comeback I would've got if I'd started making waves. Needn't have bothered, as it turned out: by the time I'd got wind of her shacked up with whatever bloke it was, she'd only bloody ditched him and gone off with someone else. Bloody hell. Wasn't so easy in my day; I sometimes wonder – how would things have gone (same way? Better? Different?) if it had been. Well, this is it – you'll never know, will you? You'll never ever really know.

The other thing I'm thinking now (nearly eight-fifteen: get the cab out in a minute) is about my name, Reg, because I'm busy with the Biro doodling it, aren't I? I do that, in the margins of the *Express*, when I've filled in a bit of the crossword. Sometimes big swirly letters, and sometimes that sort of posh writing like what you see on the credits of the old films (which ain't easy). R – E – G. There's not really much to it, and I hate it, if I'm honest. I've always been called Reg – never the long way, the full way (which I know, yeah, is a bit on the poncey side anyway): all I know, it's Reg on my birth certificate (never bothered to look, tell you the truth). What I don't like about it – apart from, I don't know, it sounds a bit thick (and I may be very many things, but thick I am not) – and it isn't sort of very, well – I would say *classy*, but I know I'll never be that – well, wouldn't want to be, they're sometimes the thickest of the lot, aren't they? Your ruling classes. But it's more than that: what really has got to me over the years (and you wouldn't think, would you, it could matter: I mean, a name's a name, right – and by any other thing would pong the bloody same, like they say); but when you write it down – and I just have, all big and loopy – it always looks like it should rhyme with, say, Leg – Peg or Keg, Beg or Meg (and I knew a Meg, once – nice woman, talked a bit) – but the only other word that goes like Reg is Veg (and it's no good you checking, cos I've been into all this, please believe) and I think maybe that's where I must get the thick bit from.

Right: eight-fifteen. Let's get this cab on the road. I used to call up to Enid, when I was leaving of a morning time (she gets up later and later, these days: says she's ill, and she could well be right) – but where's the point, is how I'm thinking now: she never ever calls back down. And it's not a question of once she used to, no no no – because what used to happen *once* is that she'd bloody already be down here, wouldn't she, fixing my breakfast (bit of egg, lot of bacon) and saying there's a clean shirt hanging, look, and will I fill you a Thermos? I have crispbread, these days – nice cup of tea, course. Midday, grab a bit of dinner in the shelter up Little Venice, don't know if you know it. Nice crowd.

So. There's just one other thing that's now on my mind, and that, of course, is Adeline. And who, you might feel justified in asking, is this Adeline, when she's at home? Well, I don't really know, tell you the God's honest truth. She can only be, what? Nineteen? Twenty? Not much more – something on a par with our Laverne. She works a checkout, some days, down the local Sainsbury's. Seems a nice girl. Always a smile. Nice little hands as she swipes through the stuff. I only know her name because of them name-tag things they all wear these days – we've not properly talked, or nothing. One time, I bought a couple of mangoes and she goes God, I wouldn't mind going to wherever it is them funny things come from – why's it always *raining* in London? I says – I know what you mean, love. tell you what, how about this: win the Lottery, we'll go off together! And she laughs at that. Nice laugh.

Right. I'm in the cab, now. Quite a fair day, for once. Maybe get myself down King's Cross – always a good bet, early. Now listen – tell me something: is all this everyday-type here-we-go sort of talk actually *doing* it for you? Maybe it is – maybe you don't notice. Me it doesn't fool for a second. My mind's *invaded* now, see, and all because I couldn't for one more second delay my very first thought of Adeline for the day (unless you count the night, and the grey and silent end of it when I just lie there next to Enid, and only my mind is alive). Oh Christ. What can I do? I try my best to think ordinary thoughts – just to be plain old boring Reg McAuley, cab number 01827, husband and father (failed); but if anyone ever got right in close to me (and now, I doubt anyone ever again will or want to) they'd know like I do that all this stuff is surface.

Oh look! That's a turn-up: punter already, waving his paper at me: a first, this is – don't think I ever picked up a fare, not in this neck of the woods I ain't. Euston Square, mate? No problem: looks like it could turn out nice – traffic's not too bad, neither.

No. See – truth is, I'm ripped by lust for the Sainsbury's girl.

*

Tony knew just what to do. Oh yeah? Oh *yeah*? Hell, Jesus – two minutes ago he did, oh yeah sure – and five minutes before that he damn knew something else. And now? Now? *Now* – sheesh – now I'm having trouble even recalling my own goddam *name*. And I gotta be cool, here – you know? Like, this kinda stuff you don't just steam in on, boy – else you ain't looking both ways at once, it turns out to be the last thing you're ever gonna get round to, yeh? But it's gotta be done – gotta be: this I knew with Gina, and maybe if I'd just had the guts to see it through then, I'd've had my Gina, oh yeah sure, and one great mother of a pile of money, I'm telling you – and then when Nan came into my life I could've said, Gina – hey, Gina? Listen, babe, I hate to – you know – *hit* you with this thing, know what I'm saying? But hey – it's been *nice*, you know? But it's kinda like *over*? You hear me? Yeah. Easy to do, huh? And how hard (you tell me) is it to take? The hardest – just the hardest. Yeah: you tell *me*.

When I put down the phone from Jake, I felt kinda high – nervy, you know? But kinda cool. It was a *step*, I guess I'm meaning – at least I got some sort of a *deal* out of the guy. So I thought – hey: Nan can't know, Nan has no idea just how low a guy she's dealing with, here. So what if I tell her?

150

What if I tell her – Hey, Nan: your big man Jake: he's willing to *sell* you, honey! How does that go down? You sweet with that? You cool with being some little *thing* that this guy will take money for? And yeh sure – I know how she'd come on to me is like this: Oh get *lost*, Tony – Jake isn't like that (you're crazy). So I'd stick with it, work away at it – soon she'd come to know it was true because she'd *ask* him, and what's he gonna say? Well *sure* he'll deny – sure he will, but by then she's gonna start *smelling* it's true, and once that's in her nose and all over her head, that lousy feeling will start chewing away, chewing away, and then it'll all fall down around the two of them. And then she'll come back to me.

Jeez. Can you believe I *believed* that? That was how my last fit of crazy went down. Now, I'm back with another one: just get the money, and cut the crap. Look at it: I got a pile of money – *somebody's* gonna damn well listen to me: if it ain't Jake, it's gonna be Nan. This is how I figure: I'm a guy who *means* it, you know? And when there's this real delicate – *balance*, yeah, to be swayed . . . well, it's money that's gonna do the swaying – every time, baby: every goddam time. And maybe it's the movies, taught me some of that – and could be too it was Gina:

'You're not much like, are you, Tony – other guys?'

'That's bad?'

'It's kind of not great. I mean – don't get me wrong: I *like* you, and everything – but hell, Tony . . . the way we have to *live*. We just don't ever *do* what other people do. We never *go* anywhere, we never *buy* anything . . . I mean: look at this room. It's *terrible*, Tony – surely you must *see* it is? Everything's just so . . . I mean . . . why don't you *mind*?'

'*Now* I mind, sure. You ain't happy, Gina – then I mind.'

'There is an *answer*, Tony.'

'There is?'

'Oh don't play *games*, Tony! Honestly – you're always like this. You know exactly what I mean. The reason everyone else has nice things and everything is that they bloody well *work*, Tony. Ever *heard* of the concept? Work? I always seem to end up paying for just everything, don't I? And I'm pretty fed up with it, quite frankly.'

'Gina. Come and sit by me.'

'I *mean* it, Tony. It's really not funny any more.'

'I ain't laughing.'

'Toe-*neeee*! You're driving me absolutely *crazy*! You've just got to start making some decisions, you know. Because if you don't, I will.'

'Which means?'

'Which means I've had *enough*. How many *ways*, Tony? You make all these promises, but you never ever *do* anything, do you?'

'Maybe I should rob a bank.'

'Oh big bloody *ha*, Tony! Can't be serious for a moment . . .!'

'No – I mean it, Gina – I mean it. Why don't I? I could be like Clint, yeh? Thin cee-gar? Maybe a poncho?'

'Tony. I'm going now. You tire me out.'

'Aw – hey! Don't go, Gina! OK – OK – I put away Mister Wise Guy, already – now come talk to me. Ya knows ah loves ya!'

'Who was that supposed to be?'

'Popeye. Whaddya think?'

'Doesn't sound anything like him. Who's Popeye?'

'Oh Gina – ah loves ya best when you's stoopid!'

'Oh stop *talking* like that, can't you? Look – I'm going. You have to decide, Tony, really you do. Otherwise I may not be back – and I *mean* it this time. You've got to give us a decent life, Tony – I need it. And I need it *now*.'

All that had been how long ago? Before Nan is all I know; everything kinda blurs, now, into Before Nan and After Nan – and Before don't count . . . and After . . . it can't go *on*. Anyhow . . . those days, Nan had not so much as entered my life, and Gina was kinda important to me. Any other guy, he woulda thought, maybe – hey, the girl's right, sure she's right: get off your ass, boy, and get it *done*. And sure – I chewed over this, and I kinda fooled around with the idea of that . . . but in the end – you know what I did? Hey – I'm laughing now, and maybe you will too: I bought a gun. Nah – not a *real* . . . not the real thing, nah (this country, they make a big deal about that). No – this is a kind of – *air*-pistol? Looks sorta like a Luger, bit maybe Smith & Wesson. Black bastard. Heavy. Good and easy action, is what we got here. I guess I just wanted to be like Clint. And also, I figured: robbing a bank – how hard can it be? Like, stupid people get away with it every day of the goddam week. So anyway – that was then, and I didn't do it.

But now I'm gonna. Oh and yeah – one dumb thing about the gun: it shoots these stupid little yellow pellets. I mean, OK – yeah, it ain't in my plan to be shooting, but hey – it, you know, *comes* to it, well then, guy, you need lead and hard steel behind you, not a handful of M&Ms – you know what I'm saying? Plus – the end of the barrel, they put a little red circle of plastic. For why? Huh? So I blacked it out with a marker: cool.

Now . . . I got me a gram of Charlie to deal with, here – chopped out and lined up nice. And then I'm *gonna*.

*

'Been helluva bloody day, can't tell you,' sighed Reg McAuley, wiggling his backside as he wedged himself on to the narrow slatted bench in the comfortingly warm and fugged-up cab shelter (up Little Venice way – don't know if you know it).

Blimey – it's always a bit of a squeeze, I'm not saying, but today it's just bloody ridiculous. There's Dave Ridley – legs thrown wide as usual and taking up enough space for two and a half of us (he's bloody huge, is Dave – how he fits hisself into a cab at all is a mystery to me, and still he goes

on stuffing his face with these big thick sausage sandwiches, just like he's doing right now; mind you, be fair –
Mavis does a lovely sausage sandwich. Tell you: talk of
the town – cabbies come from all over; that and her black
pudding and chips, with an egg just broke over the top).
Then there's Jono, Arthur, Naseem and Mike. Don't much
know this other bloke – seen him about, once or twice. Sort
of cabbie gets the rest of us a bad name; not that he's bent,
or nothing – it's just that (Bobby, he could be called –
needn't be) he's one of those gets us all laughed at: always
setting the world to rights, sort of style. Tell you – stick him
in Downing Street and he'd wipe the floor with the lot of
them.

'What's up with you, then?' shouts out Dave – and
bloody hell, he don't have to yell, do he? Right next to
me, he is – bloody mouth chock-full of sausage bloody
sandwich.

'What you *think*? Job. Some of these punters – ah Mavis,
my Love: tea, toast . . . and, um – any of those pasties? No?
Spect Dave's had 'em. Well you *do*, Dave – you *do*! You can't
deny. Appetite like a bloody horse. OK, then, love – bacon
buttie, do me lovely. No – tell you, some of these punters –
never mind where they're coming from, half of them
haven't even a clue where they're bloody well going!'

Reg thought Dave could then have said Oh too right – tell
me something I don't know, why don't you; difficult to be
sure, on account of he was well into tea and KitKats, now.

'Thinking of packing it all in,' grumbled Reg, quite
amiably. 'Get myself a proper job.'

'Yeh? Like what? You couldn't do it, son. Like what?'

'Like . . . ooh Mavis, you saved my life, girl. My stomach
thinks my wossname's cut . . . like maybe no job at all,
that'd suit me. Nice few mill on the Lottery – do me just
perfect.'

And as the general boom and rumble of You-ain't-the-
only-bloody-one-mate fairly rocked the shelter, Reg

thought No, I'm not, of course I'm not – I know that, course I do: nearly every single man jack of us is weekly dreaming . . . even rehearsing inside ourselves just what we'll do when our number comes up: the ashen look, the panicked recheck, the weak and whitening fingers and palsied glance across to whoever it is with the What's-Up-With-You-Then look all over their faces and then – as slow and trembling as you like . . . *Here*: you'll never guess what . . .! Yeh. Lovely, that'd be. And then I could pay everyone I know to just leave me alone (Enid: take this money and leave me alone; Laverne: squander this lot and then do what you like; Pauly: could you be doing with a cuppla quid, son?); and then I could scoop up my sweet Adeline and take her off to wherever it is those bloody mangoes come from and then I'd come to know again why the hell it could be I was ever bloody born. Oh God, oh Jesus – it always comes down to this: whatever is on and whatever is up, I'm just ripped by lust for the Sainsbury's girl.

*

All Tony could feel was acute and yet dreamy, slumped – he thought forward – over the table in his universally hated and yeah-so-what-the-hell room. Even as his eyes felt hard and itchy – pebbly smooth and nearly detached – bright white, almost as if emitting long stiff beams that were probing into distances so near as to surround him, still behind them Tony's mind had difficulty in quite recalling . . . couldn't seem to totally piece together exactly what, or remotely why. And then – just as if a two-handed generator had been thrown into action – he had it all clear, so registered and simple. Tony stood: he didn't stop or want to think any more: it was all as plain as day.

Everything he needed, he swiftly and quite calmly stored away into a light canvas holdall: a turquoise ski-mask and dark rubber and seriously constricting goggles (he'd rejected them once – too like blinkers, and they dug in close to his temples – but then Tony had been forced to coolly reconsider: when above a pointed gun there is a face, what else would there be to latch on to and later barge back in amid a kick of fear and trembling but the wet black eyes boring in on you, the pupils at their centres radiating waves of just reined-in violence and stricken too by their own wide-openness and lack of security?).

A thick folded newspaper and a lot of plastic bags made up the sum total of Tony's requirements; but then finally – and he flinched away from not just the breath of absurdity but also the hot cuff of dread and a terrible doubt as he did it – Tony slipped in a small carton of yellow and rattling plastic pellets (yeah – like when everyone around me has dropped down dead from laughing, I'll just coolly reload and turn the thing on myself?). Oh God. No – just the sight of the gun will see me through – snug in my jacket, now (weighty beside me), and all that's left is to get out of that door and attend to business: rob that *bank*, boy – and get yourself a *life*.

But not a bank, no: banks he'd checked out – oh yeah, back in the Gina days, that far at least I'd got – and banks were too scary: banks you just knew had you sussed out and nailed down before even you push open the door. And yeah, sure – Tony knew, sure he knew, that the building society he'd set down as a target was no less tooled up – no fewer cameras, hidden alarms, and maybe in back a whole buncha other stuff that right now I just can't get *into*, OK, but the distance between the door and the counter was, well – maybe I could run it; and those outta shape women who sat there bored and non-judgemental in their company shirts and all those damn silver rings they seem really to like, you know? They would maybe just smile with their mouths and just *let* me, huh? Hear my shame and feel my pain and just for the sake of getting me back together with the woman I love, maybe one of these dames would look at me kind and just *let* me (because with dames, it's always kinda cleaner, you know? When they give you the look and just *let* you).

The whole idea is, you get there soon before they close up. Not while they're, you know – *doing* the closing up, or else you're gonna get hit by the widest smile of all as they tell you real polite and friendly that they're open in the morning again, *Sir*, at a half after nine, and meanwhile why don't you just go fuck yourself? You time it right, they're kinda tired – already in their minds it's home time. And this here is what's getting to me now because I been walking now, what? Ten minutes. Gotta be ten minutes, and still I got a way to go. Always I planned to walk – buses you can't rely on, and even I ain't so stupid as to flag down a cab – but I should maybe have timed it: I just sorta walked the walk in my mind and came up with this ballpark figure of maybe fifteen minutes, twenty tops – but I'm telling you, already we're close to fifteen minutes and, like I say, it's a way to go, it's a way to go.

Now it rains. This won't – shouldn't – make any kind of a difference: like, I'm not about to walk slower on account of now it's raining, right? But everything's kinda harder – seems to take so much longer – with the rain coming down. Also in my mind when I pictured it, rain wasn't in the frame, so already I'm starring in a different movie. So I walk quicker – yeh, quicker, but not so quick as anyone's gonna stop and look at me and start thinking Hey: what's with that guy – where's, like, the fire? Because then later – when I'm all alone and on the run – these people are gonna look way up into the rainy sky before those eyes of theirs get to narrowing up and then they're gonna come down with Oh yeah *sure* – yeah, now you come to *mention* it, there *was* this guy – just as you describe – hurrying in that direction: sprinting – face was purple and bursting, and he had the words HOLD UP tattooed in red right across his goddam forehead and he was definitely American and his name was *Tony*, pretty sure (you want his address?), and I think he had dark rubber goggles in that grey Macy's holdall of his, and for sure there was the warm clunk of a gun hitting at his hip with every lope of his criminal thighs – even if this iron of his was crammed up to the breech with little yellow plastic pellets and not the round-nosed dumdums that you might expect so determined and coked-up a desperado to be packing: oh yes, officer – that's him, all right.

Gotta get a holda myself. I figure I'm there in no more than five, maybe: four if I step on it – six, seven if I pull right back and play it cool. I don't know I'm gonna *last* six or seven, so I'm taking it steady: I turn this corner, I'm just one block away – cross the road and then I can *see* the baby: reach out and *touch* that mother.

*

Tony stood poised at the door. This very thing meant, he knew, that already he had hesitated even if just for a second in the sort of way that was never seen in people intent on pushing through those doors and depositing their Giro or drawing out forty (actually – weekend – better make it fifty) or querying their statement or grubbing after a quarter of a percentage point of interest or assuring the sub-manager quite plaintively that they're dreadfully sorry but this balance just can't be *right* because they remember distinctly putting in a cheque to cover the shortfall as long ago as last Tuesday morning (and come to think of it, might even have been the Monday).

So he entered now with intent – and was at once quite thrown by the sight of three people idly queuing amid chromium pillars and much-strummed thick rope for the only operational window. Tony wanted to leave (why didn't I think of *people*?). Outdoors had never ever looked so good. He put his lips through a work-out that was unfamiliar to either of them, as he concentrated hard looking down at the floor. He had backed his way into the place, fooling around with what he hoped might pass as a bag of shopping, maybe (he had rootled in the holdall, and now the mask and goggles were tight in his hand); the cameras, he felt pretty sure – one up above, look, another over there, more just Jesus Christ knows where – should so far have caught no more than his long-peaked, pulled-down baseball cap. The woman at the front of the queue was leaving, thank the Lord, and the two people ahead of Tony – oldish man, young could-be mother, looked like – dutifully shuffled forwards as if they had been firmly instructed to close those gaps.

The old guy was going – near bracing himself, seemed to be, with what could almost be a sort of proprietorial pride: looked that way, as he slid his passbook into the inside pocket of his I-know-it's-smart blazer, as if the sole custodian of the truth that what it in fact contained were the title deeds of the whole wide world. The young could-be mother (why do I think that? There's no damn kid in tow, so why do I think that?) was chatting away to the chatting-back teller as if that's the reason she'd come here – but hey, even women couldn't be doing with this for too long, could they? Well could they? Never mind: concentrate. What I do now is, I duck down to the floor and make like I'm doing up a shoelace – this I worked out whenever. OK, I'm sweating, I'm sweating (well wouldn't you be? Never mind I'm scared as shit – these places are like a goddam oven, best of times). Look at this – I got elastic-sided boots on. No mind – they don't have cameras down at ground level, I guess. What I do now is – No, lady, no! Don't look down! Jeez – she maybe thinks I'm eyeing up her legs; don't be dumb, girl – I'm here to rob the place, capeesh? What the hell do I got to be doing with *legs*? OK – I got the mask on, and my face, my face – it feels like a stew. The goggles are steaming up: they're not meant to do this. When I bought the goddam things I said to the guy: these goggles – they steam up, or what? Not these ones, sir, no – the cheaper ones will: with the less expensive range you will get this, yes, but this particular pair you have selected is very much known not to. I had the guy here now, I'd rip out his throat: all I see is fog, and my whole head is burning up and plus I'm streaming with blood or lava along with all the sweat.

All I need now is for the woman to leave. Leave, honey, why don't you – on account of there's a limit as to how long a guy can be crouched down on the floor of a building society got up like a fuckin' mountaineer and doing up the lace on his elastic-sided boot. All I do is – the dame splits, and I stand up and hit them with the truth: outta here in no time, right? So now the lady's asking for a mini-*statement*? Jesus, Jesus: *believe* it? I'll give her a goddam mini-state-ment: Fuck *Off*, lady: my knees are seizing up on me, and so too is what's left of my nerve.

'You all right?'

Tony's blood-heat now switched to freezing – this, he knew, had been directed down at him. He waved above his head an all-encompassing and thick-gloved hand in some sort of direction, while his neck did its best to suck down and swallow whole all that skulked above it. A gruff and ape-like if stilted grunting rounded off his big assurance that all was well at his end.

'Bloke down here seems not all right,' the woman con-fided more softly to the teller. 'Anyway, Isobel – I got to go. I'm late already.'

Tony hissed out his relief at *that*, at least – gulped it right back in, though, as the woman continued quite seamlessly:

'How's your *mother*?'

And Tony – whose joints and spirit had practically given up on him, now – heard only a wistful sigh as did she say *Isobel* came back with Oh, you know – usual: she's just *mother* . . . There followed a burst of sororial and budgerigar giggling, a selection of farewells, and the young could-be mother turned – had maybe glanced back at him crouched there (who could say?) – and then walked away and through the door and out of Tony's life.

Now!

And do you think he could *move*? Like hell he could – locked limbs and a rising panic were keeping him down; only a further and disembodied enquiry as to whether he was all *right* (you down there, whoever you are) now spurred him on and forced him upright and in a matter of seconds the whole thing was actually going as well and as swiftly as in the endlessly previewed highlights that he had spooled on to a loop and played and played and played.

She had started at the sight of him (and to his intense surprise, Tony registered this and thought Well yeah – who wouldn't?). From where Isobel was sitting – nearly aghast – all that were immediately apparent to her were just those two thin, red and active lips (she'd never forget them) framed in blue – framed in green? – urging her to what? I can't hear – *do* something, but no: she couldn't take it in and her fingers were – could they be? – straying beneath the counter and he barked at her *No!* – very sharply at that and she did not want to but couldn't anyway make out his eyes behind the grey and thick misted ovals, but his meaning now was bright and terribly clear to her and as he unfolded that newspaper just enough – just one hard corner – so that Isobel could glimpse – oh Jesus, help me, I'm so, I'm so – I can't remember: what should I *do*?! I can't just – ?! But already she was, with dead white hands, passing over grimy piles of money, more money – just keep sliding across wads of this money and he'll go, he'll leave and then he won't hurt me, oh please don't hurt or touch me – I can't believe this is – it isn't – truly happening, and it's taking so long and why doesn't somebody *come*? They can't all have gone yet. And suddenly someone was there, almost beside her – and Tony's eyes leapt up at him (and he was thinking what, now, with the gun quite firm in his hand?).

'Oh *God*, Mister Carey,' breathed Isobel – jerkily, and yet with such softness, her eyes stuck wide – her jittery fingers still, as if paid to, passing over wodges of money (please don't let them end, the thick stacks of money, because then he'll look up and then he could kill me) – and darting back from the man's hands as they reached out with greed and fed it into the maw of yawning plastic bags.

'It's quite all right, Isobel,' said Mister Carey, low and calmly – and this in the face of the gun that a near-delirious Tony had levelled at his heart. 'Just do as he says.'

'No alarms!' rasped out Tony – his voice seeming even to him too highly pitched and yet clogged with fear and from somewhere outside him. 'No alarms! Hear me?!'

Mister Carey raised up his hands, palms outwards, and with them went the innocent, more insolent, arch of each of his eyebrows. Isobel was sobbing, now – the cash drawer was empty of all save ripped wrappers and elastic bands, and she didn't have it in her to say so.

'*More!*' roared Tony – and again he was astounded by not just the direction from which his voice came out of him, but also the very nature of his own hacked-out command. Every fibre within him was yearning to back down and tear off, and yet now Mister Carey had open the lid of another steel-grey till, and dangerous and audible seconds throbbed dead as more and more lumps of rim-soiled money – the smell rose up from it – were groped and rammed into bags now gorged with sin and maybe Tony's future.

Enough! Tony had been screaming at himself for how long, and only now it got through. He backed away – the bulk of the bags making him awkward. He wagged the gun to remind these two that, yes, he had one. Isobel's lips were shivering, her imploring eyes seeming ready to melt down her face in blue and helpless streaks: that was the last thing Tony saw as he turned and set his mind to running – he heard behind him door-clunk and then a rumble amid a rush of air, and that had been more than enough to alert his senses to a new and awful awareness that here and soon there was to be more than this – but the force and twisting power of the grip on his ankle had him falling headlong and heavily just as his hand was on the door that led out and away from any trace of this. He was toppled – face-down and sprawling, now, his gun thrown wide, the bags of money hugged into him tightly as his caught and bent-round foot just kicked out wildly – lashed back with all the ferocity and nose-filling fear of one being dragged down and under in a sea turned vicious. He could only think to struggle quite madly before defeat came – or that door was pushed open and another bad man would try to stop him: until either moment came, there could well be a kind of chance, and Tony just had to fight for it with a wild-eyed fierceness and concentration both new to him. Then his power-driven heel connected hard with let it be bone, and he heard a yelp of huge and pained surprise as the constriction about his ankle was relieved and then relinquished. Tony was on his feet before he had even worked out how to do that – and he gasped and then screamed at the hurt and imbalance of standing. He was so nearly back down again – his weighed-down arms came as close as hell to flailing as a further jolt of blunt hot pain was shuddering around his foot as it slithered madly on a rolling river of little yellow plastic pellets. He nearly fell through the door and out into the street and he tore at mask and goggles and dragged his stricken ankle just past the shop, then the café, and down this side road – the pain was almost sweet and made him faint, forcing his teeth to twist and grind down into any soft part around them – and now he was near that alley with the bins all down the length of it where years ago he had thought he would pause, take stock – listen and consider – but he loped right down it – wounded, stalked and so wholly on the run: turned left, not right as was always –

Jesus, I thought so – the idea, and soon his bearings were shot to bits but he stumbled on anyway (for what else could he do?). There had been white and moony faces along the way – not a mass, and not a rush of them, but a regular flicker, looming up and ducking down – one or two *concerned*, it seemed like, a flinch or so from largely women and a whole lot of deliberate blindness. I am not sure (my chest is close to bursting, I feel my leg is a big and dead heavy too-long thing, because the pain is spiking upwards and taking me over) . . . not quite sure where I am, now. I must must must get out of wherever it is, though – but how do I do this?

A taxi was cruising away from the smattering of traffic just down there on the corner, by the lights (and yeah yeah – I know that was the one big rule: don't hail a cab. But *look* at me!). Tony transferred the whole bulge of bags to his other hand, while trying to stand as if he were a human being and signal with a degree of calm and authority. The fucking thing just – Jesus! – sailed right past him, the bastard – *bastard*. But there was another close behind – but with bloody, those things – *people* in the back. Get them *out*, those people – chuck them, get rid of them, kill them and *take* me, can't you, because hear me – look, hear me: I have *got* to, now, get *out* of here. I just can't stand around – I stand around and people will *look* – like him over there, see him? See him? He was looking, I know damn well he was – not *now* he isn't, oh no, because I looked over and caught him, didn't I, but then he was – he was looking *then*.

And as the lights turned red, Tony just thought *Right* – I can't wait and I can't chance it for even a moment longer. He hauled open the rear door of yet another bloody taxi just idling there, and winced and tried to just hiss out the shock of pain as in two bad stages he pulled his trunk of a leg up and into the back behind him. The bags just slithered where they would – Tony's reddened and clammy fingers just too out of it even to luxuriate at their release – and only now

164

did he unclench his wound-down eyes and see the gesticu-
lations of the driver in front.

'*No*, mate – sorry. My light ain't on, is it? Going home.'

'Airport!' gasped Tony. 'Airport!' Why? Why *airport*?
That had never been in the picture, had it? Was now.

Reg sighed deeply, and wagged his head in could-be real
sorrow for all the bloody morons who ever walked this
earth, but in particular for himself, poor old Reg, who once
again for all his bloody sins had to explain the very simple
facts of life to yet another punter who don't have a clue
what he's bloody well *at*. He pulled the cab over to the side,
and very pointedly yanked on the handbrake.

'You're not listening, pal. I'm on my way home. OK?
You'll get another cab, no trouble.'

'*Airport*!' panted Tony. 'Please. Pay you.'

And Reg was really ready to get quite stroppy – but Jesus
Christ what's all this, now? He drunk, or what? Bloke's
hand just come through me partition – casual as you like –
with a bloody great lump of money in it: more bloody
twenties than you ever bloody saw in your life.

'You want to be careful,' said Reg – trying to be careful –
'flashing all that lot about. You won the Lottery or what,
mate?'

Tony had released his grip on the money, and the fritter
of notes cascaded over Reg's shoulder – was slipping down
between his legs, some caught up around his ankles,
tucking behind the accelerator, there (I can feel it move,
beneath my feet).

'What airport you want anyway, son?' he heard himself
say. 'There's more than one, you know.'

*

Blimey O'Reilly – what the hell am I supposed to do now?
This ain't never happened to me before, not this one hasn't.
Dear oh dear – here's a right story and a half for Dave

Ridley and the rest of them, come tomorrow dinner time. So what – I take the bloke to Heathrow, like what he wants – I chucked him a couple of options, and it's Heathrow he went for, dozy sod – or else I bung him down the local nick and let them sort it out (and no, I don't know what's wrong here, but *something's* bloody got to be, hasn't it? Stands to reason). Yeah – but then I'm off the road for half tomorrow, aren't I? Questions – bloody statements, all that caper: that's down to me, that is. And by the time this bloke twigs where I brought him, he's only going to do a runner, ain't he? So I'm left talking to the Bill, and he's away on his toes. So like I say – what to do, ay? What to do? Oh Christ, it's a bugger, this is: all I needed in my life (could have been well home by now).

'This the way to Heathrow? You sure bout that?'

Jesus, thought Tony, as he jerked at even that – it kills me just to *talk*, my goddam foot, it hurts so bad. It's maybe broke, that ankle – it's all swoll up. All I gotta do is just get on a plane. Get on a plane, right? Is all I gotta do. It'll take me someplace – don't matter too much where – and then I chill out, get me patched up – seen to – and then after a cuppla days, week maybe, I come back and . . . uh . . . why in hell I'm doing all of this? Oh yeh, oh yeh – Nan, my Nan. I love her. I come back and pay off Jake and get her. And then it's OK.

'Yeh,' agreed Reg quite readily – because it was, was the way to Heathrow: might as well humour the bloke while I think what to do. 'You, er – you in some sort of trouble, mate? Ay? Wanna talk about it?'

'Just drive the cab, OK? Just get me there.'

Why's he driving so goddam slow? Tell him to step on it, yeah? Nah. Already he smells a rat the size of a building: maybe I just sit tight – play it cool. Why'd I go and throw a fistful of dollars at the guy? That was me being Mister *Cool*, right? Oh yeh sure – I guess it happens to him all the time. You know what I think? I tell you what I think: this whole thing, I maybe could've planned it better, you know? Given it, maybe . . . bit more time.

This ain't gonna work. Who am I kidding? There's no way, baby, this thing can happen. Look at it: someone – some guy, right, *must* have seen me get this goddam cab (remember, I'm the crazy Yank with HOLD UP burned into his face). And is there anything in this city so easy to trace as a black fuckin' taxi? And who's got to *trace*? The guy up front, he's got me clocked – he *has* me here: Jesus – all I know, right now he could be about to turn me over, turn me in. This the way to Heathrow? Jeez – *ask* me, why don't you: all these roads, to me they're all the same. I think, maybe, I gotta get outta here . . . Look! Right now – right this second, the guy's looking at me in the mirror. Oh no – not *now* he ain't, sure, because I looked up and *caught* him – but then he was, you bet: he sure was *then*.

And still not quite knowing he was really about to do this thing, Tony narrowed his eyes and tightened his mouth in anticipation of the shock of pain his next swift actions were about to shoot him up with. The taxi had slowed as a light turned amber, and now it shuddered and purred at red. Just over there – across two lanes of angry traffic, there glowed at him a tube station. I reckon I just got to get me there, cos right now I'm swinging in a noose. So *do* it. Yeah, I'm gonna. So *do* it, Tony, Chrissake: get this *done*, willya? Yeah – you're right, you're right: this is one of those now or never scenarios, yeah? This baby ain't gonna stay red for ever, am I right? Right – too right. So right *now*, then, Tony: help me out, here.

He gathered plastic bags right up tight to him, clunked open the door and in nearly one electric movement practically leapt into the road, his howl of sheer agony on impact maybe all that alerted Reg to what in bloody hell was bloody happening now. And Tony could hear his *Oi!* And then a diminishing Oi *You!* as he blundered heavily among braking, swerving, untamed and screaming cars, his own quite passionate shrieking adding to and spiking the pure hell in which he found himself floundering badly. He got to the other side, though (I'm clutching the barrier!), and some wild motorist's horn had jammed and he'd just crudely pulled in anywhere and was fighting to get out of that car right this second and next he was making for Tony, but Tony now had hauled up his leg and his bags into the hot stale mouth of the Underground station and he found himself thinking quite lucidly that maybe in the light of the extraordinary circumstances, it would be quite OK if the business of his ticket was left till the other end (wherever on God's earth that place might be). So when some guy in half a uniform came right up close to him and Excuse Me, rudely, Tony just elbowed him aside and limped on stiffly – but this proved to be the wrong thing to do because now a heavy hand had gripped him firmly about his shoulder, this unaccountably triggering and then jacking up the pain threshold in his leg which then rocketed off the scale and so he struggled now quite roughly – had to be free and rid of this – but then the other guy, he was shouting now harshly, and that mealy-faced motorist – yeah, just had to be – was wholeheartedly pitching in with him and barking out *Mad*, *Crazy* – He's got to be *Nuts* – and all Tony could do now was bawl like a maddened animal as he lashed out in any direction left to him, though he knew he was pitching to the side, could feel himself keeling over, but it was only when the policeman muscled in and bundled aside everyone and pinioned Tony into such a lock that he felt so weak and imprisoned as to be under a spell, but still he flailed around gamely – but the crunch of his teeth as his jaw hit the ground, the weight of the copper as he screwed his knee into the small of his back and ground him down: these two further big and spreading areas of pain made Tony go limp – his hands opened up and his arms stretched out stiffly, as if unravelling themselves from the sweet soft couch of night-time dreams. Before he closed his eyes, he knew only the taste of breathy grime from the hard floor to which he found himself stapled, and the rushing sight of ruffled eddies of money kicking up and fluttering amid a cluttered woodland of incredulous ankles. All Right Son, he distantly heard from somewhere above him: You Just Rest Quiet. And Tony thought Yes, yes – I'll do that, oh yeah. A siren grew louder and then louder still before it practically invaded him and then cut dead. He felt the vibrations of heavy feet coming, and closed his eyes more tightly. I will – I'll do that: I'll Just Rest Quiet – which is maybe all I ever was doing, until turmoil came and took me. I wonder if, when it comes to it, all these bad guys will see it: I *did* do crime, oh sure I did – but listen up, man – it's *love* is all I did it for. You maybe meet me halfways in getting your mind round that?

Something harsh and heavy had locked about his dragged-round wrists: my leg I don't now feel – it's maybe run off (I hope it makes it). The rest of me, I think, is done for – my big and desperate try to be like Clint and win back love is over. And what it is, is . . . I guess I didn't make it.

*

Would you bleedin' Adam and Eve it? Tell you – all these bloody novel writers you keep on reading about, there's not nothing they could make up that'd hold a bloody candle to just one single week in the life of a cab-driver. You want stories, mate? Telling you – stories I could tell, make the best book ever (and one day, thought Reg quite candidly – when I get a bit of time – I might just bloody do it. Maybe just get in some arty-farty merchant to sort of, you know – put it good: bloody bestseller – tell you, son).

Like take today: the Yank with all the money (and *yeah* I've counted it – course I bloody have. Nearly three hundred quid, bleedin' idiot – pretty good result, yeah, for not taking no one out to Heathrow – wait till I tell Dave

Ridley and the rest of them: green won't be in it). So I suppose, yeah, despite all the aggro – not too bad a day; what I'm going to do now is get myself home, not stopping – no way – not for no one. Not that I'm in too much of a hurry to get back to bleedin' Enid, course – but tonight I reckon I've earned myself a little drink. Grab a *Standard*, get down the Duchess, maybe sink a couple – why not, ay? (Old Ted often gets in there of a Tuesday – not a bad lad, small doses.)

So what you reckon about the Yank, then? Most probably drugged up to his eyeballs, shouldn't at all wonder: they're all at it nowadays, you know – you just got to open a paper (I bloody well know what *I'd* do with them). Whatever happened to just having a quiet pint with a couple of your mates, then, hey? What do they want to be doing with all this stuffing muck up their noses and sticking bloody needles in their arms, then? Blimey – you don't see me queuing up for no jab: mainly why I never went to Tunis, that time. Not bloody worth it, is it? Having to have an injection, just to go to Nig-Nog Land. Stick to what you know, that's the way I live: you stick to what you know, son, and you won't go wrong.

What I've done is, I've double-backed down parallel the high street, look, and shot up the mews and that very tasty shortcut up by the park and now I'm well out of the whole of the contra-flow system and my back's nicely turned to the incoming traffic: reckon I'm home next to no time.

*

'Hiya, Reg – you ain't been down a bit. What can I get you?'

'Yeah, Mickey. How you doing? Pint of Directors, there's a good lad. Slip down a treat.'

'World been seeing to you good, Reg?'

'I'm not complaining, Mickey, I'm not complaining. There's a lot worse off.'

Like, I suppose, thought Reg (watching, as always – could never take his eyes off it – Mickey putting his back into pulling that pint; it's anticipation, I reckon that's what it is: long day, first of the night, it's always like that) – like, if we're counting, my Enid back indoors. Can't be much in it for her, now – life and that, can there? Like today – I get back and she ain't around and I thought Funny, I thought: not like Enid to go out, or nothing – not these days. Where would she go? Various reasons, she won't even get in the shopping no more (how I come to be down Sainsbury's in the first place, as it happens). It got to the stage – talk about queer – what with all she was getting off of the telly about additives, modified wossname, politics and all the pricing wars she'd boycotted the supermarkets. As a result, we never had no bloody food, did we? So I had to get myself down there – else I never would've met my Adeline.

Then I twig: what it is, she's still upstairs in bed, dozy cow – didn't even bother getting up. So I bring the old girl up a mug of tea, and she hunches herself around it – clutching it, she is, with both of her hands for all the world as if she's just been airlifted out of the North bloody Sea (all it needed was a blanket round her shoulders). Later I bung her one of them Sainsbury's Italians – she's a bit partial to Tallytelly Hoojamaflip, some tomatoey goo all over it, bits of green stuff. You can zap them in no time in the thingy, so it's not like it's trouble, or nothing. So yeah, you could say, couldn't you, that people like Enid are worse off than myself; particularly in light of the latest.

'You're a bleeding stranger.'

'Hiya, Ted. What you up to, you old bastard? What you having?'

'Dividing my time, Reg, dividing my time. Mild and bitter and a whisky chaser, if you're twisting my arm. I tell you, son, dear oh Lord: it can't go on. What with this and the fags.'

'Way you knock 'em back, Ted, you could be right. Serve

the man, Mickey – and get one in for yourself, hey? You only live once. Twice in Ted's case, mind – bastard should've croaked years back.'

'You're a scholar, Reg – I'll have a small brandy, if it's all the same to you. But later on, eh? Got to keep an eye.'

Reg planked down a twenty-pound note, and made it clear by a nearly regal wave of his hand that Mickey could partake of his small brandy now or whenever, mate – either way it was no skin off Reg's nose, believe him.

'Nice for some,' said Ted. 'Cash trade. Salting it away – hey, Reg? I'd do the same, son.'

'It's *graft* out there, Ted, I ain't kidding you. Every bloody penny you take in, you're sweating blood, mate. Telling you – you wanna be a cab-driver, first you got to be a bloody saint.'

'Well here's to Saint Reg! Cheers, mate.'

'Cheers, Ted. Good health. Get it down your screech, you sod. Look, Ted – don't think I'm being wossname, or nothing, but I just wanna go off in that corner there and work something out quiet, like. Bout the only place I get some peace. You sweet with that?'

'*Course*, Reg – you please yourself. Maybe catch up with you later, eh? Buy you one. Enid still the same, then?'

'Christ, Ted – you of all people. They're *all* the bloody same, aren't they? Better off bleedin' without them, aren't we? You're well out of it with that Sonya.'

'Yeh – you're on the money with that one, Reg. Right dog she was. Won't believe it – she come round the other day.'

'Joking. What you say?'

'I told her to sling her hook off out of it, didn't I?'

'You did right, son. Bleedin' nerve.'

'What I told her.'

'I'm proud of you, Ted. OK, then – maybe later, OK? You're on, son.'

As Ted sloped away, Reg opened up his mouth and ate half his pint and then moved off to that little corner table just by the serving hatch and well away from that bloody lit-up clanking machine (how many times I told Mickey about that? He says Don't blame me, mate – it's the bloody brewery, innit?). Reg set down his glass and pulled out the *Standard* from the side pocket of his jacket – lay it flat, that's right, and now let's have a good look at this: read it properly. Telling you – I clap eyes on the picture on the front, I don't hardly believe what I'm seeing. Recognized him straight off – no matter he was face-down with a bloody great copper on his back. Poor sod: I bet when he got up this morning, he didn't think his mug was going to be plastered all over the evening paper. Every bloody day it's the same – you just don't know what's coming down next.

Turns out he's only gone and turned over a building society, hasn't he? Knew it had to be something like that, if I'm honest. 'The robber,' it says here, 'whose name has not been released' – no, don't suppose *he* was, neither – 'was apprehended by an Underground inspector, a member of the public and a policeman at Earls Court Station having got away with an estimated £35,000 in a daring daylight raid on a high street building society. At the Westbourne Grove branch of the Manchester Building Society earlier in the day he had approached the only cashier on duty, 52-year-old Miss Isobel March. He was wearing a bright green motorcyclist's mask, she said, and pointed at her face what turned out to be an air-gun of the type freely available from hobby shops up and down the country. The hero of the hour was the sub-manager of the branch, Mister George Carkey, 34, who tackled the man and wrestled him to the ground. Mister Carkey sustained facial injury, and the man made his escape. Police are so far at a loss as to how the robber made his way from Westbourne Grove to Earls Court, and urge any members of the public who saw any-thing suspicious, such as a car or a motorbike driving off at speed, to come forward. By the time of his arrest, the

Manchester head office had already posted a reward of £5,000 for the man's capture, but as all the money is thought to have been recovered at the scene of the arrest, it is uncertain as to whether the station inspector and the unnamed member of the public will stand to gain.'

Reg allowed the rest of his pint to trickle on down his throat, and gassily come to rest. Tell you what – I know one bloke what definitely stands to gain, and that's yours truly. See, I'm very happy to read here, aren't I, that all the money is, what do they say – 'thought to have been recovered', because when I open the back of the cab tonight, first thing I see kicked into the corner is a screwed-up plastic carrier bag. I don't think nothing of it, at first – and then I have a poke inside. Telling you – ain't totted it all up (stashed it in the garage, didn't I? First thought) but there's got to be the best part of ten grand there, or my name's Tony Blair. Buy you a lot of happiness, that kind of money: tax-free and out of the blue. Yeh – but steady. I ain't never even *thought* like this before; let's get this clear – I'm like all cabbies I know: straight down the line. I mean, yeah – you'll give change for a ten when it's a score, time to time (clubbers, mainly – so out of it they don't notice nothing), but that's just being *human*. This, though – different kettle of wossname altogether. And I don't too much like the sound of this sort of eyewitness lark, neither. What if someone clocked my number? Or even saw the bastard get into the cab? Old Bill'll be down the Carriage Office faster then you can ... but listen – what if I just say Yeah: Yeah, I picked him up, and then he scarpered, didn't he? Well it's true, ain't it? What happened. Don't have to let on about his calling card, course. Wants thinking about, though.

Reckon what I'm going to do now, is – I'll have just the one with Ted, and then I'll get myself home and have a little bit of a ponder. (*Sainsbury's* carrier bag, as it happens: funny how it all links up.)

CHAPTER SEVEN

George Carey was frankly pretty disgusted with just about every single one of the newspaper reports, if you really want to know – save just maybe the local rag, I suppose, which sort of did him proud. I mean – fair enough, the *Standard* had me down as the 'Hero of the Hour', which I very much liked (it's got a really good sound, that has, don't you think? 'Hero of the Hour': really good ring to it) – but how, please tell me, did they manage to get my name down as 'Carkey'? Hey? Bloody journalists – they don't get anything right. Anything you ever know the slightest thing about, they always get it wrong. Famous for it. And yet we blithely continue to swallow just every single word they write about anything else in the world. It's like the weather people, isn't it? Constantly wrong, day after day – and yet we all go on listening to the reports and *believing* them: you'd be better off tossing a coin. I did my job like they do theirs and I'd be on the dole in double-quick time. Where did that 'k' come from? How is it possible? I *told* them Carey – spelt it out (because sometimes it's the 'e' that's missing; first time I've ever had a 'k' stuck into it – it's just beyond belief). And God – Pete Chalmers, won't let it alone, will he? I actually know for a fact he's acutely jealous of all the attention I've got (stands out a mile), so of course he has to try and bring me down in any way he can (childish, yes, but that's Pete). But hour after hour I'm expected to deal with all of his 'Carkey! Carkey! Is that you, Carkey? Now let me see: would that be the car key we insert into our not quite top-of-the-range and distinctly pre-owned BMW in order to generate movement? Or are you perchance named after that singularly repellent and dung-coloured material famed for cladding our valiant fighting forces?' *Yes*, Pete – ho ho, I go: exceedingly funny. Now do you think you could just *leave* it, hey? Joke over – OK, Pete? Fat chance: he'll be doing all this for just *years*.

And another thing about the papers, while we're at it – *Mail*, *Express*, *Mirror*, every bloody one of them has followed the *Standard*'s lead and said that I'm thirty-four when I'm not, I'm just not – I'm thirty-*three*, if anyone cares, and that's what I said to the bloody reporter when he asked me. So how does a three become a four? It's sloppy, isn't it? Just plain sloppy – not good enough by a mile. And they took pictures, you know: my jaw is partly taped up at the moment (not actually broken, thank the Lord) because the bastard gave me one hell of a kick, so I am not I admit looking quite at my Hollywood best – but nonetheless I was rather looking forward to seeing the pictures (never been in the papers before). Not *one* of them printed a thing: only the local paper – they did. Sent someone round. Christ, it looks like a prison mug shot, and this bloke is meant to be a *professional*, for God's sake: it's what he does for a *living*. Shirley didn't even recognize me! It was as bad as that (mind you, Shirley too – she's not at all happy with all the attention I'm getting. You'd think, wouldn't you, that the wife of the 'Hero of the Hour' would be chuffed – or at least be a *bit* pleased – basking in reflected glory, sort of thing: not my Shirley – it just isn't in her).

No – the only picture that got printed endlessly was the one of the American bastard with his face on the ground, and that policeman on top of him (some tourist took it, apparently: paid for his holiday). And most of what I told the reporters – they didn't use it. And what they did, they mangled. But they printed everything they could about the bloody *criminal*, though, didn't they? God Almighty – you'd think the Hero of the Hour would warrant just a *leeedle* bit more space than a common villain, wouldn't you? But no – this is the age we live in. Look at this bit: 'The man, who was today named as Tony Clinton, an American domiciled in this country, was said by best friend Jake Self to have always been a bit of a loner. Mister Self's fiancée, Miss Susie Black, added that Clinton appeared to have been recently under a great deal of stress, possibly due to over-working.' Well who actually *cares*? Hm? I mean – what, you're a bit busy at work so you rob a building society, do you? That's just *normal*, is it? Not in my book it isn't. God – I expect what'll happen next is that the muggins taxpayer – that's you and me, matey, and don't you forget it: out of our hard-earned wages – we'll be expected to foot the bill for *counselling*, swiftly followed by a cushy term in an open prison. Me? Hundred pounds from Head Office, I got. That and my name spelt as *Carkey*. Justice? I don't really think so.

I shouldn't, strictly, actually be at work at all, I suppose. Everyone's been saying God, George – take a few days off, why don't you? Week, even: you must be pretty shaken up – quite an ordeal. Well – I'm not pretending that this sort of thing happens to me every day of the week (although I suppose if I'm being quite frank here, I have always been aware of the possibility of danger in a job such as mine: with the responsibility there comes the risk – you just simply have to be a big enough man to knuckle down and shoulder it, that's all) – but I thought that staying at home would not be the right thing. Anyway – we've had loads of locals coming in just to have a look at me (it's easy to understand how all the big stars feel – people gaping at you all the time) and well – I didn't like to let them down. It's probably quite a great moment in their lives as well – getting to meet the Hero of the Hour! It's a rule of life my father taught me: never ever forget the little people, for they too must play their part. Very true, that: I like to do my bit.

Poor old Isobel, though – she's been knocked for six, by all accounts. Haven't seen her since. Strange – she seemed really quite together when all the Press and police were here, and everything, but when it all quietened down she just started going to pieces, basically. Doctor looked her over – said it was just shock, touch of faintness (well face it, she's not as young as she was, our Isobel – fifty-two, I read in the papers: no chicken, is she?). So they took her home in a car: look *after* yourself, they kept on saying – and if there's anything you *need* . . . She got a hundred quid too, apparently (don't quite know why, but there you go), and the next morning they sent round a load of flowers. Maybe if I'd stayed home they would've given me flowers too – I'm not too sure of company policy on that score, when it comes to men; I'm not saying a couple of M & S vouchers would've gone too far amiss, but there – let it lie. So as I say – old Isobel is a bit of a bag of nerves at the moment, and from what people say, I can't see that mother of hers helping: must be awful, looking after someone old. I say to my two – Tell you what, kids, when I'm old and useless, just stick me out for the binmen – I don't want any part in blighting your lives. They laugh and say Oh don't *say* that, Daddy – we *love* you. Sweet. They're good kids – they're the future: what I'm working for (*got* to be worth it, hasn't it?).

Still – it wasn't all bad news for Isobel: least they spelt her name right.

*

'Well don't just walk *away* from me, Isobel: explain. What do you imagine you're going to *do* in this place, for all that time?'

Isobel sighed, and tried it again. 'I told you, mother, I just don't know. No idea at all *what* to expect. Never been to one before, have I? I imagine it'll just be rest and – well, just *resting*, I suppose. That's what the doctor said I most needed. There's nothing actually, I don't think, *wrong* with me – it's just that I'm – '

'Well of *course* there's nothing wrong with you – anyone can see that. You're *young*, Isobel – *young*. Goodness me, when I was your age I felt like a *child*. You wait till you get *really* old – you wait till you have to bear what I go through daily: then you'll know the meaning of *nerves* – then you'll know the meaning of *tired*. Good God – it's *me* who should be going to this health place, whatever on earth it's supposed to be. When did anyone ever send *me* off to anywhere in the world that would do me the slightest bit of good? When you're old, they just don't care any more. All you are is a drain on resources. You're on the scrap heap.'

'*Scrap* heap, mother! *I* take care of you, don't I? It's all I do. That and work.'

'It's *only* the work, only your job that matters – it always was with you, Isobel. Can't wait, can you, to get out of the house in the morning? Never mind me – you just *go*.'

Isobel sighed again (she did it a lot). 'Jane comes in at lunch time, doesn't she, mother? It's not as if you're alone all day. And anyway – how do you suppose we *live*? It's my job, isn't it? It's how we get *money*.'

'My pension – '

'Oh *God*, mother, why do you keep on *doing* this?' I mustn't, thought Isobel, really quite feebly, get excited: it's the one thing they told me I really mustn't do. 'Your, oh God – *pension* doesn't even pay for the food for the *cats*. You've just no idea – '

'Oh thank you. Thank you very much. That makes me feel very nice. Very nice indeed.'

'Oh *mother* – you know what I *mean*. You've just no idea what things *cost*, now. The way we live, believe it or not – I don't really know why, but for one reason or another it actually costs a *lot*. I don't *choose* to go to work, do I? I do it because I *have* to.'

Which isn't, as Isobel very well knew, remotely true at all: mother is really quite right about this – can't *wait*, can I, to get out of the house in the morning. When the doctor,

Doctor English (don't know who he is, he was sent from work – but he seems very nice) – when he sat me down and said to me You know, Isobel, what with the trauma of all you have been through, and the way I can now see you live, I really think it would be best, you know, if you could get away by yourself for a little while: somewhere you could rest, where they understand this sort of thing. And just as my heart flew out to grasp hold of so wonderful a thing, there raced into my head – as usual, as usual – all the old anxieties: what about mother? Who would be here for her? What about work? How much would all this *cost*? And then the doctor told her that the Society would be more than delighted to underwrite the entire treatment for up to a fortnight – it's a nice place, Isobel, in Buckinghamshire, not too far. Beautiful grounds, plenty of time for rest and walking – and the grub, I'm reliably informed, is not at all half bad. As to your mother . . . surely there's someone . . .? Sister, perhaps?

Sister, oh yes. There's certainly one of those. It's just such an old story, all that is coming – but the awful thing is, it's my life. Geraldine – big sigh – is the young one – but not, at least, beautiful with it. None of us in this family has ever been that, but although I say it myself, I do think I always did have the edge on Geraldine in these matters: she was never blessed with the cheekbones, you see, and nor with the legs. But of course it has to be faced: I'm fifty-five years of age, now (and it still comes as so much of a shock, that – I feel that somewhere down the line I unaccountably lost track of twenty whole years, just looked the other way and they were gone: I just quite literally cannot believe it). And when you're that age, when you're a woman of fifty-five . . . and I told that beastly man from the paper, forget which one, I was only fifty-two – and they printed it, too. If I hadn't been so flustered . . . I didn't, did I, *know* it was just a toy sort of . . . what did they call it? *Air*-gun thing – not when he waved it at me, I didn't, that horrible man: he's the reason I'm now the way I am – shaking cold all the time, just quivering like a . . . and then I'll suddenly burst into floods of . . . it's so *unlike* me, so *unlike* me . . .

No – if I'd actually had the time to sit down and *think* about it, I would've told him, mm . . . late forties. I don't actually know if that would have been credible, or not – and I don't, in honesty, very much care. You look at your face so terribly often, you just don't see it any more. Now wait – what was my thread? Age . . . late forties . . . fifty-two . . . oh yes, I have it, yes yes: when you're a woman of fifty-five, you see, you're just not – unless you're one of these film star Joan Collins types with all their treatments and beauticians and *operations*, these days, of course – you're just not going to have the *elasticity* of someone even ten years younger. And that, I suppose, is what Geraldine has over me – simply having been on this earth for a single decade less than I have. Plus, of course, not having to take care of mother. That, believe me, can age you a hundred years in just the space of a morning, if it's one of those days when she's decided to be difficult – increasingly frequent, I have to say (in fact I can't remember the last time *not*).

'Here, mother – take these.'

Isobel's mother squinted severely at the cluster of pills on her daughter's outstretched palm. Her nose twitched, as if she had just detected the first tang of some pungent odour arising – one that all the conspirators in the latest attempted treachery had clearly believed to be bland and untraceable, but they weren't so very clever after all, were they? I may be old, but I'm not stupid – a little detail this band of assassins could do well to remember.

'What're *those*? More poison. I've had them.'

'No, mother, no – not this morning, you haven't. That was yesterday, wasn't it?'

'Last night – '

'Last night you had the *other* ones, didn't you – hey? The little yellow ones and the multicoloured capsule.

181

Remember? With your Ovaltine. These are the *morning* ones, aren't they?'

Isobel's mother reached forward with extreme reluctance, two arthritic fingers hovering over the selection – maybe as if spoilt for choice, or else in a bid to divine just which one conceals its deadly cyanide cargo. She settled on a pair of chalky blue ones, each of which she gingerly placed at the tip of her tongue.

'Poison . . .' she still managed to say, without expelling either of them.

'*Silly*, mother – here, here's your water. Not too much. And try not to spill. I'll write down all these tablets on a rota. This afternoon – here, mother, now the big white one: I've chopped it up. This afternoon I'm going down to Tesco's and I'll lay in stacks of all your favourites, OK? So you won't be short of anything you like. And I'll get you some more talking books from the library, yes? Still into Ruth Rendell? Still like her, do you?'

Isobel's mother's whole face contorted as she slurped up water and with huge show and plenty of neck action knocked back the bits of broken-down white pill (don't ask Isobel what it's actually *for*, this white one – she'd lost track of all their intentions years ago, and new ones kept on being prescribed: most of them were meant to counter the swingeing side-effects of the ones before, so far as she could tell). And I shouldn't really think it – she is my *mother*, after all – but when she screws up her face like that: winds tight her eyes and sort of brings up just one side of her mouth and retracts her mottled neck to show up all those dark and livid corrugations – she terribly reminds me of a lizard. Will I too end up looking like a reptile, one day? I hope, at least, no one will be there to see it, if I do; which seems very likely.

'And Morse,' grunted Isobel's mother.

'Morse, yes. I actually think you've had all the Morses . . .' started up Isobel, before closing down. Of *course* she's had all the Morses – and all the Rendells, Christies and P.D., what is it – James, as well (and God, they're long, those). It's only all these deaths that keep her going. 'But maybe there's a new one. Now – will you be OK till I get back?' Rush on, thought Isobel – rush on: don't give her time. 'I phoned Geraldine. Tell you? Yes, I've phoned Geraldine – spoken to her – and everything's arranged. Can't *wait* to see you, mother. It's been ages, hasn't it? You'll have such *fun* together.'

Fun or not, together is what they're going to be, anyway, whether they damn well like it or not. I must, thought Isobel (and the doctor kept on saying this to me, in that gentle way he had) – I must, just must think of *me*, for a change. I had to keep on reminding myself to try to do that little thing all through Geraldine's awfulness – I nearly caved in, oh – so many times. I so very nearly just said Yes, yes – OK I give up: you *win*, both of you. I'll stay here walled up with mother – and you stay home all cosy with Keith and your three horrible brats and then everyone's happy. Everyone, of course, except *me*: I'll just go into a decline, and then what? Who's going to look after mother *then*, I'd like to know. (But more than that – why doesn't either of them care about what happens to me? It is my mother and my sister I am talking about here, you know: I've no one else – have I?)

'So what you mean to say is,' was Geraldine's first and breathy, near-incredulous and certainly highly indignant broadside, when Isobel had more or less wound up the gist of what, she was very much afraid, just had to happen. 'What you're actually saying to me, Isobel, is that you're just simply taking off? Just like that. Is that what you're saying?'

'Yes . . .' said Isobel, quietly. 'I explained.'

'Oh yes may-*be*. But I'm afraid it's just not really good enough, is it? I mean – you phone me out of the blue, and you seriously expect me to drop just everything and rush over to attend to mother just because you've suddenly decided to *go* somewhere?'

'I didn't . . . suddenly decide. I didn't *know* this was going to happen, did I? I just feel so . . . the doctor said – '

'Well doctors *do* that, don't they? Go away for a while – they're forever saying that. God – if *I* went off for a holiday every time some doctor told me to I'd never be *home*.'

'It's not a *holiday*, Geraldine – try to understand. I *need* this.'

'Oh I see. You need it. Yes I see. And I suppose I need to leave my family, do I? Just tell Keith – *so* sorry, Keith, but there won't be any food on the table for as long as Isobel decides – and oh yes, you'll be in sole charge of the children, all right? His position carries enormous *responsibility*, Isobel – I don't think you quite realize – '

'It won't be for long.'

'But how *can* I? Isobel? It's all right for you – you can just up sticks and shoot off whenever you want to. I've got *duties*, here: I'm a *wife*. I'm a *mother*.'

'I know. I know. But it's our *own* mother we're talking about here. God, Geraldine – I haven't been anywhere for *years*. And you didn't even come over when it was her *birthday*.'

'I sent crystallized fruits.'

'I know, but – '

'Which are not cheap. Anyway . . . when are you planning to go?'

'Tomorrow.'

'*Tomorrow*! Oh God *no*, Isobel – you really have to be joking. I can't just – ! *Tomorrow*?! Oh no – forget it, that's out. Completely out. Can't you *wait* a bit, for God's sake?'

'Well that's the whole point. The doctor says – '

'Oh God the bloody *doctor*. Doctor says this, doctor says that – we aren't *children* any more, Isobel – are we?'

'Maybe not. But we still have a mother.'

'Well I just think it's terribly *unfair* of you, that's all. I'll come – I'm not saying I won't come. Don't want you putting it around that Geraldine's shirking her duty – but I really do think you're being dreadfully inconsiderate. It's not *me* I'm thinking of – it's the family. I'm a *wife*. I'm a *mother*.'

'I know. I know. Tomorrow, then. It doesn't have to be early, or anything.'

'Grateful for small mercies. And have you any idea just how long this little jaunt of yours is actually going to take?'

'I . . . no, I don't know. I hope not long.'

'Don't we all. God, Isobel – you really are, aren't you? You really are the absolute *end*.'

Well, thought Isobel – quite late that night, when her mother, though profoundly disgruntled, was as settled as ever she would be – I don't quite know about that, but certainly during the last few days I've felt I might be fast approaching an end of sorts. I just can't tell you how I felt, in the aftermath of that . . . gunman, I think of him. And the sheer sick awfulness of George Carey (quite a dark horse) just hurling himself at the man like that: that stench and grapple of violence – I just felt so very deeply *ill* (couldn't even *look* at the papers afterwards). I knew I had to get away, was pulled by the need: people were terribly nice – but even before I had stepped into the car, the void in my stomach had plummeted lower at the very first cold vision of what it was – all I had – to come home to. But tonight, I have approached excitement. The barely tamed fury of Geraldine, mother's unrelenting and bitter resentment – neither of these has remotely quelled it. This time tomorrow, they two will be here – they will be coping, somehow – and I shall be on my own somewhere else entirely (don't even know quite where). And my bed will have been made up by some hand other than mine; my meals will be smilingly served to me – and after, briskly cleared away. I will walk. I will rest. I will walk. I will rest. I will be all alone, with just myself.

Tonight I have approached excitement.

*

Reg was bending down and slipping on with care those panelled light greyish sort of moccasin-type lace-up maybe I suppose could be loafer kind of things he'd sent off for, one time. Lovely flexible soles, they've got (bend 'em in half: go on – *challenge* you: bend 'em in half, and they'll just spring right back into shape, just like it said on the ad). My Laverne – she was still at home, them days (hadn't yet got round to taking up live-in fornication in place of a future) – she goes But Christ, Dad, who in their right minds wants to go round bending their bloody shoes in half? It don't never occur to *me*, tell ya. I don't know why you even bought them in the first place, she goes on – they look like nutter shoes, to my eyes. What you talking about, girl – *nutter* shoes: what the bleeding hell is that supposed to mean, ay? You just make it up, you do – I don't know where you bloody get the half of it from. *Nutter* shoes, she comes back (helluva tongue on her – always has had, telling you): *You* know – you see them in the park, and that: nutters what they let out of a day-care centre for the afternoon in somebody else's trousers and a striped pyjama jacket and shoes like bloody *yours*, Dad! Oh *chuck* it, Laverne, I chuck at her – just button it, OK? You don't know what you're bloody *talking* about. Highly serviceable, these shoes are: great for the cab. But she won't leave it, will she? Like a bloody prize-fighter, my Laverne – or one of them dogs, what are they? Them that once they get their fangs well sunk into something, they just ain't about to let go, come hell or high wossname. Terriers, could well be, but I'm not swearing. Anyway: *yeah*, she goes, they're *great* – great if you're a *nutter*! Be honest – it's not your brilliant repartee, is it? Not what they call ... what do they say? Cutting ledge, is it? Not going to get her on to *Question Time*, I don't hardly think – and yet she really thinks she's it, does Laverne. Tell you – before she moved out, I used to wish she'd take a leaf out of her mother's book: yeah – why don't you just become one of the walking dead, like bleedin' Enid?

I wonder if I should go with a tie? Bit formal, is it, these days? Well yeah, reckon so – only going down the shops, aren't I? It's hard to know, now – and of course the young, well: different ideas altogether (you just got to look at Laverne: Pauly, thank Christ, still seems to have a head on his shoulders). No – tell you what I'll do: I'll chuck on that knitted short-sleeve job – polo shirts they call them now, which is pretty bleeding odd in itself: my day, your polo was one of them high-collar roll-neck pullovers (mints with the hole, we used to say) and these, these sorts of things were called Fred Perrys, though Christ alone knows who he was, when he was at home.

'You still here?'

Sour, isn't it? I don't know if you, like I did, caught in the face the smack of that, but it's turned real sour, Enid's way of speaking, all down the years – and more so lately, seems to me.

'Just off. Get you a cuppa tea before I go, love?'

'Get my own tea, can't I? You getting Boasters?'

'Am I getting *what*, love? What the bleeding hell are them?'

'You bloody get down enough of them, Reg. Them biscuits with the bits of chocolate and raisins in.'

'Oh *them's* Boasters, are they? Yeh – I like them. Like them a lot. I thought they were McVitie's.'

'McVitie's is digestives.'

'Yeah – granted – but they must do other things. Course they do – big firm like that.'

'And bog-roll. We're near out of bog-roll. And don't get the blue one – gives me headache.'

'Anything else? I got down here tea, beans, chipolatas, some of your ointment and satsumas. Ooh – and I think we could do with a few more Cheese Footballs: pretty low when I last had some.'

'Cost a fortune, them. You know, Reg – I think they *are* McVitie's . . .'

'What – Cheese Footballs? Could well be, love.'

'*No*. No! Not Cheese bloody *Foot*balls – them other things: *Boasters*. Cheese bloody *Foot*balls . . .'

'Oh right. Got you.'

'Although thinking about it, they might well be too. Or Jacob's.'

'They do a nice cream cracker, Jacob's. Always been partial.'

'I wouldn't minding owning them, anyway. Must be coining it in, mustn't they, Reg?'

'Who – Jacob's? Yeh – spose so.'

'*And* McVitie's. Must be bloody coining it in.'

'I shouldn't at all wonder, love. So – that it, then, yeah? Nothing else? You all right for Milk of Magnesia?'

'Don't bloody work, do it? I reckon they changed the formula. Old days, spoon of Milk of Magnesia'd settle you right off for the night. Now – you knock back a bloody gallon of the stuff and you still feel cut in half and not a dicky bird. Pepto Bismol, you'd maybe best get.'

'What's that? Fizzy drink? Didn't think you went for fizzy drinks, Enid. Thought you said they went for your ears.'

'Fizzy bloody *drink* – it's a stomach thing, ain't it? Colour of window-cleaner.'

'Don't much fancy the sound of it. How you spell it?'

'I don't know how you bloody *spell* it. It'll say on the sodding *label*, won't it? And Honey Nut Loops.'

'What happened to your Bran Flakes?'

'Don't talk to me about *Bran* Flakes. Bloody hell – I know I needed a right clearing out, but I didn't want bloody *gutting*, did I? Huntley & Palmer's: that's the other biscuit people – must be coining it in, all of them. Well God's sake *go*, then, if you're going, Reg. Shops'll be shut, time you get there. You doing it local?'

'Local, yeh local.'

'Tesco's got an offer this week on tropical fruit juice, reading somewhere: buy three and they give you two – something like that. No, hang about – that can't be right . . .'

'I'll have a look. Right, then – I'm off.'

Yeh, thought Reg, as he slammed that great door shut (the door now stood between him and Enid) – I'm off, all right, but I ain't about to get myself down Tesco's, am I? I'm checking out Sainsbury's: see what they got.

*

And in next to no time (I drove too fast, I know I did, and no matter how eager – my game, I just can't risk it) Reg was standing by his trolley and confronting with his customary awe the mirrored mountains of Sainsbury's fruit (and veg). Two string bags of satsumas, I got – Enid sucks on them like a bleeding vampire – and a nice big bunch of bit-green bananas, which'll do me very nicely. And no – *course* I'm not giving my mind to the business of sticking all this stuff in the sodding trolley – it's checkout time, innit? That's what's making my heart pump up and down like . . . whatever things do that, pump up and down – can't think of a bleeding one, not just now: maybe it's just down to hearts – could be they're the only pumpers we got. Yes I *do* know she's here for definite, I ain't that green, not a bit – I ain't a banana. (First thing I clocked: this branch – don't know if yours is similar, at all – they got a big glass frontage right on the street, so all the girls working the checkouts, well: first thing you clap eyes on. Plus – I saw her here, didn't I, same time last week, so I'm figuring to myself, well – regular shifts, more than not as likely.)

Honey Nut Loops. Me, I'm more of a Shredded Wheat man, myself – and I don't turn my nose up at bitesize Fruitfuls, neither: slice a nice banana on that lot, top of the milk – telling you: fit for a king. When I was a lad – and Pauly, he was just the same, little scamp – I'd drive my mum mad with getting on at her the whole time to buy whatever cereal had the best toy inside. There was submarines, one time: you put baking powder in, far as I can recall, and they'd go up and down in the bath. We ain't *got* no baking powder, my mum goes – and I come back with (cheeky sod) Well *get* some, then. And she did, too. Do anything for me, my mum – what a lady. Still miss the old girl, if I'm honest – she really did right by me, Mum did: wouldn't half mind getting her back in place of bleedin' Enid, but there you go: God works in mysterious wotsits, don't He? Not for us to say What You Playing At, Son? (They didn't, you know, *really* go up and down at all, them submarines – they just hit the bloody bottom of the bath and stayed there, didn't they – which left Mum with about half a ton of baking powder, and just that look she give me all over her face, won't never forget it.)

See, what I got to do is *time* it right: don't want to feel rushed or nothing, do I? Plus, I don't want no one else hanging about, neither. Tell you – ain't felt this nervous since . . . well, can't even remember the last time I tried on anything at all in this line (married man, aren't I?). I hope to God I'm not let down: I don't think I could take all that – not after feeling good, the way I do now.

Ain't heard no more. You know – about the looney with all the bags of money. There was just one little bit in the latest local: he got sent down, the bloke, can't remember how long – and some shrink was gonna take a butcher's. But what I mean is, there ain't been no more about no money missing, or nothing; I ain't had the Old Bill knocking on my door, is what I'm saying, so I reckon I'm well in the clear. And tell me this: what's the point of a windfall, hey? If I don't buy me a bit of pleasure my time of life, well what then? Double glazing? Conservatory? Bloody cruise with bleedin' Enid? I don't hardly think so. Nah – what I want is here and now, so what I'm going to do is, sort of just hover a bit – wait till her lane is more or less empty – and then I'm going to have to get this thing done. Grab the Pepto Wossname, yeah – maybe a nice bit of Cheddar – and then just slide over the whole shebang to my Adeline (you notice – Gawd, ain't the mind funny? – how already she's *mine*, this girl) and with it, all my hopes for any future I got.

Blimey: sod the Cheddar – time has come, mate. Just looking around her, she is, seems like she's welcoming a bit of a breather: ain't no one round her at all. Reckon I better nip in sharpish, then – else some biddy'll be down that aisle with half the bloody supermarket in her trolley – or maybe my Adeline might take it into her head to get herself off for a tea break, or something.

Reg could not account for how he now came to be so close to this girl – she was just across the counter from him, and he was so aware of this as he watched with a red intensity his selection of goods trundle on rubber and into her hand.

'Hello again!'

Yep, that must have been me, thought Reg, what just said that. She looks a bit startled, does she? Kind of smile maybe coming through, though?

'Yeh,' she said. 'Thought you'd been in before.'

'Come in most weeks. You always here of a Tuesday?'

'Yeh – Tuesdays, Wednesdays, Thursdays. Like more, but it's a bit quiet at the moment. Ooh,' she tacked on, hefting the Pepto Bismol. 'You not well? I get that tummy thing sometimes. Awful, innit?'

'No – I'm fine. It's for – it's for someone else. Look, um – Adeline . . . call you Adeline?'

'Few want.'

And her face now bore the first traces of What's-all-this-then? Yes, thought Reg – she's been here before, hasn't she? Course she has: looking the way she does, she'd be bound to. Which is why I got my secret weapon – and now might well be the time to launch it.

'I've, er – sounds daft, I know, and I hope you won't think I'm, er – well, I hope you won't think badly of me, or nothing, but I brought you a present, sort of thing. Little offering.'

'That's sixteen pound ninety-seven. Sorry – you what? Didn't catch. You done what?'

Reg put down some cash to cover the bill, and while she was attending to that (look at her neck – that young white neck, when she turns it away!) he slid across a small black box. Adeline was handing him change – her little finger just fleetingly grazing his palm – and pretended quite hard to have just caught sight of her present for the very first time.

'What's all this, then?'

Her eyes were glinting with what? Intrigue – half amusement? Or was it just anger and affront, raw and simple?

'Just a – just a little something. From an admirer, you could say.'

Oh Christ Jesus – what's she thinking? What's going on in that head of hers? She's glancing about her – almost silently calling for help, is she maybe? And oh shit *look* – bloody fat woman's waddling down the aisle, now – basket jammed full of dog food and Pampers (the lives some people do lead).

'Open it,' urged Reg. 'Or later, if you like.'

'What is it?' asked Adeline – wide-eyed and fingering the thing.

Reg glanced frenziedly at the fat woman unloading her cargo of big and vitamin-enriched meaty chunks along with all the soft and absorbent – and back again to Adeline, who held his gaze as she reached out beside her to swipe through the first of the cans.

'Well,' was all Reg could think to respond. '*Open* it.' And then – taking in a good part of the altered situation: 'Or later, if you like. Look, um – you must be knocking off quite soon, yeh? How about you come and have a drink, or something, and you can open it then. Yeh? You know the Grapes? Round the corner?'

'I know it.'

'Well – how about that, then? Hey? I won't bite! Say, what – half an hour? Half an hour suit you?'

The fat woman now said: 'Am I *interrupting* something?'

Yes, thought Reg, with rising bitterness and a touch of panic.

'No!' he laughingly assured her. 'No, um – no. *Well*? What about it? Yes? Half an hour OK?'

'That tube of toothpaste,' said the fat woman, 'isn't mine.'

Adeline picked up the box of Colgate and looked up sunnily at Reg: he nearly fell over in the dazzle of it.

'Yours?' she enquired – more sweetly, it sounded to Reg, than she maybe might have done in the normal course of events, could be?

Reg shook his head. 'So. Will you?'

'That'll be twelve pound twenty,' she said to the woman. 'OK, then. Half-hour. Grapes.'

Reg fast took in a lungful of breath – he felt so caught by the rush, he bloody well nearly forgot to let it all out again.

'*Really*? Oh great – that's great. See you there, then. Great.'

And Reg swung away with his carrier bags – couldn't even begin to tell you the half of what he was feeling, but he could say *this* much: it was a whole pile better than whatever it was what usually stuffed and bloated him and brought him down low. Adeline just watched him go, and then turned to check the fat woman's signature against that on her card. Silly old sod, is what she was thinking: makes me laugh. Not too sure about them shoes, though (what will I do if he turns out to be a nutter?).

Even Shirley, thought George excitedly – simply can't wait, now, to get back home and tell her (the kids, I know, will be over the moon) – even Shirley, surely, has got to say she's proud of me for this one: I've only been asked, haven't I, to appear live this afternoon on London Live! I know: *great*, isn't it? Actually live – me, on radio (goes out all over London, that station, you know). They're putting some programme together on crime in the capital, the man was saying, and how ordinary everyday people, when they, you know, have a run-in, how they cope with it. Well, it's fairly safe to say that it's no secret at all that I acquitted myself with something approaching honours, I rather think – and even now I can't really answer the question everyone is asking of me – exactly *why* I behaved in the way I did. I mean – man had a *gun*, God's sake; and we didn't know yet, did we, that it wasn't the real McCoy, not at that stage of the game we didn't. And even those air-guns, you know – do you a terrible injury, close quarters: don't know why they're not banned, quite frankly. This government, it often seems to me, has got its priorities all round its neck. Never mind debates on *cannabis* (which actually *is* banned, but God – you wouldn't know it, would you? You've just got to look at the news); never mind lowering the age of, oh Christ yuk, homosexual *consent* (all that lot should just be put up against a wall and boom boom: *finish*. Why should our kids live in danger, under the shadow of perverts? You listen to all these politicians sounding off about this, that and the other, but you never really get out of them a straightforward *answer*, do you?). And they want to forget about rubbish like fox-hunting, too. What the hell does it matter – who on earth cares? – if those braying Henrys want to dress up so stupidly and run off after some bloody fox or not? It just couldn't matter less, could it? No – what we want to come down hard on is crime in our streets: guns and violence and muggers – robbing old ladies and frightening half to death perfectly decent people like Isobel March (practically a basket case, is what I'm hearing; they asked her to be on the programme too, but she wouldn't even hear of it, apparently). Well, I respect her decision, of course I do, but if we all went round burying our heads in the sand then all these issues are just never going to come to light, are they? People have to know the truth about what goes *on* out there – and that's why I'm more than prepared to stand up and be counted: and we should *all* be ready to do our bit, is what I'm saying – Hero of the Hour, or no.

'Excellent. So we'll expect you in the studio around three-fifteen, then. Would you like us to send a car for you, Mister Carkey?'

'A car would be – it's actually *Carey*, my name, by the way, I should say. That's Carey as C - A - R - E - Y. Carey.'

'Oh I'm terribly sorry, Mister um – it says here – '

'I know. I know it does. But it's not my name. Believe me. Carey.'

'Carey. Right. Well I'll just make sure that's amended, then, Mister um.'

Yes, thought George: I'll believe that when I see it. Some of these pen-pushers, you know – amazing they can spell their *own* name, never mind anyone else's. Now take me – I hold a clerical position of not a little authority, and I well understand (this is why my superiors pay me) that in an organization such as ours, an incorrect surname can rapidly translate itself into potential disaster. Which is why I make damn sure that on *my* little patch, anyway, no such thing could ever occur. I hardly think this goes unrecognized. A branch managership has long been my dream – and although at just thirty-three I would certainly be one of the company's very youngest, I feel that it shouldn't, now, be very long in coming (and I'm not saying that my currently considerably raised profile will not be of some advantage, in this respect).

'So you'll listen, then – yes, Shirley? And tape it for the kids, for when they get in. The actual programme's going out at – '

'What's the *thing* for that? What station did you say it was? What's the thing, what is it – frequency?'

'Hm? Well – *I* don't know. It'll be in the papers, won't it? TV and radio guide.'

'I think we threw that bit out. Was that the one with David Attenborough on the front? I think I got rid of that.'

'Well . . . *phone* them, then, and ask them. Oh God, look: car's here now – I've got to – *phone* them, will you then, Shirley? Just phone them and ask them – and don't forget to tape it for the – '

'What's their number?'

'Look – I've got to – Christ, *I* don't know what their bloody number is, do I? Look it up in the – oh God, look it up in the bloody *directory*, can't you? I've got to – or ring up directory thing and ask *them*. Three-thirty, it goes out. Got that? Three-thirty, London Live. I've got to go now, Shirley. Wish me luck.'

'I was going to go to the hairdresser's. Appointment.'

'Well – well *cancel* it, then. You've got to *be* here to tape it for the – *Jesus*, Shirley, it's not every day your husband is talking live on the radio, is it? I've never ever *done* it before, and – oh God he's *honking*, now – I've really got to – so you *will*, then, Shirley, yes? Find out about it and get it recorded. Yes? Oh God *answer*, can't you? Speak! I've got to *go*.'

'I . . . suppose.'

'*Thank* you,' gasped George, as he more or less fell out of the house, and ran away waving to the car.

Oh yes – *thank* you, thank you oh so very bloody *much*, dear wife of mine – thank you for actually making the time to listen to me, the Hero of the Hour, live on the radio, and helping preserve that unique moment in our lives for the children, to keep and enjoy – and thank you too for actually bringing yourself to cancel the bloody *hairdresser's* in order to do it. I don't in point of fact really know why, thought George now – strapping himself into the back seat of the car, all his nerve-ends alive and chock-full of This-is-itness – she even bothers going there anyway: hair always looks the bloody *same*, to me – whichever way they tweak it.

*

It was utterly true, you know, what Isobel had said to her sister on the phone, that time: 'God, Geraldine,' she had feebly protested (suddenly felt so weary), 'I haven't been anywhere for *years*.' Had she really understood that Isobel had been talking quite *literally*? Isobel very much doubted it. Geraldine and her Keith and the three beastly boys – they seemed forever to be taking off for somewhere or other, or else they'd just got back (if neither of those, then planning the next one). A lot of it, Geraldine would urgently confide (quite as if Isobel *cared*, or something), was for Keith's *work*, you must understand – this job of his thus clearly and once again identified as being the hub and pivot – the very epi-centre of the Universe, around which it falls to the rest of us to modestly revolve as best we may. Though why Keith's work (and no, please don't even bother asking Isobel what exactly it is that Keith actually does – lucrative, clearly – because she had never in all frankness listened to any of Geraldine's frequent expositions with sufficient attention to form a firm conclusion: 'It's all a bit *complicated*,' was a phrase that tended to crop up a fair deal, and Isobel for one was more than pleased to leave all unravelling well alone). But as I say, why Keith's work should mean they're forever on holiday . . .

But for me – just being in the back of this car, right this second – on my own and *going* somewhere, oh I just can't *tell* you what a treat that is. My one small suitcase safely stowed in the boot, the quite new holdall close by my side – and I knew I wouldn't so much as touch those sandwiches, still a bag of nerves (don't know why I even troubled to do them) – and there in the front seat (he's got such broad shoulders) a strong and competent professional driver, paid by someone else to know exactly where he's going and silently and swiftly *take* me there. Oh God, what bliss. I do, if I'm perfectly honest, feel an awful lot better than I have been since right after the – you know, *incident* – but I realize now more than anything how terribly *tired* I am. You don't notice it, I think, when it's a habitual thing. It's just how you feel – physically as well as within – for just every waking hour, so you simply knuckle down and get on with it. You're running down fast, and you don't even know it. So even if nothing else comes out of all this, I'm thinking (oh look – we just slowed down there, and turned . . . I think – they were a bit high to see, but I think there were some big brick piers and gates, there – balls on top . . . yes, looking out of the back window, now, I can see I was right – I really do think this might be it, then – I think we're actually here; I would ask the man, the driver, but I'd feel a bit silly).

Now what was I saying (better be quick, if I want to finish this thought) . . .? Oh yes – even if I get nothing else out of all their specialists and regimes and goodness knows what, then at least I should be able to *sleep*, surely – sleep without the shadow of *worry*, all the time. At least, oh God, I very much hope so, anyway. Because throughout this car journey (and it's only been not much more than an hour, you know – practically no traffic at all, getting out of London) I have, if I'm honest, been going over and over it all in my head: did Geraldine really take it in, when I told and told her all about mother's routines? Will she remember to turn off the immersion? She won't, oh dear – lose her *temper* with mother, will she? I know that mother can be intensely wearing (yes, I think I can say I know that) and Geraldine always did have a short fuse at the best of times, but really, you know, you just have to remember that she's *old* – old is all she is (it comes to every one of us) and not really at all *well*. And what about the cats? Will she remember to put the three bowls down as *well* as the water? And oh God – that funny knob on the cooker – oh damn oh dear – I didn't explain to Geraldine about the business with the *oven*, did I? You see, if you don't half-turn and *then* press it in, it won't connect properly, and then right in the middle of whatever you're doing, it can just cut out. I would ring and tell her, but phoning home is one of the major things I absolutely mustn't do, according to Doctor English – and yes, I can see his point, I suppose: one has to, I imagine, try and put it all behind one, yes? Else what's the point of being here?

And we *are* here, now – oh goodness. The car tyres have crunched on gravel as if they were munching it all up – God, the building's absolutely huge, I didn't think it would be – and really rather grand (columns up the front, look) – and someone's already coming out of the door, all dressed in white. Quite a red carpet welcome – and all for Isobel March! I feel rather scared, which I expect is quite daft of me. It's funny: I was so pleased to get away from the house, mother, the cats, work – and yet right this second I would just love to be back there with all of them, instead of being alone and on the verge of somewhere different, somewhere new. I dare say this will pass.

*

What I said to my Laverne, one time – I said (she were still at school at the time, still some hope left) – I says to her, *Laverne*, I says – take a tip from your old man: get yourself an appointment with the *careers* bloke, yeh? You got one of them, your school? They all have them, pretty sure – did in my day, anyway. Course – those days, all they wanted you to do was metalwork or join the bloody Army – and as for the girls, well: typing and get yourself hitched and drop a sprog pronto was about the sum total. But there's all sorts open, these days, Laverne – so this is what you do, right? You listening? And no – it's no good, is it, pulling your *faces* – just bloody *listen*, can't you? You only got the one chance, ain't you? Hey? It's only your whole *future* we're talking about, innit? Now listen, you have a little talk with this geezer – might even be a woman, these days, there's no way of telling – and really *talk* to them, right? Tell them all the stuff what really interests you, there must be something, and then gather up any bumf they got lying around and get hold of useful addresses and write off and see what they all got to say for theirselves and then lay it all out on the floor, like – yeh? And what you do then is, you weigh up the pros and cons – whittle it down, sort of style, and then you can home in on what's really right for *you*. See? Well? What you think? You know it makes sense. Well speak up, girl – no good just *staring*, is it? Course – I'm not saying you have to get all of this done right *now* – not right this minute, you don't. Yeah: said all that to her – done my level best, didn't I? What more I could've done? And do you know all she comes back with? All she got to say to me? *Dad*, she goes – and the look on her face, you wouldn't hardly believe it: like I'm a bloody underarm *stain*, or something (a bugger to get out). *Dad*, she goes – shaking her head: I ain't gonna do it *never*.

And she never, true enough. Nice, or what? Your own daughter. What she done is, she got out as quick as she could and takes some crap job in a shop. So why then, Reg now asked himself honestly – why if that churns me up so bloody much (they do a nice pint in here, I'm not saying – do without the music) am I sat in the Grapes of an early evening waiting for and praying she bloody turns up (cos she's ten minutes wrong already, don't I bloody know it), a very young girl who on the face of it's gone and done exactly the bloody same thing? Hey? And if we're looking at it, there's this, and all: with Adeline, it ain't her *welfare* what's at the forefront of my wossname, is it? Mind. Oh Gawd – this *way* I'm thinking: can't go on, can it? Maybe I forget the whole bloody thing, ay? Get out while I can, out of harm's way. How about it? Just put the rest of this pint down me gullet and scarper back home to bleedin' Enid (bung her the Pepto Bismol)?

'Hi!' sang out Adeline – face as fresh as flowers. 'Bit late. They kept us. Ooh – I love this record!' she suddenly squealed – and her lips set into a kiss as they pouted out the beat of what very much seemed to Reg to be the bloody same awful noise that had been belting out since he bloody sat down. 'Now look, Mister – I don't even know your name, do I? We got to talk.'

Blimey, thought Reg: she's a bit previous. The way they are now, is it?

'It's Reg. What can I get you?'

'Oh thanks, yeh. Voggatonic – be nice.'

'Good as done,' grinned Reg – squirming off the banquette and making for the bar, waving a tenner as casual as you like. I don't even know, he was nervously thinking, if I'm even enjoying this or I ain't. Still – early days (wanna tread careful, though, do I? Don't even know that, no more). What do you have to do to get served round here? Die, and start smelling up the place? Sleeves on these Fred Perrys, tell you – keep on creeping up your arms.

'Haven't been in here for ages,' was what Adeline had to say, when Reg placed in front of her a very large (triple) Smirnoff and tonic (not into Slimline, are they? Not at that age, they're not). He sat before her and took a modest pull at just the half for him, this time (got the cab outside, haven't I? Even this much is pushing it). 'Used to, all the time. Then we sort of, I don't know – drifted on. Like you do.'

Reg nodded. 'We'. Her young set, no doubt. Boys and girls. God Almighty – what is it I imagine I'm *doing* here? What is it I think I'm *about*?

'Now look, Reg – something we got to get straight from the off, right? I don't know you or nothing, do I? So I'm a bit . . . well . . .' And in place of more words, she slipped out of her shoulder bag the little black box, and slid it on to the table. 'Now look – don't get me wrong, or nothing – I love it, I really do – it's the loveliest thing anyone ever give me, but . . . well I *can't*, can I? Just take it? Not, sort of, knowing you or nothing? Why me, anyway?'

But already she had the Gucci watch out of its box, and following a brief bout of twiddling with it, firmly strapped on to her wrist.

'Looks great,' approved Reg. 'Perfect on you. *Course* you must take it. It's for you, ain't it? *Bought* it for you.'

Adeline with reluctance tore her eyes away from its black and gold face. 'Yeh but *why*, Reg? You don't even know who I am.'

Reg put his hand on the table. Wanted to cover all of hers with his, but stopped a good six inches of even close.

'But I'd like to,' he said. An unfamiliar flush spread across his neck.

Adeline blinked, and then briefly chewed her lower lip. Take off the touch of eyeliner – rub away that smirch of lip-gloss and she's back in the queue for school dinners: a child is all she is. The chubbiness of her face was exercised, now – a glint of perplexity was dancing across it (here was another of life's situations that she had maybe only seen in a movie, one time) – but zips of arrogance too were darting in and around: I *can't*, can I, *possibly* accept this? And now two fingers were soothing the bright blue lizard strap and clicking on and off the buckle: this thought was actively slugging it out with God I want it so *badly*. And want, as it will, was tilting the balance.

'You got great taste,' smiled Adeline – now busy subjecting every inch of the watch to little short of a full body massage: it would seem to have become another part of her.

'Yeh well . . .' was Reg's brushing away of any of that. It

was down to Laverne, wasn't it? How long it take? Getting out of her what it was in Christ's name a young woman fancies, these days? You know – something a bit out of the ordinary run, is what I'm saying: bit special, like. What you wanna know for? That's all he got. Never mind that – never mind what I wanna *know* for – just bloody *tell* me, can't you? What you doing, Dad? What's your game, ay? Seducing little girls – that what you up to? Don't be so bloody *stupid*, Laverne – where you learn to talk like that? I'm your *father*, aren't I, so show a bit of bloody respect, first time in your life.

Well – I'm right up to my eyes in it now, aren't I? So all I could do was say it was Laverne *herself* I was fishing for, here – not too long till your birthday, is it, my precious? Oooooh you sly old bugger, she comes back with: *well*, if you're really feeling flush, I wouldn't say no to one of them really smart little Gucci watches, she says – they got them in Selfridges. About four hundred quid, but really class – you know? There's this bright blue lizard strap they do – I really could go for that big time. Yeh? went Reg. Yeh? (writing it all down as quick as he could: tell you, foreign language, all this – another bleeding country). Anyway – got the bloody thing, didn't I? And yeh – had to spring for a pair, course I did, else Laverne won't never let me forget it, will she? You know what she's like. So already I'm eight hundred and a couple of triple vodkas well down the line, and unless I start up the chat a bit quick, like, I ain't going to walk away with a bleeding thing to show for it (and I tell you one thing about money, son – no matter which way you come into it, once you start spending, it don't half go, you know: like bleeding water, I ain't kidding).

'You don't have to, like . . .' cranked up Reg. 'It's not like you have to *commit* yourself to nothing, or nothing. I don't expect nothing like that. I just thought, well – what I was thinking is maybe we could have, you know – bite to eat, sort of thing. Spot of dinner – dinner of an evening, I mean. Somewhere nice.'

'Yeah?' queried Adeline, idly. What's-all-this-then had stormed back in.

Reg nodded (how's this going? Christ alone knows). 'Yeh. Somewhere really nice. Up West. Push the boat out.'

'Yeh?' she now was laughing: 'What – you loaded, then, are you, Reg? What you do?'

'Well, I'm a cab-driver, is what I actually *do* – but I got a bit lucky lately – know what I mean? Come in for a bit of a tickle, didn't I? I've asked around a bit and they do a real nice carvery up the Cumberland, punter was telling me – you know it? Marble Arch, yeh? I was thinking Friday . . .'

'Got it all worked out, entcha Reg? I don't know about Friday, though . . . Friday's always a bit . . .'

'Yeh? Oh right. Well scrub round Friday, then.'

'I'm not saying I can't, maybe, you know – put something off. I'm not saying that.'

'*Right*,' agreed Reg eagerly, before puzzlement set in. 'So what is it you *are* saying, then, exactly, Adeline?'

'Oh God – look at the time! I gotta go. It's gonna be great, now – looking at the time. I really love this watch, Reg, it's really *large* – thanks ever so much. OK, then – let's say Friday. Cumberland – that it? I'll find it. Take a cab, yeh?! What time?'

'Well – suit yourself, basically. They have their dinners quite late in these places, I reckon. Say, what – six suit you?'

'Say six-thirty.'

'Six-thirty. Great. That's . . . just great, Adeline.'

She was standing, now, and Reg was well on his way to doing the same – but Adeline seemed to have stooped down, kissed his cheek lightly and skedaddled right out of the place before he even had time to get out a cheerio for the girl. Young people? Telling you.

So I'm feeling well chuffed, ain't I? Ten years younger don't even come into it. Floating, I was. So it was a bit of a bugger, what I heard on my way back. Had the radio on in the cab, like I do – wasn't really listening or nothing (my mind, well – had other fish to fry, if you take my meaning), but I prick up my wossnames, don't I, when this geezer comes on and starts sounding off about the bloody bank robber bloke, or whatever he done. Sounded a right stuffed ponce, this geezer – not old or nothing, just a prat – but it turns out he's the one what had a go – nearly got a hold of the maniac before he had it away on his toes. What he says is – I remember it so clear, and why bloody wouldn't I? – he says Contrary to what you might have read in all the papers there *was* a considerable shortfall in the money recovered (there are reasons, I gather, this hasn't been announced), and to have got to Earls Court from Westbourne Grove in so short a time, the man must either have had a getaway car waiting, or else got into a taxi. And if, in fact, he *did* use a taxi – the bastard goes – why has that driver signally failed to come forward?

I felt such a mixture, time I come home. I'm still sort of a bit dizzy from my time with Adeline (and also the ale, let's face it – shouldn't have touched none, not when I'm driving) and yet I'm well sick about this little lot, ain't I? (Quite literally, it turns out later: had myself a slug of Pepto Wossname.) I'll tell you, son, will I, why that driver has Signally Failed To Come Forward: on account of he got the Considerable Shortfall – and so far the time it's bought him is well on the way to being not just handsome, but really *large*.

*

When the car dropped him back, George was feeling – well, pretty on the whole not at all displeased with himself, is maybe not overstating the case. The driver had caught the major part of his thrust, he was telling him, and he for one was right behind George and everything he stood for. These bastards – this was what the driver had had to say, and what could George do but eagerly agree (the authentic voice of Middle England – too long silent: just ask anyone) – they're just lower than *scum*, aren't they? These muggers, and that: they want nailing to the bloody wall.

True, those people at London Live had seemed to have an awful lot more time for George when he had arrived than immediately after the broadcast, when he was more or less turned out into an anonymous corridor ('You'll find your own way out OK, yes?'). But look – they're busy people, aren't they? Got to keep their fingers on the pulse of this entire great capital city of ours: they deserve only our thanks, as well as a fair degree of, yes – respect (if anyone, these days, even remembers how *that* goes).

Waving away the driver, George paused just slightly before releasing the latch on his gate. His eyes slid over to the left and, registering nothing, swivelled all the way back round to the right. Anyone watching, at all? Someone, maybe, who had just happened to tune in – or maybe a habitual listener who wouldn't miss one of these regular bulletins for all the tea in China? Possibly they might have sat up with surprise and a certain pleasurable glow of recognition. Good heavens, they might have thought – I *know* that man, lives in my street: wasn't it him I read about in the local paper, just last week or so? But the whole road seemed to be even more deserted than usual: not so much as a curtain twitch – even from her across the way, which was saying something (in the normal course of events, all it takes is a visit from the postman and she's up there with her telescope). Still – they all would've heard it at work: pretty sure I told just about everyone about it, anyway.

And now I find I've paused too, in the hallway – not remotely sure quite what I might be hoping for this time around: kids won't be back from Shirley's mother's, not yet. And Shirley? Well – I didn't in all honesty expect a brass band or the strewing of rose petals (let's keep things in proportion, shall we?) but it would have been quite nice if she'd at least found it in herself to stir out of the big room and maybe just come out here and say hello. I mean, yes – such a thing would be decidedly uncharacteristic of her (oh yes – very much so) but this is hardly a typical day, now, is it?

She was sitting on the sofa – shoes off, legs tucked to the side of her, just as ever. What does she *do* all day? That's what I can't understand. Granted she works as some sort of, I'm never quite sure, PR, part-time – pretty good at it too, so far as I can make out. Money certainly comes in handy. And don't ask me why *part*-time: said she needed a break – time off to regain her bearings, she said – re-establish contact with who it was she sincerely needed to be. (This 'break', needless to say, has yet to end.) Yes well: nice for some, was my take on that. Be very useful, wouldn't it, if we all just packed in half our day's work because we happened to *feel* like it. How would it be – and I made no bones about putting it to her, this: got no *reaction*, or anything – how would it be if I came home one evening, Shirley, and said to you and the kids Well, everyone, that's it, I'm afraid – half-day working for me. The bills? Oh, I expect they'll attend to themselves, won't they? Food for the family? Oh, I'm quite sure Waitrose will give it to us for nothing. Clothes for the kids? Holidays? Oh – well maybe you could all learn to take up busking or *mugging*, or something, because I, George Carey, have decided this sunny afternoon to just lie back and try to trace my marbles or *bearings* or whatever rot you're spouting. Got to *find* myself, haven't I? Now let me see – where on earth could I have *put* me? Hmmm? Cupboard under the stairs, conceivably? Don't think so, no – or at least I wasn't in there last time a fuse needed mending, anyway: no, I'm sure not – otherwise I would have noticed me, wouldn't I? God's *sake*, Shirley: pull yourself *together*.

Shirley's comeback to that? A rueful grin of self-recognition, do we think? A sudden rush of realization as to just how much time and effort I thanklessly put into this household of ours? No – oh no. Nothing at all like that. Oh dear me, no. If I recall the incident accurately (and usually I may be relied upon in matters such as this) she simply looked me in the eye and said Christ, George: You Really Make Me Sick. No truly. Believe it or not, these were her very words: You Really Make Me Sick. I tell you no lie. And then she said she was going out. Out? I said. Out? What do you mean – *Out*? Where are you going? I haven't eaten, yet. No answer: she just went. And still to this day I have no idea where. Splendid, isn't it? And I'm the one who makes *her* sick! I sometimes am at a loss as to why or how I go on putting up with it, I don't mind telling you.

Well, thought George now – I might as well open the proceedings (it's quite *amazing*, isn't it? Just as if I'm not even here. Left to herself, she'd just go on, you know – sitting there and reading the latest in a seemingly endless succession of damned expensive glossy magazines. Well – I say *reading*, but what she actually does, quite infuriatingly, is open the things from the back and then just turn over pages at the rate of about one every three or four seconds: what sort of way is that to spend your whole life? This is the person, is it, that she sincerely needed to *be*? Oh dear oh dear).

'So,' said George – a smile breaking through despite himself, as he easily settled to reliving his minutes of glory. 'Did you, um – hear me OK? You caught it? I thought the interviewer, Steve – I thought he was really rather good, didn't you?' George was now loosening the knot in his tie, knowing that then it was time to remove his jacket and drape it somewhere. 'So – what, Shirley? This one of your days for not talking at *all*, is it?'

'Quite the reverse.'

George nodded. 'Quite the reverse. I see. Quite the reverse – right. So when is it you are actually planning to speak, then, Shirley? Do I have time to run a bath? Or is it more imminent? *Look* – just give me the tape of the pro-gramme, will you? I don't actually *care* if you liked it or not. Just give me the tape – I'd quite like to go over it. I'll play it later to the kids – you don't even have to be involved.'

'Why did he call you Carkey?'

George hissed out his frustration. 'Yes – that *would* be the one bit you actually latched on to, wouldn't it, Shirley? It was completely *maddening*, that, because I don't know if you noticed but for the first, I don't know – eight or ten minutes, or whatever it was, he was calling me, well – Mister Carey, he kicked off with, and then it was George. It was only towards the end he came in with this damned *Carkey* nonsense. I can't understand it.'

'Oh really?' sighed Shirley (God just *look* at her – it's almost as if she's just woken *up*, or something). 'That's the only bit I heard – didn't even realize it was you he was talking to. Your voice sounded so – '

'What do you mean? What do you mean – it's the only bit you *heard*? That was right at the *end*!'

'Sounded so . . . terribly drawled out and slow, I thought. Yes well – I couldn't find the *thing*, could I? I set it to what they said but there was some sort of opera or something on – I think I must have had the wrong wave thing, whatever they call them.'

'I see. So you missed it. And there's no tape, then – right?'

'Well obviously if it wasn't *on*, I couldn't record it, could I? Anyway, I don't think we've got any.'

'Oh *really*, Shirley – you really are the – ! And what do you *mean* we haven't got any? We got that multi-pack, didn't we, just last weekend at Argos. We've got *stacks* of the things. God, you know – I really think you do this sort of thing purposely.'

'George – sit down.'

'Oh what *for*? I've got to ring work – see what *they* thought.'

'Oh yes – your boss called, not long ago.'

'Really? Oh great. What did he have to say? Did he like it? What did he say?'

'Didn't say anything. Just said will you call him.'

'What – didn't say anything at *all*? Must have said *something*.'

'Didn't. Just said to ring him.'

'But he *must* have said something more than that! He can't have said Get George to ring me and then just hung up.'

'Well he did. Can we stop talking about this now?'

'Why? Is there something *else* you'd like to talk about, Shirley? Shouldn't the kids be back by now? Are they being dropped, or am I meant to fetch them?'

'They're staying over with Mummy tonight.'

'Really? Are they? Why? I didn't know about this. Why don't you ever *tell* me anything, Shirley?'

'I thought I had. Sit down, George.'

'You just don't tell me *anything*. It's always up to me to find *out*. Oh God. *Right*: no tape to listen to – excellent. I'll just go upstairs and ring work.'

'George. I'm leaving you.'

'No, Shirley, no: I'm leaving *you*, you see. *I'm* going upstairs – you're going to carry on sitting on the sofa looking at pictures of *clothes*. Why are they staying over, actually? What's all that in aid of?'

'George – how can I put this kindly? I can't *stand* you. Do you hear me? I just can't stand any more living in the same house as you. It's been building for ages – '

'What? *What?*'

'*Listen*: it's been building for just, oh God – *ages*, but all this stuff – '

'Shirley . . .!'

'Oh *listen*, damn you: all this – the way you've been just lately since this stupid bloody robbery thing has just *done* it for me, George. You've become just *too* unbearable, this time. You're always so *full* of yourself, George, and I just don't think you *see* it.'

George's upper lip felt cold, and was trembling: might have been on the verge of just anything.

'What are you – ?! What do you *mean*?'

'I *mean* . . . oh God, this is so difficult to . . . I can't really *explain* it in words, George, what it is I mean. All I can say is I'm going. I've tried to avoid this, but I can't. I'll just go mad if I stay any longer, George. I'm sorry, but it's the truth.'

George felt weakness deep down in his stomach – but although he yearned to give in to it and hug in any warmth going to block out and maybe smother even some of this rising pain – clear a way through a gathering fog of fear – he swallowed hard and manfully reasserted the control for which he was (was he not?) well renowned.

'Oh right I *see*. *I'm* terrible. *I'm* the one. I make you sick, yes? And you – '

'Yes.'

'Don't – just don't barge *in*, OK? I'm *talking*. You can't stand me – you're just absolutely *perfect*, of course, but I'm – '

'I didn't say – '

'Stop *interrupting* all the time – *Jesus*. So you reckon you're going, is that it? Just like giving up half your job. Had enough – I'm off. Very nice. Very easy. And what about our two children, may I ask? Yes? Remember them? Do they feature at all in this latest plan of yours? Jesus – '

'George . . .'

'*Jesus*, Shirley – what are you *saying*? What do you mean you're *leaving*? Where will you go? You've got nowhere to go, have you? So how can you leave? Hm?'

'Oh *George* . . .! You really don't *know*, do you?'

'No of course I don't *know*. I don't know anything, do I? How could I? I'm just the man who makes you *sick*. What? What don't I know? God, Shirley – you can't actually be *serious* about this . . .?!'

'George. I'm having – I've been having an affair. For quite a time, now. I thought you might have . . . sensed it. Obviously not.'

George's face was rigid and white: barely seeping pink, now – and then red rose into it, as if from the shock of swift and repeated slapping.

'What . . .?'

'I'm sorry. I thought you knew. Oh God, George – you *must* have known! I can't *believe* you didn't . . .! Anyway. We'll talk again when we're all a bit more . . . I'm leaving right now, George.'

George now gazed at her as she moved towards the door.

'What . . .?'

'I'll phone in the morning. Why don't you get an early night?'

George cocked his head as if to register the snapping of a twig amid a silent and tinder-dry and I thought quite safe and comforting neck of the woods.

'*What* . . .?'

And then she must have slipped out. Did she? Shirley? Couldn't really say: she's not in here any more, certainly. Whole house is quite empty. How long have I just been sitting here? Don't remember sitting down. She told me to, Shirley – more than once, I seem to recall. But I don't actually remember, um . . . doing it. But I did, quite clearly – must have, because in this chair I surely do find myself. It's getting dark. Must just phone work. No – too late. They'll all be gone, now.

Stupid bloody robbery thing – that's what she called it. Yes well. I've watched the videotape repeatedly, and stupid it wasn't. Shame they caught him, really – might have been on *Crimewatch*, otherwise . . . And Shirley – she wasn't *there*, was she? No. And where was she, then? Where has she been, all these afternoons, since when, exactly? How long? I simply had no idea. Stupid bloody robbery thing – that's what she called it. Yes well. She wasn't *there*, was she? No. I

212

was – *I* was there. I got kicked in the face. That's what made me the man of the moment: that's when I became the Hero of the Hour.

CHAPTER EIGHT

Even now, you know, thought Isobel – even now (and it's
twice we've talked, shared a quiet drink by the pool) I don't
really know quite what I should be making of him, but he
seems very nice, Mike, if a little intense. I'm just so completely out of practice, aren't I? The only people I ever talk
to are customers at work, and that's not proper conversation, is it? Answering their queries about personal loans
and compound interest and agreeing, whenever it's raining,
that the weather's just dreadful. Mother, of course – if that
can be called communication (listening, more like). And
talking of mother – well. I didn't *really*, did I, actually think
I'd be free of her? Not with Geraldine at the helm: just
wasn't going to happen, was it? I've hardly been in this
place for two minutes (lovely grounds – just beautiful; I so
adore just walking and breathing in all this *air* and then
getting back to my wonderful room and simply lying for
ages in a deep hot bath) – just more or less arrived, I had,
and already that sister of mine has – can you credit it? –
rung me three times! I couldn't believe it, the first time they
came and told me. Are you *sure*, I said (still wet behind the
ears, really, aren't I?). Because I thought in my blessed
naïveté that if you weren't supposed to phone *out*, then the
same sort of rule would apply to anyone trying to, you
know – get in touch, sort of thing. But no – they're bound to
pass on messages, they say, and then it's up to you what
you actually do with them. Yes, well – I wasn't going to
ignore them, was I? As Geraldine knows, that's just not part
of my make-up. So the first time this happened, I was only

having a *massage*, wasn't I? Never had one before – it's quite fabulous, the feeling: could get quite addicted to that, along with rather a lot else that goes with all this 'millionaire lifestyle'. Maybe I'll win the Lottery (some hopes).

'She says she doesn't want her back rubbed!' gasped out Geraldine – and Isobel was only slightly ashamed by the spark of pleasure she received like a jolt on hearing first-hand just how frazzled her sister sounded. 'Says it *hurts*. What do I do? Just leave her?'

'You have to go easy,' said Isobel, softly. Like my mass-euse did – I feel so supple and gentle and boneless and tingly. 'It's the shoulders, really. It won't hurt to miss it for one day, if she's really kicking up. Everything else all right? Cats?'

'Oh *God*, yes!' exploded Geraldine. 'Everything else is just *marvellous*, isn't it? I've abandoned my husband and my children and I've become a char and a night nurse to an intensely crabby old woman! *God*, Isobel – I just don't know how you *stand* her.'

'Yes,' agreed Isobel – quietly, but with a depth of feeling. 'Well.'

'Anyway,' resumed Geraldine – with all the customary acid, Isobel noted, again intact and back to the forefront – 'I'm sure *you're* having a whale of a time, at least. How long are you *staying*?'

'I've only just arrived. Are the cats all right?'

'Oh God I've got to *go*! I think she's dropped something or broken something or something, Jesus. Oh *God*, Isobel – I've got to *go* . . .'

Me too, thought Isobel – enjoying greatly the sensation of an unplanned smile (simply came to her, just like that). She replaced the receiver, and made for one of the lounges. She had spotted this one earlier in the day – seemed very nice, from what she took in. Large and old-fashioned chintzy big sofas and wallowy chairs, and those huge french windows opening out on to the lawn (on sunny days like this, some people play croquet – it's awfully calming to watch). And that's when – she'd just got herself settled on a garden lounger affair, just on the terrace (had fetched a glass of iced tea and a copy of *Vogue* – God, haven't seen *Vogue* for just *years*) – and that's when he first came up to her and smiled quite broadly and then said Hi, my name's Mike – mind if I join you? And Isobel – startled at first, and at pains to confirm that it was truly herself he was in fact addressing – looked up to and at him and said in her customer voice No of course not, delighted: please do. Isobel. And isn't it a perfectly lovely day?

Mike sat down heavily – more or less allowed his legs to buckle beneath him, secure in the belief that the canvas-slung director's chair would somehow contain and cushion his collapse.

'So-o-o . . .' he opened – glancing sidelong at Isobel, and then pulling briefly at whatever tall thing he was drinking (some sort of infusion, it could be, was Isobel's opinion – although he didn't at all seem to be *liking* it, or anything). 'What brings you to Colditz? No – I suppose we shouldn't ask these things, should we? Me – I'm trying to chuck the booze. It'll get out sooner or later anyway. Not easy, I can tell you.'

'Yes . . .' agreed Isobel slowly, and treading with care. 'I mean, no – I can see that that would be . . . very um . . .'

'Yeh well,' concluded Mike briefly. 'Day at a time.'

'I'm just here,' piped up Isobel – and already she was thinking Well why, actually? What is it, officially, that I'm here for? 'To relax,' is the side she came down on – tacking on a throwaway and she hoped not so much girlish as carefree little giggle.

'Yeh.' And Mike was nodding repeatedly, as if to convey the sudden invasion of gravity, here – cogitating, he seemed to be, the deeper implications of an already profound and endlessly complex conundrum. 'Relax is *good*. We all get too stressed out, that's the whole trouble. No matter how successful – no matter how much money and all the crap goes with it, what you end up is stressed out. Is all you get. Relax is *good*.'

Isobel was wearing the thin and watered smile that didn't commit her to feeling or outwardly expressing anything at all – more a public acknowledgement of her awareness that he had uttered. A rather serious young man, then, on the face of it. Well – I say *young*: everyone seems young to me, these days. What I really mean to say is, well – he's not a *boy*, quite obviously, but in common with nearly everyone, it appears, he's certainly a good deal younger than I am. Forty, could he be? Bit less? More? Forty-two, maybe. In the region of early forties, I think I'd say – but never out loud, of course: just think how mortifying it would be if he was, oh God – *far* younger than that, but was just looking a wee bit tired out, possibly, or because the sun just now was dappling and highlighting the near transparency of his blond and feathery hair at the temples. Nice hair, though – quite short and very clean-looking. I think his watch is rather vulgar, I have to say.

'How old you think I am, Isobel?' he said suddenly. 'You can be as honest as you like.'

'Oh *goodness* . . .!' fluttered Isobel, 'I'm just so totally hopeless at all this sort of thing – honestly! A lot younger than *me*, anyway – everyone is.'

'I'm thirty-five. Thirty-five years of age, is what I am.'

'Mm – I would have said about that, or even a bit younger.'

'No, Isobel – no you wouldn't. You wouldn't have said that because you strike me as a very nice and pleasant and straightforward lady who would not have told me a lie to my face. I look wrecked – I know I do. It's the way I live – it's killing me. Why I'm here, I guess. *Isobel* – !'

This last loud and nearly panted-out bursting of her name had made her immediately wary (at least, however, he had remembered it – this must surely go some small way

217

in compensating for his seeing me as no more than a nice and pleasant and straightforward *lady*, God in heaven help me).

'Mm . . .?' was all she felt safe in launching.

'Look – I've been very rude, going on about myself when we've only just met – but look: I'm alone here, yeh? I guess most of us are, one reason or another – and it just occurs to me that if I wouldn't be, you know – *intruding*, or anything . . . it might really help me – maybe both of us, who knows? You never know, do you? If, um – I could, you know, spend a little bit of time with you. Walk, maybe. Swim. Drink, from time to time. Only this foul hot water, though – more's the bloody pity. Does that sound awful? If it does, just say so.'

And of course Isobel had said No – no. Mike, of *course* it doesn't sound awful, not a bit – the reverse entirely (and she was pleased to notice that she meant it, too – yes, oh yes, she probably would have said something of the sort no matter what she had been feeling, but it was good to know that her words were conveying the truth: a bit of company, a bit of male company over the next few days – what could be wrong with that?).

Because no I haven't, in my life (if you want to know – and as you might have guessed) had very much at all of all that. I can't wholly blame mother, not wholly I can't – but she was always, to say the very least, extremely discouraging in any matters at all that carried with them even the remotest aroma of *men*, and all their doings (amazing she ever got married in the first place). If she'd ever found out about James, well – I honestly don't know quite what she would have done: killed me, probably – and at the time, the way I felt then, I don't really suppose I would have very much minded (welcomed it, in fact – yes, almost certainly). How perfectly strange – it really can't be healthy – that a woman of my age can even now be cringing within, not just from the hot flush of, oh – so painful memory of how wrenched open and coldly laid bare I had been, but also from the recall of the icy spread of fear of what would happen if ever my mother should find me out. Because before – prior to James – there had been nothing at all, really, for either of us to become in the least bit exercised over. I had gone through none of all the fumblings and gropings that I am forever hearing and reading are an integral and unavoidable part of the growing-up process (a smudge-faced and clammy-fingered cheap rite of passage). Not that the boys were exactly queuing up for me, or anything. (I tended to hunch over, as if urging my recent and almost immediately quite billowing curves to think again – change tack and grow back inside me where my abdominal acids would see to all the essential business of breaking them down so that they could be conveyed as just more waste away from me in quite the usual manner, along with all the other rotten and unwanted effluvia that clogged me up and made me heavy. Can't, can it? Be altogether healthy, thinking all that.)

I took a terribly poor degree (I had lost the ability to concentrate, soon after I left school: mother kept on telling me what an absolute fool I was) – in *politics*, of all mad things on earth – I can't even now remember why *politics* (never been remotely interested – I imagine it must simply have been under-subscribed – at some very small and dingy so-called 'college' in a part of east London that you will certainly never have even heard of, let alone been to – although now, I fully expect, it will have been 'made over' and 'rebadged' (don't they say that?) as some attempt at a glittering seat of learning, lacking only the dreaming spires (and real aspiration) of true academia. And there, yes, there had been one or two I suppose you might call them, would you – *men*, for want of a better word, whom I sort of got friendly with. The first time I, you know – got this thing over with (I do remember his name, of course I do – although still, even now, I don't at all want to) – I was surprised by not just how short a time it all took (the girls, they'd told me about that – amazing, they said, why boys are always *wanting* it so much: it just lasts two seconds) – but also how rough and sudden he had been. It was as if he was rummaging around in panicked haste amid the depths of a momentarily abandoned handbag – sweatingly eager to grasp and be away with just any small thing of no matter how little value before the rightful owner could gather back her property. And when I said to him 'Is that it? Has it happened?' it wasn't, as he seemed to think – aren't men strange? – in any way meant to be putting him *down*, or anything, because even then I was unnaturally aware of the supreme fragility of anything at all to do with just any of this, from the point of view of their oddly male way of looking at things. No – it was a genuine enquiry – I honestly didn't know. I had simply been aware of a brief and harsh invasion followed by an unaccustomed fullness, which quickly went away. It all confused me very much – and more so, I remember, when he practically fled from the room, mumbling it could have been anything, and maybe even apology.

James was much later, and yet still so long ago. Only my second job, it had been – a Midland Bank in Harrow. James was the stand-in manager for the summer, and I had thought him, oh – so terribly wise and sophisticated and all the other stupid things women can imagine men are; all he was was *older* – and, it turned out, married – but I didn't know that, of course, not at the beginning – or else I never would have . . . anyway. And even at the end, he still just stood there, red-faced and denying it – right up until I thrust at him the letter from his wife, threatening to not just blacken my name but also my eyes, before gouging them out. (We had pub lunches, and he made love to me in the filing room; once he gave me flowers.)

But James was, I suppose, quite kind while he lasted. And when that autumn evening the vast and burning pain had boiled up inside me and took me over utterly, I had quite calmly assumed I was about to die – I suppose because it seemed impossible to me that anyone at all could ever survive this. I was, thank God, at home and alone in my room; even now I can, if I dwell, practically faint at the idea of having been assailed so brutally as I was by all that ripping agony during a tea break at work or – worse, oh God, so immeasurably worse – in the little back living room, with mother. I did not think that my whole body could ever contain so much blood as was at first oozing and then just belching out of me in dark and glossy gobbets, soon to become a crimson cascade. Here was no mere period – even I could tell that much; I had not at all known I was pregnant (had no inkling) and this too late knowledge now filled me with sadness as I simply lay there, being vacuumed of everything – because I knew I would not be with child for very much longer. And I was scared, too, because even then – in that state and at my age – I could not in all honesty have laid my hand on my heart and told you where it was exactly that babies actually did come from. I found out so soon and for certain in quite the most cruel and terrible way.

Later, I – disposed of things. The bedspread had to go too – and I remember making a mental note to maybe buy a rug, small rug, next time I went across to Leather Lane, and that would cover the mark. For now I'll just (God, it's a deadweight) shift over the bed – and if mother says to me *Isobel*: that's a very strange place to have moved your divan, don't you think? Sticking halfway out into the room, like that . . .? Well then I'll just say I like it, it's a change: it's *different*. (And then I cried, for hours and days.)

Can't imagine why on earth I started dragging up all this old history (Mike has just gone off to get us both tea). Anyway – since that time, I have tended to steer well clear of men and all of their intentions, honourable or (much more likely, isn't it?) the other thing. Not that where I work now offers anything remotely in the way of temptation, I have to say. I mean, God – look at George Carey, for instance: I *don't* really think so, do you? God knows how his wife puts up with him, bumptious little man. Do you know – the day after all that awful robbery business (and I think this place must be working its magic – I've hardly given any of that a single thought since I came here) he actually spent most of the afternoon going round simply everybody and pointing out the bit in the paper, can't remember which, that had written he was Superman, or something: he'd even underlined it in *red*. Men are so often – aren't they? – so very, very silly.

And I was still waiting for Mike to come back (he's terribly tanned – maybe goes away a lot) when Polly – she's the pretty one, the nice one – came up and told me that Geraldine was on the line – again. I very nearly thought Oh *blow* it – I can't be bothering with her, no matter what she wants to know; but then you never can be *sure*, can you? Quite *what* it might be. So I asked Polly to please tell Mike when he got back just what I was doing, and that I'd only be a couple of minutes, and off I had to go to the wretched little booth they've got here, so that Geraldine could in no time undo all the good that I truly do believe is lapping at the edges (and maybe, quite soon, I will feel it deep inside me).

*

'I was really gonna go for the lamb,' chortled Reg, setting down his small but brimming plate – gravy right out to the edges – and then easing himself into the narrow banquette alongside of Adeline (and didn't she look totally cracking? Telling you, that dress of hers: *poured* into it, she is – a million dollars ain't even close; give some of these bloody so-called film stars a good run for their money, I ain't joking). 'But there's just something, I don't know – real special about a great bloody hunk of roast beef – can't never resist it. Never could.'

'I got lamb,' said Adeline.

'I know you did – I saw you did. And very nice it looks too. Course, the benefit of a place like this is you can always go back and have a second dollop. Ain't like Oliver Twist, or nothing.'

'Don't know I'll have room for more. Have a sweet, though.'

'Well – take it as it comes, ay? See how you feel. Me, I reckon I could just force down a bit of that lamb, after. And the pork was looking lovely, and all. You don't often see pork, do you? Not nowadays, you don't.'

'How they make money, then? If you keep going back. Is this one the salt, you reckon?'

'Nah – too many holes for salt, innit? That'll be the pepper you got there, love. Wanna go easy – bring tears to your eyes, that will. No – thing is, *course* you're gonna get your, you know, out-and-out pigs, entcha? But it ain't *typical*. There's always someone who's gonna take advantage, though: name of the game. You clock the Yank when we was queuing? Size of a bleeding Routemaster, he was: he'll be back, for definite. Reckon they'll have to slaughter another bloody herd before that one's done.'

Adeline laughed lightly – her nose wrinkled up, and she held on it and then let it go. 'Oh Reg – you are *funny*, aren't you?'

Reg assumed a truly reflective expression. 'Couldn't really tell you. Ain't never thought about it. Blokes in the shelter seem to think I'm all right. At home, it's hard to know. Yeh, um . . . now's probably not the time to, you know, *mention* it, kind of thing, but er – I got a wife, back home. Might as well say it.'

'Yeh well,' said Adeline, quite carelessly – digging a thumb good and deep into the crust of a roll (bleeding hard, if Reg's was anything to go by). 'I sort of assumed that.'

'Yeh? Oh right. And you don't, uh – mind or nothing?'

'Why should I mind? Nothing to do with me, is it?'

Reg smiled faintly. What was this all about, now? Is this how they are, then, these days? Liberated totty, out for what they wanted? Or did it mean that she was just out having a scoff with her bleeding *uncle*, or something, and so what bloody difference did it make to her if he was married or not?

'Yeh well,' shrugged Reg – trying to field this stray and throwaway air she had punted across, like a well cool frisbee. 'Just thought I'd, like – you know: *say*. This Yorkshire's a bit soggy, my way of reckoning; don't half soak up all the doings, mind. Doing Trojan work on that score. Lamb to your liking, Adeline? Tender, is it?'

'Call me Addy. Most people call me that.'

Yeh? thought Reg – blending in yet another daft smile with a fairly energetic bout of chewing. Why you want them to call you that, then? Adeline, I reckon, got a fair lump of poetry to it. Addy I don't much care for. What – Addy as in Subtracty, or something? Nah – don't like it. All these shortenings are crap, far as I can see – and I've said all I'm going to say on the 'Reg' side of things. Mind you – I been guilty myself – well, me and Enid, anyway: the stick what Laverne give us when she went the comprehensive, what with everyone calling her Lav, and that (You still vacant? Or have you got engaged yet? You're full of crap! – you know what kids can be like). First time she come home with all this (I shouldn't laugh) I says to her Calm down, girl: you're looking all *flushed*, Lav. Nearly *kill* me, she did.

'Yeh?' said Reg. 'Addy, then – very nice too. Here – you know what I'm thinking: I'm thinking just a nice slice of that pork, bit of crackling – set me up good, that would.'

'Don't know where you put it. I'm not even going to get to the end of this lot, don't think. Mind you, I did have those prawns for starters.'

'Yeh. Never been a big one for prawns, me. Sucker for a

nice dressed crab, though. Them rollmops was OK, with the salad. Get you another drink, can I, Adeline? Addy?'

'Yeh – why not? Reckon I could go the zabaloney.'

'Yeh? What's that when it's at home, then? Thought you was on the vodka?'

'It's an *afters*, Reg! Honestly – where you *been*? And the profitty rolls looked well wicked and all.'

'Well you're on your own there, girl. I'll be happy with my little bit of pork – spud or two. Maybe just a mouthful of Cheddar, anyone's twisting my arm. Yeh – uh – waitress! Hello? Waitress! Bloody hell – didn't she hear me, or what? They just don't wanna know, do they? Look right through you. Ah no – here she comes. Yeh – large vodkantonic, yeh? And I'll have another lager, reckon. Ta, love.'

Earlier on, when they'd both just got there, Reg had said How bout a nice bottle of wine, then, with our meals, ay? (They had run into each other with no trouble at all, in spite of the bustle and size of the lobby: Blimey, Adeline had gone – look at the size of that huge great hanging light thing. Yeh, acceded Reg: wouldn't fancy being the bloke what replaces the bulbs.) But Adeline had turned up her nose to that particular suggestion – and she was dead right to Reg's way of thinking because, look – people *always* say that, don't they? Bit of an occasion, they all go *Yeh* – and we'll have a nice bottle of wine, how's about that, then? Trouble is, it don't exist, do it? I ain't never had a bottle of wine what I could call nice – red ones are like bleeding Ribena, and the white buggers, Jesus: not much short of battery acid (strip that thing on your teeth right back to the wossname).

'It's really nice here, Reg,' said Adeline, now – glancing around her as if to check this still held good. 'Thanks ever so much.'

'Glad you come?'

'Yeh. Yeh. Thanks ever so much.'

Polite little thing, ain't she? Not like some of the kids you see about, nowadays. Mind you, I can't deny it – all this Ta very much lark, it makes me think a couple of things. One – it's like her bloody uncle's well back in the frame (assuming the bastard was ever bleeding out of it) – and Two: it's also a bit like a Goodbye, ain't it? Know what I mean? It's a sort of ending, coming out with something like that. Like when we was kids at a birthday party, when you got your balloon and a bag full of tooth-rot: Thank you for having me, you'd go, like what you been taught. Yeh well – point is, not wanting to be crude about it, or nothing – I *ain't* yet, have I? Had her. No I ain't – and tell you the truth, I ain't got a bleeding clue how it's all gonna go, now, here on in. Reckon I got to play it by ear, yeh? Reckon I don't got a choice (not kidding – it's so bleeding long since I *done* any of this).

Adeline didn't, when it came right down to it, plump for the zabba thing what she was on about (said she was crammed right up to bursting point and if she even so much as looked at it she'd throw up all over the shop). Still managed a couple of scoops of trifle, though – big glacé cherry perched right on the top by that prat with the chef's hat – altogether too chummy by half, to Reg's way of thinking. A lot of his pork got left (Know what I reckon? Reckon I overdone it) but that hadn't stopped him wrapping his laughing gear around a nice wedge of Cheddar – even went a bit of that funny runny Frog number (didn't want to know nothing about the horrible blue and mouldy job, though – what they take him for? I want bacteria, I can get it at home).

'I reckon,' reckoned Adeline, chucking to the back of her throat the flat and still just tinkling dregs of her third – could well be fourth – Smirnoff and tonic. 'I reckon I'm so full, I don't think I can even *move*.'

'Know what you mean,' nodded Reg. 'My waistband's giving me gyp. I could go a kip, right now.'

'Ooh yeh – that'd be lovely. I can't walk an inch.'

'Funny enough . . .' tiptoed Reg, 'I wondered about that.

What I mean is – what I mean to say is, you *could*, if you wanted to. We could. Take a little rest, is what I mean. Somewhere quiet. Maybe have another drink, sort of style . . .'

'Yeh? How you reckon, Reg?'

'Well, thing is . . . I've got us a . . . I mean, don't think I was, you know . . . what I mean is, you don't *have* to use it, or nothing. I ain't bothered about the money, or nothing, if we, er – if you don't, like, feel like it . . . but well, thing is: I got a room.'

'What – you mean, *here*, like? In this place?'

'Yeh. Here. Right here. Upstairs. If you fancy it.'

Adeline looked at him – dead straight, and rather hard, Reg thought. Oh blimey. Then she got up, and without once looking back, walked away from the table, and right towards the door – and oh blimey: Reg was right behind her.

'Adeline! Addy! Don't – you got me *wrong*, love. What I say? Look, don't be . . . I said you didn't *have* to, or nothing. Don't go. You going? Why you going? Stay. Look – I'm *sorry*, OK? Don't go. You going?'

'Yeh, Reg,' said Adeline – and she turned in the lobby to face him. 'I'm going.' And then she smiled. 'What floor's it on, then?'

*

George was now thinking that maybe he must almost be more or less half awake, then – could he be? Or was this just another of those terrible and splintered quasi-mad and ripped-up dreams that had torn at him all night long – at once dragging him under a clammy blanket of unreasoned fear, and then quite cruelly exposing him to just enough bright limelight to make his blinking and rheumy eyes set up an itch, and then get down to aching, but still not let him see anything clearly? Harsh and unfamiliar sounds badly jangled him and forced him into shivering – one arm limply and with no hope feebly feeling for a cover of warmth that had gone from him. The void of his mouth could well be as dry and hard as a box, if this sensation that now overtook him was even centred near there. And his head, oh dear God – a deep and heavy shifting unease was filling him up and stirring, the dull and gauzy pain inside seeming expanded and larger than the whole of him. Then came from somewhere a clanging – this was surely, was it surely, not a part of him but a real and elsewhere sound. George stretched out his cranked-up legs as far as they could go, and now was quite dreading his impending wakefulness; his mind did its utmost to cower in moist and safer regions, but a high and hurtful ringing had now set up around him – shrill, yes, and distant. George turned over and lay there crouching, trying to shut out not just that, but anything else that touched him. And then he suddenly felt himself topple – his eyes were wide open before he hit the ground, and a grunt was sent out of him as his knee came down jarringly, on concrete.

On concrete. George's eyes were tight shut now – a puny defence against the clattering rush of half-spliced and quite shocking images that now boisterously assailed him. His arms, with a weighted reluctance, began to explore – reaching out like fearful tentacles, each finger-end primed and on the alert as it went on probing this new and hostile terrain. The side of George's head was pressed flat and hard on concrete. He was cold, and deep down in his stomach there rumbled the first and nearly convulsive swell of what easily could be nausea, or just the seeping aftermath of a recent evisceration. But he had it, now – he had, oh dear God, a hold on it. George just lay there, on concrete, as his whole brain struggled to not even close to – nowhere near the tip of around the truly terrible truth that could no longer be dismissed as a wild and blaze-eyed figment of the sweat-night's imagining. He had tumbled from a hard and unforgiving, thick and brutal wooden ledge – the one thin blanket still and somehow entwined about his ankles. Because that, you see, is where they install you. If you are brought to a prison cell late at night, then this is where you are kept. Turn over too suddenly as the fragile half-light and idle clamour of early morning bleed in through open pores, well then you immediately fall, to be shocked by concrete.

My life, I think, is over: I seem to have put it to death. It's truly amazing, really, because all I felt when I went out last night was sad and astounded. I remember thinking I wanted to call someone, yes I do remember that – I wanted someone by me. But I'm not – never was – the sort of person who has a pool of mates to draw on, you see. Colleagues at work, oh yes – Shirley, of course (who has left me. Did I mention? Oh yes – Shirley, my wife, is gone). But no sort of social circle, is what I'm driving at – no club memberships, nothing at all of that order. And I suppose if I'm honest I'd never really felt I was ever at all in any way *lacking* in this department – I'd never really had the need of anyone else, to tell you the truth. You go to work – talk to people in the normal course of your office day – and then you return home in the evening, don't you? To the wife and kids. And I've never been much of a one for drinking, either – which I suppose, now, is quite viciously funny. But that whole pub culture, you know – completely passed me by. It's not just all the endless talking about *beer* (I've noticed that – you noticed that? They spend as much time talking, these people, about their pints of beer as they seem to do drinking them; and God look – it's *beer*, for heaven's sake, is all it is: what is there, actually, to *say*?). No, it's not just that – it's the whole sort of joke-telling, car-running, golf-playing camaraderie – I've never been good at all that. I don't know if they're genuine, at all, these people – I really couldn't tell you. All I know is, it's just not *me*, all that, and certainly I could never even begin to pretend. And yes I did, since you ask – I did try once or twice, but they all saw right through me, I just know they did: they knew my faking was insincere. And another thing – God Almighty, all those rounds you're expected to get in! Criminal, these pub prices, you know. I don't frankly know how they all manage it – and they're down there practically every single night, as far as I can make out: same old faces. I mean – presumably they've all got mortgages and kids and everything else like the rest of us, no? Summer holidays to think of – or else it's Christmas looming. I wouldn't dream of throwing away all that money on boozing, when some positive good could come of it. Take the little conservatory I had built on, couple of summers back: that'll be paid for in about eight years' time – eight years come August – and meanwhile the family has been reaping the benefit. Plus, an estate agent was telling me – customer, as a matter of fact: quite in the know – they're pretty much guaranteed to augment the overall value of your property, these things, so all in all it's quite literally money in the bank, isn't it really? Rather more sensible, I think you'll agree, than blowing it all on a circle of red-faced and braying sycophants in the bar of a public house! More fool them is what I say.

But let's be clear – it's not that I'm completely down on drink *per se*, or anything – I'm not a *prig*, I hope. No no – I quite like a can of Heineken on a hot afternoon – lovely in the shade of the garden, after a hard Sunday's weeding, say, or cleaning out the shed. And some table wines can be perfectly pleasant – oh yes, I'm not denying that. In Barcelona, one year, I became very partial to a certain well-chilled rosé, I seem to recall; couldn't now tell you the name of it, or anything – but it was just ideal for the time and place. And you didn't have to worry about finishing up the bottle, or anything, because the hotel operated a highly efficient labelling system so they could serve it up again on exactly the right table the following evening. I'm going by memory, but it also came very reasonably priced, I'm fairly sure. Shirley (that's my wife, who has left me now: oh yes – Shirley has gone) – she's quite fond of a gin and tonic: maybe a bit *too* fond, as I've more than once suggested to her. Fair do's when she was earning full-*time*, of course – but not so much fun for me when I'm expected to fork out at the supermarket, is it? Well – that's one thing I won't have to worry about, anyway; yes – that's one bone of contention I think I can safely put out to pasture.

So if you ask, in the light of all this, how in heaven's name it was I ended up last night in whatever godawful pub I surely did end up in (and people will, won't they, be asking that? Asking that, yes – and asking other things too) all I can attempt in addition to tartly observing that that is a very good question is just this single most lame of excuses: I did it because men *in extremis* just *do*, don't they? Well look – it's one of life's most colossal slaps in the face, isn't it? Wife walking out on you. And it's not as if there had eventually come to me the awful and crushing culmination to a heavy inevitability – no no, I had none of even the cold consolation of thinking to myself Well, George: here it is at last, I knew it had to happen: a marriage such as mine, it simply can't, can it? It can't go on. No – quite the reverse. I could never ever have conceived that it was remotely capable of doing anything else – it *had* to go on: well, didn't it? I felt so sure that it would – go on and on and on – if only because, well – that's what marriages are *meant* to do, isn't it?

Well in my case – not, apparently. Maybe I would've handled it differently, I don't know, if I could have turned to a best friend or even a brother or a father – a *mother*, for Christ's sake (I've got none of those – an only and lonely child, I was: father went away at some point, not sure why or where, and two years ago come August – I remember because I was having the conservatory put up at the time – a fair proportion of my mother's internal organs more or less overnight, it seemed to me, just ganged up and turned on her, gnawing away – ate out all of her strength, and then when she was hollow, she just faded away from me).

Last night, the house had seemed small and oppressive and yet echoingly vast and empty, without the kids and without my Shirley (who had gone, left me, my wife), and yet I panicked – yes, I remember this – right at the very doorstep because yes, oh yes – I had to get out, I had to do that, but *then* what? *Then* what? To go *where*, exactly? Where could I go? Yes well – clearer now, isn't it? I went to that place that is warm and lit and no questions are asked – where you can be easily alone, amid the jostle of others: the pub. Not just one pub either – oh no, for someone who simply doesn't *do* this sort of thing, I surely couldn't be accused of skimping the deal. The first was the Duke of Grafton, solely because it just happens to be right on the corner of our street. But the man from the newsagent's was in there with his dog, who I can't stand (the newsagent, I mean – always leafing slowly through his perfectly repellent top-shelf magazines – but the dog too, I might say, seems decidedly unwholesome). So I drank just the one whisky in there – and yes I *know*, I *know*: don't even ask me, I just can't answer you. What on earth made me order a whisky, when whisky is a thing I simply never touch? Well partly, if you push me, because the man just alongside had done exactly that very same thing and so for me to do likewise simply just cut out any form of thought (and no, I don't think I was trying to establish an affinity with him, don't think I was, but in my state – adrift and alone – who can actually tell?). And also, of course, I was well aware of the condition I quickly needed to succumb to, and whisky is hardly known to loiter – it's famous, isn't it, for getting you there with the minimum of delay.

So then I walked about a bit – popped my head round the door of that other place nearby, never ever before been in there (Red Fox? Red Lion? *Red*, anyway . . .), but I didn't at all care for what I saw there. Scared, actually, I think I quite must have been: just a hot loud wall of people, clinking and clatter overlaid by a deep bass fog of talking and growl. I felt as if I was half in the maw of a huge old beast whose late-night breath was making me retch; so I pulled myself out and away from being swallowed by that – and then I saw a taxi, yes (remember that distinctly), and my hand was well up for the business of hailing it – arm was then twitching with the spasm of cancelled command, because I didn't go through with it: taxi stops – what, then, is the next thing? They want to be told, don't they? Where to go. They assume, you see, that you know. Even if nothing at all is on the agenda, the belief is always out there that you know full well where the nothing is to happen. And I had no idea. I could have said something vague and reasonably foolish such as, I don't know – West End, but he would only, wouldn't he (only fair), have pressed me for details. So I walked on a bit further and it started to shower and then I thought Oh God blow this – I'll get myself off home, I really might as well: what do I suppose I'm doing, traipsing round the streets, in the gathering rain? Shirley is not at home, this much is true, but nor is she to be found strolling on a slime-washed pavement. And then another taxi was pottering by and so I flagged it down and said West End, please, and he nodded, the man, and I got in and we moved off and then he called back at me What part, exactly? Where you want, mate? And I said I'd let him know.

My part of London had soon hissed by me, and I felt so alone when I found me cruising somewhere different. Soon after, I remember knocking my knuckles on the glass division and saying in a voice too loud and more highly pitched than my usual way of speaking – This'll do, this'll do – here will do just fine. He said, the driver: You sure, mate? Anywhere here? And I said Yes – yes, thank you, anywhere here (and I thought as I paid him Oh yes indeed: anywhere here, or anywhere else – the choice in the end was yours).

So soon I'm in a pub. That's one of the things about London, isn't it? And maybe other cities too, I'm not really qualified to say. But in London, you can be miles from anything you've heard of or even ever seen, but you're always quite close to a pub. So I went in. And this was no more vile than you would expect it to be: not at all nice, but not so bad as to make me leave. I drank whisky at the bar. After the first two, three maybe – could have been four or more, thinking about it now, because the absolute first had been only a single and that was clearly silly: I would never reach journey's end if I was travelling on *samples*. And then the bloke there – the man behind the bar (not grossly unfriendly, as I sort of recall) he said, when I'd ordered again – he said to me: You want anything in that, do you? And I said Yes, yes – put more in it, why not? And he looked at me for a second (it was the first of the looks I garnered that evening, the very first of the looks before all the glaring) and then he jammed the glass back up to the optic and as the squirting came, I gazed at the rising bubbles in the upturned bottle and the level of gold in the glass grew higher. He hadn't meant that, I remember dimly realizing one or two more drinks down the line, but I was already a good way beyond minding even remotely about that: it became a kind of a joke between us, which even made me smirk (and all my lips felt funny). Large Scotch, I'd go – and he'd say Yes sir, right away sir: you want anything in it, do you? And I'd maybe snort (and all my nose felt wrong) and came back with Yeh go on, then – put in another one. He laughed. He laughed. And I'm not surprised.

Time was passing, and then it put its foot down – nearly knocking George off his feet as he hurtled along in its wake. The moods he went through – each of them lasted for seconds and years, and all were seeming to him life-changing, or at the very least profound. A sort of calm and floating pleasure, he recalled with vivid affection: he really liked this one a lot. He felt not only OK about being cast-away and turned upon, but just so utterly self-absorbed and *good* about it all – for so long as I had *me*, for God's sake (and *I* wasn't going anywhere, was I? *I* wouldn't leave me because I need me too much) . . . well then as long as I was still here for me, what else then could I ever go wanting for, let alone need? But as, I suppose, is the way of moods, it didn't come close to seeing him through – and nor did it merely darken or filter softly into something quite near, not too far from him. No. The change was immediate – violent and abrupt: he nearly was drowning in hell. His chest was heaving – he was fighting for breath, quite as if he was literally being hauled down into the swelling undertow of something murky and without foundation, as thick as ink, and just as black. Such despair was spiked by anger – George resented very badly being made to feel like this, and he eyed the people around him, as if to size up, single out and finger the culprit. His head was so swollen, and a thudding surge of sound enclasped him before receding into a somehow even louder rowing and the tink-ling of glasses set all of his nerve-ends on to jingling points of appalling liveliness, while the rest of him was practically dying.

George's chin was now touching the bar – as would maybe yours if your thin and sappy neck could no longer be coaxed into supporting a three-ton head, filled with rubble and sponges. The voice that seized him emerged from the hubbub at first just dully – even the words meant nothing at all. He was aware of a hand squirming into the side of him – they were shoulder to shoulder right along the bar and last orders, maybe, were soon and looming. But why should he respond or recede – why give an inch or a damn about this? It's *my* bar, he thought: bought and paid for – I have lived here all my life, and in consequence I ignore all insinuation (I'll put up with none of its goading).

And then 'Excuse Me'. It's then he made it out for the

very first time – the fingers were waggling some money at the barman, and Excuse Me was being softly roared right into George's rubber and rapidly expanding skull, and was met with only disdain. He did not want to feel the seeds of anger – all he wanted was to be left to live his life in peace. But when again this Excuse Me hit into him, he felt a surge in his neck as if it was purple – he imagined it livid and alive, like slashed-open fruit – and he hunched down lower so as to contain the boiling, pound back the fury. And then *Excuse* Me, he heard – *Excuse* Me was coming in at him from all directions and he slugged back drink and was clutching hard the empty glass and now he was barely clinging on to the tail of his rage which was heaving away from him, desperate to be loose and do damage. And so when *Excuse* Me! slid in again, and this time like a hot knife (cold inside him), he felt himself clenched and cooked, tight and in a ball. Hard fingers were prodding his back and shoulder – his braced-in limbs were being poked and provoked and *Excuse* Me *Excuse* Me *Excuse* Me was all over his mind and driving him wild and he swivelled so suddenly his eyes were amazed and his legs were nearly having none of it as he reasserted quite pointedly all the control he could lay his hands on and with a deep and now quite undisciplined bellow that released from him just everything that clamoured and clawed he lashed out to the left and then hard to the right of him and silence was vying with calamitous noises and amid much smashing and thick-barked outrage George felt himself pinioned and struck and saw only amid the uproar the woman reeling backwards and away and clutching at her face – her warm blood spattered and had licked his cheek and then all the heat and sound and sliced-up lights cut right out as he first caved in, and then closed down.

CHAPTER NINE

It's really so terribly odd, thought Isobel, to see that old blue dress of mine in so different a context, just flung there like that. Mind you: I say old – I've got far older, of course. God, you maybe wouldn't credit it, some of the things in my wardrobe . . . museum pieces, I shouldn't at all wonder; keep meaning to have a good old clear-out but, well – you know how it is. Once I did – made a brave and concerted effort at gathering together a bundle – really awful and frumpy old things, hadn't for the most part so much as looked at them for *decades*, if you can believe it. More to the point, I doubt I could even have struggled into the half of them, which is fairly depressing just by itself. And all those crusty old bent-up shoes: they didn't really look or feel like leather any more – just hard and lightweight and cold, like old things are. I could not imagine my feet had ever been in them – particularly those bright apple-green horrors (I think they were for a wedding that I don't now recall having been to; in a sale, Dolcis pretty sure – and I had a vague sort of plan to dye them later). All this ancient stuff that hangs around you . . . and yet once, once I had twirled and twisted before mirrors in a shop, catching glimpses of myself this way and then from that angle and quickly and excitedly deciding Oh yes, I must have it – expensive, too expensive, but of all the things in the whole of London, this one is truly it. And then years on, it just hangs there, all forlorn, like the sad little rags of someone else altogether. (And they're all still there, is what's so awful: I hadn't even worked out a way of getting all these boxes down to Oxfam when *mother* descended, didn't she? Spent the whole afternoon unpicking and unpacking like a sage and fastidious totter, exuding waves of virtue – diligence and thrift – as she countermanded my decision on just about practically all of it. You don't just get rid of a thing, Isobel, she had admonished me sternly, simply because it happens to be *old*: some such items have *years* in them yet. And I nodded.)

I was worried, you know, yesterday, about my underwear. And the point is here, I suppose, that I cannot recall the last time when my underwear has even so much as crossed my mind. In common with maybe a lot of ladies of my age, now (and yes, I can well see that it would depend upon your position, your husband, conceivably, and maybe your income – not to say your legs) I simply buy batches of the same old comfy things in good old You-Know-Where, whenever the last lot gets dingy or starts to sag at the sides, like they do. I haven't yet had a swim in this place, either – although my swimsuits (I have two, because sometimes after work when I've fed the cats and mother, I quite like to do about twenty or so lengths in the local pool: it cleans and empties the mind) . . . now what was I . . .? Oh yes – the swimsuits are perfectly fine (from Harrods, no less! Sale, of course – one is striped, one is plain) but some of the women you see lounging around here, well . . . you don't like to, do you, brazenly display your pretty glaring defects among all that brown and long-legged perfection? Most of the younger set here remind me of palominos – do you know what I mean? The colour, as well as the grace. But swimsuits are one thing, and underwear quite another. Who is underwear for, after all, apart from oneself? Putting it on, and taking it off. So how did I know (when could I ever have dreamed) that someone else would ever again be a party to any of that?

Last night, Mike and I had supper together – the far part of the dining room, just by the fretwork screen (you can see the ornamental pond from the window). I started off with smoked salmon – very yum, very moreish and not at all greasy, like it sometimes comes – and Mike had some sort of Continental sausage, looked like to me, sliced very thinly and served with what seemed to be gherkins and olives (which you can keep, quite frankly – not my sort of thing at all). After, I went for the supreme of chicken – and it was quite a tussle, I can tell you, because the people at the next table had ordered the rack of lamb with new potatoes, and it did look very lovely, I have to admit. Mike was just toying with a small and plain grilled fillet steak, picking out only the cucumber from a colossal mound of undressed salad.

'You've got to *eat*, Mike,' said Isobel. 'You're only picking.'

'Yeh . . . you're right, really. Can't actually understand it – ought to be raving hungry, by rights. Haven't had a drink for what seems like a year. And the fags I'm struggling with too. So I'm meant to be ravenous, aren't I? If you listen to them all, that's what's meant to happen, you give up drink. Maybe I'm dying, ay?'

'Oh don't even *say* that, Mike! You're young – you're a young man. You're just a bit *tired*, that's all. It's nothing to be ashamed of! You'll get over it. We all do.'

Mike smiled, slow and lazily – Isobel saw this much before she glanced downwards, one hand flying up to the beads at her neck (they were a deeper shade of blue than the dress she had at last and finally determined to wear).

'Yeh – you're right. Right again, Isobel. You're always right about me. It's so easy, so plain *nice* to be with you. Special.'

Isobel blinked several times in very rapid succession and her mouth, she felt, was behaving in a horribly similar manner.

'This chicken is wonderful,' she said quite softly. 'How is your steak?'

I cannot recall, thought Isobel, the last time I was actually sitting opposite a man – in a situation, I mean to say, where looking over to him is an accepted part of what you do. The angularity of the face – such an unfamiliar thing – that touch of raw stubble, just peeking at his cheek like a smattering of granite. The quite thick hairs trapped beneath the strap of that actually, I suppose, not too bad watch of his – and how they catch the light, like that, when his big hands go to break bread. And just look at the easy amusement in his eyes – an acknowledgement of complicity: it was just him and Isobel, is what she read there (in this thing together).

'The steak? It's fine. I'm just not . . . I thought a walk, maybe. Later.'

'It's a lovely evening.'

'Yeh – I thought that. Why I thought, maybe – a walk. Later.'

'Are you having a dessert? They've got strawberries, I saw. And some sort of looks like summer pudding. A walk would be nice.'

'Good,' approved Mike. 'I think just coffee, for me.'

And later, they had walked – and Isobel even now could not have told you whether it truly had been so very warm and still a – did they say *balmy* night? Or whether all that came from just the glow that seemed to be coating her from both without and within, basting her gently and all over (she wondered if such radiance would be palpable to others). The formal lawns sloped away past the pool, old brick steps taking them both down a grassy ramp and on past ancient trees to the wilder edges, stuck with stumps and strung with wire. Beyond there lay bristling fields that folded into hedges, where the curves of more reared up softly and then curled away into the darkening sky. Isobel stood quite still and said It's so beautiful, and Mike just whispered: Isobel. And then he put his lips to the side of her throat.

'Why, Mike?' And her voice in the air had sounded to Isobel surprisingly strong, for waves of weakness were breaking all over her – washing in and rushing right up to her rotten defences that had never been tested.

Mike stood before her, his fingers just resting on her shoulders. He kissed her cheek.

'What do you mean: *why*? What can you mean?'

Isobel tried to draw back, swinging up her eyes to the tremendous sky.

'I mean *me*, Mike – why me? Why not one of those other women back there? I'm ... they're *young*, Mike. Aren't they? Like you. So why me?'

'I told you,' said Mike, quite simply. '*Special*.'

Isobel smiled, with caught-breath hesitance – glancing up for just any true assurance that Mike could, oh please, give to her. He smiled broadly and slipped his hand around her lifeless fingers, tugging at them gently. And hand in hand, with arms so loosely swinging, they retraced just part of their walk and easily circled a small thicket of bramble – Isobel quite girlishly pleased to see a half-circular and greenly mottled grey stone bench there, just sweetly nestled and inviting her. She sat, and opened her mouth to fearfully utter maybe quite the wrong thing – but that mouth was held now and kissed with insistence, her whole face relaxing into the bliss of giving in. Mike was just slightly away from her, now – grinning like a lad – and Isobel, with eyes alight, was laughing quietly in anticipation of whatever his own were telling her was coming. He hunched up his shoulders like a pantomime villain, darting his eyes first this way then that as if to make doubly sure that their relentless trackers had at last been thrown off – that the scent was just theirs again. Isobel's gaze was so wide when he produced like a triumphant conjuror that flat half-bottle of Bell's: I just don't *believe* it, they were gently chiding – you utterly naughty, naughty boy!

'Just the one won't hurt,' laughed Mike. 'You won't grass

me up now, will you, Isobel? Remember – you're my *special* friend.'

They took it in turns to swig the whisky – they kissed and then they kissed. Isobel felt lost and near mad with the lavish freedom of just that drizzle of release – and when Mike stroked her breasts, each in turn, all she felt was wonderful. Back in his suite, he had flung off his clothes, all of them so quickly and with no care at all – and Isobel too had felt just like doing that and so she kicked away and scattered her old blue dress just anywhere it would go . . . and only then did she become so coy. Mike had deftly caressed her shoulder, softly saying Hush and moaning gently, as if to bring calm to a small half-shattered and shivering bird. Slowly she had given ground, because she so much needed to – and when he moved away and towards the bed, she walked there with him, both brave and docile.

Mike's brown and sinewy body had shocked her, and so had the billows of her own as she quivered with a nearly stinging disbelief while that raw stubble at his cheek dragged and rasped as his mouth set to plucking, and pulling in parts of her. Her very own *O!* of astonished delight was the trigger for her total abandonment, and she clasped that man to her – so hard and tightly and with such hot conviction that she no longer knew or cared just where it was she ended, and at what point something so big and new might just have now begun.

*

Reg had had a leaf through one of them sex books, one time – you know: setting down fair and square for all to see the ins and outs and ups and downs of the entire bleeding gubbins. They don't mind what they publish nowadays, do they? They just don't care. And never mind publish – it's all there, plain as you like, now, on *wossname*, innit? Video. Take it home: freeze-frame, rewind – God Almighty. Jesus –

my day, you'd be passing round a set of airbrushed black-and-whites of a couple of tarted-up chorus girls – all tits and sequins, with a blur between their legs. You remember all that *Lady Chatterley* lark, must be . . . Christ, nigh on forty bloody years, now (where's it go, ay? The bloody time – where's it bloody go to?). I had that off a fella, that *Lady Chatterley* – they was all over, at the time; can't remember the bloke what wrote it, but word got round he was a right mucky devil so we all thought *right* – you plank down your three-and-six and you're sorted. Bloody hell! Telling you – you ain't never in the whole of your natural read such a boring load of old claptrap, couldn't understand for the life of me what all the bleeding fuss was about, not none of us could. I was just starting up the Knowledge at the time and my oppo, who's-his-face – Denny, yeah that's it (wonder what old Denny is up to, these days; ain't heard hide nor hair since Gawd knows) . . . yeh anyway, old Denny had marked up what was meant to be the best bits and I had them clipped on to my piece of hardboard at the front of the moped, didn't I? So while I should've been thinking Mansion House and Guildhall I was just going So when's this stuck-up cow gonna get her bloody leg over, then? Amazing me and the bike didn't end up totalled.

Anyway, all I'm saying – them days, you couldn't get your hands on proper filth even if you was willing to pay for it (Amsterdam, you could – but I'm a cabby not a bloody bargee, so where's the goodness there?). *Today*, well – chalk and cheese, innit? Everywhere you look there's naughties: telly, posters, *Sun* – wall-to-wall, yeah? So I suppose what it is, us older geezers, we got this feeling, right or wrong, that all the young lot, you know – they're totally sussed and cool about whatever might happen their way, and we're still practising our scales, sort of style. They're all concert wossnames, and we're sodding about with 'Chopsticks'. Like everything else, innit? You get taught in school about pounds, shillings, pence and you got that cracked and you're well away, aren't you, with your bobs and tanners and your thruppenny bits – and then the bastards go and change it all, don't they? *Course* they do – and there you are back with the *learning* again. Christ – it's quids up next for the chop, you know – soon I'm gonna be messing about with *ecrus* or whatever these Krauts is foisting on us poor old Brits. And it ain't just the cash in your pocket, neither. Blimey, you go – It's a real scorcher today, innit? We're sweltering – must be up in the eighties; and some clever kid like my bleeding Laverne, she comes up with What's the *eighties*, then? And you say What you *mean*, what's the eighties?! The eighties translates as bleeding *hot*, don't it, Laverne? Cuts no ice. They ditched Fahrenheit – they even ditched Centithing, far as I can make out. Yards and inches, they got the axe – it'll be pints next.

What I'm saying is, you grow up to be a, you know – good and responsible adult, pay your rates, make sure there's bread on the table, raise your kids best you can – and suddenly you're made to feel stupid, like you don't count for nothing, and all these kids is king. Course, now with these bleeding computers and bloody faxes and bleeding e-mails, well – you might as well be a mummy in a tomb (what's wrong with licking a stamp and bunging it on a wossname, ay? Envelope. Say that nowadays, they laugh in your face). What I'm *really* saying is – me and Adeline, we get up to our room at the Cumberland, right, and she gets the top off that champagne what I laid on quick as a flash, like she been doing it for years (me – few times I done it, I always made it go like the fountains down Trafalgar) and then she come up to me bold as brass and gives me one hell of a bloody great smacker right plonk in the middle of my mouth, like, and the look on her face, right, is what I been dreaming and praying for since first I clap eyes on the gel – and yet all I can feel is sort of stupid and *old*, you know? On account of she knows the new rules, yeh? She knows the score. And I'm just stuck way back, frightened to open my bloody mouth for fear of whatever come out of it she's going to just *laugh* at – which I couldn't, quite frankly, really take, not at the moment. Other hand – can't just hang about, can I? I mean – time has come, mate: time has come.

'You having some of this or what?' says Adeline, holding out the bottle by its neck. 'Bed's all lovely and bouncy. Wish I had a bed like this – mine's all sad and small. I said I wanted a really big metal one – huge, you know? With bars on. But my mum, she says Nah: what you want a big bed for? You're only little. Mums don't get it, do they?'

And as Adeline set up a ripple of cheeky giggling at that, Reg convulsed under the weight of the evidence: *Yeh* – you see? Exactly what I mean. People of her *mum's* generation (what is to say *me*, shouldn't bloody wonder) are just *out* of it, aren't they? Want locking up in a bloody museum.

'I'm still full up from my tea,' managed Reg. 'Don't know I could go no bubbles. Dinner, I should say. Seems funny calling your tea your dinner . . . whole new language.'

Adeline set down the bottle, and her glass beside it. She then stood up and Jesus – such a bloody saucy look was creeping all over that perfect little dolly face of hers (telling you – you just wouldn't credit it). You see this in films, sometimes, a look like that, I'm not denying – didn't never think it would happen to me, though – not in real life, I didn't. It's like that *Lolita*, innit? With the girl and the old bloke. Never read the book, or nothing, but if it was anything like the film, well – they can stick it. Another bleeding boring old load of talk, that was. I don't frankly know how they get away with it, them so-called book writers. I mean – the come-on is this sexy kid having it away with the geezer, right? So why don't you never *see* nothing? Why's all they do is just *talk* and *look* and that? Anyone else, they'd have them up under the Trades Wossname Act, wouldn't they?

Point is, though – never mind all that. Nah – scrub all that, because as I been thinking all that pile of old cobblers, what Adeline's gone and done (while all that was, like, passing through my mind) is she's only reached behind her and undone that long zip in the back, ain't she? And that tight little dress of hers (blimey – she's a little madam, and no mistake) has sort of wriggled down and right off of her – she's stepping out of it altogether, now. The sight of her limbs has just about stopped up my throat. There's little tits there, yeh, in a little shiny bra thing, and the same sort of pants, look, just about keeping back all the doings – but it's her limbs what seem to me to be all over the place, now: long legs – loosely walking over – and outstretched arms what are getting nearer: those and her eyes are all I can see.

'Reg . . .?'

'Yeh?'

I wanna touch it, don't I? *Course* I bleeding wanna touch it – *made* for touching, all that, innit? Well bleeding *touch* it, then, you manky prat: this ain't no dream, mate – it's hanging there in front of your face, Reg – so what you standing about for, ay? You want a copperplate invitation, do you, or what is it?

'You still up for that kip, then, Reg? Bit of a lie-down, yeh?'

'Yeah.'

'Well come over to the bed, then, yeh? Come on, Reg.'

'Yeah.'

'Well come *on*, then. Wassamatter? Don't you . . . fancy me or something? You want me, Reg?'

'*Yeah.*'

'Well bleeding come *on*, then: I'm here. Wassamatter with you? You shy, or something?'

Reg looked down: might as well.

'Yeah . . .'

Adeline smiled and took his hand – and Reg felt an impulse shoot up and through him: he had touched her hand before, oh yes granted – but it was different now because of all these limbs: those and her eyes are all I can see.

Adeline led Reg to the bed, and she lay there. With one hand she pulled back the counterpane, and then she half-slid beneath it.

'You gonna take your clothes off or what, Reg?'

'Yeah.'

And he sort of did: the jacket, tie and trousers were easily discarded: no problems there (the nutter shoes he shuffled off). Then he undid the buttons of his shirt and while practically expiring with his efforts to suck in the more pendulous elements of that round and distended gut, he eased himself down, and then into the bed beside her. Adeline grinned very broadly and nestled right up to him. Her legs now seemed hot and clamped all down the length of his, and he gasped out loud quite as if he were a virgin, newly invaded. The flat of Adeline's hand lay softly on the grey and matted fluff of his chest, and pressed in as it slid on downwards. Reg concentrated very hard on just two things: willing himself, on the one hand, to become rampant and excited right up to and beyond the point of combustible frenzy – and on the other, striving really quite desperately not to explode in an altogether other sense, and disintegrate entirely.

Adeline's fingers were now done with rummaging (not going to work, is it?) but her voice was gentle, and not without sympathy.

'You tired, Reg – yeh?'

'Yeah.'

'That's OK. We can just lie here, OK? That OK with you, Reg?'

Reg compressed his lips, and shut tight his eyes.

'Yeah,' he said. Yeah, tired in one way, I could be – but then there's the other thing: I ain't for how long never done all this, have I? Not since my Laverne was barely on solids, I never. And then quite suddenly: 'Oh God I'm *sorry*, Adeline – I just don't know what's *wrong* with me – I mean I just – !'

'Sokay, Reg. Sokay.'

' – no but I mean I just been *yearning* for this, you know? Thought about nothing else, day and night – in the cab – back home with bleedin' . . . back home. I can't tell you . . . I really like to be with you, Adeline. You're like a ray of . . . it's just I'm a bit – oh Christ, I don't *know* what I am, I'm just – '

'Shy, Reg. You're just shy, and a little bit tired.'

'Oh you're . . . *wonderful*, Adeline. Just *wonderful*.'

Adeline chortled, and flung herself flat on her back.

'I ain't! Not when you get to know me, I ain't.'

And suddenly, again (all was sluggardly, and then it was sudden), Reg was intense:

'You happy, are you, Adeline? Your line of work? Is there – is there anything *else* I can do for you, Adeline? I mean – help you out, sort of style? Is there something, you know – that you need, or want, or anything? Ambitions, like . . .?'

'Oh yeh!' laughed Adeline. 'What I always say – five thousand pounds!'

Reg tucked in his chin, and nodded hard and sagely.

'OK . . .' he said. 'Fine. Done. Give it you tomorrow. Grapes suit you? Dinner time?'

Adeline was laughing quite wildly, now – very in tune with the joke.

'Oh yeh *great*, Reg – dinner time in the Grapes. And what – I'll bring a Sainsbury's bag along with me, will I? For the cash?'

'No need,' said Reg, quite casually. 'It's already in one.'

Adeline wagged her head at the silliness of Reg, and slithered out of bed. He watched her limbs as she sauntered over to the champagne bottle – watched her limbs as she poured out two glasses (longed for those limbs as the wine rushed up and coursed down the sides).

'Oh bloody hell!' yelped Adeline, picking up a flute in either hand and licking at their bases.

'I mean it, Adeline,' said Reg, quite gravely. 'Honestly

I do. I don't need money – it's better with you: you're young.'

Adeline looked at him.

'Don't mess about, Reg.'

'I *mean* it, Adeline! I really do. I'm not joking. Wouldn't do that.'

Adeline looked at him, and far more closely.

'Blimey . . .' she whispered. 'You really *do*, don't you? But Christ, Reg – I was only *kidding* you . . . I didn't expect – '

'I know,' said Reg. 'That's why.'

'But hey – you don't think I'm – ! I mean, you don't think I said that because I'm – !'

'No,' responded Reg, softly and with certainty. 'I don't.'

Adeline put the glasses just anywhere, and rushed back to him. She hurled herself on to the bed – and although Reg was quite winded, he loved it, of course he did – really did love it a lot.

'Oh Reg you're *fantastic*!' shrieked Adeline – and she had his face tight squeezed between the palms of her hands as she covered his red and protesting, thrilled and bursting lips with kisses. 'I can finally get to do that *art* course if you really mean it, Reg – I've just been wanting to do that since before I left school! I *hate* what I do – just *hate* it. Do you really really *really* mean it, Reg? Five grand? Cos that's what it costs. You really not joking? Oh *God*, Reg – I'm so happy!'

Reg looked up at her.

'I *love* you, Adeline.'

Her face was still, and Reg reached up a finger to catch that first fat tear as it rolled over her cheek. She subsided on top of him and he kissed her with a weight and tenderness that came close to overwhelming his entire understanding. Adeline was easing more clothes off both of them and Reg nearly was hurt by sweetness as she guided him tight and deep inside her: not one of them moved as the shudder of his coming sent up waves both in and around them. Reg felt dizzy with living and nearly asleep as Adeline kissed his eyelids. (My little Adeline – my own little Sainsbury's girl: it wasn't lust what ripped me up – I were torn by something else entirely.)

*

They brought the letter round by hand, and George – shocked into sobriety and knocked by it too – could only assume that they had done this, the high-ups in the Manchester, in order to ensure not just that it arrived without mishap, but also that it did so absolutely right now, this minute, no messing. It made for pained and appalling reading, and yet there was a curious thick blanket of inevitability huddled about its cold and skeletal form. George was still maybe stalled at the stage they call stunned (don't they?) and he knew that when that grew thin and wore away, then things would be worse, oh yes – much worse than this.

They had told him at the police station – as they got him to sign things, God knows what (and usually, you know, I'm really so punctilious about forms, and suchlike), and then handed back to him, oh God, his belt and tie – they told him that bail had been . . . (oh my Lord, I can't have heard right – could you, would you mind saying just that bit again? *Bail*, yes I see – bail: mm, yes, that's what I thought you said) . . . that, sweet Jesus, *bail* had been posted by his employer, and so until such time as . . . (But wait, please wait just a minute, sorry to interrupt you again, but . . . my *employer*, did you say? But how come my employer . . .? That is to say, I have been here just the one short and endless night, so how come my *employer* . . .? Oh I see, quite, yes – I understand: you're not at liberty to say, mmm, mmm, mmm. But as a result of this 'bail', I am at liberty to go: thank you, officer, thank you. A car home? Yes, thank you again – thank you so much, that would be very . . . because I don't in truth know quite where I am.)

And until such time as *what*? Sorry, sorry – I'm just a bit . . . oh yes, until such time as I am summoned, I do realize (don't I?) that I have formally and in writing agreed to remain in Greater London and to be contactable at all times at my sworn place of residence? Well, I may in all honesty have on some level realized that, and equally it may not have remotely registered – but now I surely *do* realize that this is very much the truth of the matter (the facts of the case). Thank you, officer, thank you. You know – I'd just like to say, um – *apologize*, really, to all of you, everyone – because last night, last night – it was so terribly *unlike* me, you know? So completely out of *character*. I mean, normal course of events, I don't even – Ah no, of course, I see: you are not at liberty to discuss the matter – no of course I see that – I didn't want to burden you, or anything, I simply just wanted to *say*. Someone is ready to take me home now? Oh good. Then I'll go. And thank you again – and sorry.

The letter from work had been signed by his immediate boss (George had always called him Jon, but it said Mister Jonathan Hawkins, here) and it was printed on Head Office paper – which you don't often see, it has idly occurred to me (not at branch level, you don't). It starts quite coldly – as well, I suppose, it might: I didn't phone back, it says here – I had *failed* to respond, is how they actually put it – despite at least two messages left at my home address. Management was extremely disconcerted by my unwarranted statement on live radio that all the monies from the robbery had not entirely been accounted for; even more irresponsible was my suggestion that a London taxi-driver might have aided and abetted, knowingly or not, the criminal and his crime. The police had been keen to keep both of these pieces of information to themselves, in order not to alert any other party concerning the direction their enquiries might currently be leading them. This, however – the opening of the second paragraph made quite chillingly clear – was no longer the major issue in this case. Initial reports of my quite scandalous behaviour the previous evening put my position within the Society in an altogether different light. Jon – Mister Jonathan Hawkins – would be obliged to me if I would at the very earliest opportunity . . . (You know, it's just as well I'm no drinker, because despite the fact that my stomach is in turmoil and my head feels practically detached from the rest of me – while nonetheless bearing down hard – I could, and I know it's early, quite early in the morning, I could quite go a small shot of something harsh, right now) . . . if I would at the very earliest opportunity . . . (Or maybe, you know, if I had a best friend to turn to, or a brother or a father – a *mother*, for God's sake: I have none of these) . . . if I would at the very earliest opportunity . . . (I thought that could have been the front door slamming, just then: but it couldn't have been because you see the only other people who actually live here – or, I should say, who *used* to live here with me, in my home, are my wife, Shirley, who has gone, yes, left me – and my two children, who are, if memory serves from so long ago, still with Shirley's mother, unless Shirley has seen fit to remove them elsewhere – I wouldn't, of course, know; so that couldn't, you see, have been the front door slamming, because everyone's *gone*) . . . if I would . . . at the very earliest opportunity . . . (But there is noise, now, you know – in the hall, it very much seems: do you suppose, on top of all this, I might have *burglars*? It seems unlikely; and what would they take? Not me, I imagine – me they wouldn't touch) . . . so, in short, to sum up: if I would, at the very earliest opportunity . . .

'George. What's wrong with you? You look like hell.'

George let the letter flutter to the floor as his head was practically disconnecting itself in its effort to spin round and concentrate on just where, exactly? On where this sound has come from.

'Shirley! Oh my God – *Shirley*! Oh thank heavens – you're

back, you're back, you're back. Are you back, Shirley? Are you safe? Where are the kids? Are they safe? Are you back?'

Shirley looked down.

'Yes, George,' she said, so very flatly. 'Yes I am. Back.'

George trod on the letter as he stiffly moved a little way towards her. As he stood just one pace distant, wide-eyed and wondering whether he should or even could reach out and touch her, his heel ground down on the letter's conclusion. His mind had long ago taken it in, even if his eyes had failed to focus: he was to report without delay, so that a dialogue may ensue . . . vis-à-vis the terms of his termination.

*

George, now, was doing his absolute best to feel quite wonderful. I mean – this *is* wonderful, isn't it? I mean – yesterday, well: life fallen apart because wife and kids gone, yes? Now they back so wonderful, right? Well no not really, in the light of other things (They Took My Fingerprints: I've got a record). But let's just dwell on this one new good bit, yes? Cope with other things later.

'Shirley, oh Shirley – I knew you wouldn't, couldn't *really* leave me. You were maybe – tea, yes? Make tea, will I? Then we can sit down and – *look*, Shirley – I think I understand: I had to be taught some sort of a *lesson*, that it? Well I *have* – I will, I'll – look, I'll just make us a nice pot of – I'll get the kettle on, mm? I could actually do with a good cup of – and then we'll talk. But I have to say, Shirley – things are not, um, looking all that great. But I'll tell you. We'll get through, yes? Anyway: *tea.*'

Shirley slumped on to the sofa, and watched him go. In the sudden silence of seclusion, she felt her face crease up, and her hands rushed up to catch it, before it fell away. Her wet, hurt eyes revolved to the side and then rolled above her, as she mindlessly plucked at the scarf at her neck. What on earth could bloody *George* have to say that could make me feel worse than I do? What in hell could have happened during the terribly short time since I left this life for a new one (and now I'm back)? The storm of release I had felt as I closed that door behind me – the excitement had me so nearly delirious . . . and then came this: I'm *back*.

He'd been pleased enough to see me, Max – and yes, I was a bit nervous about that, because I hadn't actually told him that I'd be coming, or anything, and sometimes he could get a bit ratty about that sort of thing. Because I hadn't sat down and planned, you know, that this was to be the day I would finally break clean and walk away from this stale and terrible marriage that somehow had woven itself around me. Been *dreaming* about it for, oh God – months, months and months . . . since not long after me and Max started getting properly serious, I suppose (and how serious, actually, can he have been? *I* was serious, oh yes: I told – I told him just how much last night . . . maybe he thought I was serious enough for the both of us). It was just George going on and on in that prattish bloody way of his: *Applaud* me, people – because *I* work in a *building* society (why did he always feel so bloody *proud* about that? I mean, OK, it's a living, yeah sure – but it's not exactly *Downing* Street, is it? Although you listen to George and you'd hardly know the difference). And the kids were with Mummy and I just suddenly thought Right: that's it: if George is going to tell me how bloody great he is – on account of he *didn't* foil a robbery (get that!) – if he tells me this just one more time, I'll stick a bloody knife in him – and he's just never going to *stop*, is he? He won't ever *stop* because this is just *George*: the bloody way he is. So I'll go. Right now. Just take off.

'Shirl!' comes Max's cackle, crackling over the intercom. 'What a pleasant bleeding surprise. Get yerself up here, gel – saucy little sex-pot, you.'

So you can see, can you, how time spent with Max was

such a blessed release from George. I mean OK – Max is a bit of a, well – what they call a rough diamond, well yes I know that, it's plain to see – but it's his tremendous sense of *life* that I find so . . . well: anyway.

By the time I got up to the flat (penthouse, actually – absolutely fabulous in a bit of a Seventies *Playboy* sort of a way, but the views are sensational) Max already had a huge Gordon's and tonic mixed and waiting for me – in that wonderful fluted glass he knows I love: great rocks of ice, two whole quarters of lemon and a fresh mint leaf right on the top (I didn't actually go for that, first time he did it, but I really do like it now; doesn't seem right without. God – at home, you say you want a gin and bloody George, he practically has a fit – but then, he hardly ever drinks, George: can't imagine him drunk).

'So what brings you round, then, Shirl? Couldn't keep away, ay?'

Just as well you didn't turn up an hour ago, though, sweetie, else you still would've been hammering at the door. Had that new little girl round here, didn't I? Working on the advertising side. Bloody Monica, that po-faced secretary of mine – PA, whatever the fuck – she goes *Honestly*, Max, I really do think that that particular department is well up to strength – I don't at all believe we *need* a new girl. Ho *yus*, Monica, but I was doing the interviews, see, and I takes one look at Charlotte (I call her Charlie – she's a posh bit of thing, and she goes for that big time) and I says to Monica Oh yes we fucking *do*, love. And turns out she's a good girl, Charlie – well, be fair: catch 'em young and they all are, aren't they? Now look – get me straight: I'm very happy to be seeing old Shirl the Twirl this evening, don't think I'm not, but it is, isn't it? Bit naughty, eh? Just coming round uninvited, like some sort of *salesman*. She's getting just a bit beyond herself, is Shirl – PRs go like that – and she just might want slapping down, if you know what I'm meaning. See, what it is – they take advantage. Even the ones that are so bleeding humble and grateful, when they're new to the game (and I'm not saying Charlie won't get to be one of them, neither: early days yet, so who's to say? But look at the way even Feebs went well to the bad. That Annie, she was a non-starter from the off – didn't even want to be called *Annie*, bleeding hell: what's she think she was? Just wanted her mortgage paid, seemed to me. But Feebs I thought was a right fucking gem: didn't never think that Feebs would turn on me like that; but there you go – that's just what I'm saying, isn't it? You can't never tell).

Now take Shirl the Twirl as a for instance – part-time PR with the company, she was – couldn't tell you what that is, nor if she was any bleeding good at the job or not, to be honest (don't take much of an interest, that side of things: for myself, I reckon I can handle my own PR, know what I mean? And as to the company, well – what's the fucking publicity boys up to, ay? What they're paid for). But she was a right little cracker on the bed front, I tell you that for free. And always very nicely turned out too, which I like (that's one thing about PRs – lovely, aren't they? Slim little skinny black legs, tight little short-skirted suit on 'em). So how it went was, I'd be saying Tell you what, love – let's go out and hang on the nosebag and then we can fuck off back to my place, what say? And she'd go Oh I'd *love* to, Max, but I've got this presentation to work on – and I'd be back with Sod the presentation, Christ's sake, and she'd give me that look she give me and go (saucy little sex-pot) *We-e-ell*, Max: you're the boss. Else she'd maunder on about her bloody kids. In the end it turned out she couldn't handle it all – as Monica kept on pointing out to me, day in day out (bless her: don't know where I'd be without her, miserable cow) – so *official*, like, I get rid of her, Shirley, but I still slip her whatever few quid she was earning, like, and now everyone's sweet. So you'd think, wouldn't you – light of all that – you'd get just a bit of respect: know her place, yeah? Not just turn up when she fucking well feels like it, you know? Not that I ain't pleased to see her, or nothing: always nice for a tumble, is Shirl the Twirl. Look – I even fixed her her favourite drink, haven't I, with the mint leaf and all (so what's she want? *Jam* on it?).

'What's with the suitcase, Shirl? You taken up, what – selling brushes door-to-door? That your new game, is it?'

'*Daft*, Max! No, I've um – mmm, this drink: God I need it. No, I've *come* to you, Max. Finally. I've come to stay.'

'Yeh? Well fair enough, love. Only what you normally say is you can't stop the night cos of the kids, don't you? They fucked off to your mother's, then? Or that deadbeat bloke of yours stuck with them?'

'Don't . . . don't call him that, Max. It's not *his* fault.'

'Well – I only got it off *you*, didn't I? Don't know the guy.'

'Anyway . . . I'm not just talking the night. I mean I've *left* him. God it feels so good! I feel so, oh – God, I just feel so *free*: it's *wonderful*. I do so love you, Max.'

Max was energetically stabbing down into his highball glass with a chromium stirrer, mashing up the fruit in his vodka-based Pimm's – something he drank, Christ, bleeding jugs of, once the thirst and the mood came over him. I do hope, was filtering through his mind, I do so hope for her sake that this bird's having a high old joke. Cos if she don't know she's being funny, then it's down to me to bleeding tell her, and pronto.

'Don't mess about, Shirl, there's a good girl. Now – you eaten, or what? Only we can get food in, if you fancy it – else – '

'Max – listen: I'm not – '

' – or else we can go round Sophie's, but I don't know I'm up for all the palaver of changing, you want the truth. There's cold muck in the fridge.'

Shirley's eyes were questing and imploring: why is he talking about food? Why isn't he talking about *me*?

'Max – did you *hear* me? This is the start of something different! This is the beginning of something great and new for the both of us. You always *said* it killed you, when I had to leave . . . well I'm here – I'm *here*, Max – for you. Permanently. It's wonderful.'

Max snapped on his smirk of reluctance: what it said to him (and sod everyone bleeding else) was *Right*, mate: dirty work to be done, it most surely would appear – and you, son, are very much the man to get it seen to.

'Shirl. Correction. This ain't the end or beginning of nothing. You got all this wrong, girl. See – trouble with women is – '

'*Women*? What do you mean – *women*? I'm not just a *woman* – !'

Max allowed himself the shadow of a smile: oh yes you *are*, darling – and that's exactly and bloody all you are (they just don't get it, do they?).

'Don't interrupt me, Shirl: *talking*, aren't I? Like I say, the trouble with women is – they got something good, like, and so instead of thinking Hey, I like this: this I like – they go *Right*, mate: I want *more* – more will be better. I want *all* of it, for ever, twenty-four hours a bleeding day. And that's a big mistake, Shirl. Big mistake. Like your gin and tonic: you wanna drink it round the clock? No more tea and coffee? No nice nip of Scotch? *Course* you bleeding don't. More just messes you up, girl. More just spoils the whole bleeding thing. Get me?'

'Max – why are you talking about *drinks*, now? I'm talking about – '

'I *know* what you're talking about, love – I know it bleeding well. And what I'm saying is No. Enn Owe. No. Got it? I don't do all that – I got my life the way I want it, see? It took me a while, and it don't come cheap, living like this – and I'm sorry, but I ain't about to screw it up for you, darling – and nor for no one else, neither.'

Max paused now, because by rights it was her turn, yeh? And for a moment it looked as if Shirley was on the point of some stuttered utterance – she believed she was, though nothing she felt would gang up and form; and so silence accompanied by a look of hurt and shock and maybe a glimmer of temper was all that confronted Max's unwavering eye.

'*So,*' concluded Max, in as kindly a tone as he could frankly be bothered with, 'let's have no more prat-talk, OK? Now – what you wanna do about food, love? Or you wanna just come over here and give your Uncle Maxie a nice little cuddle?'

Shirley had stood, and was quivering now.

'Max – *please* . . . you don't *understand* . . .'

'Shirley, Shirley – how many *times*? Hey? It's *you* what don't understand, love. It's you what don't get it. What can I say, ay? What bleeding more can I say?'

'But *Max* – *Max*: I've *left* him. Don't you see? *Left* him. I thought you *wanted* me . . . I thought . . . oh Christ – I feel so – !'

'*Do* want you, Shirl – course I bloody do. But like I *always* wanted you, see? There ain't nothing different.'

And then a flush of anger rose and blossomed at the base of Shirley's throat – was spreading across her cheeks.

'Max – you just can't *do* this – it's not *fair* to me. I've given up *everything* for you, Max – you can't just – '

And Max too was not now far behind in the rising fury stakes:

'Now you just wait a bloody fucking *minute*, Shirley! What you mean – you give up *everything*? Hey? What's all this "*everything*"? What you give up is some thickhead loser in a dead-end job and your crap little house – and what you was hoping for was – ' And here Max threw wide his arms, the better to encompass his entire magnificent empire, this to include the emperor himself ' – all of bleeding *this*. I don't, quite frankly, call that much of a sacrifice, do you? Sounds to me like more of a *con* – take my meaning? What you think – I was born yesterday? You reckon you're the first bird, do you, what took a gander at this lot and thought Ooh yeah: very tasty – I'll have myself a slice of that? The reason I got it all, girl, is cos I bleeding don't hand it *out*. I been *nice* to you, Shirl – '

'Max! Max! God's *sake* – !'

'Fuck *off*! I'm talking! I been *nice* to you, Shirl – done good by you – and this what I get. And here – here's another thing: what about your kids, ay? Just going to abandon them, were you? Like they was nothing?'

'Of *course* I – of *course* not, no. I'd take them with me – course I would. Christ, Max – please don't *do* this – '

But Max was staring at her now, as if mesmerized – his wide flat face caught as if in a spotlight.

'Oh I *see* – I *see*. Oh *very* nice . . . oh *very* bleeding nice I must say. I didn't see the whole picture, did I? Not only was I going to get wall-to-bleeding-wall *Shirley* all over my fucking life, but my pad was going to be overrun by snot-nosed kids belonging to some other bastard what I was going to raise – that it?'

'Max . . . oh *Max* – !'

'Well I'm very *sorry*, Shirley love – and this is maybe the worst business decision I ever made in my entire bloody life on *earth*, OK – but having weighed up all the undoubted advantages in your extremely tempting offer I find myself with huge bloody reluctance coming down on the side of You Must Be Fucking *Joking*! You gotta be taking me for a right bleeding idiot, Shirley. Well listen – news for you, girl: I *ain't*. Now: listen even more carefully. What I want you to do – '

'Max – don't. Please don't. Oh God – *please* don't – '

'*Talking* – shut your face. What I want you to do, right this very second, is pick up your case of brushes and fuck off back where you come from – got it? We're *done*, Shirley – over. Should've seen it coming a mile off – you been nothing but trouble from the off. And you can kiss goodbye the money and all, ungrateful cow. Bleeding *nerve* . . .'

Shirley now was practically hysterical – afraid to live

260

through another moment. She kept on shrieking out his name: *Max! Max! Max! Max!* Even as he bundled her out of the flat and into the lift, she was sobbing and coughing out his name; only the cold of the street served to smack her to rights – and the hotel she booked into, she couldn't later as she lay on the bed there, softly weeping, even have told you its name.

*

And back with George, breathless again, with these same four walls around me, time was somehow passing. It had not been decided to leave the children with Shirley's mother for just another day: simply, neither Shirley nor George had thought to phone or collect them, nor even to mention their names in passing.

George, thought Shirley, seems for some odd reason (can he really care about me that much?) quite as stunned as I truly am feeling: stunned and amazed, and maybe still just on the brink of a deeper and longer-lasting sadness that, I am well aware, yes, could lay me low. I have drunk quite a lot of that gin (maybe, um eat something, should I? It hasn't really occurred to me to be even slightly hungry – and George too, he seems quite unbothered) and I know that it is more than possible that a degree of this blanked-out astonishment that I am, in truth, so very grateful for – it is possible, yes, that this is little more than the numbing touch of alcohol. So better keep doing it, I think I better had – because I don't frankly believe I could bear it, if feeling started seeping back.

George was in another room, and drinking whisky (he didn't even know they had any, but he was, oh God – so very pleased they had). The lowering pain in his head as the day wore on he had found to be almost literally unbearable (I have never felt this, never) and yes I am appalled to discover that only more of this poison is all that will help, but I find it difficult now even to think in terms of *damage*: in the light of all this, what more harm can I come to?

I haven't told her. I haven't said so much as a single word about it. Well I don't want, do I, to frighten her away again? I don't know where she went, last night (and do you know – just glancing at the window, it very much seems as if night, or at least evening, certainly, is with us again). I imagine to a girlfriend: friend from work. Very pally, you know, PRs. Not at all like my job, the job I used to do: you could set your watch by me, you know (ask anyone) – same time leaving, same time coming home. But in the PR world – in that world, Shirley was forever explaining to me, you never know quite *what's* going to come up, you see, and nor when, no: nor when. So she's been out a lot of evenings, lately – launch parties, Press do's, all that sort of thing – and look, the very nature of PR is, well . . . friendliness, isn't it? Being nice to people. So I doubt if she was short of a bed for the night. Because no of *course* – of *course* I don't believe for a single second that she was having a, God – *affair*: quite obviously nonsense, isn't it? First of all, people who *are* having affairs would never ever dream of *calling* them that, would they? Affairs are what *other* people, people of whom you don't at all approve, are slyly conducting behind the backs of those who care.

Shirley, in such a situation, would have been bound to have considered herself part of a loving and mutual relationship – well, ridiculous, isn't it, as I think must be plain to all: it's *me* she loves – me and the kids. But I'm not so blind – and even after the shock of the wreck of the rest of my life, and all this punishing booze, I can, you know, put myself in another's place – and so no, I do see clearly why, of course I see why, she *said* it. People – women, anyway – they'll say these things to give you a *jolt*: jerk you, maybe, out of a sort of complacency which, yes, I will admit, I was possibly guilty of sliding quite close to. But you *see*, don't you, the terrible cost of this irresponsible gesture? If she hadn't *done* that (and why then – why did I not see it then for just the empty statement and feminine wile it so very clearly was?) – if she had not told me to my face that she was *leaving* me, well, ask yourself: would I have gone to pubs? Drunk things? All those things? And somehow hit a (Christ, oh Jesus Christ) woman in the face? I've . . . got to have a drink, bit of a top-up – just a drop. The smell of the cell still clings to me: I ought to wash, I ought to change.

Shirley wandered into the room, a tumbler hanging loosely from her arm: she seemed startled to see George, half on and half off the sofa, looking quite dead (but of *course*, yes – George lives here too, doesn't he? With me). The gin was over; she had upturned and shaken the bottle to be sure – and yes, it was empty: no more came out. And so she was determinedly prowling, in quest of something else – anything, really, would do.

She rummaged in a cupboard and found only sticky and old unspeakable Christmas things, and so made for the whisky on the table. A huge irritation burst right through her quite suddenly, brittly invading the miasma of gloom and aching that wrapped her up: because in many ways, oh Christ help me, Max had been *right*, hadn't he? It was good, what they had – so why did she have to go and so spectacu- larly mess it all up? What had *possessed* her, at all? Well it was George, wasn't it? Bloody *George*: if he hadn't gone just that bit too far – if all his cockiness had not come to a gloriously awful peak as a result of those stupid little bits about him in the paper, then she might, Shirley – she just might have managed to keep it all down. And now all that and a lot else was spewed just everywhere, which was just sick-making in itself.

A clattering somewhere quite close alerted them both – George jerking up and over as if it were gunfire. Together, and over so many dead hours, they had woven a stale cocoon of hot old rags wound tightly around, and this new and outside noise was not just intensely surprising, but charged and alarming too. The realization hit into George the very next second: the papers. It was not evening he had glimpsed, but the callous insinuation of yet another day: the scorn of morning was as harsh to George as it was unexpected, and new bad things were reaching out to take him.

The *papers*! He lurched into the hall and tugged at the bundle, wedged quite tightly in the slot. He roughly stashed behind his back the local weekly, and let the others just fall around. Shirley was there, now (what *was* that noise? I don't *understand* . . . oh it's the papers, the papers – only the papers. But how can it, though, be the *papers*? They come in the morning, don't they? So it's morning, then, is it? Must be, must be). She stooped down to them – a sort of automatic reaction, she now was imagining, because the papers were in her arms as she moved slowly and loosely back into the room, but she could not recall actually picking them up.

George stayed put (had she gone? Yes, she'd gone) and was leafing through frantically – and here, oh dear God, here it was (not too big, not too big a piece, thank Christ – no picture of me, thank Christ – who's that woman?) but here, nonetheless, it bloody well was:

'HERO' ARRESTED IN PUB BRAWL

Local man George Carey, 34, described in one newspaper recently as the 'Hero of the Hour' as a result of his 'having a go' when a man – since apprehended – attempted to rob the Argyle Street branch of the Manchester Building Society, where he is an employee, was yesterday morning released on bail, accused of having allegedly lashed out for no apparent reason at Lucy Keyes, out with friends in the Feathers pub, North Road, shortly before closing time on Tuesday evening. Miss Keyes (pictured), 23, of Camden Town, who works in Dixons, said to our reporter: 'I just couldn't believe it – he was well gone and just started hitting out. I'm getting married the Saturday after next, but the doctor says it will have gone down by then.' Her fiancé, John Post, 25, also of Camden Town, said: 'I just don't believe the police letting him out like that, bail or no bail. He's mad, bonkers – an animal. I know what I'd do with him.' Miss Keyes and Mr Post met while working at Dixons. Carey's case comes up next week. No spokesman from the Manchester Building Society was available for comment.

George's eyes flicked up, down and across the piece, sucking in the odd bit, dreading the next – misconstruing a good deal of it, working backwards – rushing on forward and dizzily to the end. He took in too, very vaguely, a crammed-in postscript to the story: 'An unnamed cab-driver was today said to be helping police with their enquiries in connection with the Manchester robbery.'

George stuffed the paper behind the chest in the hall; he would retrieve it later, and with fanatical zeal go over every single word – in order – and then again, with care. (*This* time they got my name right, didn't they? Oh yes – *this* time they bloody did.) Back in the room, Shirley had the daily in front of her, but she was idly glancing out of the window (one curtain, anyway, she had tugged at until finally it was more or less drawn). I've got to. Max. Get him back. *Got* to. Must.

George said: 'Do you want tea, Shirley? Anything?'

Got to make a phone call. Have a meeting. The terms of my termination.

Shirley raised her glass, by way of reply – it now had in it a good inch of Scotch, and she snuffled in a vaguely embarrassed way at the incongruity of, oh – not just this, but so much else.

'Isn't that that woman . . . ?' she said then (sort of curious, she could easily have been – but not, really, very). 'That woman you work with? Didn't we meet her at that awful Christmas thing?'

George wandered over and looked down at the out-spread paper. And then he looked closer.

'You're right,' he said – quite immensely surprised, this latest odd thing serving to spike and heighten his confusion. 'Isobel March. Good God. Good God Almighty. How terribly *strange.*'

CHAPTER TEN

Isobel had been sitting on the stone bench, in the shade of what she now thought of as their very *special* tree (the weather, you know, has been utterly delightful – I'm just so lucky: this, on top of everything else). I got up terribly early, this morning – Mike's just awful: he loves to sleep in till much too late. Last evening was bliss: he arranged to have this most wonderful picnic packed up for just us – fed up with the dining room, he said he was – all those fat blokes and skinny women *looking* all the time (and he was right, you know – people *do* stare, right at you; it's terribly rude – I wonder, sometimes, if they even know they're doing it. A lot of them are foreign, of course, and I well remember from that time in Florence with mother – don't *ask* me when – the people at cafés: just didn't stop. Didn't try to hide it, or anything: just looked straight at you). And he'd got a bottle of champagne, which was terribly naughty of him; *Look*, Mike, I said – if you really *are* meant to be giving up drinking, I can help you. I mean to say, honestly – I really couldn't care two hoots either way if I have a drink or not. And he said – that really wicked, lovely smile he's got – he said Don't be so silly, Isobel; you can't have a picnic without champagne – and anyway, champagne isn't *drinking*, is it? Champagne is just *fun*.

It's hard to believe, now, that I came here because I was stressed. God – never *been* so unstressed, so relaxed, as I am right now: I think what I feel could even be happiness. It's this place, really – must be; this place, yes, and Mike, of course. I said to him last night, when he was spooning out strawberries, I said Mike, tell me – tell me honestly: what is it that you see in me? (And I really wanted him to tell me, I really did, because whatever little thing there might be about me that anyone might find even a little bit appealing, I've quite lost sight of.) He just said: You're lovely. And he kissed me.

I'm not getting up my hopes, or anything: a little too long in the tooth for silly thoughts of that kind. We're both in an unreal environment here, aren't we? We each just happen to be in this very singular place (and when in my life did I ever imagine that I would be somewhere like this? Didn't even know they *existed*) – yes, we're both of us just here at the very same time: coincidence, yes? And life – real life – is different. And Mike, of course – he's still a young man. Successful, I should guess (he doesn't talk about what he does, but you can always tell, can't you? If someone's confident. And that watch of his – which I really very much like now, like it a lot – it very clearly cost him a great deal of money). So I couldn't tell you (I don't dare ask) if this, whatever this is, can go, you know – on, or anything. With mother, of course, nothing of this nature can ever be easy. So just enjoy the moment, is the way I'm feeling. Well. Not really. I can't actually do that – never ever could. I would love to build, and Mike – he is, you know: so very gentle and kind; now that he has come, I would hate to lose him. But look: it's best not to dwell.

Isobel now rose and stretched out her arms far more extravagantly and for a good deal longer than she needed to, as if rehearsing a vast and all-enclasping welcome – and loving, too, the sun as it warmed her upturned palms. I think I'll see if His Majesty is awake yet – maybe he'd like some coffee, or a bit of breakfast. Hee – this is funny: last night in the room I told him about the cats. I didn't actually mention mother – I just was talking about cats. He said, I've got this theory about cats and dogs: the reason why women like cats so much is that they see them as a cross between soft toys and babies – but when men like dogs, shall I tell you why? Because they remind them of *blokes*. I don't know why I find that so funny – maybe it's even true, I really don't know. (And – for the record – I'm not, actually, one of these lonely and dotty old women who's besotted with her cats; I wouldn't in truth really mind very much if they left or died or something – one less thing to see to.) I put all of that right out of my head at the time, though, because his hands were moving across me, and I quivered, I quivered – I remember just shaking with much more than anticipation: it was more a pent-up and nearly desperate keenness to have again all those feelings of the night before.

Isobel wrapped around her quite tightly the white towelling robe – *another* marvellous thing about being here, actually: you don't have to keep on deciding what to *wear* all the time, which is just as well in my case. I never really realized before just how pitiful my so-called wardrobe actually is – even the best things are more or less invisible. Most people here just wear track suits or these robe things in the daytime – and you get to *keep* them, too (it said so in that big brown leather sort of book affair in the room). It's lovely, the feeling of the grass as it brushes your ankles as you just amble along: something I'll miss, when I'm back in London. There's a lot I'll miss, when I'm back in London – and nothing, in truth, I really want to have again. Job, maybe (it gets me out of the house).

Already there are three or four people in the pool. There's an indoor one as well, with a rather worrying bubbling bit attached, but in this weather everyone seems to want to splash about under the sky, and I'm not a bit surprised. I envy them – love to join them, really, but the state of my thighs at the back is just perfectly shameful (these full-length mirrors – they spring on you such terrible surprises). And I never properly noticed it before but both of my swimsuits almost make a feature of the criss-cross wrinkled and puckered old tawdry skin just above and between my breasts: quite as ageing as hands, to my mind. Mike doesn't seem to mind – seems quite blind to any of all that.

And here's another of these awful people – just staring, like that. What on earth does she imagine she's *staring* at, in heaven's name? I'm not *that* funny-looking, am I? And God – she *is*, you know – that woman with her silly orange tan and all that jewellery – she's actually (can't be, can she?) *sniggering* at me, quite openly. I wish I had the nerve to stare right back at her – see how *she* likes it. And now her friend – another very hard-looking woman, to my eyes (does she really think that hair looks even remotely natural?) – she's laughing too! Yes: *laughing* – I *mean* laughing, more or less out loud and right at me! Right – get away from this (I don't want them to see me blushing): I'll use this side entrance here and work my way round to the main hall (how can people *be* so rude? I wonder if Mike's awake yet). There's a cleaner coming towards me; I suppose they start at dawn, must they, to get everything right before the guests start filtering down (could do with one of them at home). And no – he can't be (I'm imagining it, I must be) – but he is, he is: he's looking right at me and his face is split by all that grinning and now he's *spoken*: he's said to me *Well*, girl – *you're* obviously enjoying your stay with us! Can he *really* have said that to me? He's passed, now – still wagging his head, though – and I haven't of course *responded*. How on earth *does* one? What in heaven's name is actually going on, here?

I am ordering some breakfast, now, from the girl in the hall. Coffee, yes – and tea as well, actually. Toast – brown, I think. And I'm pretty sure that's all – but I can ring down, yes, if I want anything cooked, can I? And the girl has said Absolutely, no problem, Miss March – and that will be in *your* room now, presumably? Well *honestly* – I mean, *really*. That really is a bit much, isn't it? I mean, what – have these people really nothing better to do than . . .? *My* room, yes. That's all I can utter. I'm really very affronted. Ah – here's

Polly (the pretty one, the nice one) and I can at least say to her, because you can talk to Polly – *Well*, Polly, I say, what's *your* opinion? Hm? Do I look like a circus clown to you? Have I grown donkey's ears during the night? I don't know if I'm becoming paranoid in my old age, but all morning people seem to have been, you know – looking at me, and things. And Isobel, now, attempted mirth: Have they got me confused with Elizabeth Taylor, do you think?

And what's this? Polly has lowered her eyes – and in order to say whatever it is, she is consciously subduing her voice. *Ah*, is what she has come up with so far. Well, I don't get much from *Ah*, do I? But something is about to be said, I feel, and I'm nervous, frankly. Polly is beckoning me into an office, and I'm following her, I am, of course I am. We're in there, now, the two of us, and next she shuts the door.

'You don't know, do you . . .?' started Polly, with enormous reluctance, it seemed to Isobel, as well as considerable embarrassment. 'I'm terribly, awfully *sorry* about this, Miss March – we do everything we can to stop all this sort of thing, but sometimes these awful people . . . they just get in, and . . .'

Isobel looked at her blankly. 'What are you saying? Look I'm really very sorry if I'm being *obtuse*, but – ?'

By way of reply, Polly opened a tabloid newspaper, and slid it over to Isobel, who – quite irritated – glanced down at it. And then she looked at it hard – her lips just shook, beyond her control, as she watched her own two hands reach out for the thing. Then she looked sharply at Polly: tell me, please, I have taken leave of my senses – or that this is some sort of very poor and misplaced joke? But Polly was intent upon the floor, and barely muttering: 'I really am so terribly . . . we all just feel *awful* about this . . .'

Over half a page was a grainy colour picture of Mike and Isobel on their own stone bench, beneath their very *special* tree. One of Mike's hands was full on Isobel's breast, and in the other there teetered a flat half-bottle of Bell's. Their lips were touching. LOVE-RAT SANDY IS AT IT AGAIN – these were the huge accompanying words that made no sense to Isobel, now, and she felt so simple as she heard herself quite feebly ask of Polly, Who is *Sandy*? I just don't understand . . .

And Polly looked even more alarmed, now.

'Oh God,' she whispered. 'Don't you really *know*?'

Isobel just softly shook her head, and found herself reading:

Actor Mike Bailey, 40, better known to the viewing millions as The Road's love-rat and boozer Sandy Hall, is at it again! Allegedly packed off to £300-a-night The Meadows clinic in Buckinghamshire by an exasperated producer and instructed to chuck his real-life womanizing and drinking – but whoops! He doesn't seem to be doing very well, does he? And blimey – this one looks old enough to be his granny! Not like last month's model, 22-year-old game show presenter Lana Hendrix. Wonder what long-suffering wife Cheryl will have to say when Mike gets home! A spokesman for Granada Television said last night: 'Mr Bailey's private life is his own affair. We have no comment to make.'

When Polly judged that Isobel had stood there long enough to have read all this a hundred times, she tentatively reached out a hand, halting its progress well shy of Isobel's elbow.

'Can I . . .? Get you some tea, maybe? Would you like to sit down, Miss March? Oh God – I just can't apologize enough for all this. We *try* to vet everyone who comes here, but . . . did you really not know about . . . who Mike Bailey is?'

Isobel seemed surprised by the sound of a voice in the room.

'Hm? No, I . . . no. I don't watch any of these, um – soap

272

things . . . never really seem to have the time . . . I think I'll just go and, um . . . has Mike, Mister Bailey seen this?'

And now Polly's mortification was set to be complete.

'I, uh – imagine so, yes. His PA faxed him quite early.'

'I see.'

'He's, uh – gone, actually, Miss March. Checked out a while ago.'

Isobel nodded slowly, and with narrowed eyes – as if a riddle that had confounded her for simply years and years was at last unravelled before her eyes.

'And also, Miss March – your sister telephoned, about twenty minutes ago. Sounded quite urgent. We did have a look for you, but . . .'

Isobel nodded more briskly, now, and indicated the phone on the desk. Polly nodded back as if she had been programmed to do so, and gratefully backed out of the room, gently closing the door behind her.

Geraldine answered on the second ring.

'Isobel – thank God. Come. Get *back* here. It's mother – oh God. She's had a – doctor thinks it's a stroke. Oh God, Isobel, I'm so – it's *your* fault – you never should've – '

'I'm coming. I'm leaving,' said Isobel, quite automatically. She looked out of the window, at the sun on the plane trees. 'I'm finished here, now,' she nearly whispered.

*

It's very nearly time I went to phone my Adeline. Seven minutes, I reckon, it'll take me to walk down that phone box. Well – I can't go phoning from here, can I? Bleedin' Enid – she's as close as you can get to a bloody great corpse, most of the time, but the ears she's got on her, I'm not joking – like a bleeding elephant. And no I *can't* take the cab, Clever Dick, can I? Wouldn't risk it, even that short a way. And yeh I know – it's my own bleeding fault – I'm just not thinking straight, lately. See, what happened was – I went up the Grapes of a dinner time, like I says I would, and there was Adeline, good as gold – even got me in a pint, hadn't she? Drop of vodka for herself. And I can't tell you – brought a right lump to the old throat, that did. Can't never recall no female ever buying me a drink, like, and it got to me, that did – right there.

'Reg,' she starts up right away, no messing. 'Listen to me, Reg – I been thinking, ain't I? And I don't mind if you changed your mind, or nothing. I mean – I know you sort of said all that – you know, the money and that – in the heat of the, like, moment, and so I just wanted to say that I really don't mind if – '

Reg just grinned like a looney and dumped the carrier bag down on the table in front of her: counted it out last night, hadn't he? Five grand exactly, mostly twenties – tidied it all up with elastic bands, made it nice. Thought of sticking it into a Jiffy sort of envelope or something like that, but in the end, well – the Sainsbury's bag just seemed right what the doctor ordered, somehow. Poetic. And I'm telling you – there's loadsa gelt left: least the same again, shouldn't wonder. That'll come in handy for more of them slap-up meals down the Cumberland (not forgetting my bit of afters, after).

'It's all there,' said Reg – quite proudly, and loving the moment. 'They do a nice pint in here.'

Adeline, her eyes so bright, risked placing just the one finger at the edge of the bag (little Gucci watch looked right lovely on her) – fearful to set off the alarm: or maybe it would blow up in her face.

'I just – don't *believe* it . . .' she whispered. 'That anyone on earth would do this for me. Thanks *ever* so much, Reg – I really really mean it. I'm just choked. Honest I am.'

'Love you, girl – don't I? Now here – tell me: what's this art course all about, then, ay? What – you going to be like that Picasso bloke, are you, pickling dead sheep?'

Adeline laughed. 'Nah – it's not nothing like that. It's

design, is what it is. Sort of packaging and display kind of stuff is what I'm really into – seen enough of it down bloody Sainsbury's, I can tell you.'

'Speck you have. So what – you wanna design, what – cans and boxes and stuff like that, is it?'

'Yeh – and whole ad campaigns, and that. I'd really like to work for one of the big companies, one day – Saatchis, Max Bannister – Bartle Bogle, or some buggers – one of them. Honest, Reg – I just never ever thought I'd get the chance. Only reason I done all the Sainsbury's crap was I was meant to be *saving* – only I spent it all, didn't I? And even if I didn't, I reckon I'd be sat there at that checkout till I was a bloody hundred, before I got this sort of bread together.'

'Yeh? Well,' smiled Reg, 'now you don't have to.'

And then I went and got in another pint, didn't I? I know, I know, you don't have to tell me: ain't never done it before – not of a midday, and the cab outside. But look – there I was in a boozer with my (would you Adam and Eve it?) teenage girlfriend what I just bunged five grand in used twenties instead of out there on the street, pulling in the punters; tell you – not thinking straight (and what's more it's *great*, not kidding you).

Then what happens? Well – I fix up with Adeline to meet down the Cumberland tomorrow (can't hardly wait) and then I nip back here on account of I forgot to take out my bag of change with me (telling you – I gone all to bits) and blow me if I don't hang that corner on Bluecoat Avenue just a bit too neat and so I puts on the brake and shoves her into reverse and yeh – talk about reverse! Tell me about it. I only go and back right slap-bang into a bollard, don't I? No one looking, thank Gawd. So that's the bloody tail-light well crocked, innit? So I got back here, fast I could – and I'll have to get that done, now, before I go out tomorrow else the Carriage Office, they get wind of it – they'll be down on me like a ton of wossname. And it's down to me, what it costs, cos this manky insurance I got – the excess'd bring tears to your eyes, know what I mean? Tell you what, though: I don't reckon it was the ale, what done it – nah. Know what I reckon? Reckon it was love.

And all that little lot's been going through my head as I'm walking down the road, like: timed it perfect – and no one's even using the blower. So I nips in, and now I'm dialling my Adeline's number.

'Hi, Reg!'

Blimey O'Reilly – I'm telling you, just that great first hit of her voice, like, and I'm floating on wossname.

'Wotcher, darling. You OK, yeh? Love you, girl.'

'Oh Reg I'm just *fantastic*! I got the forms, and everything – put down the deposit. I'm just so excited! Jacked in Sainsbury's – should've seen the old witch's face when I tell her! Going to *art* school, aren't I? Told my mum. She says, where you get the money for that, then? And I'm going It's a new thing – it's free, yeah? And she's, like – *free*? Oh – that's nice of them! She's such a laugh, my mum – you can say anything to her and she just sits there, basically.'

'Looking forward to tomorrow?'

'Tomorrow? What's tomorrow? Oh *tomorrow* – oh yeh, right. Cumberland, yeh? Yeh – course I am, Reg: course. They give me a whole list of stuff I got to get – port . . . whatever they are – folios, I think. And pens and colours and big sort of instruments and that.'

'Yeh? Bung you a few bob tomorrow – all right? Take care of it.'

'Oh thanks *ever* so much, Reg. You really are great – you know that? Meeting you – it's changed my whole life!'

'Me? Nah. I ain't nothing. It's you what's great. Adeline.'

'Oh look there's someone at the door, Reg. I gotta go. Probably only Steve.'

'Who's Steve?'

'Oh just somebody. Nobody, really. So I gotta go – yeh, Reg? See you tomorrow. Look forward.'

'Can't wait. Love you, Adeline.'

'See you, Reg, yeh?'

'Yeh – bye. Love you, girl – OK?'

'Bye Reg.'

I reckon, thought Reg, as he was strolling back home, I reckon I know now how that Romeo bloke in the film felt. Me, I'm just an old git, right? But I ain't never known it before, this feeling – but what I'm saying is I ain't a bit surprised he was so hot for that Juliet, is what I'm saying: if she was anything like my Adeline, he was well sorted, wasn't he? Didn't end good, though – but that's Hollywood, innit?

Reg turned the corner into his road, and the first thing he sees is the police car smack outside his house. Says Police on it, look – sort of limey yellow and orange bits and just the word Police in black, there, plain as day. Bloke sitting in it – driver, like. I'm a bit closer, now. And now I'm just about there. Oh Christ – copper at the front door, ain't there, looking through the glass bit. Right, mate. What am I gonna say, then? What am I gonna say? What shall I say to him, ay? How am I gonna *do* this? Well, Reg? *Think.*

'Afternoon,' said Reg, walking up the path and jangling the keys of ownership.

'Afternoon, sir. You the owner of this cab, are you?' And he consulted a notebook. 'Number 01827?'

Reg glanced sideways – looked at the taxi in the driveway. What a strange-looking object: ain't never seen one before.

'What – this cab?'

'Yes sir. This one here.'

'Yeh. That's mine. That's me.'

'So you are Mister Reginald McAuley, then. That correct, sir?'

Reg nodded. Yeh. Correct. Got it in one (quite like the Reginald). His mouth was well on the way to spouting a whole load of butter-wouldn't-melt (felt it rising) and then

suddenly he was amazed to have been mugged by a con-
vulsion – so surprising and all-pervasive as to almost make
him double up. Every atom of all the muck he's been
stamping down on because he didn't at all care for its whiff
or texture was immediately released and it at once over-
whelmed him. He was practically weeping, now, and he felt
so weakened – didn't really catch the policeman's glance of
concern, his asking Reg if he was quite all right, sir. He
simply whispered, I think you had better come – come
inside; your mate all right, is he? In the car?

And once he was in the room, Reg sat down heavily and
gave him the lot: *Yes* it was my cab what picked up the guy
– I didn't come forward because of all the money he left,
see, and I was *going* to hand it in, *going* to report it – yeh I
was, I was – you gotta believe that . . . but then time had
passed, see? And it would look bad. Wouldn't it? And then
things went quiet, and so I just sort of kept schtum, like. But
I knew really there wasn't a snowflake's chance in
wossname that I'd actually pull this bloody thing *off*, like,
because it's a *cab*, ain't it? And cabs, up or down, get *traced*,
don't they? Like I just found out.

The policeman was nodding quite impassively, as he
quickly scribbled in his notebook. Not much more than a
kid, Reg was idly thinking now: nicked hisself shaving.

'Well, sir,' he said, when Reg had more or less dried up.
'That about wraps it up. Anything more to add would be
best done at the station, OK? We'll take a formal statement,
and then you'll be allowed to make one phone call and if
you don't have a brief we'll – '

'Thing is – I never *meant* to do wrong. Know what I
mean? I ain't never crossed the law before. Not me. Not
never. My mates'll hate me for this, cos they're all as
straight as a die, you know, my mates. All cabbies is. Well,
not me, of course. I ain't.'

'Come on, sir. Keep it for the statement.'

'Half the money's gone. Invested it.'

And then Reg dug out a package from the drawer.

'Here's what's left. Don't know how much.'

'Right. We'll get it counted, down the station.'

And as Reg settled himself into the back of the car, he was thinking Oh dear Christ – what will Pauly think of his old man? And then he was thinking this: One phone call, eh? Great – I can ring my Adeline (looks like tomorrow in the Cumberland's a no-no).

The driver of the car arched his eyebrows into a form of enquiry, and the other policeman responded with a widening of his eyes. You might well *ask*, mate, is what was running excitedly through his head. Didn't expect all this little lot, did I? Only stopped off to tell the silly bugger his tail-light's fucked.

*

Isobel had gone straight to the hospital. The train journey into London had been, oh God – just *awful*. It seemed to Isobel (hiding behind sunglasses and a muffler, and God she was hot) that just everybody in the carriage was perusing *that* paper: no one at all seemed to be reading a broadsheet. *Isobel* was; well – not actually *reading*, no, but certainly she held the *Daily Telegraph* in front of her face. She tried to think of mother, but all she thought was Mike. I am both surprised and pleased, though – she warily observed – to discover that I do not find myself disgusting, and nor do I feel in any way cheapened; the reverse, I think – despite just everything, I am enriched.

The doctor patiently told her that as strokes go, her mother's attack had been reasonably mild, but that at her age, it was far from good news – did Isobel understand? Oh yes, she did – she understood too terribly well: the shock of seeing her daughter being fondled by a drunken soap star in a national scandalsheet had triggered off a could-be fatal reaction; oh yes – it could have killed her.

Didn't, of course. No – all it had done was render her even more dependent on Isobel's every waking moment, her entire life on earth. The first few days, the doctor went on soberly, are critical (and yes, Isobel supposed – they generally are, aren't they?). Some movement and ability will return to the left side, but we have no way of knowing at this stage quite to what degree – did Isobel understand? And yes indeed, again – there was no ducking understanding: Isobel saw the future quite clearly. Her mother would recover sufficiently to become effectively useless and practically intolerable and the resultant stress levels imposed upon Isobel would bring her right up close to breaking-point. Close, but not quite there: people such as Isobel did not break – they simply got on with their mending.

And how had her mother, then, come upon the photograph? Need you really ask? Isobel could just see Geraldine now – grasping with almost hysterical relief at this blissful gift from heaven: she will have folded the paper just so, and placed it neatly on the tea table, just to the left of the Minton cup and saucer that mother always made such a song and dance about if the handle was not pointed inwards and towards her, because that is now how she had decided it was most convenient for her to clutch it and slurp – clutch it and slurp.

Geraldine was already packed and waiting, by the time Isobel got home (a cab was standing outside). The house had a smell, funny smell – a mix of the new and the horribly familiar.

'It's no good *looking* at me, Isobel,' started up Geraldine, picking up cases. 'It's your fault, this – it's all your fault.'

Isobel sighed, and sat.

'I expect you're right,' she said quietly. 'I think I'll make myself some tea.'

'I'm not sure there is any. I didn't get to the shops, what

with all this, oh – *upset*. Anyway – I'm going now, Isobel. I don't know if Keith and the boys will even *recognize* me.'

'Only been a few days,' said Isobel. And it's very true, that – that's all it's been: just a few days.

'It seemed,' sulked Geraldine, 'a *lifetime*.'

'Did you really have to, Geraldine? Show her the picture? You might have known it could nearly have killed her.'

'*What*? Now *look*, Isobel – don't you go blaming *me* for any of this. It's *your* fault – all of it. You're the one who just upped and left – did whatever you did. *I* was the muggins left here to cope – so don't you dare try shifting any of the blame on to *me*. Let's just get that clear right at the start.'

Isobel regarded her. 'I'm sure you're right,' she said softly. 'Go now, Geraldine. Get back to Keith and the boys.'

And Geraldine did just that. God – can you *believe* it, is what she was thinking, as she bundled her bags into the back of the cab (they never think of *helping*, do they?). That's just Isobel all over, isn't it? Always been like that. It's never *her* at fault, oh no: it's always someone *else*. And what on earth was she banging on about a *picture* for? I don't know anything about a *picture*. No – but if I'm perfectly honest (but I'm not going to tell *Isobel*, am I? She'd just love that) what I think maybe might have done it is all that bloody mix-up with the *pills*. Oh God – it was all so bloody *confusing*: the red ones, the square ones, the bloody blue ones. I lost track of what on *earth* she was swallowing, half the time – and then I think I could've doubled up, last night (might have) because oh look, *God* – I can't be expected to remember *everything*, can I? Anyway – they're all meant to be *good* for her, aren't they? I wasn't even meant to *be* here: I've got a *husband* at home, you know, and three young boys. *That's* where I should be. And that's exactly where I'm going.

*

281

Looking back now on that phone call from George Carey, Isobel could, she supposed, see the lighter side of his rampant egomania and that awful flat-footed rudeness that is always with him.

'Isobel,' he had opened – almost as if pronouncing on her the sentence of death. 'George. George Carey from, you know – work.'

'Yes, George. I do know who you are.'

'Right. Well yes of course. I suppose you've, um – heard of my little bit of unpleasantness? Everyone seems to have.'

'I'm not quite sure what you mean, George. I know you've left the Manchester. Is that what you mean?'

'Well no. Well, that is to say – *yes*, yes I have left the, um – work. Well – sacked, basically. Look, it's all a bit – I got into a bit of a scuffle in a, oh God – *pub*, you see, and my case comes up this week and – '

'*You*, George? *You* did?'

'Well I know! That's exactly what I *mean*: crazy, isn't it? And that's my, as it were, point here. My solicitor says it would help a lot if someone could, you know – vouch for my character, sort of thing. Say how sober and hard-working and all the rest of it I am, you know. And I thought maybe . . .'

'That I could do it. Well I don't really see why not – it's *true*, isn't it? You are all that.'

'Too *right* I am – I mean, look: I made a mistake. Even *I* am allowed to make just *one* mistake, surely? God – I've already lost my *job* over this . . . wits' end, I don't mind telling you.'

'Poor George. But do you think my word would carry enough weight? A woman who has been seen cavorting with a married TV star?'

'Mm . . . yes, take your point. I did think about that. But I really do still believe you're the best I've got. There's no one else, really, available. I've seen that bloke, you know, once or twice – Sandy, or Bailey or whatever his name is. Absolutely dreadful. Can't imagine why people waste their time watching such dross.'

Dear George Carey: ineptitude on a truly epic scale as, I think, simply anyone would agree. Anyway – I did, did what he asked of me – just back from there, as a matter of fact, and it was nice what George's solicitor had said to me afterwards. That without my testimonial, George might never have got away with just a suspended sentence. Can you *imagine*? George himself said nothing. Well – I didn't really wonder at it: puts all my little problems quite firmly in the shade, really. No job, criminal record – and God that *wife* of his, Shirley: she was there, scowling throughout. I'd almost prefer even mother to her. (Who is, yes, more or less exactly as I predicted – home, and just about well enough to be as ill as she chooses for ever and ever: I think I mustn't dwell on that. I dutifully attend our deaf-and-dumb breakfasts and teas, and between us there looms unmentioned the *picture*: my guilt, and her forbearance.)

And then afterwards, there was that frightful occurrence in the corridor. This dreadful man came right up to George and snarled into his face 'That was my bloody future *wife* you hit, you bastard! Suspended sentence! Suspended sentence! I'd give you a bloody suspended sentence – I'd effing *hang* you!' (except he didn't say effing). And then he punched George hard, right in the stomach – and oh my God you should have seen the shock and hurt all over his face! He looked like he was about to *die*! And there he was on the floor, doubled right up and clutching his midriff with his solicitor there looking deeply embarrassed and muttering Come *on*, Mister Carey – get *up*, get *up*! And George was panting hard and stuttering with difficulty and considerable disbelief again and again: 'He *hit* me, he *hit* me, that man *hit* me – why has nobody arrested *him*? Oh God – my *guts*. This is supposed to be a court of law! So where's the bloody *justice*?!'

I now am aware of a little brass bell going ting-a-ling,

ting-a-ling. The specialist had said that this would be a good idea – a simple and effective method, the specialist said, whereby mother could alert me to her needs. Her needs. Is what the specialist said. Except, of course, it is not the *specialist*, is it, who has to live with the infernal little thing – day and night going ting-a-ling, ting-a-ling, ting-a-*ling*. But there. It's not as if any of this comes to me as a *surprise*, or anything. It's how, I suppose, it had to be. I'll see what she wants in a minute.

And Mike? Well no – I haven't heard so much as a single word, not that I remotely expected to (he has my number: he'll call if he wants to). And have I myself attempted to make contact? Via the television station, or something of that sort? Well – I thought of it, very fleetingly, yes I did – but no, no no: it's best, on the whole, left, I think. A reporter was shuffling around at work, they told me, but already Mike has been seen in town with some new woman, apparently – and so I have been, I suppose quite mercifully, forgotten. (He must, in his life, I imagine, know a lot of women: people generally.) I've watched the programme, now – did I say? Oh yes, once or twice – well, whenever it's on, really – and I must say I don't at all fall in with the verdict of that absolute buffoon George *Carey*: I think Mike's quite wonderful in the role (but then I would, wouldn't I? Because I do, don't I? Yes, yes – I do. Will always).

So there. The end of my own little brief encounter. Regret it? Oh good heavens no – how could I possibly regret it? Wish it *away*, you mean? Oh not at all – no no, not a bit of it. I shall keep it warm, and keep it by me. Because after all – I'll *need* it, won't I? For looking back on.

CHAPTER ELEVEN

'*Mike*, you silly old bastard! What you been up to, ay?'

Mike Bailey closed his eyes and flattened his lips into tacit acceptance of yet another heavy round of telephone joshing, courtesy of yet one more (well-meaning?) mate. He hissed in the direction of the hands-free cordless and wagged his head in a very actorly parody of Dear oh dear, it's a fair cop, guvnor (you got me bang to rights).

'This and that,' he sort of laughed – indicating the phone as he did so, and mouthing over to Sally this latest lowdown: *Max*, was the message – Max Bannister, yeah? Sally – pretty irritated, as per bloody usual – chucked up her eyes, briefly squinting as they took in glinting from the chrome-rimmed row of inset halogen downlighters. Then with the glistening nails of four spread fingers, she raked back into place her heavy and blunt-cut fringe and shook her head impatiently so that the whole glorious mane of quite fabulous long and bright blonde hair reasserted its tenure around her cheekbones, while still leaving handfuls (skeins and hanks) to tumble on down to her breasts (always a hint of lace, before the pouting brownness of them dived for cover). Then she continued to thump her way almost viciously through the glossy pages of one more magazine, as she blindly glared at the pages.

'This and fucking *that*!' roared back Max. 'That's one way of bleeding putting it – and *putting* it, it very much seems from the papers, is just what you been doing, you naughty boy. Just can't keep it zipped up, can you, Mikey? That's why I love you so much.'

'Yeah well,' conceded Mike. 'You know how it is.'

What, he supposed, he was trying to somehow telegraph to Max by way of short and cautious responses was *Yes*, Max – fine: I'm up for all the banter and pub talk you want, mate – but not right now, all right? *Sally's* here, OK, and you know how she *gets*, yeah? (Even now she's giving me that *look* and tap-tap-tapping on the face of her watch – she'd be like this, probably, whoever it was on the phone – but God, that Sally's always the same when it's one of my mates.)

'I know *exactly* how it bloody is!' boomed back Max. 'Now listen up, mate – this do of mine, yeh? You on or what?'

'Yeh yeh, Max – great. Got the invite. Looking forward.'

'Bloody well hope so. Why I always gotta ring round toe-rags like you what never arr ess fucking pee? Party to remember, my son.'

'All yours are, Max. No one does it like our Maxie boy. And you OK? Ducking and diving?'

'Dunno about that. Making money and fucking around. There's more?'

'You don't *change*, do you, Max? Look – Sally's making noises at me. Got to do a bloody interview.'

'Yeh? Well just remember the golden rule: *lie*, mate. Always works. Start telling them the truth and it comes right back at you, don't it? *Upsets* people – know what I mean? Who *was* this old boiler you was poking, anyhow? Not your usual make of chassis, was she? Just handy, I expect.'

'You got it in one, Max. Tell you more when I see you, yeh? Look I *got* to go now, Max, else Sally'll kill me.'

'Now *she's* more like it. I'd give *her* one, no problem.'

'I *bet* you bloody would. Max – I'm outta here, OK?'

'Go on, then, Mister Bloody Telly Star. You wanna pack it in, son – all them fucking photographers and fucking reporters around every time you pick your bloody nose.

You wanna get into *my* game, mate – more bloody moolah, for a start!'

'You're probably right! Max, I . . . Max? Max? You there, or what . . .?'

'No he's bloody *not* there,' hissed out Sally – muscles in her neck all bunched up (never a good sign) and her hands are clenched, look. 'I cut the bastard off – you'd be rabbiting on all night. Come on, Mike – we can't keep this bloody woman waiting any longer – this interview's *important*. Damage limitation, OK? Just put across the Really Really Trying *Hard* bit: doing your best to *improve* – people are suckers for that.'

'Yeh yeh – you told me.'

'And keep on saying Cheryl's right behind you – and call her your *wife* a lot, OK? It's all I could do, Mike, this time, to stop her going straight to the Sundays. She will, you know – one day.'

'Christ. I know she will. How many more of these bloody things have you set up? I just can't keep on answering the same bloody *questions* all the time . . . Do with a drink, right now.'

'After. Absolutely *not* before. There's just two more after this. One at four – *TV Quick* – '

'Oh *Jesus* . . .'

'I know – but it sells. And the last at five. That's with – '

'Doesn't bloody *matter* who it's with, does it? They all of them ask the same bloody *questions*: Who was the woman at the health place? Who is your latest girlfriend? Was it the woman with you in The Ivy last week? Are you still seeing Lana Hendrix? What does your wife Cheryl think of all this? Are you ever going to *reform*? (What's it to *them*, anyway?) How's the fucking *drinking*? . . . Jesus, Sally – I'm just so sick of it.'

'Yeh well,' said Sally, quite briskly. 'Your fault for being a soap star, isn't it? I'm going to buzz her up – yes, Mike? Her name's . . . what's her name, got it here somewhere . . .

Heather something, pretty sure. Anyway – be *polite*, OK? And don't mention any names apart from – '

Mike sighed. 'I *know*, I *know*: Cheryl's. Why do you *do* these things to me, Sally? Do you *enjoy* seeing me stressed out, or what?'

'I do it, Mike, because you *pay* me to do it. Jesus – if you didn't have me to run your life, you'd be dead in a ditch by now.'

'Maybe better.'

'Maybe.'

'You don't *like* me, Sally – do you?'

'I'm buzzing her up right now. I like you as much as I *have* to, Mike. More than you seem to like any of these women of yours.'

That's harsh, thought Mike – watching Sally's profile as she talked so sternly into the phone. I only ever fancied her the once – quite early on. And when she said No I thought Well fuck it. Which is how I am, I suppose. I don't really *get* to wondering if I *like* them or not: it's just Yes? Or No? And if it's Yes, then great – and if not, not: fuck off. But that one at the health place ... Christ, do you know ... I've forgotten her bloody name – isn't that awful? No I haven't – it's ... no, I have you know – it's gone. But she was nice – I quite liked her. Liked her a lot, as a matter of fact. I know she was, what – fifteen years older? But so what? I could *talk* to her, you know? Rare, that.

Oh Jesus, look: another bloody kid reporter's just walked in the door. Great pleasure to *meet* with you, Mister Bailey, she'll go – then she'll plonk down her little recorder and we'll just quickly check the fucking *sound* level and off I go again, down the same old route. And after – as she's deciding just how she'll go about stitching me up – she'll go: *Mike* (cos it'll be Mike by then – always is). *Mike*, she'll be – Could you just sign this for me? My friends would never *forgive* me if I didn't get your autograph. Oh God I'm just so *sick* of it, you know? It can't go on, can it?

Isobel. That was her name. Quite liked that one – liked her a lot, as a matter of fact. Wonder if I should . . .? *Nah!* Forget it, mate: after that bloody picture in that fucking paper, Christ . . . she'd spit in my face, shouldn't wonder. Jesus – the things I do to people, without even *meaning* to. And just look at what I do to *me*. This is how I wind up: alone again, and on the loose.

'Great pleasure to *meet* with you, Mister Bailey.'

Oh Christ. Off I go again: down the same old route.

*

Hugo was swivelling like a kid on the bright red leather and aluminium chair – maybe he was attempting to encourage the blue and fragrant smoke from his Cohiba Esplendido into describing an ethereal series of haloes about his balding head. The meeting had ended just minutes before, and only he and Max lingered on in the board room – fourteen more sleek and sexy leather chairs were scattered haphazardly at various distances around the steel and maple table – littered, now, with a scattering of glasses, ashtrays, knocked askew blotters and Max's doodles of spaceships.

'No, Hugo – I'm telling you, son: fair's fair. You're right to be well fucking pleased with yourself,' allowed Max, expansively. 'Gawd Almighty – just take a dekko at the look on your bloody face! Like the cat what got the cake, or whatever that crap goes like. Here – how can you smoke them bloody great things, ay? Bleeding expensive way to do yourself in, ain't it?'

Hugo leant across to an ashtray and eased with care a briquette of ash from the tip of his cigar.

'I can afford to top myself any bloody way I want now, can't I?'

'Yeh, you're right, Hugo! You do exactly what you like, my son. You've earned it, telling you. I'm well pleased. Tell you, though – when the Creatives first come up with the doings I thought Yeah oh yeah – *lovely*, no denying: but are these clients going to bite? Don't mind telling you – I was worried.'

'It was a brilliant campaign, they came up with.'

'Oh yeh, *granted* – oh yeh, I'm not *saying*. I said from the off, didn't I? Good *work*, lads – that's a brill campaign you come up with. Yeh but the *budget* – know what I mean? Five times anything before. Would they *commit*? You know what I'm saying?'

Hugo was smirking, fatly. 'That's where I come in.'

'Too *right* that's where you come in. Telling you. Hugo, you silly sod – there ain't *no one* can get them signatures on the dotted line like what you can. You wanna be in government, son.'

And Max was already well into gear with the scoffing laughter as Hugo hooted out *Government*?! You're *joking*! Less than a hundred bloody grand a year?! I don't really *think* so, do *you*?!

'You're right – you're right, son! Reckon your bonus after this little lot'd buy up the whole fucking cabinet!'

'Who'd want them?'

'You're right! You're dead right – just as well they're stuck in the Houses of Thing, ain't it? No one else'd have them. So here – what you up to tonight, then, Hugo? Celebrating up West, or what? Who you gonna be fucking blind tonight, then – ay? Who's the lucky lady? You're coming to the do, though, aren't you?'

'*Course* I am, Max – course. Wouldn't miss it. No, I thought I'd, you know – ask Anne out first. Bite to eat.'

'You know what I think, Hugo?'

'Yeh yeh – I know what you're going to say. You've said it all, haven't you? I've just really got a *thing* for her, you know? Always have had, if I'm honest. Seen quite a bit of her, over the months, matter of fact. And at first, I don't know, I reckon I was just a bit of company: meal ticket, if you like. But lately – there's a *change* in her, Max. I really do think she's seeing me in a new, sort of – light. I could really *be* with her, you know – I'm not kidding. Love her, really . . .'

'Can't understand it. She never rang my bell, telling you. Bleeding gold-digger, far as I could tell. And yeh I know they *all* bloody are, fucking bitches – but this one more so. Know what I mean? And when we was anywhere, she'd go all superior – like I wasn't bloody *good* enough for her, or something. Couldn't hardly believe it. *And* she never put out! Christ – what bleeding game did she think we was playing? Here, Hugo – you ever, er . . .?'

Hugo shook his head. 'No. Not yet. No. Far as the money goes, she can have all she wants . . . far as I'm concerned. It's only for the kids she wants it, really. They're nice kids, Adrian and Donna. Need a father.'

Max sat bolt upright, and goggled hard.

'*Here!*' he warned, with great solemnity. 'Here here here here! You don't wanna go talking like *that*, Hugo old son. You don't wanna go nailing yourself *down*, do you? Hey? Where's her husband fucked off to, anyway?'

'Far as I know, he's still with Phoebe.'

'Who the fuck's *Phoebe*?'

Hugo looked up sharply, as if caught out.

'What – you don't mean – not *my* Phoebe – not *Feebs*, you don't mean?'

Hugo stared him out. 'I thought you knew. Yeah, Phoebe – the lovely young girl who nearly killed me with a bottle.'

'I haven't heard a dicky bird since the day she fucked off – and I don't want to neither, ungrateful cow. Yeh – she did, didn't she? Clocked you one. She's a nutter. Tell you one thing, though – we was dead right for each other, Feebs and me. She done wrong, for leaving. Mistake, by my way of reckoning. Anyway. So what – she's with Annie's husband, yeh? Bit of a turn-up. And you got the hots for Annie. Like bleeding musical chairs round here, ain't it?'

'And what about you, Max? Who's the latest? Still that girl in PR?'

'Shirl? *Nah*! Her twirling days is over. Got shot of her, didn't I? Only wanted to move *in* with me, didn't she?'

'Joking.'

'Telling you. No – I tell you what I got going now: kid in adverts – Charlie. Lovely, she is.'

'What – as in Charlotte? Bloody hell, Max – she only looks about fifteen! The tallish one, you mean? The one with the legs?'

'Yeh. And knockers like – '

' – torpedoes, yeh – I know the one. Nice.'

'*Nice*? She's bleeding *lovely*, telling you. Here – this'll give you a laugh: when I done the interviews, right . . . old moaning Monica, she goes – We just don't *need* her, Max: what would there be for her to *do*?'

'Dear old Monica. Just doesn't see it, does she?'

'Well she's a *woman*, isn't she? Least I *think* she is – hard to tell, with Monica. Anyroad – *I* soon found something for Charlie to do, didn't I? Not bloody half, I did. Fact – I'm due to give her a seeing-to right this minute, if you'll excuse me, Hugo.'

'*Course*, Max – *course*. First things first, eh?'

'Swot I *like* about you, Hugo: you *understand* – you understand cos basically – you're a *bloke*, right? Here – you know what Mike, Mike Bailey tell me, one time?'

'Mike. Haven't seen him in yonks. He OK?'

'Coming to the party – tell you hisself. No – I'll tell you what he said to me, one time: said – *women*, right? Women – they go for cats on account of they're like babies and teddy bears and crap like that, right? And men like dogs cos they're all like *blokes*.'

'Never thought of it.'

'No – me neither. But he's right on the money, though, ain't he? I reckon if dogs could talk and have a drink, the only birds that'd still be living would be in the fucking whorehouse!'

'Christ Almighty, Max! You've got a bloody funny mind.'

'Yeh I know. Be the death of me.'

And while they wheezed and chortled their way through that lot, the intercom at Max's elbow set up its warble.

'Yeh, Monica?'

'Max – Charlotte is outside to see you.'

Max was winking and mumming to Hugo.

'Oh yeh right – nice one. Send her in, Monica – there's a love. Hugo's just off.'

'Oh and Max – Shirley Carey's been ringing again. Can't you tell her to stop? Five times today already.'

'*You* tell her to stop. Don't want nothing to do with her. Send her a one-off severance – five hundred, say . . . grand, if we gotta – and tell her to fuck off out of it.'

And as Hugo ducked out, and Charlie ambled in (great big smile on her, as well as her wotsits – like that in a girl), Max just wagged his head in big-eyed wonder.

'They just don't get it!' he called after Hugo. 'Do they? Come over to your Uncle Maxie, Charlie love, and get yourself up on that table like a good little girl, ay?'

*

'*Sophie's!*' almost shrieked out Anne. 'I do take it you are *joking*, Hugo. God Almighty – that's where Max bloody *Bannister* took me, that ghastly, awful day. You're getting – '

'It's a nice restaurant . . .'

'I'm speaking, Hugo: you're getting – are you aware of this, actually? You're getting more and more like him with each day's passing. I mean, does *everyone* in advertising have to be so utterly cocky and *vulgar* all the time? Is it written into the *constitution*?'

'Oh Anne for heaven's sake,' grumbled Hugo. 'Always overreacting. I just thought you'd like it there, that's all. If you don't want Sophie's, we'll go somewhere else – it's no big deal. Go anywhere you like.'

'Well not *Sophie's*, that's for sure. Far too flash.' No – nothing whatever and nowhere to do with that man. I tried, you know – I really did try to even slightly like Max Bannister – give in, even a bit, to his constant pressures. Just couldn't (how *do* people, actually?). So of course all the handouts very quickly packed up; last I heard, he'd switched his attentions to some poor unfortunate he called, oh God – Shirl the *Twirl*. Jesus: what a man. And poor Shirl, whoever she is. 'Why don't we just go to that Italian round the corner? I'm not actually that terribly hungry, if I'm honest. Or we could stay here, if you like – I don't mind.'

'Well,' conceded Hugo – a bit bucked up – 'I'm all for staying here – yeah, sure. What – order something in, you mean? Yeah sure. All for that. And then we go to the party, yes? What about Adrian and Donna, though? Are they – ?'

'They are *dining* – not at Sophie's, I rather think – more Burger King, I imagine. They're with their *father*: it's his day. And Nan's with them too, so there's no great . . . what *party*, Hugo? You know I don't go in for all that. Spent just years trying to tell Jeremy all that.'

'Does he, um – see the kids often, then? Come here much? Did you say *Nan*, Anne? What, Nan of old – old Nan, the nanny Nan? I thought you – ?'

'Oh God *don't*. I *did*, I *did* – I got rid of her simply *ages* ago, when Jeremy went – but Christ, Hugo: you know what I was *like*. I was just going *mad* looking after those two and they never ever stopped going *on* about her – Mummy Mummy Mummy is she coming *back*? When is *Daddy* coming back? On and on. I didn't actually *mean* to get her back but I phoned the agency for just, oh – *anyone*, really, to stop me losing my mind, and . . . well, she was *available*, quite extraordinarily, and so I talked to her, and everything, and she told me how much she still missed the *children*, and so on, and . . . I don't know – it just seemed the right thing to do, in the end. She's terribly *good* with them . . .'

'But I thought you said that she and Jeremy – ?'

'Yes well that's what I *thought*. I really *did* think that at the time but the way Nan and Jeremy are still swearing blind there was absolutely nothing between them – I sort of believe them. Well more than that – I *do* believe them, I do – God, I can't even remember now why I was even so suspicious in the first place. Must have been a little crazy, I reckon. Do you want a drink, Hugo? Wine or something? Maybe we could get some pizza . . . and she *is* absolutely brilliant with the children, I have to say it – they do everything she says. Me, I'd be screaming blue blazes and they'd just sit there and *look* at me.'

Hugo nodded – did it slowly, and pursed his lips.

'Yes, right – I see that. Wouldn't mind a drop of Alsace, or something, if there's any. I'll open it, shall I? I didn't know it was Nan, you'd got.'

'There's masses in the fridge. Well of course, Hugo, I *know* – I haven't forgotten that without your really marvellous generosity – '

'Oh God's *sake*, Anne . . .'

'No truly – if it wasn't for you, Hugo, I could never have afforded anyone at all – and I truly am grateful, Hugo – truly. Without Nan, I think I'd be in a straitjacket, by now.'

Hugo was keeping up a fair deal of nodding.

'Kids still need a father, though . . .'

And then it was Anne's turn to nod – and she narrowed her eyes as she did it.

'Yes . . . you're right about that, I know that. I know it more and more.'

'Well, Anne . . . you know what I've always said. Don't you? Hm? I mean – I've always said this, haven't I? I'd be *more* than happy to – '

'Get the wine, would you, Hugo?'

'No but hear me: you know what you mean to me, Anne

295

– and I'd never walk out on you – never, you know – *cheat*, or anything – and the children, well – '

'Hugo: listen. You've been frightfully kind, and I'll never ever forget it. And I quite understand if now you'll want to *stop* being kind, but . . . the way I'm thinking, Hugo, is *yes* they need a father, of course they do . . . but I'm thinking it ought to be *their* father, their *own* father . . . do you see, Hugo? What I mean?'

A stunned and big-eyed numbness on Hugo's face slowly began to make room for doubt and incredulity – these then obliterated by sheer amazement, before the wincing of pain began to wind down the curtain, prior to the closing of the whole damn show.

'I . . . see . . .' he managed. 'And how long . . . um . . . you've obviously *discussed* this with him, with him – have you?'

'With *Jeremy*, Hugo. Jeremy's his name – don't be silly.'

'With *Jeremy*, yes – you've discussed it, then – yes?'

'It's been . . . mentioned. Floated as a *possibility*, is absolutely all. I'm not saying it's going to *happen*, or anything . . . Look, Hugo – never mind all that for now. Hm? Tell me about the party – what is it, exactly?'

'Hm? Oh. I told you. Told you last week. Max's.'

'*Max's*! Oh God no – does that mean he'll be *there*? Oh no – I really don't think I could face that, Hugo.'

'Well . . .' said Hugo, slowly – almost as if working through again some recurrent and perplexing bit of mental arithmetic. 'Yes, I – I rather imagine, Anne, he *will* be there, yes, seeing as it's his party in his flat, I really do think that that's the way the odds stack up, quite frankly.'

'Don't be – you don't have to bring in *sarcasm*, Hugo. I was simply asking. Anyway – I don't think it's for me.'

'No. Well. I don't actually mind whether you come or whether you don't.'

'But you *are* going – is that the message I'm getting? Well that's just fine. I think you're being rather *childish*, but still: your own affair, yes?'

'I'll get the wine.'

'If you want. I've gone off the idea of wine, to be perfectly honest, but do please open whatever it is you want, Hugo, and then decide about food.'

Hugo shook his head.

'I'm not hungry.'

Whereupon Anne sat back and closed her eyes.

'Good. Nor am I.'

*

Jeremy was mightily relieved by the fact that Nan was around, let him be the first to tell you. It astounded him, frankly, how he would always feel so terribly self-conscious and awkward in the company of his own two children. Never really used to – well, not to this degree, anyway – when things were, you know, more *normal*; when I was still, as it were, in residence. And it's odd going back to the house now, too: couldn't actually bring myself to sell it, in the end – actually took on board Anne's point about that. How could I remove any *more* from them, Adrian and Donna? Not their fault, is it – any of this? And Adrian, you know – done most fantastically well (awfully proud of him) – and I know, yes I do, I well understand that all this guff from parents is quite hideously sick-making, but you just can't help yourself, really. I mean – getting into Westminster: no mean feat.

So anyway, yes – *somehow* I've scraped up the first term's fees (don't ask me how much, just don't) and I've arranged a personal loan to cover, oh, you know – the uniform and a list of kit and extras that you would think might easily equip a regiment for a midwinter campaign in the most hostile of climates, but there it is – it's like this, nowadays. I've been attending rather more to the work side of things, just lately (just as well – and Maria, she doesn't seem to mind so much, not any more), so the mortgage too, I'm just about on top of that (give or take just a bit of arrears) – but I just had to draw the line at a nanny or a cleaner because otherwise, oh God – *Maria's* bloody mortgage wouldn't get paid, would it? You see. And I do, after all, *live* with her, don't I? (But not, I sense, for too long – and how much *my* decision that will be, well – I'd rather not say: let's just see what unfolds, shall we?) But somehow Anne has seen to Nan, as well as some Mexican woman, apparently, who comes in every morning and generally rattles around with a Hoover, and so forth. I don't at all know how this is actually possible, because even now Nan has come back to us – back to them – Anne still seems quite resolute about not ever working again. I suppose you just get into the habit – when change comes, you just go along with it, maybe. She's sold my pair of Barcelona chairs, you know; I simply observed on their absence, last weekend when I was there to pick up Adrian and Donna and, oh God – do *what* with them this time? Oh yes, she said – quite as casually as only Anne can manage: sold them. Maybe accounts for Nan's salary for the first few months, I don't know. And quite apart from the fact that they were in themselves extremely beautiful – aesthetically quite ideal – (I sometimes could spend an hour, simply prowling around them as if ready to pounce, drinking in their spare and leggy loveliness from every conceivable angle: I don't think I ever sat on one, for all the usual reasons – why spoil something perfect?) . . . yes, as I say – quite apart from all the *art* side of things, they were in point of fact unequivocally *mine*, not shared – and I would have, I suppose, made quite a thing out of this, in the old days (except, of course, for the fact that in the old days it wouldn't, would it, have happened?). But . . . everything seems poised on the most precariously delicate balance, just lately, and I so terribly feel stranded between two worlds – separated from quite distinct comforts by unattainable distances – and so on the whole, I think, it is better to let things lie. Which is maybe what I should have seen was clearly the thing to do *then*, when first I met . . . her. Because change, you know, is not something I actually go for – which seems, I am well aware, a more than usually pathetic thing to come up with at this late stage of the game – but there, what can I say? It's the truth.

Anyway – these odd afternoons and evenings with the children have become so much more vastly easy (less fraught) now that Nan comes with us. I mean – these ghastly brightly lit fast-food dumps that they all seem to love so much: I just feel so *alien*, you know? And they rattle off like a Bren gun all these fearful things they yearn to put inside themselves and I'm there grinning and nodding and not understanding a *word*, quite frankly, because it's not a bit, is it, like ordering food anywhere *sane*? (And even when Adrian was a toddler, I was still like this: Anne did it all.) So there I am at the counter trying to remember whether it was a Double Whammy or a Triple Dipper or a different multiple altogether of some other unspeakable thing entirely, and also if it's the mayo or the other fearful glop they are supposed to 'hold' (is what they say, here) and if the fizzy drinks should be Regular (big), Medium – which is enormous – or Large (frankly obscene, and so typically American). Then Donna would always – *always* change her mind at the very last moment because she would see that with this week's special children's package (what – you mean to tell me the other rubbish on offer is seriously intended for grown-up *men* and *women*?) you get a *Barbie* toy, or something – so it's, oh God: let's all just start this *again*, shall we? *So*, Donna – you want the kiddy's Bigg Snak (a wonderful way to educate them, isn't it?) and the still orange with that, yes? And three straws. Right. Sure? OK – *that*, then . . . and Adrian, you're having . . .? (And I pause here, hoping to God he'll gabble it off again to the wholly justifiably comatose woman whose finger hovers over a touchpad, whatever mountain of garbage he's finally settled on, and it usually works – he sounds almost proud, you know, as he orders this stuff.) And me? Oh – I'll just have a coffee, thanks very much. You don't *do* espresso, do you? Or cappuccino. Latte? No? No – right, well just a *coffee* coffee, then, yes (one like last time: scalding slurry in a melting beaker and a white and brittle shard of debris with which to coax around the impossible-to-bloody-wrench-*open* little potlet of radioactive emulsion – yes, thank you: that will be *lovely*).

Anyway – Nan sees to all this nightmare, now – and Adrian's there to help her carry back the trays. I sit wedged in behind a small Formica table, my nostrils doing their damnedest to deny and refuse admittance to the overriding whiff of disinfectant that hangs about the place (they are forever cleaning – which, and I suppose this is perverse, only serves to remind me of the *dirt*). And I have to try my level best too to contain Donna's practically hysterical excitement over the Barbie mini-pony that is so soon – but not soon enough – winging its way to her, complete with a tiny micro-comb, the teasing out of its lavender tresses, for the purpose of. Other worlds: we all seem to inhabit these other worlds, which once or twice collide.

Here they come now (look, Donna – look: Adrian's got you your Grottie Krapp Muk – he's waving the box) and now all I have to concentrate upon is not looking, not even glancing over, as they demolish it all. She's a lovely young thing, isn't she? Nan. One of life's truly good people, I reckon: just lives for the kids, you can tell. She cares for others (do I, I wonder?). Just before we got here, she said to me So, Jeremy: how is, um . . .? And I said What, who – Maria? Oh fine, so far as I can tell. Which is maybe where I should have just left it – but I don't know, the frank and youthful openness in her eyes and all over her face somehow encouraged me to add on quietly, You see, Nan – the thing is, I don't really *know* her: all I can do is divine her instincts. She smiled, quite simply, and said to me so lightly: I'm no good at that – knowing people, and things; and as to their instincts – *forget* it. Touching, really: how can so young a girl know *anything*, frankly?

'You sit over here, Donna,' said Nan – setting out polystyrene bricks and leaning against them stiff and brimming envelopes of orange and carcinogenic death-sticks, to Jeremy's way of thinking. 'Adrian – you go and sit next to your daddy, yes? And don't *pick*, Adrian: wait till we've all got ours. Don't open the box like that, Donna – you'll tear it. Adrian – help her open the box. Because look, Donna – there's a colouring picture on the back, isn't there? So you don't want to *tear* it, do you? We can do it at home, before bedtime.'

Had there been room, Jeremy could have practically fallen off his too damn small chair as quite without warning, as ever, the high-pitched howl rose up from Donna (it shattered him, he didn't at all mind admitting, every single time she did this: how could such a little thing make all that *noise*?).

'What's *wrong*, Donna darling?' urged Nan, her face a picture of true concern, but also set in professional calm. 'Are you *hurt*?'

'God's *sake*, Donna!' went Adrian, as her boo-hoo of protest carried on regardless, its volume – much to Adrian's dark and intense embarrassment – ever cranking up a notch or so (How can she *do* this? People are *looking*!).

'What's wrong with her?' was Jeremy's twopence worth of take on the matter – he pitched it in with as good grace as ever he could muster (better be seen to be a part of this, yes?).

While Adrian charged with purpose into the bulk of his burger and Jeremy tried hard to set aside and avert his eye from the glittering allure of being anywhere, just anywhere else at all but here, Nan was softly stroking back the hair from Donna's crimson and tear-stained face, encouraging at least a degree of grudging abatement in the wall of sound as Donna's breath now was caught in a rapid series of choking hiccups – it sounding to Jeremy as if on every inhalation she was newly amazed.

'This – is – the – *carriage*!' she eventually got out of her system. 'This is the week for the *pony* and they've gone and given me the *carriage* and I *got* the – !'

'Oh *honestly*, Donna,' hissed Adrian. 'Nothing to *cry* about.'

'It *is*! It *is*!' piped up Donna, in high indignation.

'Hush, Donna my sweet,' said Nan, very gently.

'But it *is*, Nan – *is* something to cry about because I've already *got* the carriage – got it *last* week and – '

'All right, Donna,' shushed Nan. 'We'll see what we can do.'

And Donna watched Nan, with wet wide eyes now charged with faith, as she smiled and slid out of her seat and made her way back to the counter.

'*Baby!*' went Adrian.

'Oh shut up, *Adrian*!' spat out Donna, with – to Jeremy – quite surprising ferocity. 'How would *you* like it if you had a Summer Princess carriage and no Barbie's Best Pony to *pull* it? It wouldn't be *funny*, would it?'

But all the pain and outrage were instantly forgotten when Nan was suddenly back at the table and dangling enticingly from her fingers not just the pink and lilac pony, but a lollipop each for Adrian and Donna.

'Oh *thank* you, Nan!' burst out Donna, as her fingers scrabbled at the cellophane wrapper. 'You can have the carriage, Adrian.'

And Adrian spluttered through a mouthful of chips:

'*I* don't want your pathetic Barbie carriage, *do* I, Donna? Actually – yeh, I *will* have it, actually – Action Man's rocket-launcher can blow it to bits.'

And as Donna was stroking the little pony's mane and Nan just laughed once with affection and Adrian resumed stuffing full his face ('I'll have Donna's chips and dips – she never ever eats them, does she, Nan?'), Jeremy simply surveyed the scene and thanked the Lord that it had not fallen to him to in any way deal with this latest and small domestic anxiety. How would I have? I think in all honesty I would have just got up and walked straight out and hailed the nearest cab and left them both to it. God: all these years, and I don't really know, do I, how fatherhood *goes*. (My trouble is, I've got this carriage, maybe – but there's nothing to pull it.)

Jeremy glanced across and smiled at Nan his complicit and brotherly appreciation, but she hadn't been aware (had missed it entirely) and Jeremy thought Oh well OK, then – leave it: I think it might appear too forced and clumsy, if I tried it again. He gave his attention to the filthy coffee before him and was wondering idly whether he might just risk a sip, when Nan looked right at him, but saw only carelessness in the blank aversion of those runaway eyes of his.

*

It had been, let Nan tell you, a tough time – the toughest. Worse than the whole of just everything that had gone before – ten times harder to bear than all of the hurt and sad to date. She had thought she was safe – safe and settled for the very first time, with Jake (her man). At first, she did not believe him when he had stared right into her and said so starkly Get Out – Get Out Now, Nan, And Take All Your Junk Out With You. Yeah right, Jake, she had gone – that's not a very witty or warming welcome home, is it? Is there anything to drink, or have you had it all, you pig? And then Susie had appeared from virtually nowhere – it was almost as if she had stepped out of Jake's own body, or something: at one moment there was Jake (her man) before her, and now somehow she was confronted by the two of them.

They each wore a reined-in and almost plastic expression – endeavouring, maybe, to be not out-and-out accusatory, no, but still never giving in to kindness: summoning all the muscles around their cheekbones to rally round and stonewall all yielding and combine quite stoically to mount a united front.

And Nan had gone wild. This can not be *true*! That is what she had shrieked repeatedly: This can not be *true*! Susie had been *vanquished* – *annihilated*, don't you see? No woman on earth could rise again from the utter death of Nan's devising. And Jake! Jake! I *love* you – don't *do* this. How *can* you? Don't *do* this! All he said darkly, again and again as he held apart and firmly her flailing wrists, was *No*, Nan, *No* – you *don't* love me and I don't love *you* – I never did, did I? I was *Susie's* – and now I am again. And Susie? Susie had just stood apart and away with her hands resting lightly on her hips, regarding the floor and slowly shaking her head in time with the ugly scene being enacted before her: *wounding* – oh God so far more wounding to Nan than if she had attacked her with knives: such detachment in victory just had to be the cruellest gashing before the kill, in the eyes of this mad and conquered thing.

But Nan had not rushed away, raw and covered in grief. How could she? She was standing at the centre of her *home*, can't you see? Being held by Jake (her man) – but he was holding her away, not to him, physically urging her back and back towards the door. Nan was resisting with every vestige of strength still in her – careless of her shame and blossoming hurt, blind even to the thick red pain in her thin wrenched wrists. Her feet kept slithering backwards, her whole body was – still tensed – giving in under the immense and ceaseless pressure of Jake (her man!) bulldozing her out of the door (and one hand she jerked free – clawing wildly at the doorframe, the handle, any last thing) and then most surely right out of his life. She still was twitching and out of control as the clang and bolting of the door ran through her like a shock. Only then in the pale and endless corridor did she consciously still herself and try so hard not to cry out piteously and failed quite utterly and her shoulders kicked her in as she convulsed into racking tears and slowly, step by step, she walked away.

She had nowhere to go. This, she realized with a shudder many days later, must have been very evident to any and all of the faceless people into whom she could well have collided. Because one man – an old hand, maybe, at sniffing out the vagrant – had said to her, not unkindly, Hey Missy: You Got Nowhere To Go? And Nan, she thought she just about remembered, had dumbly shaken her head, and the man (small, wiry – might have been some sort of Asian, or something) – he had grinned quite broadly and Nan, so desolate, had been pitifully grateful and momentarily lit, even by that. He took her to a tiny and shabby, they called it 'hotel' in what the next morning she discovered was some part of Paddington. He wanted no more of her, it seemed, than whatever it was the man at the desk would slip him across – and Nan, despite the cramped and not clean ugliness of her grey and crudely truncated section of room, lay down on the narrow bed and envied the couple just to the other side of it, who seemed to be, amid their hoarse and desperate accusations, slamming each other face first into the wall; envied them simply for being together.

She had woken, or been woken, so many times that night – and around about half-past five, six o'clock sort of time, she decided with a kind of sad resolve (and despite her pain, she felt so weary) that the big long day had now better begin. There was a kettle, and she boiled it; she drank hot chocolate, it said on the sachet, because it had lain there – adding no sugar because there was none. This horrible little non-room was thirty pounds a night (she had numbly paid, cash in advance) – more than was affordable for much over a very few days (which was longer, surely, than she could bear it).

The building reeked of bacon, as she left it, which for some mad reason nearly made her cry. Knowing she would hear her own voice on the answering machine, Nan dialled Jake's flat. She listened quite intently to her own voice on the answering machine and – closing her eyes to blank out all images – softly replaced the receiver. She phoned the agency. The twins were on for tomorrow, as arranged, but then – didn't Nan remember? – the family was going away for the rest of the month and No, I'm afraid not – nothing else in at the moment, but we'll call you the minute something suitable arises. Well, um . . . Nan had faltered: I've actually, um – *moved*, is the fact of the matter, so the number you've got won't actually, er . . . reach me. So I'll keep in touch. And knowing she would hear her own voice on the answering machine, Nan dialled Jake's flat. She listened quite intently to her own voice on the answering machine, and then she said – quite hesitantly at first, but then a bit more bravely as she picked up speed – that she needed her things: this is, for now, my address (where I am staying).

It was – predictably enough, if Nan had thought about it – poor old Carlo who had eventually been lumbered with all her stuff. He carried the cases and boxes up the three flights of narrow staircase, and once in the tiny room with Nan, he apologized for being quite unable to find just anywhere to put them.

'Oh – just dump them on the bed, would you, Carlo? I'm so terribly grateful – I'm sorry you had to . . . yeh yeh, just there: fine. Sort them out later.'

'Right. Well – better be off.'

'Oh don't go, Carlo – stay for a . . . well, haven't actually got anything to offer you – I'm not, obviously, here for long, so I haven't laid in any . . . no, I've got somewhere super lined up, actually – this is just a, you know . . . But stay anyway, yes? I'll clear a space.'

'Well . . .' relented Carlo (oh *thank* you, dear sweet Carlo,

thought Nan – I haven't spoken to *anyone*, since . . .).
'Maybe just a couple of minutes.'

But Nan couldn't really bring herself to chattily go *Well*,
Carlo – so how *is* everyone? Because she didn't, quite
frankly, believe she could actually stand to know that. So
maybe only to fill in the uneasy silence, Carlo fairly elabor-
ately cleared his throat and came up with:

'Did you hear about Tony? I expect you did.'

'Tony? Oh – *Tony*. No. What about him?'

'Don't you know? It was in the paper. Picture and everything. Amazing.'

'What? What was?'

'Well – God, it sounds so . . . I actually can't believe it, but
– did you *really* not hear? I thought everyone knew.'

'Knew what? What?'

'Well – the bugger robbed a bank!'

Nan just looked at him.

'He robbed a – !'

'I know. Unbelievable, isn't it? They caught him, of
course. Could've told him he wouldn't be any good at all at
anything like that. Yes. He is, as we speak, residing at Her
Majesty's pleasure.'

'*Kidding*!'

'Fact. Two years. Probably won't have to *serve* it all, of
course – they never do. But still. Apparently he was in
cahoots with some taxi-driver is the latest, if you can
believe it. That's what the papers say, anyway – they split
up the money between them. He's gone down too.'

'But Jesus – why on earth would Tony do something so
stupid as, Christ – rob a bloody *bank*, for God's sake?'

Carlo coughed lightly. 'Well, um – I'm surprised you
don't know, Nan. He did it for you.'

This time Nan was goggling.

'*Me*?! He did it for *me*?! What on earth are you talking
about, Carlo? How could he have – ?!'

'He *loved* you, Nan. He thought that this way, he might

get you back, that's all. Crazy, yes – but love does that, doesn't it, Nan? Makes you crazy.'

And later, when Carlo had eventually managed to ease himself away, covered in relief, Nan lay back on the horrible bedspread and thought things over. Only one thing pleased her: Carlo had not once asked the whereabouts of the lavatory (just as well – you should see it) and Nan had joshingly remarked on the fact. Ah *no*, he announced in triumph: I have *conquered* – I have *been*. It turns out now he's quite regular due to a wonderful new drug from America (has you gagging for a mean evacuation the minute you get so much as a whiff of something like, well – frying bacon, say: it was then he left). All this made Nan quite ridiculously pleased on Carlo's behalf: it made her feel so unaccountably good.

But as that mood fizzled and died, even more quickly than it had arisen within her, Nan settled down to staring the facts in the face: she had to get a job – somewhere to live. She needed a home, somewhere to *be*, and then the means of making some money. Neither of these should be impossible, but Nan well knew that once she had them, they would not be enough. Having children in one's care wasn't – how could it be? – any substitute at all for being cherished by a man. And now that man – who was never, Nan was aware, any sort of cherisher – has well and truly gone, and is with another. This is, oh – not good. Bad: it's bad.

And talking of children – have you heard the latest on the Nan front? Oh yes – her own would be born, by the end of the year: they weren't that specific on dates, but mid-December, they rather thought. That one thing, you know, could be the big weapon to smash up Jake and Susie. Yes it could, if the baby were Jake's; trouble is, the father is a jailbird. Ah well: I'll have it anyway, because I love kids, really – really I do. (Maybe Tony'll send me a mailbag, to help keep the little thing snug and warm.)

Your old employer has been on the phone, Nan, the woman at the agency had confided: didn't, of course, *commit* you, or anything, because, um – do I not recall that you left her under something of a cloud, as it were? Or did I wholly misread the situation? No, Nan had assured her – you didn't misread it in the slightest: that was very much how it had been. But Anne can't surely want *me* back, can she? Oh God – if she really really does I'd just *love* it, love to – I'd even go back for less money than before (it's such a lovely house – and Adrian and Donna, I really have missed them, you know). Well *yes*, the woman at the agency very easily confirmed: she does indeed seem to want you to return (Is Nan *really* available, Anne had gone – well *ask* her, *get* her, *plead* with her, will you? Tell her I'll pay her more than before).

This call, thought Nan, has saved me. I have given the awful man downstairs a hundred and twenty pounds, now, in return for four whole days and nights holed up in this dank and dingy cell, slipping out only to buy biscuits and glossies (all I can cope with). Haven't given much thought at all to Tony, following on from those initial whistlings of amazement. Tell you the truth, I think Carlo was making up the whole damn thing – but Tony could be very weird, so you never really know. He was *alone*, you see – and the best blokes (the only ones ever worth having) are already caught and wanted. Because if no one else catches and wants them – well then why in hell should I?

Anyway – now I just strum through magazines – and even *they* are driving me crazy, and particularly the new crop of housey ones. Look at this – just take a look at this stupid article (typical):

The two-up, two-down was little more than a gutted shell when David and Rebecca took on the challenge –

lesser mortals might have been daunted, but not these two. 'There were moments,' admitted Rebecca, 'when we thought Oh Crikey – what have we *done*?' But two years and a lot of hard graft later, they are the proud owners of the lovely home you see pictured here.

Yeh well, thought Nan – I thought the ripped-up wreck looked better: who actually thought that inventing wallpaper borders was a wise thing to do? Hm? And what, actually (please tell her), is the *point* of throwing an unbleached calico bedsheet over a simple wrought-iron pole? Like bloody Susie's bloody muslin – it's just plain *dumb*, isn't it? And this! Look at this one!

Stuck for a coffee table? Why not copy Simon and Marion's idea? Simply find an old five-panel door and cut down into three sections and plane the edges and carefully assemble as shown with butt joints and impact adhesive and then apply up to five coats of sealer.

Well Jesus – how simple is *that*? Why not just go and buy a bloody *table*? And the language they use: have you seen this piece about doorknobs? Yes – you heard me correctly: a piece about *doorknobs*: 'We just *love* this funky new take on a much-loved old favourite . . .' Not real, is it? And in the ads, all anyone seems to do is loll around barefoot on sofas the size of a boat, laughing their bloody stupid heads off – and on the table in front of them (possibly quickly knocked up from their front and back doors, could well be) there are always two big goblets of red wine standing next to a bottle that is full right up to the bloody capsule (now *that* would be a trick worth learning). And the fashion mags just make me feel *fat* and *lonely* and that's when I eat more biscuits. Much more of this – God, I'm not kidding you – I'll completely lose my *mind*.

So you can see, can't you, how the call about Anne was

not just the most undreamed-of bolt from right out of the blue, but also quite literally a lifeline. I was nervous, of course, about facing Anne again (she could so suddenly seem mad), but God – I'd barely walked into the hall when Adrian and Donna came rushing right at me and whooping their welcome (Donna had wrapped herself around me and was squealing with delight – she nearly had the both of us over).

'They seem to remember you, anyway,' smiled Anne (oh please God, she was thinking, make her stay! I love the kids to bits, of course I do, but I've just got to, got to get them out of my *hair*).

'I've missed them so much,' said Nan, quite simply. And then the tears came freely.

'Adrian – Donna – please go into another room for – don't *argue*! Just for a few minutes, OK? Nan and I have to have a little *talk*, yes?'

'But you are *staying*?' implored Donna. 'Aren't you, Nan? You're not going away again and *leaving* us?'

Nan's lips went some way in forming a sort of response – but she was so overcome, no words made it.

'*Course* she won't,' said Adrian, with big assurance. And then his eyes tipped into open enquiry. '*Will* you, Nan?'

Nan just smiled like an imbecile and shook her head, as Anne chivvied the children out of the room.

'It's good to see you again, Nan,' said Anne quietly, once they were on their own. 'Would you like a glass of wine? There's Alsace in the – or *tea*, maybe? Yes?'

'I'm actually fine,' said Nan – taking in and remembering well the sofa, the rugs – that mirror over there (where have those two funny chairs gone?).

'Well look – first I just must *apologize*,' continued Anne, at quite a lick (if I don't say it now, I know I never will). 'I realize it was stupid and wrong of me to have accused you of . . . you know – you and Jeremy. Wrong, quite wrong. I see that now.'

'I did *tell* you,' is all Nan managed.

'Yes. And so did Jeremy. All I can put it down to is . . . tension. It was a bad time for me – what with Jeremy, you know – just walking off with – with whoever it is he now lives with . . .'

'Is he – ?'

'Coming back? Who knows? We don't know. We have talked, but . . . Anyway, *you're* back, aren't you? That's what we're here to discuss.'

Nan nodded. 'Yes. I am. I'd love to be.'

'Oh I *am* pleased. The children are quite thrilled, as you saw. I think your leaving, you know, did them damage. I so much regret that.'

'Kids are tough,' smiled Nan. 'They'll be fine.'

'You're very . . . generous,' said Anne, quite unexpectedly – aware of the onset of a rush of shame, and unable to move out of its way.

'I think,' said Nan, 'I'll go right now and get my things.'

'Your room's all ready – so whenever. Nan?'

Nan looked across at Anne, nearly wary.

'Mm . . .?'

'I just wanted to say – *thank* you.'

Nan sniffed. 'Nothing to thank me for. You rescued me.'

Anne touched her lightly on the arm.

'Maybe we rescued each other,' she said.

*

'She *will* stay, won't she, Adrian?'

'Oh yeh – course. No worries. She wouldn't be here otherwise, would she? Still don't know why she went in the first place.'

'It'll be lovely again, now,' squealed Donna – once again caught up and near throttled by the gargle of excitement. 'I can take out my Crying Barbie, now. I put away in that drawer a Barbie with hair just like Nan's, so she could cry and cry, all on her own. But I can take her out now and dry her eyes and blow her nose.'

'You're *crazy*, Donna – you know that?'

'I'm not. It's *worked*, hasn't it? It brought her back. I've still got a Crying Ken, though. He's in there waiting for Daddy.'

'I'd like it,' said Adrian, 'if Dad came back. I liked Mum best by far when it was the two of them here, but I don't know, now. Maybe he will. Maybe he will.'

Donna peered into a drawer in her bedside cabinet.

'I think he will,' she said. 'Look, Adrian – look. Ken's not crying nearly so badly as he was before.'

And despite himself, Adrian looked.

'I think,' he said, 'you could be right.'

CHAPTER TWELVE

Max felt sure – and only as of now – that all the disparate and essential strands of a party to remember had been successfully tautened, teased, and were plainly plaiting together ('Keep going round with the bloody *champagne*,' he had admonished one perfectly cowed and very nervy waitress, while tugging straight her white and frilly apron: 'Don't just bleeding stand there – what's bloody wrong with you? Just do what you're paid to do, girl – keep it bloody *moving*').

The penthouse was looking its grandest (he'd only gone and had the Steinway newly french-polished, hadn't he? Telling you – gleam in it now: knock your fucking eyes out); and the views across the Thames from the three larger terraces – strung with white lights and hung with awnings – were not, Max knew, ever to be forgotten (not by this mob, they won't be). Just about everyone has turned out tonight – and why would they bloody not? There's a few nobodies, yeah – couple of lost souls hanging about the edges, but you get this, don't you? Some brainless bird what's been heaved along at the very last minute: well – you can't blame the lads for it, can you? You wanna impress the tits off some dumb bit of totty, you can't do much better than one of Max Bannister's parties, can you? Hey? Stands to reason.

Noise level's good – the music's still lurking around, somewhere under there (tried a live band, once – bleeding hopeless, everyone yelling), but it's that throb of talk and laughter – that's what you really need. So what I'm gonna do now is, I'm gonna grab hold of Charlie by her tiny little waist, and amble quite casual through the throng, glad-handing anyone I reckon deserves it (and I love the roll of her hips, as I do this: older I get, the more I reckon it's the hips what's got it, if you see my way of thinking. More subtle altogether, ain't it? More *discreet*, is what I'm saying. I mean – you see all these tits in the street with women wrapped around them, and yeah: I'm not saying it ain't good – adds to the sum total of human happiness, I ain't a bit denying – but at the end of the day, it's them bleeding hips what does it for me every single bleeding time: that and the legs what come off of them. Which is why I miss my Feebs, you want me to be honest: I mean – *nutter*, right? Oh yeah right – she's well up there in the Looney Tunes stakes, no question – but in the other department, well: princess, ain't she?).

And do you know – unless I am very much mistaken (Yeah all *right*, Charlie – *OK*: don't bleeding rush me, all right girl?) – yeh – *nah*, can't have been. Just I thought I caught a glimpse of her, my Feebs, way over there, just a second back. And Jesus – she's not short of the balls, you know: never mind an invite, she'd just sail on in, if she's got half a mind to – and who on the door's gonna try and stand in her way, hey? Would you? No you bleeding wouldn't.

'Max – caught up with you. How you doing, you bastard?'

'Mike! Mike, baby: *nice*. They seeing to you OK, yeah?'

'You'd string them up if they weren't, wouldn't you, Max?'

'Hello,' said Charlie, meekly.

'Oh yeh,' grunted Max. 'Forgot. Yeh – Mike, this here's Charlotte, Charlie to her betters.'

'Hi,' said Mike.

'I feel I know you already,' simpered Charlie. 'I never miss an episode.'

'Yeh?' responded Mike automatically. 'That's nice.'

'You here alone, Mike? Here – I was just gonna show

Charlie my new artwork – come over and have a dekko, yeh?'

'Yeh fine, Max. Sally's around here, somewhere – lost sight of her. Telling you – hardly ever lets me out on my own – and look at this bloody drink! There's more water than Scotch: that's Sally.'

Max laughed. 'You wanna get down on your hands and knees and thank her, mate. Without her, you'd be dead.'

'Yeh,' said Mike. 'That's what she says.'

'What's going to happen next in the programme?' Charlie wanted to know. 'You going to leave Wanda, or what?'

Max was hissing through his teeth as he raised up his eyes and smacked her firmly on the bottom.

'Don't be a pain in the *arse*, there's a good girl – ay, Charlie? Mike's at a *party*, right? He don't wanna *do* all that.'

And as Charlie blushed and murmured her apology, Mike was thinking Yeah – Max is right: I really don't want to. I was checking the storyboards with the writers just this afternoon, as it happens – and yeah, since you ask, I *am* now slated to dump old Wanda – and have you any idea what *that* means, in this mad bloody parallel world I live in? It means I'll get a sackful of hate mail – believe it? Oh yeah. Sally'll be ploughing through piles of it – all these nuts and crazy bitches going How *could* you? How could you walk out on Wanda and her two little kiddies? She's never done *you* any harm, has she? She's a lot better than you deserve: *Men* – all the same. Jesus. They just can't see the difference between pretend life and real life – and oh yes, I've had it all explained to me a thousand times: to them, the lives up there on the screen *are* more real than their actual existences on earth. Which – if you spend half your life in the guise of some lowlife called Sandy Hall, and the other half wondering bloody why – either makes you howl with fear for all that remains of our collective sanity, or else just tempts you to take another drink and slope away quietly. You know – when I get like this, I think back to Isobel at the health place. She genuinely didn't know who in God's name I was (and who, in God's name, was I?) – and look, I didn't exactly hold it back from her, no – I just didn't want anything to change and be broken. It got broken anyway, of course. Always bloody does. I think I'm going to ring her. She's not like all the others – I really could *talk* to that woman, you know? My special friend. Who could I talk to here? Yeah: won't stay too long, I think. And then I'll ring her: why not?

Without quite realizing he had been moving at all, Mike now found himself with Max and Charlie in a shallow and dim-lit bay close by the most spectacular of all the picture windows. And then he did sort of remember, yes, his hand being pumped by various utter strangers as they glared redly into his face, their mouths jerked aside into complicit grins of wholly illusory *friendship*, or something. Max had filled in the journey with a practised repertoire of hair-ruffling, shoulder-slapping and neck-nuzzling – while Charlie had silently coped with hard and made-up women and their sour-lipped glances of deep disdain, while men just narrowed their eyes at the jut of her breasts.

'You see,' Max was now explaining – indicating to both Mike and Charlie a large square canvas, heavy on mauve and scarred by acid lemon – 'what you don't wanna get into, these days, is one of them Warhol Marilyns: *common*, they are – know what I mean? See them everywhere. Mind you – by the same token, Warhol is still your top man as far as décor and investment is concerned, so what's a bloke to do? Well – you don't want neither to go for one of them Chairman Maos – ugly git – and nor do you wanna be staring at a couple of chewing bloody cows or a can of sodding soup all bleeding day long – get my drift? So where you put your money is right here, mate – one of the early series Liz Fucking Taylors. A classy lady – and a very sweet artwork, in my very humble opinion. What you think?'

Max had his wide open face fine-tuned and ready for any applause going (I'm well pleased: just had a glance about, and yeah – party's really gelled, now: people getting oiled up a bit – girls looking naughty, flashing their bits about) and so at first he didn't react badly to the tugging at his sleeve – party situation you get this, yeah? Mauled to bits is normal – but the urgency is beginning to irritate, now (get to him, yeh?) because my dear old mate Mike Bloody Bailey is saying some damn thing or other about Liz Fucking Taylor and it's bleeding hard to get down and concentrate if someone's forever, like, pulling your bloody arm off and hissing in your ear.

'*Please*, Max, *please* – please let's talk, yes?'

Now look, whichever way you cut it, this just ain't *party* chat, is it? So what I reckon is I'm already a bit pissed off cos I'm talking to a *friend* of mine, aren't I? But then when I finally turn round and see bloody little Shirley Carey there – hopping about, her eyes all tragic on me – I just come down hard and go *Right*, girl: this is *well* out of order, I am telling you now. How you get in here? Never mind – out is where you're going. Hugo! Here – Hugo, get over here, will you? Get this sorted. Sorry about this, Mike – little lady seems to be lost. Hugo – yeh, Hugo (and now Max's tone lowered to the murderous and was for Hugo's ear only): Get this fucking mad bitch *out* of here, OK? I don't care how you do it – break her fucking legs, if you have to: I just want her *gone*.

'Please, Max – *please*!' bloody Shirley was going. 'I *love* you!'

'Come on,' said Hugo, quietly. 'Come on, Shirley – let's go and get us both a drink, shall we?'

'*Move* it,' muttered Max. 'Hey, Mike! Don't go wandering off like that – come back here and have a natter. You don't wanna mind *her*!'

'*Please*, Max!' went Shirley. '*Need* you – *want* you – *love* you – !'

And under the threat so deep in Max's eyes, Hugo firmly and sort of gently steered Shirley away (but God – she wasn't helping) – past the conversation pit and then the bar, and on through the dance area and towards the cloakroom.

'Look, Shirley,' said Hugo, quite kindly. 'You see how it is.'

Shirley's eye make-up was a wet and plastered wreck – and knowing this full well made her weep all the more bitterly.

'Why won't he – ! Why won't he even *talk* to me – ?'

'With Max, there's a time for talking – and a time, I suppose, when there's nothing to say.'

Which, reflected Hugo, must be exceedingly pleasing for him. For my part, I just seem to stand back in awe, these days, and gaze on the women he has newly outgrown – all of them better than anything I can ever get. I mean – take Shirley. Never really paid her that much attention before (well – when a woman's with Max, you don't, of course) but even now – with her lips all quivering and her hair a bit of a haywire mess, quite frankly, you can see the potential, can't you? Trim little figure – she'd clean up quite beautifully, I reckon: take her anywhere, woman like this.

'Tell you what,' said Hugo. 'You eaten? I doubt you have. Had any dinner? No?'

Shirley compressed her lips and shook her whole head in defiance, like a child with her heels well dug in, and refusing to tell on a chum.

'Well look,' went on Hugo, 'bit too noisy here anyway, isn't it? Why don't you, er – sort yourself out a bit . . . You know, I expect, where the bathrooms . . .? Yes yes – course you do: sorry. And then maybe we could, I don't know – grab a bite at Sophie's, maybe.'

'*Ha*!' burst out of Shirley. 'That's where *Max* used to take me.'

And this provoked in Shirley a fresh bout of sobbing, and in Hugo yet another round of reflection: this surely does seem to just keep on happening to me, all this – doesn't it? But with Anne, I only now have the courage to realize, the writing for me is very much on the wall (foot-high letters) and so what harm, I am asking myself, can come of a bite with Shirley? Who reined back the tears, now, and said quite jerkily:

'You're very . . . kind, Hugo. I'd like to do that. Let's go now.'

Hugo smiled. Yes I am, he thought; and yes again – let's go now.

*

Shirley, now so aware of how she must to just everyone around, oh my God – *appear*, was very eager indeed to get into that bathroom. She pulled wide the door and swung right in – so large and sparkling were the peachy marble and mirrored spaces that at first she didn't even notice Charlotte idling way over there – pouting at her own reflection: tossing her hair, letting it settle, seeing how it went with the latest expression in her eyes. Shirley was on the point of backing away and out of there – flustered and immediately ill at ease (sick at heart) with this latest unwelcome confrontation: the girl, the girl here, was not only quite clearly her supplanter, but she had witnessed too and no doubt jeered at Shirley's thoroughly sad and so clumsy attempts to get back close to Max, even if only to *talk* for a minute (*talk* – please talk: oh sweet God, Max – why won't you even *talk* to me, now? Is this really how it works?).

I am content, in not a great way, to slip away with Hugo – but how can I handle this girl, here, coolly observing my effective demotion? But Hugo, or someone like him, is an absolute must now, you see: having done what I've done with Max, how can I simply and quietly retreat? Closet myself back and deep down into the festering nest of George, oh God, and then just the children? Because George was bad before – oh yes, quite bad enough, I do assure you – but now that his insufferable smugness has left him (and what else, actually, did he turn out to have? What, if you see what I'm saying, was in fact behind it?) he has become just another of those maddening mooners and moochers – hanging about the house, because still no job (and when, if ever, will anything loom?) and constantly making coffee, oh God – for the *two* of us . . . He drinks quite a lot of, well – alcohol, now, which he never used to do – but then he is, of course, a criminal. And he surfs the Net. I know, but there you are: it rather says it all, I think. He has decided, poor George, that classical music (which never before, so far as I knew, played any sort of a driving role in his day-to-day existence) is now the single and most compelling impetus on earth, come to shake him. He posts things on a website. Some or other wistfully remote and larky fellow surfer gave George the moniker 'Elvis', and George – poor George, with his customary grasp of irony, seems to revel in that. He posts things on a website – and now he signs them: 'Elvis'. Few, very few people visit this thing: George is rarely hit or called on.

'You don't have to back away,' smiled Charlie. 'Just leaving.'

Shirley was shocked by the gentleness of tone. She had been braced for abrasion, if not a cat-like onslaught – but here was something different. Still, though, she felt she had to defend what was clearly no longer her corner.

'Don't feel so *clever*,' is what Shirley stuttered out – not quite meaning that, but better than nothing (it'll have to do).

Charlie grinned quite broadly and made to touch Shirley just glancingly, at some point about the head and shoulders.

'I'm not *complacent*, if that's what you mean. Don't worry:

I'll get him. I'll get him for both of us – and all the poor bitches before. Got it all worked out.'

A spasm of confusion drizzled very fast across Shirley's dulling brain, and it still hung around as Charlie went on talking:

'The way Max behaves, right? It can't go on. Mustn't. See – I was naïve enough, maybe you were too . . . to think I was special, chosen: singled out, yes? It took me bloody ages to see that all I was, was just the *latest*. So when he's had enough – or when I put a foot out of line, he'll drop me, yeah? Give me the sack.'

Shirley could only nod numbly, feeling the kick of tears working her over.

'Right,' confirmed Charlie. 'But I've got *evidence*. I tape him, most times – all his lies and sexist abuse. Plus there are people who'll speak up for me, when the time comes – people here, who I tell everything. Even *Monica*. Her in particular, actually.'

Shirley felt so young and stupid.

'So . . . you'll . . .?' is all she ran to.

'I'll threaten him, yeah – when the moment's right. A splash across the Sundays? He wouldn't welcome that. Sexual harassment? Wrongful dismissal? *Rape*, even. No, if I know Max – he wouldn't fancy any of that. And if he wants to avoid it, he's going to have to shell out, OK? Big time.'

Shirley could feel an unfamiliar yanking at the corners of her mouth: it felt as if her lips could soon and quite involuntarily be busy forming themselves into that rare thing, lately: a smile.

'So you'll take his money . . . and keep quiet.'

'Oh *no*!' Charlie, for an instant, appeared ecstatic. 'I'll take the money, oh yeah sure. And then I sell the lot. I feel I owe it to women in general. And especially me.'

Shirley maybe would have spoken, but Charlie had kissed her lightly on the cheek and strode right out of there, leaving Shirley still wide-eyed, and thinking it through.

The blast of party hit Charlie in the face, as she squeezed herself back into the much more intense and stronger hubbub – the odd whoop and shriek cranking up the atmosphere to a higher plateau, teetering on maybe wildness.

'*Charlie*, you naughty little sex-pot, you!' called out Max. 'Where hell you been? Been looking all over. It's with *me* you're meant to be, yeah?' And he pinched hard on one of her breasts – pulled and wrenched round the nipple. 'Gonna fuck you blind when this lot's over, telling you, girl.'

And Charlie laughed. She laughed and laughed and laughed until Max was bleeding fed up with it – What, she taken leave of her bloody senses, has she? Here – shut the fuck up, Charlie, there's a good girl: showing me up, aren't you? (Stay schtum till I tell you.)

Max ploughed his way back again through the flushed and braying masses of increasingly drunken people – accepting thanks and congratulations, chucking out the odd half-obliterated wisecrack – and dragging behind him Charlie, like so much gorgeous ballast. They eventually fetched up on one of the terraces (Nice, ay, Charlie? The air is as sweet as whatever sweet air pongs of – and at least you can hear yourself think).

'*Mike*! Thought you'd buggered off out of it. Come and get a drink, mate.'

'I've just actually got to make a quick call, Max. Maybe just the one, then, and then I'll – '

'You've had enough,' said Sally, from close behind him. 'Filming in the morning, remember.'

Mike chucked up his eyes to the stars.

'You see what I'm up against . . .' he sighed.

Max was nodding with energy – and prodding nearby Monica's shoulder while he did it.

'I *do*, son – I *do*. This one's just the same. I reckon they been plotting plots against us, all snuggled up cosy in the corner, here. That what you been up to, Monica?'

'*Silly*, Max . . .' admonished Monica.

'I'm just going to slip off somewhere quiet . . .' said Mike, very nearly to himself. 'Make a quick call. Someone I really want to *talk* to . . .'

'Make sure you come back,' said Sally, shortly.

Mike was soon gone, and Max and Charlie then filtered away (Over here, Charlie girl – some poor bastard I wanna show you off to). Sally was intent on the sight of Mike's retreating head – the odd jerk of his shoulders as he eased himself sideways through the crush.

'He's stopped,' she said.

Monica nodded. 'Woman . . .?'

'What else? Does this all the time.'

'It's what they do. It's what they all do. Still – in the end, does it really matter to any of us *what* a man gets up to?'

Sally chewed briefly on her lower lip, and looked away.

'It does,' she said softly, 'if you happen to love the bloody bastard.'

Monica glanced up at her.

'It doesn't do, that. Believe me. You get nothing in return. But it's hard, isn't it? When they've no idea.'

Sally stayed focused on all she could see of Mike and the woman, so far away and wedged between bodies.

'Yes,' she said.

*

It was the waist – that so slim and swooping waist, thought Mike much later: maybe it was, yes, or could it have been the hips that burgeoned away from it – and then the long brown slim legs jacked up so high on those extraordinary shoes? She had actually stood in his way – practically barred him.

'Hi,' she said. 'Shall I tell you something?'

324

Mike smiled at her, of course he did (why wouldn't he?) – did his best to step around the mass distraction of all the glorious protrusions of this exceptionally striking young woman, but in so few seconds was caught by the glint just winking out of each of her eyes; there was a promise there, yes (did he see it at the time?), of impending diversion, and the threat of real intimacy, maybe too deep.

'I've just actually,' said Mike, ' – Christ, what a scrum. Can you hear me? Yes? It's just I've got to make a quick phone call, somewhere a bit . . . Someone I have to, you know – talk to.'

And quite as if Mike had not spoken a word, the woman repeated, in precisely the same tone:

'Shall I tell you something?'

'What? Tell me what?'

'What I had for breakfast?'

Good, thought Mike: she's mad. Or drunk. Or coked. Whichever way, I can slip away now and just quickly phone up –

'I had,' she went on implacably, 'a cup of hot water, three sticks of celery, a charcoal tablet and a newborn baby.'

Yup: as I thought – nuts. But God – her face. And the fall of the limbs – that one brown arm there, look – reaching out and just touching my hair. These coloured lights, which I had not noticed, are caressing the sheen of the dress that holds her.

'Mike,' said Mike. 'Mike Bailey.'

'So what? It's only a name, like any other. I ought to be called Vesta Jameson. That should be my name.'

'But . . . it's not, right?'

'Phoebe. But it really ought to be Vesta Jameson – and I'll tell you why. Just a moment before I was conceived, my father ate two huge ready-made take-home-type curry things, yes? And followed them down with a bottle and a half of Irish whiskey. And after, he rolled off my mother, stone-dead. It was me you were looking at, wasn't it?'

Mike thought No – wasn't looking, hadn't even noticed. Was now, though (now I have).

'What a very interesting story, Phoebe. You must tell me more.'

'Maria. My name is Maria. What more would you like me to tell you?'

'*Maria* . . .? Oh. But I thought you said – ?'

'What? What did you think?'

'Phoebe. I thought you said . . .'

'No. Why would I? It isn't my name. Freebie. That's what you heard me say: freebie. Because that's what I am for you . . . a freebie.'

Mike was watching her closely – less aware, now, of the party booming and the jostle of others, to every side of him.

'Can I get you a drink?'

'No. Drink, I think, just clouds you. I would, however, like to lick you to bits. You know – I very nearly didn't come to this party: wasn't even invited.'

Mike was glancing to the left and right of him, his mind working hard behind the blinking of his eyes; he was passing his tongue across his sweating upper lip, and then along the lower, with care.

'Why don't we – get out of here, actually? Hm? I've got a place – not too far away. Quiet. I nearly didn't come here myself but, well – you know, do you, what Max is like? Very insistent.'

'Yes. It's simply a question of approach, though, with Max.'

Mike was now urgent: the palm of his hand was at the side of her throat – and that, he well knew, just had to be the decider, here: I feel uplifted, yes I do – and yet also (and Christ, by my standards, tonight – I've drunk practically nothing) somehow as if I am falling right over.

He took her by the elbow. 'Come on, Maria – let's *go*,' he hissed at her. 'Before, oh – anyone . . . *sees*. Let's get out of here *now*.'

Maria looked up and full into him, and smiled her smile. 'I thought,' she said, 'you had a phone call to make?'

'Hm?' checked Mike, genuinely startled. 'Oh – oh *that*. No – forget it. Doesn't matter. We go *now*. Christ I *want* you.'

Her eyes never left him as she brought in her lips to just softly graze his – he was charged now with a rush of sweet heat as she kissed him so fully, and let her mouth idly linger. And he was lanced by the same dark intensity in those deep eyes shattered by light as she gently drew back and beheld him; he only could gaze at her, as he struggled with the loss of his senses.

'I'm *yours* . . .' was all she barely whispered.

*

And now it is done. Mike just lay there in his devastated bed, squinting away from the strips of white sunlight that the vertical blinds could no longer contain. Never before – no matter how terrible he had felt or been – never ever before had he gone this far: he could barely believe he had done it – couldn't even begin to seriously wonder how or why. She was only a *woman*, for Christ's sake (wasn't she?) – what had possessed him to *listen*? Ah well – it had been more, much more than her words, Mike dully supposed: yes – it was the essence of she herself who had somehow exerted what felt like total ownership. The essence of she herself. She herself.

He had missed filming. Altogether. He winced whenever he thought it. He had been *late* before, oh yeah (many were the filthy glances and muttered asides from the rest of the cast who had been hanging around and resenting him since daybreak – waiting for Mister Mike Bloody Who-the-fuck-does-he-think-he-is *Bailey* to get his arse into make-up and wardrobe and emerge in his own sweet time as the only slightly less reliable and just about more irresponsible

Sandy Bloody Hall). Oh yeah – been there; but to just not turn *up* . . .!

And of *course* Sally had been on the phone since dawn: the first time was her usual wake-up call, the second more insistent. The third and fourth were both shrill and resentful, and by the fifth she was openly abusive. And Mike, still, had just lain there, the panic and guilt alternately teetering on top of one another as each of her messages squawked out of the machine and kerranged its way into his skull; and then there was Maria, stroking his chest and suffusing this same void and gummed-up skull with something close to scent.

'Sh. Don't worry. Sh. It's nothing. Sh. Just leave it. Sh.'

'I . . . *can't* leave it . . . it's . . . what I *do* . . .'

And he left it, he did, because she slithered down and all over him, Maria, and the alarming sensations just made him cry out. By the eighth or ninth call, Sally had been frantic – real concern now colliding with high anxiety – and Mike just knew he would have to in some way respond: pick up the phone and lie and lie – or else she would have the police come round to break in the door. But what can I *say*, oh Christ, oh Christ? This is *Sally*, for God's sake – she's heard me say just *everything* – so . . . *what*?! I can't, can I, pull the Dodgy Prawns number again, can I? Not possible. Oh God – already I can taste her sour disgust. It is too late now even to sprint for the studio (but do you know, even if there was still just the chink of a chance that I could make it in any sort of time at all, I truly do know that I would continue to sprawl and bask in this new and wicked enchantment, until all such danger had passed).

He watched – his eyes were caught by the rhythmic and easy amble of her hips as, cool and naked, she walked slowly away. She says two things: her real name is Marsha (which I don't understand) – and at what time, do I think, should she send for her things? And I hear me saying (it's my voice and it isn't) Whatever time, any time – whenever, Maria, you like or want to.

She stops at the doorway, and just her head turns back to face me.

'You're *mine* . . .' is all she barely whispers.

CHAPTER THIRTEEN

Jeremy was sitting on a Barcelona chair. Yes, he thought – I am pleased, gratified, that me and Mies are together again: I've been apart too long from the things that I love. I have, at present, just the one chair – paid for out of the bonus I quite unexpectedly received as a result of having turned in that pair of duplex apartments (and God had I been relieved to land that commission) both ahead of schedule and well below budget. I nearly bought two – things are best in couples, don't you think? – but then I thought No: first get back just the one thing you need and love, and then look forward to completion.

It is, thank God, at last the evening – and I am content to be alone. At first, when I came back home, I found it very hard to adjust – fit in, I suppose is not too strong. I had assumed that I would simply, you know – as I say, sort of slot back in and blithely carry on from where I, um – left off. But in the event it was odd – unsettling, very. The children, I felt, were nervily padding around me – lavish with their love (which speared my heart: Dadd*eeee*, went Donna: Dadd*eeee*) but treating me almost as a newly beached and rickety bomb: handle, if at all, with care – or I could (again) go off.

Anne too – she was gracious in taking me back, and I certainly am sincere in saying that – but she as well is still *regarding* me: assessing the shifts of the daily situation. Does neither of us think it will go bitter again? Maybe we are just waylaid, the two of us, by a placid desperation (I find myself, I suppose, in the coolness of the aftershock).

She's working again, Anne: seems, what? Happy enough (in the light of the circumstances). She appears to me to get more easily tired, these days; she surely goes to bed quite early. I'm actually in the spare room, still, so it can't – not directly, anyway – be anything to do with that side of things, I shouldn't think. And so in the evenings I am quite often alone – Adrian and Donna safely in bed, of course, and Nan upstairs somewhere, attending to whatever it is she does (she plays, quite softly, bass and very blue jazz – reads a good deal, she was telling me once: when we were talking).

I have lit a cigarette – I seem to be doing that again. I now pick up from the coffee table (Mies again – X-frame and plate glass: highly pleasing) what must, I suppose, be one of the latest batch of her paperback novels – she leaves them all over the house. Who's this, now? Never heard of him. Right – Page One: 'It already was dark when Martin left the house.' Yes. I think it's just that sort of opening, you know, that put me off reading, oh heavens – ages ago: fiction, anyway. The sheer and cold randomness of where you just found yourself – the people with whom, quite suddenly, you were expected to consort: it chilled me – and I know that sounds strange. Just the very fact that here was 'Martin' – and we don't at all know who he is – and he's left some house (his house? Not his house?) and it is just about night-time. Pick up another book, and you're somewhere else entirely, of course – say with a woman, maybe fifty years old, who, I don't know – cowers in a back room, plotting. It's rather like – what can I say . . .? When you're coming back into London on the train – I don't know if you . . .? And all of a sudden –

'It's *dark* in here,' was what he heard – it filled the room and made him start.

'Nan,' he gasped, quite relieved that here was no intruder. 'Didn't hear you come down.'

'Just looking for my . . . oh there it is. You're not reading it, are you, Jeremy? Because I can always – '

'Hm? Oh no – no. Just picked it up. No – I've just been thinking about how . . . how can I say – *arbitrary* the whole process must actually be for all these writers and film-makers and those sorts of people. It's like when you come back into London on the train – there's wine open there, Nan, if you fancy it – you know . . .? On the train, when you're nearly pulling in to, I don't know – Paddington, Victoria, one of those – and you see all these funny little lit-up rooms: flickering televisions and the backs of dressing-tables and people clattering about in a kitchen – yes? You pass them so quickly – and every single one of them is a miniature drama – a story on its own. And the fact that everyone one *does* know – no matter how well or slightly – it's just because, isn't it, at some point in life we just *met* them, yes? Everyone else in the whole bloody world, well . . . we just *didn't* . . . Scares me, I think.'

Nan was nodding as she poured out wine. 'Yes . . .' she said thoughtfully, coming across to the sofa. 'I think I know – yes I *do* know what you mean, actually. Do you remember that Hitchcock film? The opening? *Psycho*, could have been – God, now *that* was scary – or maybe one of the others, *Vertigo* or something. But the camera starts way up in the sky, and all you see is the whole of New York, or some-where – '

'Oh God yes *I* know that one: and then it pans on down – '

'And suddenly you can make out separate buildings and streets and windows – '

'Yes!' went Jeremy – quite excited and leaning forward – 'And then an *individual* window – and the camera, it almost seems to hesitate before zooming right on in to just that one of them, yes . . .'

'But it could,' put in Nan, '. . . is this what you mean? It could have been another one altogether?'

Jeremy nodded very quickly. 'Yes. Exactly what I mean. Frightening.'

'Why frightening?'

'Why frightening . . .? Because it means . . . because it means we're not in control. And I *know* we're not in control, of course I know that – you'd have to be a right bloody fool not to know that . . . it's just that, I suppose, I don't actually want to be *told*. Have it made so clear. That's all.'

Like that day – that day that really can't even now be all that long ago – when Maria did, eventually she did, come back to the flat. She said nothing at all – didn't really have to. And I, me too – I barely spoke. Didn't ask her where it was she'd been all night – nothing at all like that. Because where she'd been (who she'd been with) it didn't really remotely matter: all that was of concern to me was that she had not been *there* – the rest just didn't touch. Well how *could* it? If you think about it, look – if you're absent, you can't possibly, can you, have any real effect on other lives? If you're not around, Christ – it's hard enough to believe that other lives even continue to *happen*. And not just people but *stuff*: all the time I was with Maria, my perceptions were both heightened and dulled. There was just me and Maria (her hips and limbs) – nothing to do with all the *stuff* that didn't even so much as once cross my mind: Weather (Is it raining? Could be) – TV (What's on? Don't know) – Eating Out (Shall we? Can't be bothered) – Holidays (You going? Must be joking). But in other and wider contexts, all these things went *on*, presumably . . .? (I was heavy with hurt, when she told me I was going – and yet, in the usual way, relieved that the end had come. Because I never *really* thought I would know her for ever – it wasn't as if she was even very nice: I didn't even divine her instincts. But still – oh yes – still I miss that kiss of danger.)

'It's like on holiday,' said Jeremy, suddenly. 'You know – I mean at the end of a holiday – beach sort of holiday, say. Every morning you've watched all the pool attendants, yes? Setting up the loungers, spreading out the cushions, putting up umbrellas. And round about eleven they get the barbecue going – same in the evening when the band strikes up. And then later, everything is dismantled again and things get hosed down. You've *seen* it – you've *lived* with it: you know the *routine*. And yet, your first night back at home, it's just impossible to believe it still goes *on*. Simply because you're no longer there it just *can't* go on – yes? And yet the awful thing is – !'

'God, Jeremy: you're so *intense* . . .'

'Intense? I don't know about that. But look – the *awful* thing is, we, I, just don't *matter*. When all's said and done – just don't *register*. And never mind in the grand scheme of things – not even *remotely*, is what I'm meaning. I make no difference. I mean – I *thought* I had, when I – you know, *left* here . . . wasn't *proud* of it, or anything, but at least I thought I'd made a *mark* of some sort. But now I'm back, well – it's clear, isn't it? Nothing's *changed*, has it? Nothing. Nothing I can do or say can have the slightest bearing on anyone or anything. And it's true, it has to be, of *all* of us. No?'

Jeremy had been hunched over in his chair and addressing the floor – and yes, intensely – but now he looked across to Nan for maybe reassurance and was surprised to not see her still sitting on the sofa: even more so to find her on the rug right next to him – looking quite energized, and certainly at him.

'I don't believe that, Jeremy,' she said so quietly. 'I am sure – I know it – that the *reverse* is true. It *can* go on – it *will*. Don't you see? It just *has* to.'

Later, much later that night, Jeremy found it hard to put back together even the nature of what he'd been talking about. He remembered only leaning over to kiss her hard, and the way she had held him tight.

BOYS AND GIRLS

Joseph Connolly

'Connolly unfolds a rich and compelling drama of life'

DAILY MAIL

Susan wants another husband.
Which comes as a shock to the current one.

But not instead of you, Alan, my sugar – as well as. You see?

Yet once Susan has brazenly commandeered her boss's rich, elderly hand, Alan finds himself curiously cherishing the company – sharing wife, whisky and other, odder peccadilloes. Indeed Susan is forced to root out alternative amusements – and with their teenage daughter copying her disintegrating moral code, the complex machinery of their lives soon begins to break down.

Joseph Connolly plunges the reader into a tumultuous medley of inner monologues with keen, unabashed relish; exposing marital bedroom and male bonding in this biting, excruciatingly funny observation of men, women and adolescent girls.

Quercus

www.quercusbooks.co.uk

ALSO AVAILABLE

JACK THE LAD
AND BLOODY MARY

Joseph Connolly

'An exuberant, often powerful and moving reading of the
underside of the Second World War'

GUARDIAN

London, 1939.

Mary and Jack.

In love, unmarried and happy.

Until the outbreak of the Second World War.

With every tone and cadence of this novel, from wireless to
air-raid siren, Connolly conducts with masterful hand and
compassionate grace the voices of a once hopeful working class
couple – now blitzed, battered and breaking into a desperate
new dawn.

'Proves Connolly to be an original and masterly novelist'

DAILY MAIL

Quercus
www.quercusbooks.co.uk

STUFF

Joseph Connolly

'A bleakly hilarious look at people obsessed with furniture in their lives, both actual and emotional'

SUNDAY TIMES

When Emily, a successful interior designer and utter bitch, has finished throttling her startlingly dim-witted husband Kevin one morning and packed him off for a day's labour, she never expects him to achieve anything but the usual myriad incompetencies: let alone seduce a young, attractive woman in Portobello Road.

And when she's done screwing her husband's best friend Raymond in his dingy office, little does she know Raymond will be consecutively screwed over by his shrewd, secretly lustful PA with a fusion of blackmail and bankruptcy.

Emily's a maelstrom of malice and cares not for the mess she leaves behind.

But there's only so far she can push Kevin and Raymond before the storm finally breaks.

Quercus

www.quercusbooks.co.uk

SUMMER THINGS

Joseph Connolly

'Connolly has established himself as a very English comic author, in the tradition of P. G. Wodehouse'

THE TIMES

Joseph Connolly's bestselling novel goes straight to the secret heart of that sticky promenade of lust, adultery and snobbery: the British seaside.

Casting aside rose-tinted sunglasses, he undresses the foibles and fears of the middle classes in a riot of one-upmanship, lechery and deceit. Summer Things is a novel that slips from one set of startling mishaps to another as easily as melting ice-cream from its cone.

Surprising, irreverent and hilarious, this new edition of *Summer Things* brings one of Connolly's best-loved novels to a new generation.

'Viciously funny'

DAILY TELEGRAPH

Quercus

www.quercusbooks.co.uk

POOR SOULS

Joseph Connolly

'Vigorous, amusing and sharply detailed'

TIMES LITERARY SUPPLEMENT

On their way to a tedious dinner party with a couple they loathe, Barry and Susan find themselves in a stranglehold amidst a smashed bottle of whisky.

As Barry's gambling debts propel him to desperate measures and Susan's boredom finds relief in Barry's best friend, the poor souls tumble from miserable mundanity into social apocalypse. In an acid portrayal of boozing, fornicating, money-grubbing and extreme marital angst, Connolly shows himself to be a master of the genre with wickedly comic panache.

'Remorselessly points up social pretensions with the eye of Dostoevsky . . . This satire on human behaviour is timeless'

INDEPENDENT

Quercus
www.quercusbooks.co.uk

THE WORKS

Joseph Connolly

'Entertaining, but emotionally and intellectually involving too'

DAILY TELEGRAPH

Lucas Cage loses his father and gains a disused printing works in east London, the only part of his father's legacy he has ever cared for.

Casting aside the shackles of his life, Lucas transforms the building, swimming against the tide of gentrification to create a refuge for the misfits and malcontents he meets: marital asylum seekers, a couple obsessed with resurrecting Blitz-era Britain, three washed-up cockney criminals – and the charismatic Jamie Dear: a man who shares a past as troubled as Lucas's own, and a gift for bringing people together.

The nuclear family has exploded. Welcome to the factory for lost souls.

Quercus

www.quercusbooks.co.uk

S.O.S.

Joseph Connolly

'Horribly funny . . . a snarl, a hoot, a howl'

OBSERVER

The luxury cruise ship *Transylvania* takes six days to cross the Atlantic – just enough time for the passengers to find their sealegs and lose their heads.

Whether it's husbands pining for their mistresses back on shore, stewards with a raging cabin fever or mothers sweating to outshine their daughters, they transform the *Transylvania* into a floating purgatory of Pacific proportions.

S.O.S. is Joseph Connolly's brilliant boat-bound comedy, a novel of holiday-makers and holiday-haters running aground on each other's lives and loves. 'Getting away from it all' is hopeless – and hilarious – when you've brought it all on board with you.

Quercus
www.quercusbooks.co.uk